Acknowledgements

Lots of love and thanks to: Mum, Dad, Paul, Stephen, Alexander Hewitt, Tristan Rogers, Victoria Connelly, Simon Trewin, Sarah Ballard, Claire Scott, Faith Bleasdale, Eric & Felicity, John & Nicky Collins, Martyn Webber, Lewis, David W and Lyra, Matthew Wherry, and Kirsteen Brace.

Special thanks to my editors at Time Warner: Tara Lawrence and Joanne Coen.

Very special thanks to S.L.K. for everything.

Prologue

Sean O'Mara gazed out of the kitchen window. Just what the beejaysus was going on next door? All morning he'd seen girl after girl knocking on number 33's door, flittering in and out like gorgeous butterflies. Sean, who was very nocturnal, liked a good lie-in and normally didn't feel his days began until at least 2 p.m., suddenly found himself feeling very awake.

'Maybe they're having a big group orgy,' his grandfather, Kieran, mused.

Sean bit back a smile. The Wilkins family lived in a large four-bedroomed house in the heart of Richmond. Their house was hardly red-light district material; their windows were framed with expensive buff blinds, showcasing opulent, elegant rooms.

'The Wilkins having an orgy – as if!' Sean threw up his hands. 'They're hardly going to get down to it at—' He gazed over at the silver clock sitting on the washing machine, which had always been two hours, forty minutes fast. 'At . . .' Sean was feeling a little too hungover for mathematics at the moment. 'At – at this time of the morning.'

His grandfather, who was frying up a huge sizzling pan of tomatoes, sausages and bacon, let out a thoughtful sigh. 'Well, maybe they've hired out their house for a porn film,' he said eagerly. 'They might need extras!' He flexed his muscles, smoothed down his wispy grey beard and proudly adjusted his thick glasses (the arms of which were held on with yellowed Sellotape).

Sean sometimes wondered about his grandfather. He was eighty years old but he talked like an eighteen-year-old schoolboy on Viagra. He seemed to get worse as he got older. Whenever Sean suggested he, er, might tone it down, Kieran merely scoffed at his grandson, saying he didn't care what people thought. Old people, Sean mused, were like kids – they could get away with murder, with saying whatever they liked.

Sean looked outside again. Hey – *another* girl. She was waddling up the driveway, her bottom sashaying in a rather unattractive floral skirt which looked as though it had been made from leftover sofa material.

'Maybe they're having a car-boot sale without the car boot,' said Sean. 'A kind of garage thing.' Knowing the Wilkinses, instead of old jigsaws and soft toys they'd be chucking out antiques and oil paintings.

'Maybe they're having a swingers' night,' said his grandfather hopefully. 'The trend is passing over from America – I read an article about it.'

Okay, fine, thought Sean. They ate their breakfast in a companionable silence; Kieran flicked through *Loaded* while Sean nursed his hangover. He'd been out late last night at a party and his head felt as though a bunch of inebriated bats were flying around in it, knocking and clashing into each other – ouch, ouch, ouch. Still, the greasy grub was a comfort. That was the great thing about his grandfather – he was a smashing cook. When Sean had moved over from his birthplace, Cork, to England, his grandfather had offered him a room in his house to keep him company after Kieran's wife had died. Sean had been very dubious. He didn't know his grandfather that well; he'd only met him at family occasions and had a vague, unpleasant memory of Kieran farting at embarrassing moments – normally right in the middle of a speech. Sean, who was thirty, had worried that his grandfather would be a sad old git who shuffled around in green carpet slippers, muttering to himself about the war and wanting to play Scrabble. He'd been relieved to discover that his grandfather possessed several pairs of trainers, kept himself to himself and let Sean do whatever he liked, when he liked.

After breakfast, Sean climbed the stairs to the bathroom. Like all the rooms in the house, it was full of his grandfather's junk – a cage of scuttling mice was kept in the airing cupboard; the bath was currently full of motorcycle parts and, bizarrely enough, an old-fashioned black telephone sat on top of the toilet. Sean washed out his toothbrush carefully before using it, then swabbed on a blue line of toothpaste and cleaned his teeth vigorously. He showered water into his palms to flatten his hair, which was sandy, slightly curly and liable to spring up like wild bedsprings. The hot weather had tanned his face; there was a splash of freckles over his broken nose and clefted chin, and lemon highlights in his fringe. He fastened his silver St Christopher around his neck, then put on a pair of black jeans and a T-shirt.

He was still curious about all these girls. He worked as an odd-job man and a gardener; he wasn't due at the Wilkinses till 3 p.m. but today he decided to start early. The front garden didn't really need any work but sod it! Sean pulled on his gardening gloves and, armed with his shears, set to work trimming about three-quarters of a millimetre from the already perfect rosebushes. He could see into the lounge window; Andie and Nick were sitting on the couch, deep in discussion. He tried to lip-read through the glass but it was frustratingly impossible.

Sean started to sweat and was just pulling off his T-shirt when he saw another girl walking up the road. She was so entrancing that he paused, his elbows at an angle, his T-shirt pulled halfway up his chest.

The sun was behind her and for a moment she appeared like a mirage in the desert; a shimmering goddess of light and beauty. As she came closer, she took on shape and form. Sean felt his blood stir and slowly pulled his T-shirt back down, a delicious smile spreading over his face. He resisted a sudden urge to wolf-whistle.

The girl was tall and willowy and dressed from head to foot in black, from her V-neck top to her long flowing skirt and sandals. Silver crosses dangled at her ears and bracelets jangled around her wrists. Her hair was dyed blonde and tied back into a plait, wisps framing her beautiful face.

As she came closer, Sean quickly busied himself, pretending he hadn't even noticed her.

'Um.' She came halfway up the path and then stopped uncertainly, gazing at his T-shirt with a giggle.

Sean looked down in horror and realised that he'd still been moving his shears automatically. In the process, he'd been snipping off the hem of his T-shirt; red cotton shards were strewn in the flowerbed.

'Shit.' He felt like such a prat.

'Is this number thirty-three Cherry Tree Lane?' she asked. When he nodded, she added: 'Sooo . . . er, are you Mr Wilkins?'

'Christ, no. They're in there. The door's ajar.' His Irish accent, suburbanised after nine months in London, always deepened when he was nervous.

'Great.' The girl let out a long, fluttery breath. 'I'm applying for the job of nanny, wish me luck.' She gave him such a glowing smile that she looked as though she drank sunshine for breakfast and ambrosia for lunch. Sean had never really believed in God before but, as he watched her enter the house, he looked up at the sky and prayed feverishly that this angel would get the job.

1
Cara

'Okay, Cara, you can come in now,' Nick said, popping his head around the door.

I took a deep breath, said a quick prayer to Dionysius and stood up.

It's going to be fine, I told myself as I entered the living room. *Just be normal. Put on a convincing act and they won't spot a thing. Remember: you are Cara Broad. You are twenty-five years old. You are the best nanny since Mary Poppins. You come from an ordinary family. And you are normal.*

The living room was very plush. A coral carpet with thick rugs. Flowers arranged in a rainbow spray on top of a marble mantelpiece. A grandfather clock with a somnambulistic tick. Everything was neat and tidy; tables shone like mirrors, mirrors gleamed like the sun and there wasn't a speck of dust to be seen anywhere.

Andie and Nick, Mr and Mrs Wilkins, were sat on the sofa. We stared at each other for a moment, drinking each other in. Andie looked to be in her late twenties. She was short and voluptuous with curly auburn hair, a beaky nose and fierce brown eyes. She sat on the edge of the sofa, legs coiled and arms crossed. In contrast, Nick was tall and all sprawling limbs. He had short dark hair, a goatee beard and a slightly wicked sparkle in his dark eyes. He looked me up and down, grinned appraisingly and said, 'You've got the job.'

I laughed, a little confused, and sat down. Andie gave him a sharp nudge and then held his hand tightly. She opened her mouth to speak when a voice shouted from out in the hallway: 'MUM, I'M BORED OF BEING IN THE KITCHEN! CAN I COME IN YET?'

We all laughed, the tension dissolving for a moment.

'In a minute,' Nick called back, 'we won't be long, Freddy-boy. Now, Cara, would you like a cup of tea?'

'Bat-wing flavour would be fine,' I almost said without thinking, but stopped myself just in time. 'Erm, no, I'm fine thanks.' I gave myself an inward slap. *Normal, normal, normal,* I repeated.

Andie had obviously taken an instant dislike to me because she looked at my CV and said, 'Well, Cara, you don't seem to have much experience, do you?'

'This would be my first live-in post,' I said hurriedly. 'I did only graduate from the Princess Christian college recently, but I've worked with another family, looking after two girls, and it was great . . .' *Well, until they found out my secret,* I added silently.

'But only for six months,' Andie said doubtfully.

'Oh come on, she's not applying to be chief of the Bank of England,' said Nick, adding, 'your CV looks great.' He gave me a beaming smile. 'You should have seen one of the girls we had in here this morning. Her CV said she had "wide-ranging experience". When she turned up, she explained this translated to the fact she'd once baby-sat for her cousin. "I only dropped him twice," she said.' Nick was obviously exaggerating wildly now, enjoying making me giggle.

Andie gave me a cold look. God, I was completely alienating her. I quickly remembered the body language tips my grandmother had given me and adjusted my body so that all my attention was angled towards Andie. Nick looked slightly put out. I couldn't win.

'So, what would my hours be?' I asked, trying to sound enthusiastic, but Andie raised a dubious eyebrow as though I'd asked to have three days a week off and a private Jacuzzi installed in my bedroom.

'Five days a week, though obviously if we go away at weekends we may need help then.'

'Great. Are you, erm, working at the moment?' I asked Andie.

'No,' she snapped, then added with a tight, sarcastic smile, 'I'm just a boring old housewife.'

So why does she need a nanny? I wondered, hoping Andie wasn't going to turn out to be a lady-of-leisure type who would drape herself across a chintzy sofa, sipping Earl Grey and dispensing regal orders.

'And I work in computing,' said Nick, 'so you see, we're a very strange family. I've had a sex change and my real name is Jennifer, Andie is secretly a closet lesbian and our son Fred, aside from the horror of his nut allergy, deals in cocaine—'

'*Nick!*' Andie shrieked. Nick reached out and rubbed her hand gently, as if to say: *Don't worry, I'm just flirting.*

There was a slightly awkward silence.

Then: 'MUM, CAN I COME IN YET?'

'All right, Fred, you can come in!' Andie called. There was the sound of running footsteps and a boy of about six or seven entered the room. He had dark hair cut very neatly and a slightly shy air. He wriggled on to Andie's lap, darted a look my way – I saw that he had his father's dark eyes – and then hid his face in her jumper.

'Don't be shy, Fred.' When she spoke to her son, Andie seemed to thaw, her voice softening. 'This is Cara; she might be the new girl to look after you.'

'Hello,' Fred whispered.

'Fred's got an allergy. He can't eat nuts,' Andie said. 'Isn't that right, Freddy?'

'That's fine, Fred,' I smiled warmly at him. 'I can't eat nuts either – my skin goes really red and itchy, so we're in the same boat.'

'You do?' Andie smiled at me properly for the first time. 'Well, that will make preparing meals easier.'

She's coming round, she's coming round, I thought victoriously. I smiled at Fred again and he sat up on his mother's lap, giving me a strong stare, his shyness replaced by a slightly cocky air.

'I like her; Daddy said we should hire someone pretty,' he said.

'That's my boy!' Nick laughed. Andie gave Fred a playful nip but he pulled an innocent face. *Hmm*, I thought. In my experience children often have a much sharper idea of how to put the knife in than adults give them credit for. I gave Fred a slightly reprimanding look. He merely sneered back.

The interview continued for another five minutes as we hopped from topic to topic, from bathings (every evening at 7 p.m.) to bedtimes (bed by 8) to banned TV shows (no *Buffy*: too violent) to school (Fred was dyslexic but, of course, that didn't stop him from being a genius). I said yes, and yes, and yes again to everything they asked, desperately trying not to sound too desperate, to not give away how much this job meant to me, how it was my one chance of escape.

'Well, we'll need to check your references,' Andie said more kindly. She coughed. There was a tray with a jug of water and two pitchers on the coffee table. Just as she reached out for it, I leaped up, saying, 'Allow me.' We both hit the handle at the same time and the jug spun on its side, the water flushing out on to the carpet.

I stood frozen. *Oh God.* Andie stood breathless, watching the dark stain spreading across the rose and green twirls of her rug; the water beading her blouse and skirt.

'Oops,' said Fred, shaking his head at me.

Nick defused the tension by bursting into laughter. Tossing down a hanky on to the water, he shook my hand and grinned wryly.

'Don't worry, the carpet needed a clean anyway. We'll be in touch . . .'

Outside, my heart felt heavy. How could I have been so clumsy? I hoped I might see the gardener again but he had gone. Grey clouds had formed over the sun and there on the lawn was a single magpie, bouncing about as though silently laughing at my ill-fortune.

2
Cara

Oh my Dionysius. It was there, in the post on Tuesday morning. I woke up as soon as I heard the crash of letters hitting the mat, ran down the stairs, startling Jether, our black cat. There was a Barclaycard bill, a Thompsons catalogue and – aha – a stiff cream envelope bearing the W11 postmark. From the nanny agency.

I was still hoping I had got the job. The interview had softened in my memory over the past week. Okay, so I'd spilled a little water, but it wasn't going to stain, was it? Plus, I'd laughed at Nick's jokes, and shared a nut allergy with Fred. Surely there was still a ray of hope?

I went into the kitchen. It was disgustingly messy. There was a bottle of homemade apricot liqueur on the table and two sticky glasses, suggesting my mother had brought home male company last night. Wincing, I put them in the sink, then sat down, kissed my letter, said another prayer to Dionysius and tore open the envelope. *Dear Miss Broad, I regret to inform you that you have not been offered the post of nanny for . . .*

Fine. I tried to control my frustration but I couldn't help it: I tore the letter into neat, savage squares, scattering them over the floor in a blast of angry confetti. A moment later, I swept it all up and threw it into the bin. I had to accept my fate; it clearly wasn't meant to be.

And yet. I sat down at the kitchen table, aching with disappointment. I'd fallen in love with that big house in Richmond the moment I'd seen it: it was so grand, so beautiful, full of light and flowers. A big change from the dump of a house we had in Shepherd's Bush, full of dead moths and dust, spiderwebs laced everywhere because my mad mother gets superstitious about cleaning ('You'll sweep out all the angels and good spirits, my dear!'). Not to mention the black Madonna statues cluttering the mantelpieces, and the fact the curtains have to be kept closed at all times as Mum loathes the daylight ('My vampire genes!'). And though Andie had given me a tough time, I thought she and Nick made a nice couple. They just seemed so refreshingly *normal*. The parents I'd always wished I'd had.

Just at that moment, Mum came creaking down the stairs and swept into the kitchen. My mother never sidles or walks into a room – she struts in like an actress going on stage, waiting for all heads to turn to her.

I purposefully flurried through a copy of *Mind Body Spirit* magazine, pretending to be engrossed in the 'R U LONELY' dating column.

'Darling . . . did you hear the phone ring?'

'No,' I frowned. How interesting – *Wizard, mid-30s, seeks young witch protégée: I've got a wand but it doesn't work very well; it needs some massage to get the spark back in—*

'Did the post come?'

'Yes. And before you ask, no, I didn't get the job.'

'Oh dear, what a shame,' she said cheerfully, sitting down at the kitchen table.

She was looking a state this morning. Her long hair,

streaked with grey, trailed down her back, yesterday's make-up was still smeared on her face and she was wearing one of her flamboyant bargains from Camden market – a dreadful cerise-coloured dressing gown with black Spanish-lace frills.

She watched with narrowed eyes as I made her a cup of tea.

'Whose turn was it to do the shopping on Friday?' she demanded.

'Um, my turn.' It was *always* my turn.

'Then why the hell did you buy *triangular* tea bags? How am I supposed to read the tea leaves with those monstrosities?'

'Just rip open the bag at the end,' I shrugged.

'I,' my mother said icily, 'had a client yesterday morning and as a result of *you* I got her reading quite wrong. I told her she was a widow with two illegitimate children who was about to suffer a financial disaster.'

'What happened?'

'She'd had a hysterectomy, was happily married to a property developer and had just won the lottery. It was those bloody tea bags. I shall write and complain.'

I gently laid the teacup in front of her and, after pushing it away several times and much huffing and puffing, she took a sip. She kept moaning that it just didn't taste the same, that the flavour was cheap, but it didn't stop her drinking the whole lot. I hid a smile and started on the huge mountain of washing up in the sink.

And then I heard more footsteps on the stairs. Instantly my mother fluffed out her hair and loosened the belt on her dressing gown so that a 'V' of crêped skin was revealed at the top. I cringed in painful embarrassment, thinking: *Oh great, who the hell has she brought back this time?*

He had to be seen to be believed.

14

In the doorway stood a tall man with gladiator-style muscles. His dark hair was soaped into spikes, his face blotted with eyeliner and his mouth smeared with pink lipstick. He was wearing nothing but a few tattoos, a pair of lacy women's briefs, a suspender belt and some very laddered stockings on his hairy legs.

'Darling, darling,' my mother ran up to him and gave him a coy kiss on the cheek, 'this is my daughter, Cara. Cara, this is Carlos. I met him last night at the *Rocky Horror Picture Show*!'

I made a hasty exit. Upstairs in my room, I called Grandma.

'Did you get it?' she asked breathlessly. I didn't even need to reply; she could hear it in my voice. 'Oh Cara, I'm so sorry . . .'

My mother, who believes in reincarnation, says: 'We choose our parents, darling. Every soul chooses the little baby body they're going to inhabit in their next life – and you chose me!'. Well, if I did choose her I was obviously drunk at the time. Or else stuck in hell and desperate for any way to get out.

Sorry. That's mean. But I'm twenty-five years old now and I realise that parents, like the swing of the seasons, the rotation of solar systems, are a force of nature. You can't undo them; better to accept them. But believe me, being born the daughter of a witch is certainly never easy.

I was an accident. During her twenties, my mother met a man at an outdoor party which descended into an orgy of drug-taking and sin. They united on a mossy bed of long grass under an apple tree and made me.

I've seen a blurry photo of him, standing on Brighton beach, and he looks perfectly sweet: blond hair tossing in the breeze, eyes to match the sea. But according to Mum,

15

my father, who grows blacker and blacker in her memory every year, was a foul, evil, alcoholic, gambling, womanising bastard who got her pregnant by refusing to use condoms, was always stealing her money before disappearing off to the pub, and was known to smash furniture up when he returned in a bad temper. And then he left. Apparently just as I was emerging from the womb. He removed his hand from my mum's hysterical grip, calmly told her he was just popping down to the hospital canteen to get some cigarettes and never came back. I guess those cigarettes must have been too good to share.

My mum brought me up alone. It wasn't easy. We were very poor and my mother didn't exactly go down well at the job centre when she filled in 'Mediumship' in the 'What work would you be interested in doing?' section of the form.

School wasn't much fun for me either. My mother succeeded in making me the most unpopular girl in my primary school because I was known as 'the kid with the mad mother'.

And then came the day that changed everything.

For weeks, I'd been the subject of subtle bullying: I was always last to be chosen for any teams when we played sports; I would come into the cloakroom to find my coat on the floor, stamped with muddy footprints. But that day, the day they ganged up on me, was a strange one: wild clouds billowing across the sky, the wind slap-spinning the weathercock like a petulant child with a toy. I'd been sick with 'flu and my mother had been forcing cough medicine down my throat – a thick, homemade syrup that looked like treacle and tasted like bitter blackcurrant and tar. I'd taken too much that morning. My head felt sticky and woozy, my vision was blurry, and when I looked up at the weathervane it seemed to spin and spin until I hallucinated that it was a black metal bird, ready to fly off into the sky.

I didn't even notice the other children creeping up on me. They surrounded me in a circle, a daisy-chain of locked hands, a blur of white faces, mouths in little black 'o's, yelling, unifying into one chant: *CARA'S A WITCH, WITCH, WITCH!* The school cat, a ginger tabby, came sniffing into the circle to join in; even animals were against me. I suffered a huge rage like I've never felt before or after. It was as though a tornado began in the pit of my stomach and whirled into a huge white demon, blazing into every corner of my body . . . And then I heard an eerie silence. The chanting stopped. The weathervane creaked. I opened my eyes. Their faces were scared, their hands had dropped away. My anger was gone: I felt weak and weary. I heard a teacher shouting across the playground. I gazed down at the cat with a gasp. It had turned into the strangest mutated *thing*. That's the only way I can describe it: its fur was standing up on end, its eyes were gleaming like purple supernatural diamonds, its tail had slithered into a tapered end with a hissing snake's head.

I ran home and told my mother.

Luckily for me, my mother, for all her battiness, realised that if I carried on like this we were going to end up in real trouble. After shouting for ten minutes that I must never *ever* use magic in public again, she calmed down and looked rather proud of me. 'I was worried that I'd brought up some kind of freak,' she said with her usual bluntness, 'but it looks as though you do have powers after all. Thank God for that!'

Even so, I had to change schools. And again, and again. At each new school I found it difficult to make friends so I cocooned myself in my own world. My imagination was a magic carpet, sailing me away to other lands. I learned to tame my wild psychic energy into concentrated channels. I learned to practise magic subtly, when people's

17

backs were turned; like sending the odd stick of chalk flying across the room when a teacher annoyed me.

By secondary school, however, the magic of magic had worn off. I was tired of being different, and determined to finally fit in. I attended the local comp, where most of the lessons were riots. Like a typical teenager, I took revenge on my mother. I rebelled. But while all my friends were ruining their parents' peace of mind by smoking and drinking and all the usual stuff, I turned on my mother by becoming a Christian. I got the idea from my best friend Gemma, who taunted her Jehovah's Witness parents by pretending to be a Satanist.

I dyed my hair blonde. I sprayed our black cat with pink streaks (poor thing!). On Sunday mornings, instead of joining Mum's friendly 'psychic healing hands and communion with the dead' group, I went to church. I purposefully returned right in the middle of lunch, loudly humming hymns. My mum would cringe and mutter apologetically to the other hags: 'I'm sorry, I just don't know what's got into her. It's just a phase . . .'

'It's not a phase, Mother,' I'd interrupt, lovingly stroking the crucifix around my neck, my hair woven into two angelic plaits. 'I love Jesus and he loves all of you too.'

They would all quiver and shake their heads in outrage at my cheek.

'Oh, Mum, by the way,' I'd add, 'I've got a lovely new boyfriend. His father's a vicar and he sings in the church choir. He wants to marry me so that we can go to Africa and be missionaries together!'

'Cara,' she would hiss, her voice shaking with rage, 'I forbid you, you – you – you can't go out with filthy, disgusting, depraved boys like that! I won't allow it!'

When I became head of the local Sunday school, my mother wept. And when I was baptised, she spent an entire weekend in bed, tearing out her hair and praying to Dionysius to deliver me from the evils of the church . . .

Eventually I calmed down. I matured. I took down the LET GOD INTO YOUR LIFE posters from my walls and threw them away; my crucifix ended up in my jewellery box. I didn't want to belong to an extreme any more.

I just wanted to be normal.

And so I got through life by making a promise to myself: I would put up with my mother until the age of twenty-five and then I'd leave home. I'd get my own flat. I'd get a *normal* job. I'd get a nice boyfriend, get married, have 2.4 children and instead of getting bored, I'd *revel* in it, because for once nobody would ever be able to say I was a weirdo.

And I'd nearly pulled it off. Nearly.

I never made it to university but I studied for a diploma in nannying at the prestigious Princess Christian college. My decision to become a nanny was fairly arbitrary (although I figured that after years of looking after my mother, looking after difficult children would be a piece of cake). I passed with flying colours, signed up with an agency and got my first job with a lovely family in Primrose Hill, looking after two kids.

When I told my mother the news, she pulled her patchwork cardigan tightly around her shoulders and said: 'Oh?' Pause, then: 'Why leave? Why? Don't you like it here? Am I so dull and horrible and such a dreadful mother? What, is it a man? It's always a bloody man. Well, I'm telling you now, Cara – men are trouble. He'll just use you and abuse you and walk out on you . . .'

My job lasted three glorious, happy months until fate intervened. My mother came down with a mysterious illness that none of the doctors could diagnose. She spent weeks in hospital, surrounded by beeping machines, while they took test after useless test.

'It's Morgan, Morgan Le Fay,' my mother groaned into her pillow, referring to her worst enemy. 'She's never forgiven me for cursing her with shingles at Stonehenge last year. She's getting me back, I know she is . . .'

Eventually, reluctantly, I had to give up my job and stay at home to nurse her full time. Slowly, the tables had turned. Instead of feeling like her daughter, I became my mother's mother. Despite everything, I loved her deeply and worried about her continually. The iller she got, the more she lived life with reckless abandon. Before she went out on the town with her cronies, I always tucked condoms and a rape alarm in her handbag; I poured bottles of wine down the sink and topped them up with Ribena. But she carried on living life like one big orgy, permanently tipsy, chain-smoking until the house was a haze of coughy smog.

Finally, my grandmother came to the rescue. My grandmother is simply the most amazing woman I've ever met.

She doesn't look like a witch at all. She is very small (about five feet tall) with a neat blonde bob and thick spectacles. She always wears power suits and looks as though she ought to work in a bank rather than selling potions to heal warts or ward off spirits. I only wish I'd known her as a child – but she spent most of her life in Canada. Then she got divorced and returned to London, where she opened a New Age shop called The Mistress of Magic in Soho.

My grandmother soon took us under her wing. She was as calm as my mother was wild. She was our peacekeeper, my confidante, my mentor in magic. She sorted out our finances and saved us from losing our house (my mother had neglected to tell me that she hadn't paid the mortgage for the last six months). All in all, she was an absolute saint.

It was my grandmother who took me aside one day and said, 'Look, Cara, if you don't get away from your mother, you'll go crazy. You go and get a job, *I'll* move in and look after her.'

'But, you can't, you—' *won't have a life*, I added silently.

'I'm sixty-five years old and I've done all the things I want to. You're only just beginning, you've got your whole life ahead of you and you shouldn't let anybody take that away.'

I gave her a grateful hug and for the first time in a long while I felt truly happy.

Only here I was, with a CV with more holes in it than a sieve, unable to get a damned job. I couldn't help wondering darkly if my failed interview had been my mother's work. Had she cursed it? Maybe she'd been responsible for that jug of water tipping over . . . Suddenly I felt as though I'd never leave this house, that I'd be stuck here at the age of forty, my mother white-haired and as withered as a rotting apple, still screaming orders at me. Oh God. I looked outside at birds swooping across the sky and longed to fly free.

Be positive, I told myself firmly. *Go back to the agency and ask for more work.*

I was just about to give them a ring when I heard the front door bang. I heard my grandmother and my mother talking; my mother sounded agitated. Then my grandmother called up the stairs: 'Caaarra . . .'

Oh God, what now?

I peered down over the bannisters. My mother was looking sulky; my grandmother was positively beaming.

'That was the agency on the phone,' she said. 'They say poor old Sally Hargreaves can't be the Wilkinses' new nanny because she had an accident cycling – isn't that a *shame*, darling – but the good news is that they want *you* instead. You'd better hurry up and start packing . . .'

Five days later, I was in my new home, my new room. I liked it: it was one of those attic rooms with sloping roofs and windows cut into the wood. If I lay down on the bed, I could watch the ever-changing sky: white clouds racing across the turquoise blue, melting into the smokiness of twilight. The room was slightly bare: rugs on the wooden floor, a few pieces of antique-looking furniture: a chair, a table. The wardrobe was a big Narnian one; it smelled musty when I hung up my clothes so I lit a sandalwood incense stick.

I'd been so busy today, with Andie showing me around, introducing me to their two dogs (Mozart and Beethoven), giving me a list of foods to avoid due to Fred's allergies, not to mention all the house rules, that I hadn't even had time to unpack. It was lovely to have a moment to myself now, to stop to take a breath and digest everything.

I unzipped my suitcase. The trouble was, I had more to hide than unpack.

I had painted my little cauldron golden so that it looked like an oil burner; I also had loads of those little Body Shop bottles, though instead of containing lavender or ordinary essential oils they held various potent herbs, from jimson weed to damiana. Some even contained dreams; frothy liquids which, when opened by the ear of a sleeping person, would slither inside the ear canal and give them the most delicious dreams ... or nightmares. Others contained coughs and colds, curses and hexes. Though I wasn't planning to use them, I laid them out all the same; their familiar presence was comforting, brightening up the bare white ledge.

There was a ton of other stuff in my suitcase: spell books, wand, athame, boline, chalice, robe, pentacle. But I couldn't turn my room into a pagan shrine so I locked up my suitcase and shoved it all back under my bed.

I was just tidying the bottles on the windowsill when there was a sudden *crash!* – one overbalanced and hit the floor.

Bugger.

Bugger, bugger, bugger. I cleared up the shards, cursing as the dark liquid sank into the carpet. I had no idea what the hell it was; the label was too old and blurred. It left no stain but the smell was lethal. A violently sweet, sickly smell, like rotting flowers or overpowering incense.

I was just squirting perfume into the room when I heard voices below. A few seconds later, a dark silhouette appeared at the door. Nick.

He stood there, arms folded, his mouth grim.

'Look, I'm afraid, Cara,' he wouldn't meet my eyes; he started pushing up the corner of the rug with his shoe, 'we can't condone drugs in this house.'

'*Drugs?*'

'Andie – she could smell it yards off, coming down from your room.'

'What?' Had they found out I was a witch? Already? Had my mother tipped them off? I'd kill her.

'Cannabis.'

'*What?*'

'You heard me. Pot, grass, cannabis; whatever you call it.'

'Look,' I said, improvising quickly, 'I've never taken drugs in my whole life.' I went to the window and picked up a saucer smeared with charred crumbs, together with a packet of sandalwood incense. 'Is this what you could smell?' I asked.

It was a long shot but he seemed to buy it. I think he realised I just wasn't the type.

'Yes – oh God!' He frowned. 'Shit – sorry – um, right. Sandalwood incense. Look – I'm really sorry, Cara, we just got the wrong end of the stick. This is all a bit new to us, having a nanny, we're nervous. God, just ignore me, okay?'

Nervous? I was touched. And here I was thinking I was the one who might not fit in.

23

I opened my mouth to tell him I was just as nervous – when I saw it: a taut black spiral of smoke uncurling from the stain on the carpet. I glanced at Nick but, thank God, he couldn't seem to see it. Like most adults, he was obviously dull to magical happenings. We create our own realities and that which we don't believe in we rarely perceive.

The black smoke hovered in mid-air, in the shape of a question mark, as though debating which one of us to attack.

'Are you okay, Cara?' Nick stepped forward and rubbed my shoulder gently.

Big mistake. The spiral went whizzing up his right nostril.

'Atissssosssh,' Nick sneezed violently.

'Bless you,' I muttered guiltily, quickly passing him a Kleenex.

'Sorry,' said Nick, 'it's probably just my hayfever coming on. Anyhow, feel free to help yourself to a bite to eat tonight if you're hungry, or maybe you'll just want an early night. Fred's already in bed, but you can get to –' he sneezed again, wiped his nose '– know him better in the morning – *atissosshh*. Urgh.'

Despite his rapidly declining state of health he lingered, still feeling guilty about his earlier mistake. 'It's a lovely view from this window, isn't it?' he nodded.

We both looked out. The large detached houses in the road all boasted huge gardens that stretched out in sweeps of green and eventually dissolved into grassland.

Down in the garden next door I could see my friend from the interview drinking Guinness. An old man with a hoary beard had put a Kylie Minogue album on his portable stereo and was jiving about on the grass in a pair of purple flares as though he was in a nightclub.

'God, our neighbours!' Nick groaned. 'Those guys next door are seriously weird – like an Emerald Isle version of

Steptoe and Son. They're harmless, but still. They've probably knocked about ten grand off the property prices by their sheer presence.'

I burst into laughter at his rudeness.

'I just hope the old git trips over and gets confined to a zimmer frame.'

'*Nick!* That's mean!' I gave him a shove and he laughed, winking at me. He sneezed again and rolled his eyes. 'Shit, I'd better take some antihistamine. Goodnight, Cara.'

'Goodnight – and – oh, sorry about the incense thingey – I mean, it's all fine, forgotten and . . .' I trailed off.

Nick paused, giving me a funny, fond smile.

'You are sweet,' he said, before disappearing out of the room.

After he'd gone, I gave myself a telling-off. I debated clearing up Nick's cold with another spell but I'd only been there five minutes and I was supposed to be avoiding magic. No, I decided, I'd let it lie. Perhaps I would cook him a nice breakfast the next morning to make him feel better.

Feeling exhausted after such a long day, I went to bed early. But around 3 a.m. I was woken up again. No matter how much lavender I crush under my pillow, I'm a very light sleeper. Hearing agitated voices, I realised that Andie and Nick's bedroom was directly below mine. Great. I couldn't catch their argument, though I did feel guilty when I heard Andie, clearly a fellow insomniac, hiss: 'How can I sleep when you're sneezing every other minute?'

When I went down to breakfast in the morning, however, they were all bright smiles and happy couples again; and I was left wondering if I had just imagined it . . .

3
Andie

Andie couldn't believe it.

The bathroom door was locked.

Cara was *inside*.

At *7 a.m.* Andie's time. Twenty minutes before Nick would then claim the bathroom for his half-hour slot before work.

Andie let out her breath and tried to loosen the tight knot coiling in her heart. She told herself to just let it go, not to turn it into a big deal. Cara would be out soon, surely?

She went back into the bedroom and started to make the bed, yanking sheets with ferocious energy, pounding pillows and plumping the duvet. Nobody said that getting a nanny would be easy; it was bound to take time to adjust. She looked at the clock. Five minutes had passed. What the hell was Cara doing in there? Suddenly Andie flipped. *It's my house*, she thought. *This isn't a hotel. I'm paying Cara to be here. I'm the boss.*

She marched back out to the bathroom and rapped on the door. 'Cara, could you please come out now? I really, really need the bathroom.'

'Sure.' Cara came out wrapped in a towel, her hair sticky and obviously still gunked with shampoo, her face slightly panicked. Immediately Andie felt guilty, remembering Nick's words: 'It's as hard for her as it is for us, remember.'

'Look, at least finish washing your hair—' Andie began.

'No, it's fine.' Cara darted off up to the attic like a frightened rabbit.

Andie supervised Fred's wash and then sent him down to the kitchen while she dressed and did her make-up. She didn't normally bother but there was something about having a beautiful girl in the house that had suddenly made her conscious of her own appearance.

Down in the kitchen, Andie found Nick reading the *Daily Telegraph* while munching his way through about ten slices of toast. Despite her matted hair being scrunched into a ponytail, Cara was looking horribly, offensively gorgeous in a summery top and a pale pink skirt that flowed around her knees. Andie swore Nick was flicking more glances at her legs than his crossword. Humph.

Andie ran a hand through her messy curls and swung open the fridge door, taking out bread to make sandwiches for Fred's lunch.

She was just raking butter on to a piece of granary bread when she became aware that Fred's lunchbox wasn't in its usual place on the worksurface . . .

. . . it was in Cara's hands, being snapped firmly shut.

Cara met her eyes. 'Sorry,' she said as she realised their cross-purposes. 'I just thought it might help you if I . . .'

'Well, let me check it.'

'Yeah, because Cara might have slipped in the odd nuclear bomb,' Nick said.

Cara smiled sheepishly and chewed her nails as Andie looked into the lunchbox with the attentive fervour of a UN inspector.

An apple. A carton of pure orange juice. Marmite sandwiches (Fred was a Marmite-aholic). And a Twix bar.

'This will have to come out,' said Andie.

'But *Mum*!' Fred cried.

'Sorry – Fred told me that he was normally allowed one,' said Cara.

'These are a *special treat* for Fred,' said Andie firmly, removing the offending item. She patted Fred's head, for he was moaning – though not much, having known he was pushing his luck.

Out in the hall, Andie held out Fred's coat to him only to find Cara was by his side, helping to put on his shoes. Andie did up the buttons on his coat as Cara did his laces. Fred grinned, enjoying the attention.

Then Cara grabbed one hand and Andie the other. Both stared at each other.

'What are you doing?' Andie asked.

'I thought I should take him to school . . . since I'm the, ah, nanny,' Cara whispered.

Andie couldn't help it. A rush of images flashed through her mind: Cara forgetting to remind Fred of the Green Cross Code, letting him run into the road; Cara taking Fred down by the river and Fred jumping into the Thames; Cara scooping up Fred and saying, 'You're the child I always wanted but could never have' and running off with him, never to be seen again . . .

'It's fine, I'm taking him,' said Andie, 'you don't know the way.'

Cara opened her mouth. Nick appeared in the hallway, looking cross. Andie didn't care. She grabbed Fred and rushed out through the front door.

Outside, they walked down past the Thames. Andie watched Fred dancing down the path, thwacking a stick and pretending the willow trees were attacking aliens, and felt a wave of love for him. She was doing the right thing, she was. They didn't know Cara yet; she had to earn their trust first.

'Mum, what's that bird?' Fred asked, pointing to a large, pinkish-brown bird with beady eyes that had darted across their path.

'I don't know, darling,' Andie said, smiling. Fred had recently developed an obsession with nature and they had filled a whole scrapbook with feathers and pressed flowers, dead butterflies and discarded eggshells.

Then Fred made her laugh by miaowing at the bird and frightening it away.

'Don't be mean!' She ruffled his hair. He grinned up at her and she took his hand in hers, pressing it tightly. 'So what do you think of the new nanny?' she asked tentatively. *Please say you don't like her*, she added silently, then felt mean.

'I like her,' said Fred. 'But I liked Sally better. Mum, why couldn't we have Sally?'

'Ask your Dad,' Andie grumbled under her breath. She'd been taken by Sally too, whom they'd interviewed right before Cara. Nick had complained that she'd been 'dumpy and spotty' but they were hiring a nanny, not bloody Miss World, weren't they? Sally had had three years' experience and gleaming references.

When Sally'd had to drop out due to a broken leg, Andie had wanted to wait until she got better, but Nick had insisted they go for Cara. It was funny – most people who knew Andie and Nick thought that Andie, the feisty one, was the boss in their relationship. But Nick, despite his joking veneer, could be very intense when he wanted his way, and he'd been dead set that Cara was the one.

Andie dropped Fred off and walked back home slowly. She'd been planning to enroll for art classes this morning but now the thought of having to shave her legs, wash her

29

hair and then get on a hot tube seemed way too much effort.

So when she got home, she took the dogs for a brisk walk. Back in the kitchen, she let them off their leashes and picked up her lighter without thinking. *No, Andie*, she reprimanded herself sharply, putting it back down on the table. On the wall was a large chart, drawn up by Fred, with MUMMY AND DADDY MUST STOP SMOKING written on it in wobbly felt pen. She and Nick had to tick each day they were good – starting from today.

In the living room she settled down with a magazine and a cup of tea. She had to get on with the hoovering and go to Sainsbury's, but she'd just squeeze in ten minutes of indulgence. She was just enjoying a particularly juicy letter in the problem pages when an annoying noise started to bug her. Had Nick left the radio on? Then she realised it was Cara, singing in the kitchen. She was quite out of tune. Andie tried to read on but the lyrics kept tossing little hooks of irritation into her brain, reeling her concentration away. Oh bloody hell.

Suddenly the house felt like a prison. Andie jumped up, grabbed her bag and dashed out of the house, leaving Cara to call out behind her, 'Um, shall I get Fred this afternoon or will you be back . . .?'

Fuck off, fuck off, fuck off, thought Andie.

On the underground, she calmed down. She realised she'd been overreacting. Again.

Getting a nanny definitely wasn't something that Andie had ever planned to do.

Mind you, very few things in Andie's life had ever been planned. Andie might have looked like your average middle-class housewife, but her background didn't match the cliché.

Andie was an only child. Her parents had conceived her late in life, with the help of fertility treatments, and her forty-year-old mother had named her Annabel. Andie had never lived up to the sweet cloying girlishness of her name; she'd been trouble since the day she was born. She'd been a noisy baby, crying all the time. At school she was always bottom of the class; as a teenager she dyed her hair pink and joined a rock band. She even managed to get herself expelled for setting off fireworks in the girls' toilets.

She'd met Nick at a cousin's wedding. She'd been the bridesmaid and he the best man. The *gorgeous* best man; the dark-haired man in a suit who looked like Keanu Reeves; the man half the female congregation had their eye on – even Andie's aunt muttered, 'God, he's a dish' under her breath. To this day, Andie wasn't quite sure how she'd managed to nab him. Particularly since she'd drunk too much champagne and when Nick had appeared next to her, smiled at her with his lopsided, sexy smile and asked if she wanted to dance, she'd puked up over his trousers. But Nick, the sweetie, had looked after her, taken her home and brought her breakfast in bed the next morning (with a few paracetamols for her hangover). Andie hadn't really expected it to last, but their one-morning-stand turned into a fling which turned into a relationship and suddenly, six months later, she was amazed to find that she had fallen madly in love.

And so Andie had defied everyone's expectations. Instead of joining a rock group and travelling the world, throwing TVs out of hotel windows as she'd always boasted to her friends, she ended up shocking them all by conforming, settling down and getting married by the age of nineteen.

Several of Andie's friends fell away, declaring that she was being 'boring'. But Andie felt that her life had never been more of an adventure. Nick wanted to start up a computer business but they were both completely broke. They rented an insalubrious flat in a graffitied block in

Wood Green, borrowed shocking sums from the bank, lived off baked beans and only treated themselves to one meal out a month. Andie helped to raise extra cash by taking her PCGE and working as a primary school teacher. She felt as though everyone was waiting for them to fail, which only made the bond between them stronger; it was her and Nick versus the world! When Nick's business took off, she'd never felt so proud or triumphant in her life; now it was their turn to stick two fingers up at everyone for doubting them. To celebrate, they flew to Paris for a crazy weekend, making endless, ecstatic love and knocking back so much champagne that – to their giggling embarrassment – they found they couldn't afford the hotel bill. That night, Fred was conceived.

That was when the trouble started. Andie and Nick were thrilled about the pregnancy. But once Fred was born, Andie found things tough. She realised then that the price paid for money and success was time. Nick simply didn't have any. He worked late nights, he worked weekends, he had no energy to change nappies, no energy to get up in the night. Andie and Nick took it in turns to soothe Fred, marking points like a score card – *I've got to go to work on three hours sleep*, Nick would cry in the mornings; *we've had this baby together, you can't just run off and expect me to do everything*, Andie would yell back. Andie felt increasingly down. All her friends were out having fun, clubbing, setting up careers in marketing and publishing and fashion and other glitzy-sounding industries. And here she was, stuck in a big white house all day with a thing that wouldn't stop screaming. She couldn't work out why she felt so tired either – a grey, moth-eaten tiredness that fell over everything like a veil. Andie had always regarded herself as being quite tough, both physically and emotionally. She was the sort of person who breezed through winters without even catching colds and secretly felt most illness was really hypochondria.

It was a relief for Andie when she was diagnosed with post-natal depression; she'd been so lacking in maternal feelings that she worried she was a bad mother. She got better, Nick sold his business and got a new, less stressful job and life became sunny again. But that was the trouble with their relationship, Andie mused. Their marriage seemed strong but she'd realised in recent years that it was as fragile as ice. The moment they suffered pressure or stress, things began to fall apart.

Like last year.

Andie's mother suffered a fall and broke her hip. It was a massive shock for Andie to see her mother in hospital, scared and confused. Even though she gave up teaching to help look after her mother, once again things started to get on top of her – the whirlwind spin of school, lunchtimes, trips home to help her dad, trips to the hospital to help her mother. Once again, Nick just hadn't been there. She wanted someone to be with in the evenings after a tough day, to hug her and talk things over, to heal her aching heart, but by the time Nick got home at ten or eleven at night Andie was normally crashed out in bed. Eventually it all got on top of her and she came down with glandular fever and ended up in bed for six weeks.

That was when Nick suggested she get a nanny.

'Look, Andie, you're a wonderful, wonderful mother. I think you think you're some sort of failure by giving in and getting a nanny but you're not. It's perfectly normal. You deserve it, you deserve all the help we can get you . . .'

And he pulled her into his arms in a deep hug and to Andie's surprise a huge wave of relief washed over her, in admitting that yes, she wasn't superwoman, that yes, she needed help, and she kissed him in tearful gratitude.

The trouble was, Andie couldn't help secretly feeling

that getting a nanny was creating *more* stress, not less. When she'd asked her friends for advice on hiring a nanny, they'd all said, 'Just don't get a blonde.' And now they'd bloody ended up with some sex kitten who looked like she belonged in the centrefold of *Playboy*. Jesus. Nick was bound to fancy her, *and* he was a horrific flirt. Andie knew he did it partly to tease her, but still.

As Andie got off the tube, she realised the other problem was that, despite her tiredness, she found having nothing to do all day deeply boring. Nick had suggested she take up art classes (Nick was full of suggestions for her, Andie thought somewhat bitterly, as though she was a kid who needed to be kept occupied.)

Still, it might be fun. She went through the door to Richmond Library and enquired about joining their art class. The receptionist suggested Andie take a look at a class in progress to see what she thought, so she found her way to the art studio and sat down. She was slightly shocked to discover that she seemed to be the only person there below the age of fifty. How sad am I? Andie thought, if my social life equates to that of an OAP.

She was even more shocked when the art teacher informed them that today's class was life drawing. An old man appeared, lounged across a bed and threw off a sheet. Andie took one look at him and decided that she had no desire to translate Kieran's tangled beard, withered skin and crusty-looking knob into watercolour. Pretending she needed the loo, she made a quiet, giggling exit.

Outside, she was so tickled that she phoned up Nick, knowing he would find the story hilarious.

'Sorry,' his secretary said, 'I'm afraid you can't speak to him. He's in a meeting all day.'

4
Cara

Dear Cara
Please can I remind you that the milk goes in the bottom *left-hand corner of the fridge, not the top shelf. If it gets knocked over it spills on the rest of the food.*
Thanks, A.

I tore the Post-It from the fridge and threw it at the bin. It missed and bounced off into one of the dog bowls.

In the last week, Andie had got into the habit of leaving pernickety little Post-Its for me around the house. Like the bathroom (*Toothbrushes in the pot, please!*), the dining room (*Please remember to keep the dogs out, the rugs are new*) and the hall (*Could you take care not to brush or knock the spider plants when going down the stairs, it damages the leaves*). For a moment I was tempted to take revenge and turn them all into butterflies – the thought of a wave of fluttering Post-Its clouding around Andie was amusingly tempting. But – no magic. I was trying to be normal.

I sat down at the kitchen table, suddenly overcome with tiredness and despair. In my last job I'd settled in relatively quickly, but things at the Wilkinses seemed to be going from bad to worse.

Andie was still snapping at me all the time; no matter what I did, I couldn't get anything right. At first I thought she was just moody from giving up smoking. But it was more than that – she seemed to have taken an instant dislike to me but I couldn't work out why. At least she'd finally trusted me to look after Fred for (whey-hey!) one hour this morning. But Fred had been very difficult over the last week. The novelty of a new nanny had worn off; plus he'd picked up on Andie's mistrust and was now manipulating it.

Whenever Andie did pluck up the courage to leave him with me, his eyes would fill with tears and he'd say in a small, bewildered voice, 'Doesn't Mummy want me any more, doesn't she love me?', causing Andie to hug him and look wretched with guilt. The moment she'd gone he'd forget about her, zooming round the house doing aeroplane impressions.

Worse, whenever Andie came back, he'd jump up from playing quietly and turn into a young hooligan. So Andie never saw me helping him to colour in a picture; she came back to find Fred jumping over her double bed while I tried to tussle him off, or trying to climb up onto a stool – 'Mummy, I just wanted the matches, Cara said I could play with them!' That day, I'd already overheard Andie saying to Nick: 'The agency said she was *good*. I dread to think what a *bad* one would be like.'

Fred, all in all, was a problem child. More than once I thought longingly of the last children I'd looked after, the dull but placid Julie-Ann and Mary, who spent all day dressing their dolls in their thirty-seven different outfits.

Sighing, I got up from the kitchen table and decided to tackle the washing up. Strictly speaking, housework wasn't part of my duties, but I was determined to make a good impression or at this rate I wasn't going to last much longer . . .

'Hi,' said a voice behind me. I turned to see a guy wearing nothing but sandals and a pair of frayed denim shorts that showed off his luscious brown tan.

'Um, hi,' I smiled.

'Hey, glad you got the job,' he said with a wry grin. 'All thanks to me.'

'What d'you mean?'

'I put in a good word for you with the Wilkinses,' he winked. 'And twenty quid.'

'Oh. Well. I guess I owe you twenty quid then,' I said, laughing.

'You'd better repay me soon,' he added, and I thought he raised a flirtatious eyebrow.

'*SEAN!*' Fred had been playing in the garden with his wormery (though, rather worryingly, this had mostly involved decapitating them with his spade). Now he ran in and threw his arms around Sean's thighs.

'Hey, Fred, how'yer doing? Having a good day?'

'Have you got a nice willy?' Fred jumped up and down, pointing at his shorts.

'Fred!' I cried, laughing and clamping my hand over his mouth. It was the same every time I took him up to the toilet; Fred would wave his genitals around, saying, 'Look, Cara, it's a willy, it's a willy!'

'Sorry, Sean – he's just – er – got a bit of a fascination with body parts at the moment, ever since a lesson last week at school.'

'School?'

'You know, forward-thinking education. They think kids might get pregnant at six these days,' I joked. 'They'll probably be handing out free condoms next.'

37

I liked the way Sean's eyes crinkled up when he laughed.

As they nattered away, I went back to the washing up. I couldn't help feeling a tad jealous. Why couldn't I handle Fred the way Sean did?

'Can Maeve come and play?' Fred asked.

My ears pricked up. Maeve? Sean had a kid? He was *married*? I was surprised. And, I admit, a little disappointed.

'Maeve's in Ireland at the moment. She might be visiting soon, though not with her mummy.'

Oh, so he was divorced. Hmm.

To my annoyance, Fred got bored of the conversation just when it was getting interesting, and Sean went off outside to start mowing the lawn.

I took Fred outside again and we started a game of hide-and-seek. 'I'm bored of being outside,' Fred complained.

'No, you're not,' I said fiercely. Sean's muscles were rippling as he unloaded the mower; I resisted a girlish urge to wolf-whistle. 'There's lots of lovely things to look at. Throw the ball for the dogs or something.'

Fred, thankfully, became engrossed in a new game: putting sheets of paper over the bark of trees and scratching with a pencil to form a knarled etching. I felt hot and thirsty. So did Sean. He'd laid down his mower and was rubbing his sweaty back.

'I made some lemonade earlier,' I told Sean. 'D'you want some?'

'Thanks,' he said.

In the kitchen, I poured the pale fizzy liquid into some glasses. Sean followed me inside. A Post-It was hanging off his dirty forefinger.

'Oh!' I laughed. 'You've got one too! One of Andie's notes!'

And that broke the ice. Soon we were sipping our lemonade and having a good old bitch. Nothing is more bonding, especially when you're first making friends with someone. Seeing that Fred was content with his trees and worms, we sat and cheerfully slated Andie to death.

Sean, getting completely carried away, picked up a sheet of paper and a pencil. 'Come on, let's write her a note.'

'Sean!' I laughed. 'Okay, what about this: "Every time you leave us a Post-It, we regret to inform you that there will be a new charge of five pounds (each!) for administration and processing fees."

'Point two: "Please could you remember to take the Haagen Dazs ice cream out of the fridge and leave it outside Cara's bedroom door with a freshly washed spoon every morning."

'Three – I know: "Please could you remember to leave your toothbrush by the toilet bowl—"'

'Cara, where's this one heading?' Sean nudged me, cracking up. 'You filthy girl!'

I was laughing so hard I couldn't finish.

By the time we reached point ten we were in hysterics. After suffering the weighty responsibilities of my job all week, it was wonderful to be so childish.

Then our laughter died away and we sobered up, a silence passing between us.

'So, seriously, how are you finding life at the Wilkinses?' Sean asked. And suddenly I was tired of wanting to appear perfect, of pretending everything was fine. I wanted someone to see that I was human for once.

'I'm having a really, really hard time,' I burst out. And then it all gushed out: my problems with Fred; Andie's mistrust; Nick winding up Andie by flirting with me all the time . . .

'Look, I know I've just spent the last twenty minutes slagging Andie off, but she might soften up. I hated her when I first started here but her bark is worse than her bite. She's got a good heart.' Sean gave me a reassuring pat on the back and I curled in as though to hug him; but then we both became self-conscious, aware that we had only just met, and pulled back awkwardly.

Suddenly I felt a little tearful. I hadn't realised how much Andie was getting me down; Sean's kindness had moved me.

'I just need to go to the loo,' I said. 'Can you keep an eye on Fred for five minutes?'

Upstairs in the bathroom, my tears dried up quickly. I felt glad that Sean was next door. At least I had an ally to help me through the rocky times, and it looked as if there was going to be plenty of those ahead.

Then I heard a scream from downstairs. I instantly shot out of the bathroom, doing up my trousers as I jumped two-at-a-time down the stairs.

'CARA!' Andie bellowed from the living room. So she was home.

'Mummy, I didn't mean to be naughty, I'm sorry,' said Fred, not sounding very sorry at all.

Oh God. What had he done this time?

Andie was standing in the living room, jangling her keys, the other hand planted on her hip. 'Look!'

I looked. Andie had a beautiful beige sofa, decorated with embroidered green and ochre cushions. On one of these cushions was a large clod of earth. Ants were scurrying gleefully in all directions. The dogs were nuzzling the debris, earthy paw prints everywhere.

'Oh Fred!' I stared at him and tears filled his eyes.

'I – I just wanted to make a nice home for them. You said they needed a nice home – so I wanted them to watch TV – and play on the cushions—'

'Well, you'd better help Cara clean up, hadn't you!' said

Andie roughly, then sighed in exasperation as he burst into tears, scooping him up in a cuddle. She carried him into the kitchen. I heard the angry clatter of a bucket being yanked from the cupboard under the sink, water blasting from the tap.

'I'm really sorry, I'll clean it up,' I said when she came back in.

'No, I'll do it,' she snapped, her voice rising again. 'You'll only spoil it. Jesus, this sofa cost over two thousand pounds,' she added, kneeling down and gently brushing it off with the utmost care.

Then she muttered something about the cloth not being suitable and went stalking back into the kitchen. I followed her lamely.

'Mrs Wilkins, I just came by to see if you had my pay—' Sean came in through the back door and I gave him a look of warning that this was a danger zone he should keep out of. He stopped short.

'Can we discuss it later? Fred has just deposited an ant's nest on my settee,' Andie said tartly.

'Oh God. That's my fault, I was supposed to . . .' I shook my head at him sharply but he carried on. 'Mrs Wilkins, I was supposed to be looking after Fred while Cara went to the toilet. And I, being the stupid eijit I am, forgot about him and let him go wandering off. It was only for a few minutes.'

'A few minutes is all they need. Well. I don't know,' Andie said, but her voice was much softer. Then she shot me another frown, as if she was quite upset that it wasn't my fault.

'Sorry.' Sean put on his best boyish wince.

Typical, I thought, *if I was a nice young man, my job would be a lot easier* . . . All the same, I was grateful to him for covering for me.

41

'"Dear Andie"... what's this?' Andie suddenly spotted the note lying on the kitchen table.

Sean and I froze in horror. Then Sean, quick as a flash, pulled the note away, folding it up briskly.

'What was that?' Andie enquired again, her tone deadly.

Sean and I stood before her, quivering like two naughty school kids before a headteacher.

'Nothing. Just a note about my pay,' said Sean.

We both visibly slumped with relief as Andie pursed her lips and then went back to searching for a new cloth.

'By the way, Andie,' Sean said, as he turned to go.

'Yes?'

'I'd just like to say, I think Cara is a fabulous nanny. I was watching her this morning with Fred and she's so good with him. You must be pleased you've got such a good catch.'

Andie turned around, rolling the cloth in her hands.

'Er, yes,' she said with a fragile smile that slowly widened into something more confident. 'Yes, she is.'

I blinked at Sean and he winked at me, giving me a surreptitious thumps-up. *Thank you, thank you, thank you,* I whispered inside. I felt like running up and giving him a great big hug. Instead, I just smiled a shy goodbye.

Later that night, I sat up in bed in my nightie, trimming my split-ends and churning over what an awful day it had been. Except for Sean.

I flashed a glance at my window. It was directly opposite Sean's next door and I could see straight into his bedroom: the bookshelves piled with clutter, the chaos of clothes on the floor.

He is sexee, I thought dreamily, but then I stopped myself.

You see, I really wasn't interested in romance at the moment.

I've always been wary of men. I guess my mother is responsible. From a young age I was used to hearing that men were the cause of all sin. It was Adam's fault that Eve got kicked out of the Garden of Eden – 'So she wanted to eat a bloody *apple*? So what? They had to eat something, they were hungry . . .' And, of course, there were my mother's witchy coffee mornings where the hags would sit around cackling at sexist jokes, such as, 'What type of men hang around in singles bars? Married ones' And so on . . .

When I was a teenager, I always pretended to agree with Mum but deep down I was a romantic. I was in love with the idea of love, and, more worryingly, tragic love; I adored *Wuthering Heights* and *Les Liaisons Dangereuses*, and I think perhaps I secretly felt a love affair wasn't real unless it ended in tears or lifelong agony.

I first fell in love most unexpectedly – when Mum dragged me to a tantric sex class. These were held in someone's back garden and consisted of lots of scuzzy men with New Age beards and women wearing ankle-bracelets having sex at various places on the lawn while the instructor cooed: 'And let your energy rise, rise, RISE upwards.'

The instructor took me by surprise because he was (a) tall (b) had a spruce dark haircut (c) didn't smell and (d) generally looked as though he could be working behind the desk at a bank. I never joined in, just sat on the sidelines humming and pretending the shrubs were fascinating, but I was aware of him flicking looks at me throughout the class. A few nights later, we went for an illicit drink; I was only seventeen but I lied about my age. He kept telling me how beautiful I was, touching my face and enjoying my blushes, making me laugh by saying he thought tantric sex was a load of bull; he was only doing the classes to pay off a big tax bill. That night, we ended up in a hotel bed. I lost my virginity and it was satisfyingly painful.

I fell deeply, madly, tantricly in love. I skipped A-level classes to be with him. We made plans to run away together, move abroad. And then I made a fatal mistake. I told him that I was a witch.

I know it was crazy, but as every teenager who lacks proper parental guidance knows, you've got to seek advice from somewhere. I couldn't extract any wisdom from my mother so I buried myself in romantic books and movies. And at that point in time I'd just finished a trashy romance about a rich man falling for a poor girl who tried to hide her embarrassing background. The book had made a big impression on me because, in the end, the man found out the truth, took the woman in his arms and said gravely, 'Matilda, I don't care who your family is, or how much money you make, I'll always love you for you.' The moral of the book was: always be honest and allow a man to accept you for who you are.

Yeah, right. My lover told me that he was very, um, glad I was a witch. He said he thought it was cool. But everything changed. His supply of kisses and hugs, white roses and Godiva chocolates slowly dried up. I broke down one night and confronted him tearfully: 'Every time we make love, you have this look on your face as though I'm a total freak!' I was reassured when he cuddled me and said, 'Cara, of course I don't! I think you're very interesting . . . very unique . . . and if we were all the same the world would be a very boring place.'

And then one day I bunked off school early. I crept into his flat and knew at once that something was wrong. I saw them through a slit in the bathroom doorway: lying in the bath, wreathed with bubbles, sipping post-coital glasses of red wine. His arms were circled around her and she was laughing, 'God, if she found out about us, she might put a spell on us . . .' And he choked on his wine and spluttered, 'God, I know! Every time I fuck her I'm convinced she's going to turn me into something. I just think: what a freak!'

I walked out of the flat and went home to cry in my mother's triumphant arms. She told me she wasn't surprised and concluded, 'Darling, I did tell you – there are only three certainties in life: death, taxes, and that all men are bastards.'

I didn't laugh. I confronted him hysterically and he confessed that, um, he'd forgotten to mention that, yes, he had a 'girlfriend' (so what the hell did that make *me*?). I didn't eat for a week. For the first time in my life I used black magic. I melted a black candle into his shape and slowly sliced pins into it; I buried a bad egg with his name scrawled across the shell in the garden, knowing voodoo wisdom believed he would decay with it . . .

A few weeks later, when I found out that he'd split up from his girlfriend because he'd discovered she was actually married, I felt triumphant. And then guilty. And then very sad. There is nothing more upsetting for a teenager than finding out your mother was right all along.

My sadness hardened into a shell of cynicism. If all men were bastards, I was going to take revenge. I took vicious pleasure in one-night stands; I took delight in leaving fake numbers so that when they tried to call me they'd get a premier sex phoneline or the local psychiatric ward.

But one morning I woke up in a bed smeared with cigarette ash, lying opposite a spotty back and a bald head, a black hole in my heart. And I thought: *I'm turning into my mother. A woman who loathes men but is still desperate enough to have sex.*

So since then I've been celibate. A nun. Seriously – for the last four years, I haven't so much as kissed a man. I've been so busy sorting out my mother and her lovelife I hadn't had time. *And now I'll be so busy looking after the Wilkins family I definitely won't have time*, I thought firmly.

All the same, it would be nice to have an ally, a friend next door, someone to laugh and bitch with when times got tough. As I switched off my light, I could see a warm yellow glow spilling over from Sean's bedroom window and somehow it comforted me as I drifted off to sleep . . .

Later that night, I was woken by another of Andie and Nick's loudly whispered bickering sessions, only this time it was much, much worse.

I switched on my lamp groggily; the golden light sent shadows flitting across the walls like Egyptian spirits. 12:03 a.m. God, what was the matter with them, were they closet vampires who got a seductive thrill out of domestics? And then I heard Andie saying, '. . . she's just incompetent.'

'Andie, that's because you won't let her do her job properly—'

'No, there's something weird about her. I can't put my finger on it, there just is. I never wanted to hire her. As far as I'm concerned, she's on probation for the next week. After that—'

'Tsch—'

'No, Nick, I'm *serious*. If she doesn't improve after a week, we're hiring someone else.'

And I realised, with a horrible chill, that they were talking about me.

5
Cara

The next morning I woke up feeling awful. I'd barely slept, tossing and turning between bursts of indignation and worry. I sat up in bed and glared at my bedside clock. Seven-thirty. I didn't feel I could face going down to breakfast and forcing myself to be nice to Andie.

Maybe it's never going to work, I thought, sinking into a grey gloom. *Maybe I should resign and accept that I'm never going to have a normal life.*

I thought of my mother with a pang. I thought of what we'd normally be doing at this time of the morning: cooking up a fried breakfast, nagging and teasing each other, and I was surprised to find tears stinging my eyes. Overwhelmed with homesickness, I picked up my mobile phone and dialled home. After about twenty rings, my mother answered.

'Oh, it's you,' she said, rather haughtily. 'So, how's the new job, hmmm?'

'It's okay . . . kind of . . .' I said in a ragged voice.

'*Kind of?*' I could hear the triumph in her voice. Suddenly I stopped missing her and all my usual irritation came flooding back. She was just waiting to say, *I told you so.*

'Actually, it's great,' I said. 'Fabulous. Everyone loves me. I'm like Mary Poppins.'

'And look what happened to her – she fell down a chimney and ended up hanging out with a man with a strange pseudo-Cockney accent,' said my mother.

'Mum, Mary Poppins never fell down a chimney! She glides around gracefully on an umbrella!' I yelped.

'Well, how absurd is that. The tube is so much more sensible. Look, I must go,' she cut me off, 'the new lodger is coming.'

'*Lodger?*'

'Yes, lodger. Since you don't live here any more, I thought it was a waste of space leaving your room empty.'

I felt my throat grow dry. What if I got sacked? I'd be homeless. Oh God.

'Your grandmother wants to speak to you,' my mother added, without saying goodbye.

'How's it going, Cara?' my grandmother asked. Her voice was so warm and stable compared to my mother's.

'Fine, fine. I just . . . I'm having a bit of trouble with, um, the head of the house, Andie, but I'm sure she'll get used to me.' I gave a hollow laugh.

'Well, try not to get bogged down in negativity,' said my grandmother, seeing straight to the heart of the situation as always. 'Andie's behaviour is probably more a reflection of her own worries than anything to do with you. Try to be positive, try to help her. Treat her like a friend, don't let her turn into an enemy.'

That was the amazing thing about my grandmother; she always told me just the right thing at the right time. After I'd put down the phone, I felt much better. Yes, I thought, I'll be positive. I'll work out what's going wrong with Andie and Nick and I'll help her.

The only trouble was, how? In order to gain her

confidence, I was going to have to befriend her, and how was I supposed to befriend someone who clearly hated me?

There must be something I could *do* for her . . . Often it's the little things in life that make big differences . . . Like cooking her something nice . . .

Yes, that was it! I'd cook her breakfast, the biggest and best breakfast ever cooked by any nanny in the history of nannydom.

Downstairs in the kitchen, Fred was doing some homework at the table and Nick was reading a paper; Andie was still in the shower.

'How about if I cook you a fried breakfast?' I asked brightly.

'That would be fantastic!' Nick's eyes mooned like an excited kid being promised sweets as I set to work. 'Would that include fried eggs . . .?'

'Bacon, fried bread, baked beans.' I smiled. 'Don't you normally have time for cooking? I guess you have to dash off to work in the mornings.'

'Andie's cooking is pretty dreadful,' Nick lowered his voice, shooting me a sidelong glance. He shut up and gave me a quick wink as Andie came in.

I saw her breathe in that lovely scent of hot oil and butter and sizzling bacon curling at the edges. I waited for her to beam with delight.

'I won't have any, thanks,' said Andie, knocking back a handful of vitamins and then forcing them on to Nick. 'Go on, darling, they're good for you.' The sub-text being: all that cholesterol won't be.

I bit my lip, swallowing back my disappointment. After Nick's remark about her cooking, though, I deliberately let the breakfast burn. Just a bit. Just so it wasn't too perfect.

At least Nick appreciated my cooking. He sighed and groaned with pleasure.

49

'Dad, who was Florence Nightingale?' Fred asked, looking up from his schoolbook.

'She was a footballer. Christ, this food is *amazing*.' Nick grinned at me, mouth full.

'She was *not* a footballer,' Andie suddenly clicked, a moment too late.

'Oh, I've written it in now,' Fred cried. '*Dad!*'

He laughed, and Andie giggled, and I chuckled, and Nick joined in and for a moment we were all encircled by laughter. I felt I belonged, and the pinched feeling in my heart loosened, and I thought with happy relief: *Just maybe, maybe I can fit in here.* I think I got carried away at this point, because Nick started chatting about the horoscopes in the *Daily Mail*, asked me if I believed in astrology and I ended up offering to read their palms, adding as a quick caveat that I wasn't any good really, it was just something I'd learned out of a book.

As Nick held out his palm, I hesitated. I'd promised myself no magic, but palm-reading didn't involve any spells. It was just harmless fun, right?

I took his palm and smiled back.

I'd learned palm-reading from my grandmother, who had taught me that it was an intuition rather than a science. Yes, she'd showed me what the basic lines were – the love line is the highest line, that curves upwards towards your fingers; a fork at the end indicates marriage; a double fork indicates a love triangle, affairs. The middle line is for career and money; if it joins the love line, you'll meet your future spouse at work. The line swerving down by your thumb is your life line. A long line indicates a long life; jagged crosses or bumps indicate illnesses, accidents . . .

But she also taught me that the lines are superficial maps: *Look beneath the lines, look for the pulse.* There are tiny pulses in the body, she taught me, that flicker everywhere like snakes, carrying vibrations, impressions, histories. I took Nick's palm and closed my eyes, searching for the clues to his personality caught in the whorls and swirls of muscle . . . But no, there was nothing. No sensation. Just blankness.

I felt a flicker of frustration. Now that I'd stopped doing magic, my psychic powers seemed to be out of practice too. For one frightened moment I wondered if they would ever return or just crumble away to grey ash.

'Well?' Nick demanded.

'You're going to have a very happy marriage. You're going to be such a sweet couple,' I improvised vaguely.

'I hope we already *are* a sweet couple,' Andie said wryly.

'How boring,' said Nick.

'Oh, thanks very much!' Andie flared up.

'No – I mean, I was hoping Cara might predict that I'm about to win the lottery so I can buy a Porsche and retire to the south of France for the rest of my life,' Nick grinned. 'Oh well, you have a go, Andie.'

Andie rolled her eyes and let her palm droop before me. I only touched it once and then it happened: a series of visions, striking in lightning flashes. Andie and Nick rowing . . . a broken coffee cup . . . a hotel room . . . keys . . . screaming . . . moonlight on water . . . and for a moment I was drowning, water swelling in my lungs, a tightness in my throat as though a rope had been tied around my neck, tighter and tighter, screaming in my ears, Andie running through dark woods, Nick shouting: *Where are you?* I shuddered violently, opened my eyes and recoiled.

Thankfully, Andie wasn't even interested in my verdict. She pulled away, standing up.

'Come on, it's time for Fred to get to school.'

'Sure.' I shook myself and stood up too, letting the visions subside and dissolve away. I should just forget them, I decided, as soon as possible. I had no idea if they were past, present or future. If I started to act on them it would lead to magic, and I wasn't a witch, I was just a plain old normal nanny. 'Great,' I said, more firmly, 'let's go. Look, why don't I take Fred to school today?' I asked very tentatively. Though I'd been entrusted with looking after Fred at home, I'd yet to enjoy the honour of Taking Him Out of the House.

'I don't—' Andie began.

'Yes, Andie, that's a *very* good idea,' said Nick, giving Andie a stern look.

Andie gave Nick a look back. Nick said, '*Andie!*' and she darted a glance my way and said, 'Nick not *now*, okay?' I quickly pretended to be fascinated by the fridge magnets. So this was why they fought at night; Andie was embarrassed at bickering in front of me, of letting me see the faintest hairline cracks in her marriage.

Desperate to resolve the tension, I quickly said, 'Look, why don't we both go? You can show me the way.'

'Okay,' Andie looked relieved.

And that was when I found the answer to Andie's problems.

We took the scenic route via the river. Trees rustled with leaves and the morning sunlight shimmered across the Thames in liquid pools. Fred took my hand on one side and Andie's on the other and turned us into a human gymnasium, bouncing along with little jiggy jump-steps.

'There's my bird, what's that bird?' he cried.

'It's a jay,' I said; I'd been a bit of a bird-spotting spod as a kid.

'Oh wow!' He tugged Andie's sleeve. 'It's a jay, it's a jay!'

For some reason, Andie gave me an absolutely foul look. We walked on in silence for a few minutes. I was churning inside. What was Andie's problem? She was so *Jekyll and Hyde*; one wrong word and the coin of her mood flipped right over.

I tried to remember my mantra from this morning: *Be positive. Help Andie.*

'So, how long's it been since you stopped teaching?' I asked her.

'Oooh, a year or so,' she said. 'I was only part time after Fred was born and then my mother fell ill and I had to look after her.'

'D'you miss it?'

'Miss it?' she laughed incredulously. 'Miss the crappy pay? Miss ghastly Ofsted inspections? God, no. In the end, it was too much about paperwork and no time to bloody well teach.'

'Oh.' My mind ticked away. Maybe there were other careers Andie might be suited to. Unfortunately, all I could think of was a traffic warden. I could just see Andie with a cap, a grim look and a notebook. I hid a smile.

Then, to my surprise, Andie blurted out: 'Though, to be honest, I wouldn't mind working with children again. It was so incredibly rewarding.'

'I'm sure it's something you're really good at,' I enthused.

'Well, I suppose I am good with children – Fred, don't pick up dirty Mars bar wrappers, put that down!'

By now we had reached the school, a large Edwardian sprawl of red brick and knobbly chimneys and sash windows. The playground was filled with children playing, forming a giant panda in their black and white uniforms, their bright plastic lunchboxes and satchels darting about like tropical fish. Andie reached down to give Fred a kiss but he wriggled away in embarrassment. I called 'Goodbye' after him too but to my dismay, and no doubt Andie's satisfaction, he didn't even notice. He ran up to a teacher with fizzy blonde hair and loud red Christopher Biggins-style spectacles.

'That's Suzanne. Ms Hampton,' Andie sighed, 'his favourite teacher.'

'Why don't you go and ask her if they have any teaching posts?' I nudged Andie.

'Oh no, no—'

'Go on!'

'Don't be silly, I can't go back,' Andie said sharply.

Another teacher entered the playground then and grabbed our attention at once. He was tall, with a loping stride, and an allure of messy sexuality: mussed-up brown hair, sleepy turquoise eyes, an old jumper and a fag tucked behind one ear. I saw a little girl run up to him shouting, 'Mr Yates!' He had a fabulous smile too.

'Maybe I'm in the wrong profession,' I joked to Andie, who smiled.

'Actually, I do just need to check with Ms Hampton about Fred's trip next week,' she mused.

Ten minutes later she returned, looking bright.

'Well, that's all sorted then.'

We walked back home in a slightly uncomfortable silence until Andie said casually, 'So, would it be okay if you collected Fred during his lunch hour from now on?'

'Sure.' I repressed the urge to whoop out loud! Surely she wasn't going to sack me now? I wondered what had provoked her sudden change in mood.

'It's just – I was chatting to Suzanne – Ms Hampton – and she said that they are actually looking for a supply teacher to cover their Year 6 for the summer term. The permanent teacher's away on maternity leave and they got someone in who was dreadful, so they need to fill the space urgently. I know the headteacher already so Suzanne's going to put in a good word for me. It's a real coincidence, isn't it?' she said breathlessly. 'And I really feel it's something I'd like to do.'

I rolled my eyes. Andie was acting as though the whole thing had been her idea. She clearly didn't like taking advice from others.

Still, there was a brightness to her face, an excited catch in her voice that made me glow inside. I could see she was going to be great at her job, and she and Nick would start getting on better again and they'd love me for suggesting the idea and we would all live happily ever after. God, it had been easy. I ought to set up a Cara-Broad-Will-Fix-It agency, I giggled inside. Plus, I hadn't even used magic. Suddenly I decided that I didn't care if my powers were fading away. In fact, perhaps it would be best if I let them rust and disappear; that way, I wouldn't have any temptation to use them. I could get by just fine on my own, I realised with a warm conviction, and it made me feel strong, and independent, and good about myself for the first time in a long time.

Later on, I went out shopping to do some errands for Andie.

I was feeling in a fantastic mood. After picking up some smoked salmon and crème fraîche from the supermarket, I lingered in the clothes' shops for a while, drifting from Top Shop to Next to Dorothy Perkins, trying on clothes just for the hell of it. I found one particularly gorgeous outfit, a shimmering white summer dress, and as I twirled in front of the mirror I found myself imagining what Sean would think of it, pictured his eyes trailing over me. The price tag sobered me up. On my paltry salary I might be able to afford it if I saved for the next twenty years.

As I was walking home I caught sight of a familiar dark-haired figure weaving through the crowds.

'Nick!' I called, but he was too far ahead of me.

I followed him from the high street to the river path, struggling to catch up.

It suddenly struck me that he should be in work at this time of day – 3 p.m. So what was going on? Intuitively, I pulled back and watched to see where he was heading.

On the riverbank, I hid in the green shadow of a willow tree. Nick sat on a bench for a while, looking depressed; then he pulled out a packet of cigarettes from his pocket and lit one up. A second later, he stubbed it out and put the packet away. Then he drew it out again and fiddled with the wrapping. I remembered seeing Fred's wall chart and Andie telling me they had both given up smoking and I smiled fondly – poor guy, he was obviously struggling. He suddenly leaned forwards, burying his head in his hands and letting out an angry sigh. He really *is* struggling, I thought.

A girl with a blonde ponytail, wearing a smart blue suit, came up and sat by him. He offered her a cigarette and she lit up, teasingly slapping him when he tried to steal a drag. I decided I'd better walk away before I saw any more.

I felt my sunny feeling trickle away. *It's nothing*, I kept telling myself, *I'm sure she was just a friend*. But I couldn't help feeling uneasy as I recalled their night-time arguments. There was a lot going on beneath the surface of their marriage that I knew nothing about and I realised that if I was going to sort the Wilkinses out, it might take a lot more than just helping Andie get a new job.

6
Andie

The first thing Andie normally did when she woke up was reach for a book.

Andie loved reading, especially the classics. She'd been a voracious reader in the early days of their marriage – it had been a running joke that Nick had to forcibly prise the book from her fingers and hide it in order to get the bedroom light turned off by midnight. But since Fred had been born, she'd had less time; even after she dropped him off at school she usually got too tangled up in housework and shopping to truly indulge. So first thing in the morning – that glorious window when Nick was in the shower or downstairs having breakfast, when Fred was in bed, when the world was shut out by the curtains and the room was bathed in quiet, golden light, when bills could be forgotten, when nobody wanted ironing, breakfast, love or anything from her – was her precious 'Me' time. Time to escape and dress in glorious floating gowns for Mr Darcy, or relish the love affair between Dorothea and Will.

In more recent months, however, her 'Me' time had turned into 'Aimless Worry' time. She found her concentration sliding away until she ended up lying with the book on her chest, fretting: *Is life just going to carry on like this, day after day?* In her early 20s, life had been full of buds of possibility – glittering oceans, places with exotic names she might travel to, children she might have, books she might write, houses they might buy and do up. It was only recently that she'd become aware that somehow life had solidified. They had a nice house, Nick had a steady job, they had Fred, friends, a routine . . . but it didn't look as if they were going to do much more than that. They didn't feel ready for another baby; she'd suggested moving abroad but Nick wasn't keen. *So this is my life*, she thought, and it bothered her, because she felt she ought to like it, but there was always a sense of something missing . . .

Her 'Worry' time was always invariably brought to an end by Fred barging into the room, shouting 'Good morning'. And then, when she kissed him, she remembered how much she loved him and life seemed like it might be all right after all.

This morning, however, everything was different.

'MUM, YOU'RE COMING TO SCHOOL WITH ME TODAY!' Fred kindly informed her, waking her up.

So she was. New job. *Argh.*

Andie suddenly felt like a little girl on her first day at school. She ran down to the kitchen and grabbed Nick, who was in the middle of ticking the first 'AM' box on the 'NO SMOKING' chart on the wall.

'Darling, can you come in with me?' Andie begged him.

'Andie, I can't. I've got this massive Japanese deal, it's going to be wild, I should have been in an hour ago.' He gave her a tight hug and a big kiss. 'You'll be fine, darling. Phone me at lunch time and tell me how you get on.'

'Okay,' said Andie in a small voice. 'Have fun.'

As she got dressed, she couldn't help thinking about the first time she'd started teaching, before Fred was born. Nick had woken her with breakfast in bed, given her a pep talk and a thousand kisses of support, then driven her to work, nearly crashing several times because he was so busy holding her sweaty hand he kept forgetting to shift gears. Still. Things were different. They were grown-ups now.

But, after a fraught half hour of whizzing about dressing, showering and breakfasting, as she bundled Fred into the car she suddenly became conscious that half the street was doing the same as her. She paused to look at them all: mothers and fathers snapping and jangling car keys and swinging briefcases and kissing kids goodbye. There was a vibrancy in the air, a sense of energy and fresh beginnings, that suddenly made Andie proud to be part of the commuter crew. The whole day ahead of her was now zinging with possibilities and challenges.

She got into the car and clicked Fred's seatbelt with a smile. *I can do this*, she thought. *I'm going to be great.*

She was terrified

Absolutely fucking terrified.

It had been all right at first. The moment she'd entered the school, she'd breathed in that familiar smell – a mixture of disinfectant and glue and glitter and the toxic whiff of those fat squeaky marker pens – and felt at home. Then she'd had to pop in to see Cloones briefly. Cloones had been the head for the last ten years and she looked like a cross between a gorilla and Jane Eyre: very large, very tall, with an incongruously twee grey bun perched on top of her block-sized head.

'We've had three supply teachers in three months,' said Cloones, her currant eyes winking in her doughy face, 'and as I emphasised in our interview, if you could handle the class and take them through to their SATs, I would be most grateful.'

And despite the faint nervous rumblings in her stomach, Andie had smiled her Julie Andrews smile and felt strong and confident.

And now. Now she was standing in front of her class. Thirty pairs of eyes stared back: some frightened, some naughty, some bored, some challenging. And an unexpected terror struck her dumb. *I can't do this*, she thought, *I've lost the knack*. The minutes ticked by. The kids stirred, sensing delicious trouble ahead. *I wish I was back home. I don't want to be here. I want to be in bed with Fred. I want to be lounging on the sofa watching daytime TV and reading problem pages. Why did I decide to do this?*

It's all Cara's fault.

She suggested it.

The kids started to chatter. One threw a paper aeroplane. Another tossed a pencil. A third sneaked some chewing gum out of her desk.

Andie suddenly became aware of a presence outside the door. Cloones. She was pretending to check the doorknob while oh so obviously checking Andie out through the window.

GET IT TOGETHER, ANDIE! she shouted at herself.

'Right, class!' Her voice sounded weak; she had to tug it from the back of her throat to try to sound confident but it only came out hoarse. 'Settle down!'

The kids looked at her, wavering.

And then she made a fatal mistake.

She smiled.

If there was one rule of teaching that Andie had learned it was never smile in the first lesson. It was a mistake she'd made during her first day of teaching years back, when

60

she'd been under the delusion that all kids were little angels, and – still singed with faint memories of nasty teachers from her own schooldays – she had been determined she would win them over by being *nice*. As a result, the class had been a riot from start to finish. Nice did not work with kids. The classroom was a battleground. You had to stand your ground from lesson one; show them who was boss.

'*I said*, QUIETEN DOWN!' Andie bellowed.

The class, looking slightly bewildered, gazed up at her testingly. Andie gave them all her most ferocious don't-mess-with-me glare. They calmed down.

Behind the door, Cloones frowned. Andie bit her lip. Shouting wasn't good either – if you got kids into a Pavlovian habit of only behaving when you shouted, you ended up losing your voice within three days. She needed to be more subtle.

'Right,' she said slowly. 'If any of you start misbehaving again, you will all have to stay behind for one minute at the end of class. Now, would someone like to hand out the pencils?'

Instantly a girl at the front stuck up her hand. She was obviously a teacher's pet – good. Andie needed all the allies she could get.

'Thanks,' she said, passing her the pencils with a warm smile. The girl smiled back. The whole class groaned as though they wanted to puke.

All the same, it seemed to satisfy Cloones. She moved away from the door and Andie felt herself relax. Suddenly everything started to flow. She went through her lesson plan; she made it fun for them; she alternated between toughness and tenderness, laughter and strictness, and they were with her, on her side, eating out of her hand, when she heard a sudden *bang!* against the window. She was about to demand to know who was throwing things when she realised the noise was coming from outside. From the playground.

It was most bizarre. Outside, about thirty kids were behaving like inmates in a lunatic asylum. Some were crouched into balls; some were dancing; others lying flat out on the tarmac. And they were all shouting. Shouting gobbledegook: 'I'm HAPPY!' and 'I LOVE EVERYONE!' and 'LEAVE ME ALONE!'.

Andie was about to tell them off when she realised there was a teacher with them. The boyish one who'd wolf-whistled her earlier. What the fuck was this? *Dead Poets Society*?

'And so we all know that prime numbers are . . . are . . .' Andie tried to pick up the reins on her lesson. But she'd lost them; the class were fidgeting and looking out of the window.

'I'M ANGRY!'

'. . . numbers are . . . very . . . nice and . . .'

'I HATE YOU!'

Oh, this was hopeless!

She yanked open the window and called out: 'Um, excuse me . . . you . . . you . . . ah . . .'

But no, he was too engrossed in swirling his arms about and yelling, 'HAPPY! I'm A HAPPY TEACHER!' at the blue sky.

'Miss, his name's Mr Yates,' the teacher's pet informed her helpfully.

'Right. Mr Yates? Could I have a word please?' Andie called out.

He finally noticed her and came up to the window.

'Yeah?'

He grinned – a cheeky, lopsided grin that was so relaxed, she felt intimidated.

'This – rabble – is disturbing my class,' Andie said crisply.

'Well, it's a drama therapy group,' he said, sounding rather excited. 'Part of the new National Curriculum. The kids are pretending to be different emotions.'

'Drama therapy?' said Andie slowly. Suddenly desperation took hold of her. 'Bullshit more like,' she said savagely, ignoring the squeals from her class. 'I'm trying to run a *proper* class here!'

'So am I!'

'Well—' Andie paused, suddenly aware that there was someone behind her, someone who had just crept into the classroom.

Cloones. Uh-oh. She was stood there, arms crossed, waiting to see how Andie would handle the situation. After all, getting on well with the other teachers was just as important as getting on with the children.

'Mr Yates,' Andie concluded sweetly, 'I would be so grateful if perhaps you could take your class on to the playing fields.'

Mr Yates stared back at her. Andie felt sweat on her forehead. *Please don't do this*, Andie begged him silently.

Then he smiled – a twisted, furious smile – and said in a voice of utmost gentlemanly politeness: 'Sure.' He clapped his hands. 'Okay, class, let's make a move!'

Andie slowly turned back to face Cloones. The kids gazed at them as though they were about to enjoy a shoot-out in a Western. All in all, it had been a very entertaining morning for them.

But Cloones threw down her gun. She smiled thinly and said in a metallic, utterly unconvinced voice, 'Very good.'

And although the rest of the lesson went well, those two little words churned in the back of Andie's subconscious

63

all day. Very good as in very good? Very good as in completely shit and you'll be fired next week? Very good as in how dare you insult Mr Yates like that?

At the end of her first day, however, Andie felt deeply satisfied. Especially when Sophie West came up to her and said, 'Mrs Wilkins, you're the best teacher we've ever had!' Teacher's pets, Andie decided, were just great.

She felt a deep pinch when she thought of Fred. She'd arranged for Cara to pick him up and as she hurried home she had visions of poor Fred in tears, wailing for his proper mum. She was pleased but slightly miffed to find Fred completely happy, playing Monopoly with Cara and not missing her in the slightest; when she tried to hug him, he merely wriggled away and said, 'Mu-um, can't you see we're playing!'

Fine, thought Andie, I may as well get on with some marking.

She found herself in for a shock.

She made herself a mug of Earl Grey, then shut herself in the dining room with a pile of thirty exercise books and started to work her way through them. They were all terribly messy: dog-eared, graffiti-splattered, and Andie was annoyed to see that the first in her pile, belonging to Sophie West, was written in pink neon pen with all the 'i's dotted with silly circles with happy faces in them. Worse was to come. Her spelling was awful and her most recent essay, What I Did in the Easter Holidays, consisted of just one line: Not much. To Andie's appalled amazement, the previous teacher had actually *ticked* it and given her a *gold* star. What did pupils have to do to earn two stars? Write nothing at all? Well, it made marking quicker, Andie supposed.

Perhaps Sophie was just the worst of the bunch, she

thought; she'd have to give her special attention from now on. But the rest were the same. The spelling mistakes were alarming, but this was probably explained by the fact that the last supply teacher hadn't been able to spell herself: *This is a grate piece of work* was scribbled at the bottom of one page.

Once she'd got over her shock, Andie briskly clicked her pen and went through the pile methodically, making a note of all the things that needed to be covered. She found herself slipping into a trance and some time later she suddenly heard a bang and Fred yelling, 'DAD's home! Dad, Dad, Dad, I've been playing Monopoly with Cara and I *beat* her! Three times!'

Andie did a doubletake at the clock. 7 p.m.! Time had flown. She felt tired, but very satisfied.

'I'm starving!' Nick announced, strolling in. He looked at the table blankly, as if wondering whether the lack of cutlery and tablecloth and plates of hot dinner was really a painful mirage. 'Oh. It's not ready yet.'

Andie was double-knived with guilt and anger.

'I thought we'd order pizza,' she said, waiting for him to ask, 'So, how was the new job, then?' But no. He was far too engrossed in jabbering on about *his* day, *his* boss, *his* Japanese deal.

In fact, it wasn't until they'd all sat down and were halfway through the pizzas that Nick suddenly choked and said, 'God, Andie – how was it? You were supposed to phone me at lunch; you didn't!'

'Well, I had my hands full with thirty kids. But it was fine,' Andie said tightly. 'Fine. I really enjoyed it, actually.'

'You're sure you're not tiring yourself out—'

'Well, I will be if you expect me to come home every day and then rustle up a three-course meal for you, yes,' she couldn't resist snapping. As she got up to clear the plates, she swore Nick rolled his eyes at Cara behind her back. *Bastard*.

By nine o'clock Andie was completely whacked. So was Nick. They collapsed into bed together. Andie couldn't help hoping Nick wouldn't want sex; she'd probably start snoring halfway through.

But to her relief, Nick was tired too. He read Tolkien for five minutes, then gave up – he was yawning more than reading – turned off the light and cuddled up against her.

'So have you had any more thoughts on Cara?' Nick asked. 'I thought she was on probation.'

'Well, she seems to be settling down with Fred now, so . . . I suppose she can stay. We'll see how she goes.'

'Ooh, you are tough,' said Nick, rubbing his nose against hers in an Eskimo kiss. 'I'd hate to be in your class. I'm sure you're very *strict*.' And they both laughed. Andie suddenly felt love sing in her heart and she held Nick so tightly she felt she would suffocate him. Then he annoyed her by adding, 'See, all that stuff about Cara was just worrying because you had nothing to do. Now you're working you don't have time . . .'

Still, Andie conceded as Nick dropped off to sleep, it was probably true. All the same, work hadn't stopped her worrying. It had just given her a new set of problems, that was all. That night she tossed and turned, fretting over her pupils, Cloones, spelling. And Mr Bloody Yates. God, he was such a git. As she finally fell into a nightmare-fragmented sleep she suffered a nasty feeling that she was going to have a lot more trouble with him in the future . . .

7
Cara

Another week passed at the Wilkinses without hassle; and then, on Tuesday morning, something highly embarrassing happened.

We were running late because Andie had woken up with a terrible cold and a muzzy head. Nick gave her a stern lecture that she ought to take the day off work but she knocked back some paracetamol and insisted that she simply had to go in because she'd arranged a 'Show and Tell' pets session at school.

'I can come and help too,' I volunteered, and to my surprise Andie agreed. She really must be feeling ill, I thought.

Or maybe it was just another sign that she was starting to trust me. Over the last week I'd started to feel acceptance trickling out of her, little by little. I really thought the teaching job had worked – she seemed tired but she shimmered with a new vibrancy, as though she'd regained her appetite for life.

Anyhow, we came galloping out of the house – hair, books and lunchboxes flying – and clambered into the Wilkinses' Ford Fiesta, only to find Sean's car blocking our driveway. Sean's car was so embarrassing it was comic. It was an old pink '60s Beetle with psychedelic green and blue squiggles spray-painted over it. The engine was chugging and his grandfather was sitting in the passenger seat, picking his nose unselfconsciously.

Beep! Beep! Andie pounded her horn furiously, looking ready to mow them down.

Kieran casually flicked a bogey in our direction and shouted out idly: 'SEAN'S COMING IN A MINUTE . . .' Several minutes went by. Andie started to swear under her breath and beeped again. Kieran, oblivious, gazed at me (I was poking my head out of the window, looking disapproving) and said: 'We'll move the car if you agree to come out with us on a date next week. I tell you, Sean's been nattering on about "the pretty lass next door" all weekend.'

I went pink and beside me Fred crowed loudly: 'Sean fancies Cara, Sean fancies Cara.'

Finally, Sean came running out of the house carrying a pair of gardening gloves and some shears.

'Cara's coming out for a drink with us next week,' Kieran said loudly.

'Okay, if the Kieran O'Mara Dating Agency has quite finished, can you bloody move!' Andie yelled.

At the mention of the word 'date' I saw Sean blush. He quickly revved up the engine and as they drove away Kieran shouted: 'WE'LL SEE YOU NEXT THURSDAY! IN THE GOAT AT EIGHT!'

'You don't have to go,' Andie said to me, rolling her eyes and shaking her head. 'God, that guy is completely mental. We should be on that *Neighbours From Hell* programme.'

I pulled a grimace too but inside I couldn't help glowing. *Sean's been nattering on about 'the pretty lass next door' all weekend.* I was flattered. I had to admit that I liked

Sean and I was looking forward to getting to know him better, if only as a friend.

By the time we arrived at school, the stress of being late had taken its toll on Andie. Beads of sweat danced on her forehead; her eyes were red and Fred took great pleasure in yelling, 'BLESS YOU!' every time she sneezed.

'Are you absolutely sure you're well enough to go in?' I asked her after we'd dropped Fred off at his Year 4 class.

'Oh, I'm fine.'

She didn't seem to like me fussing over her.

Her class were wriggling restlessly in their seats. Their pets were lined up at the side of the classroom in their cages, beady eyes swivelling, claws stretching, tails swishing nervously.

'All right,' said Andie, clapping her hands. 'Quieten down now!'

But the class, overexcited by their pets, didn't respond, chatting and shrieking like a miniature zoo themselves.

Andie turned and slowly drew a '1' on the blackboard. Then she crossed her arms and surveyed them all with a steely look. The class nudged each other and slowly settled. Finally there was silence, except for the occasional miaow or squeak.

'That's one minute you will have to stay behind after class,' she said calmly. 'If you don't pipe down, I'll keep adding more.'

God, she's good, I thought admiringly. She managed to get across a perfect blend of firmness and fun.

'Now, we've got a special helper joining us today. This is Cara.'

I smiled at the chorus of 'hi's and 'hello's, some shy, some cocky, some shouted, some whispered.

'So today—' Andie sneezed violently, provoking laughter and a chorus of 'Bless you, Mrs Wilkins.'

'This cold is driving me *mad*,' Andie sniffed.

'Here's a hanky.' A boy at the front with squiffy hair, a sallow face and large glasses offered her a rather revolting-looking scrap of grey cloth.

'No, it's fine, Nigel.' Despite her bright smile and warm voice, Nigel looked rather hurt. He's a sensitive child, I thought.

Next to Nigel, a girl with red hair in plaits, a violently freckled face and a pair of beady green eyes said, 'Yeah, Nigel, Mrs Wilkins doesn't want to eat your snot.'

The class tittered.

'Sophie, don't be unkind. Now, you've all written little pieces on why you like your pets, so you can come up to the front and read them out. Yes, all right, Sophie, you can come up first,' Andie said as Sophie cried, '*Oh, me, me, me.*'

Sophie smiled smugly and collected a box from the side. Her cat, a white Persian, glared out through the bars crossly.

'Can I take her out?' she asked.

Andie sneezed violently.

And again.

And again.

'Andie, why don't you go home?' I said gently. Then, when she shook her head emphatically, I said, 'Well, at least go to the staff room and take some Lemsip. I can look after the class.'

'Thanks,' Andie said and, after instructing the group that they'd better behave, she sidled out. I turned back to the class with a bright smile and, despite the fact that I am a nanny and have plenty of experience with kids, I couldn't help suffering a tickle of fear in my stomach. The moment

Andie had walked out there had been a change in the atmosphere – subtle, but there all the same – a sense that the children wanted to see what they could get away with.

'Okay, Sophie,' I said, a little more firmly. 'Tell us why you like your cat.'

'Can I take her out of the box first?'

What would Andie have said? Well, it was supposed to be an interactive lesson.

'Er, sure, why not.'

Sophie pulled out her beloved Persian and I offered to hold it for her while she read her essay.

'We got my Persian, Fluffy, like, three years ago 'cos my mum likes cats and I . . .'

Unfortunately, Fluffy didn't seem to like me very much. She wriggled violently, embedding her claws in my breasts.

'. . . I didn't like Fluffy at first as I thought she had too much hair so, like, I put her in the washing machine and my mum said that was mean but—'

I lost control. Fluffy bounced on to the floor and scuttled under a table. Children yelled and tried to pick her up. Sophie flew after her, tugging at her tail; Fluffy turned on her and slashed her arm with her claws. Sophie burst into noisy sobs. I found myself reaching out, an incantation dancing on my tongue, but I quickly stopped myself. I don't need magic, I thought firmly. I can handle this, I can take control.

'WOULD EVERYONE JUST CALM DOWN!' I roared.

Nobody took the slightest bit of notice. Several other girls, upset by Sophie, started to cry too. And then I couldn't help remembering a spell my grandmother had used a few years back. We'd had an annoying Rottweiler next door who had tried to eat us every time we left the house, and had caused the postman to leave our mail at the end of our path rather than put it through our letterbox. I remembered my grandmother whispering sounds to the dog and from that day onwards it had not only licked the postman every day but had even collected our post in its meaty jaws and brought it to our door. Oh God, surely one tiny weeny little spell wouldn't do any harm? It was an emergency, after all! I gulped, waved my hand and whispered a feline incantation.

Instantly the cat, who was now prowling around the back of the classroom, stopped. I stared at it until all I could see was its eyes: two round green orbs with black knife-slits. I gently called out a series of miaows, irrs and purrs. Slowly Fluffy crossed the room and walked calmly into her box. I slammed down the lid. Phew.

Sophie stopped crying and blinked in astonishment. 'Fluffy,' she muttered, hugging the box to her chest.

'Miss, how did you do that?' asked one kid, his eyes like moons.

'Do what?' I asked innocently. 'Now, let's continue . . .'

I resisted the urge to run out of the classroom. Where the hell was Andie? At least fifteen minutes had passed. Why hadn't she turned up?

'So,' I said, 'who would like to go next?'

The one good thing about children is that they have a very short attention span. The cat-magic was quickly forgotten as they all waved their hands, crying, 'Me, me, oh, me, please!'

And there, at the front, sat Nigel. His hand was limp and he was muttering 'Please' as though he didn't expect to be chosen, as though he was always the last to be picked for team games and class dramas.

'Nigel!' I said brightly and he jumped as though I was a gameshow host who'd just shone a spotlight on him and told him he'd won a million pounds. 'So what's your pet?'

Nigel stood at the front and pulled a dirty mustard-coloured matchbox out of his pocket.

'Miss, you can't have a matchbox for a pet,' Sophie called out, and the class laughed. 'He's got a lesser-spotted matchbox, how sad!'

'That's enough, Sophie. So, Nigel, tell us what's in there,' I said kindly.

'A spider,' Nigel said. He lifted up his card and read his speech in a mumbling monotone that nearly broke my heart: 'I am Nigel and I have this pet spider. I'd prefer a dog but my mum says we can't afford any pets 'cos my dad walked out so now we don't have any money and we'll have to move soon if he doesn't cough up and I don't have any friends but now I've got a spider and I love him and he's called Fido.'

All the way through the kids, led by Sophie, cat-called and feigned imaginary violins. By the end, I had to blink back the tears in my eyes. I knew I was over-reacting but it all reminded me too much of my school days, of being taunted for being the witch's daughter, of never fitting in.

'Shut up, Sophie,' I snapped, so sharply that she looked surprised and was silenced for a moment.

Then, a few seconds later, she screeched, 'OH MY GOD!'

'What *now*?'

'It's – oh – my leg!'

Oh bugger. Sure enough, Nigel's spider had slyly scuttled out of its box and was now climbing its way up Sophie's leg. Sophie jumped to her feet, screaming and shaking. The spider clung on for dear life. The next thing I knew, she had brushed it off and impetuously stamped on it. Fido had been reduced to nothing but a black splat.

Nigel stood very still and gazed down at the mangled remains as though his world had fallen apart.

Oh God, could things get any worse?

'I'm really sorry,' Sophie cried shakily. Then she burst into tears for the second time that day.

I bent over the spider, muttering an incantation and gently breathing on to it. The reversal-of-death spell seemed to work. The spider's legs uncurled and straightened; its flat body plumped back into a healthy round ball. Nigel gasped; the other children echoed him.

'There you go,' I said, 'I don't think Sophie stamped that hard. Spiders are really very robust little creatures . . .' I trailed off.

Something was wrong.

The spider was looking rather large. Worryingly large, in fact. It was now rapidly reaching the size of an apple.

Argh. I'd obviously gone slightly overboard with my resuscitation.

The spider's legs spindled out like spools of wool. Its body now filled the gangway.

Oh God, how to reverse it, how to reverse it?

Crash! went a desk. A boy fell on to the floor and started bawling. The class screamed and hid under their desks, huddled in frightened groups (though, it must be said, a few of the boys were pointing and saying, 'Is that the coolest thing ever!').

Bigger and bigger, bigger and bigger. Soon it was as tall as me. And it was starting to look a little threatening.

I gave the spider a pleading smile and whispered, 'Down, Fido, down boy.' It glared back at me with its huge, glittering eyes. *Think, Cara, think*, I yelled inside. *The spell to reverse growth, the spell, the spell, the spell* . . .

And then, in the corridor, I heard the click of Andie's footsteps.

74

The spider's head hit the ceiling. It reached out one long leg and slowly trailed it over my head, as though savouring something it was about to gobble up.

'I know, I know, I know – *abrashrinkusspiderus*,' I called out.

Andie was nearly at the door. The spider's leg had frozen by my ear. Why wasn't it working? Had I got it wrong?

And then the leg fell away. Like some warped film played in reverse, the spider curled and melted in on itself, a black blur of shifting shapes, until it had shrunk into nothing but a little creature the size of a two-pence coin once again. I quickly scooped it up into the matchbox and pushed it into Nigel's shaking hand.

'Well done, Nigel, that was the best talk so far today. Now, everyone, what on earth are you doing under your desks! Will you please sit down or I shall keep you back for another minute myself. Come on, surely you aren't afraid of a little spider, are you?'

The class went back to their desks just in the nick of time as Andie came in.

'Well, you are all looking very quiet, aren't you?' she said, pleasantly surprised.

None of them could speak. All they could do was gaze up at me in awe.

And I was so shellshocked that I failed to take in Andie's pinched face and the way she was muttering, 'That bloody, bloody man . . .'

'Well, I'm glad to see you've got everything under control,' Andie said.

'Where were you?' I cried desperately, sweat wet on my forehead.

'I bumped into Jonathan, Mr Yates, in the staffroom; we were just sorting out our differences,' she said, rather icily. 'Now, it's time for lunch – but you've all got to sit in silence for one minute.'

I don't think I've ever suffered a more excruciating minute in all my life. I just wanted to shepherd them all out of the classroom and slam the door before they could start telling tales.

To my relief, they got up meekly after the minute's silence. As I watched them file through the door with their pets, I thought in relief: *They're too shocked. I'm okay. I've got away with it. And I've learned my lesson. That's the last time I ever EVER use magic—*

'Mrs Wilkins.' Sophie couldn't resist. Shooting me a sly glance, she said, 'Mrs Wilkins, Cara talked to my cat Fluffy and then she, like, brought Nigel's spider to life and then she did this magic thing and it, like, turned into this huge monster.'

My heart stopped. I waited for Andie to tell me I was a Satanist and march me home to pack my bags. But she merely chuckled and said, 'Nice one, Sophie. You always did have a good imagination. Now behave, okay?'

'But Mrs Wilkins, she *did*, I saw her—'

'Sophie, that's enough! *Shoo!*' Andie pointed at the door gently. Sophie left, looking sulky and tearful, muttering, 'Grown-ups never really know what's gong on.' I gave a little shrug, as if to say, 'Kids, hey!'

We picked Fred up from his class to take him home for lunch. I was still shaking by the time we reached the school gates.

I felt so deeply disappointed in myself. The whole incident reminded me of how once, as a teenager, I'd been desperate for a pink skirt in Top Shop and had used magic to shoplift it. Every time I wore the skirt, things would always go wrong, like someone throwing a cappuccino over me or racing past and spewing a puddle of dirty water over it – whether it was due to my guilty conscience or the Wiccan Threefold Law that bad magic will return with repercussions thrice as strong I never could tell. Either way, I ended up taking the skirt back.

I'd realised then that I could only use magic when I really needed to: for emergencies, not luxuries. And even then, there was something unsatisfying about using magic to solve problems; I felt hollow, as though I'd cheated at life, leaned on a crutch rather than sorting things out by myself . . .

Okay, I promised myself firmly, *I won't use magic again. Today was just an exception. From now on things will be different . . .*

It was strange; when I first met Nick and Andie I thought they were such a happy couple. I wasn't being naïve; I realised that like all couples they see-sawed up and down, faced bad times as well as good. But Andie and Nick had tensions that lurked beneath the surface, which somehow I found more disturbing than if occasionally they'd let off steam and chucked crockery at each other. Every night, when I sat down to have dinner with them, everyone wove a web of polite conversation; Andie asked Nick about his day; he asked her about hers; they asked Fred about school. But I sensed a perpetual pressure cooker tension in the air; often I had a funny feeling that one day one of them was going to say something tiny like 'Please pass the salt!' and the other was going to explode.

After one of these dinners, I had just put Fred to bed when Nick asked if I wanted a game of chess.

'Well, to be honest, I'm a bit crap at chess. What about Monopoly?' I asked. 'Then Andie can join in.'

'Monopoly?' Nick pulled a face. 'Andie can't play, she's got masses of marking. Besides, I'm a chess master,' he added nonchalantly, unfolding the board.

'Are you?' I asked in shock.

'Well, I was the chess champion at Nickelby Boys' School Sixth Form a long time ago,' Nick admitted. 'But chess is a passion of mine. Don't look so surprised.'

'No – I just – I just . . .' I blushed, feeling that he was enjoying making me squirm. 'You just don't seem that type . . . you seem the sort of *masculine* type who would, you know, go bungie jumping or stock-car racing or whatever . . .'

'Oh, so chess makes me boring. Well, I do have diamond-patterned V-neck jumpers in my closet because, of course, chess is second only to trainspotting,' Nick said sarcastically, rolling his eyes. 'As a matter of fact, I think chess requires a sharp intellect. It's not too dissimilar to business, or anything in life. I think the way that people play chess reflects the way they handle life.'

I normally get quite competitive with games; there is nothing I hate more than losing. But tonight I couldn't focus; I had an agenda of my own.

'Hmmm. So how's it going at work . . . oh damn, that's my knight,' I winced.

'Not bad. You shouldn't have put your pawn there,' he said, taking it.

'Do you, um, have time for fun . . . and nice lunch breaks?' I asked. I searched his face for a flicker of emotion, but he was staring intently at the board. Maybe his game was indicating that he didn't give away any secrets.

'Well, not really,' he shrugged, taking another of my pawns. I shuffled another pawn forward. He took that too. 'Really, I'm pretty busy.'

'Yes, but the weather's lovely, it must be nice to go outdoors . . .' *And sit on benches with mystery blondes.*

I could have sworn Nick's eyelashes flickered. Then I realised it was because he'd won.

'Checkmate!'

'Damn.'

'Another game?'

'Okay. Look, if you want to take Andie out to dinner sometime, I'd be happy to look after Fred. I mean, it's just that I overheard Andie . . .' Oops, now I was confessing to openly eavesdropping.

'What?' Nick glanced up for a second.

'The other day, when I was collecting Fred from school, I overheard Andie saying to Suzanne – I mean, Ms Hampton, Fred's teacher – that you and she never go out to dinner much anymore . . . or do anything romantic . . .'

'What Andie doesn't understand is that I'm *busy*,' Nick snapped. 'Things are hectic, I can't just drop everything.'

But here we are playing chess when you could be out with Andie right now, I thought. Suddenly I understood Andie's frustration with him. Nick really was like a rat in a pinstriped-suit, obsessed with ambition, who was going to end up having a heart attack at fifty-five and spend his retirement regretting everything.

And then a tiny thought popped into my head. I thought of my grandmother's shop and the left-hand corner with the cluster of blue glass bottles covered with dust. There was a potion there . . . wasn't there? . . . a potion my grandmother had once tipped into my mother's boyfriend's tea. A potion to soften the soul, ignite a lust for life. One week he had been working twelve hours a day and surviving on coffee; the next he was taking three days off a week, buying us all presents and suggesting trips to Disneyland—

'Checkmate,' Nick said. 'Tsch. The trouble with you, Cara, is that you're too hasty and impetuous. You make moves without thinking them through.'

Suddenly I felt mortified. *That is me*, I thought. *That's why I used magic in the classroom and nearly blew my cover.*

I'm impetuous and I act on whims and I end up flying headfirst into trouble. And here I am, about to consider doing it again.

'Don't worry,' he said, seeing my face. 'It's only a game, okay?'

'Right,' I said. 'Right.'

After we played another game, I said goodnight and went upstairs to bed.

Okay, so I did lose three times. But I did at least persuade Nick to take Andie out for dinner. I thought it was a sensible idea, a safe idea. No magic involved. What could go wrong?

Unfortunately, I had no idea just how disastrously it was going to turn out.

8
Andie

Andie had hoped that her enmity towards Jonathan would heal as she settled into her new job, but unfortunately it became much worse.

Andie had once read in a magazine that starting a new job was on a par with divorce in terms of stress levels. She could definitely vouch for that. The last supply teacher had been so dreadful that Andie had masses of work to do to get her class up to standard. And Cloones still kept dropping in at odd moments. Even so, it was rewarded by good spells. Sophie writing a whole paragraph on What She Did at the Weekend. Or Nigel having the guts to volunteer to read out his poem in class. And she was getting on well with the staff too – especially Suzanne (Ms Hampton), whom she already knew as Fred's school teacher.

Yes, she was getting on well with everyone except Jonathan.

It was a Wednesday morning and Andie was in a good mood. Her cold was much better and Nick had suddenly surprised her by suggesting they go out for dinner that evening. She had a staff meeting after work so she'd brought along a change of clothes so she could go straight from school. It was ages since they'd had a night out together; Andie could hardly wait.

The first person she saw when she entered the staff room was Jonathan, lounging in a chair, feet propped up on a table, telling Suzanne a rude joke. As Andie went into the little kitchenette adjoining the staff room, she mused that Suzanne's laugh was nearly as loud as her clothes – but not quite. Today Suzanne looked as though Dame Edna Everage had collided with a Technicolor movie in a mustard yellow jumper and a bright pink flouncy skirt with black lacy stockings. Norman Brett, who taught Year 3, was sitting behind her taking alternative sparrow bites out of his egg sandwiches and sips from his faded Thermos while reading a copy of a trainspotting magazine which was folded across his lap.

Now, where's my mug? Andie thought, searching through the cupboard. The mug was a lovely blue one Fred had made for her in pottery class which had 'Andie' painted in wobbly red letters on the side. It seemed to have disappeared. And – hey! – her box of Earl Grey tea – which clearly had *her* name on it – was lying open.

'Suzanne, have you seen my mug—' Andie broke off, her eyes fixed on Jonathan's slender fingers. They were curled around the stolen item.

'Erm – is this yours?' Jonathan looked sheepish and ran his hands through his hair.

Andie made it clear his boyish act wasn't going to wash with her. 'The name on the mug might have given you a tiny clue but never mind. Maybe you'd like to clean it out once you've finished with it,' she said coldly.

'Well, you can borrow mine,' Jonathan called over. 'It's the pink one with the, um, naked lady that lights up when it gets hot.'

Andie picked it up. It had gritty brown lumps in the

bottom and more brown rings than a tree stump. She glared over at Jonathan, but he was chatting away again. As she finally selected a clean cup and made her tea, she felt irritation simmering inside her. Jonathan's loud, fast-pace voice seemed to echo in her head like a migraine . . .

'So, I've got this nightmare kid in my PE class,' he was saying now. 'He's a real little bastard. Every time I ask him to do something, he has to show off in front of all the others.'

'God, which one is that?' Suzanne asked, grinning as Andie sat down next to her.

'Oh, his name's Fred Wilkins,' Jonathan rattled on.

Andie felt motherly outrage tornado through her. Suzanne coughed loudly and gave him a kick.

'What? He is a *total* nightmare – ah.' Suddenly Jonathan clicked. 'Mrs Wilkins. Andie Wilkins. Mother of Fred Wilkins.' He swallowed hard and stared into the depths of his cup as though the watery brown dregs were particularly fascinating. Then he got up, said a breezy, 'Well, must get back to class,' and left quickly. Without washing up her bloody cup too.

'Don't mind him,' said Suzanne, patting Andie's knee. 'Jonathan is infamous for putting his foot in it. When he first came here he called Ms Cloones Mr Cloones for a whole day before someone took him aside and corrected him. He only got away with it by sending her three massive bunches of flowers.'

Andie couldn't help laughing, despite herself.

'But everyone loves him because he doesn't mean any harm. Also, he is very new – he's only been teaching a year and this is his first school.'

'Really?' Andie was surprised; Jonathan looked so tall and confident, she'd assumed he was an experienced teacher. 'So how old is he?'

'He's only twenty-five. He's a mere pup.' Suzanne giggled again and lowered her voice. 'Don't you think he's a dish?'

Andie didn't want to be rude so she replied tactfully: 'Well, why don't you ask him out?'

'Ask him out! God, no way. I don't date men, I just shag them!' Seeing Andie's face, Suzanne shrieked again. 'Well, what's the point, men are crap and life's short, so I just believe in having a good time. God, I wouldn't mind shagging Jonathan though.'

Beside them, Norman coughed, looking embarrassed, and screwed the lid on to his Thermos.

'Sorry, Norman, we're having a bit of a girly chat over here,' said Suzanne. 'Ooh, by the way, are you still on for your birthday party next Thursday?'

'Well, erm . . .'

'Oh, come on, Norman! I've invited everyone!' Suzanne turned back to Andie. 'It's Norman's fortieth soon—'

'My thirty-*ninth*,' Norman corrected her.

'Right,' Suzanne winked surreptitiously at Andie, 'and I've organised drinks at All Bar One. You've got to come.'

'Oh, I can't,' Andie said automatically, 'I've got to look after—' *Fred*, she was about to say, then realised: *Hang on, no, I don't. I have a nanny!* 'Well, sure, maybe I could bring Nick along.'

'Oh, definitely!' said Suzanne. 'Norman's well excited, aren't you?'

Andie hid a smile as the bell rang for the first lesson, for poor Norman looked as though he would much rather be sitting at home playing with his train set.

The day went by in a rush of lessons, grammar and sums. Every time Andie hit a problem, she found herself thinking of dinner that night as a mental sweet to suck and get her through the day.

By the time she reached the staff meeting, Andie was knackered. As Ms Cloones went through point after point, most of the teachers looked close to falling asleep.

All except Jonathan. He was in charge of organising the school trip to Wales later in the year and he persisted in outlining safety, transport, timetabling, blah blah blah. Andie was quite surprised; he seemed so jokey that she'd secretly felt he must be a bad teacher who messed about all the time. It was clear that Jonathan was in fact deeply passionate about his job.

Passion was all very good but Andie wished he would bloody well hurry up. She looked at Suzanne, who rolled her eyes and gave Jonathan a kick. He yelped and got the message. Finally, the meeting wrapped up.

Glancing at the clock, Andie saw that it was now 6 p.m. Shit, she was going to be late for Nick. Thank God she'd brought the clothes to change into in case things overran. As she made for the Ladies', she heard Jonathan call, 'Andie, have you got a minute—' and pretended not to hear him. In the toilet cubicle, she made a Supergirl transformation and emerged wearing a white suit. She untied her hair and brushed it until her curls were a haze of static, added some make-up, exchanged her flat shoes for heels and her everyday handbag for a snazzy black one.

The heels were a mistake, Andie thought as she teetered across the playground. As a horn beeped, she jumped and nearly tripped up, just catching hold of the school wall, her handbag strap sliding down her arm.

'Watch out,' Jonathan grinned from behind the wheel of his car. 'I was going to offer you a lift home, but clearly you've got a date.'

'I do have a date. With my husband,' Andie said coldly.

She yanked up her handbag strap with as much haughty dignity as she could muster. 'We're going out to dinner in Richmond.'

'Well, can I give you a ride? I really wanted to make peace with you after the whole, er, mug debacle.'

Andie paused, checking her watch. It *was* 6:20, and it might be quicker than waiting for a bus.

'Okay,' she said, slightly ungraciously, and climbed in. Jonathan zoomed up the school drive. Andie quickly put her seatbelt on. 'Er, you couldn't drive a bit faster, could you?' she said as Jonathan swerved on to the main road, cut in front of a Mini and overtook three more cars.

'I'm too impatient,' Jonathan said, shrugging, putting his foot down on the accelerator.

A small silence. Andie turned and glanced at the back seat.

'What a mess,' she said, eyeing up the clutter of letters, unopened junk mail, tweedy-coloured animal hair and crushed Coke cans.

'Well, you're welcome to clean it the next time you have a spare moment.'

'Oh sure, I can't think of a nicer way to spend my spare time.'

'So where are you going tonight?'

'Luigi's. It's a little Italian place on the high street.'

'Oh really? Hmmm. I've got some friends coming over from the US tonight, maybe it would be a good place to try.' Seeing her face, he added hastily, 'Don't worry, I shall keep as far away as possible from your romantic soirée, I know you don't want me breathing down your neck. Look – I really am sorry about the Fred thing. Am I forgiven?'

He glanced over, his brown eyes wide open, and she couldn't help melting.

'Yes,' she smiled. 'You're forgiven.'

As he dropped her off, they both said cheery goodbyes. Andie strolled into the restaurant to find Nick hadn't arrived yet. He'd booked them into the smoking section, the naughty man, so she asked for it to be changed. She ordered a glass of white wine and started to relax, feeling the splinters of the day ease themselves out. The restaurant, filled with crawling green plants and soft lighting, was gorgeous. God, she and Nick hadn't been out together for so long. Suddenly she felt the warm pleasure of anticipation line her stomach. That morning at breakfast Nick had circled his arms around her waist, kissed her ear and murmured, 'We're going to have a great time tonight, I promise, promise, promise. We can order truckloads of wine and you can have two desserts and then when we get home, we'll . . .' He had licked her ear and she'd giggled girlishly, arching back her head for a kiss . . . until Cara had come in and they'd sprung apart, blushing.

As her mobile rang, her heart sank.

'Nick?' she sighed.

'Darling, I'm so sorry, I'm going to be late.'

'Maybe I should just go home,' she snapped.

'No, stay. I'll be half an hour.'

'*Half an hour?*'

'Have a starter, okay? And order me a main course; the usual?'

'Okay,' Andie sighed and hung up sulkily.

She ordered another glass of wine and a goat's cheese salad. It was funny; she couldn't help feeling self-conscious sitting in a restaurant on her own. She felt relieved when the salad came; it gave her something to do with her hands. She ate it slowly, trying to make it last.

It was now seven-thirty. Nick was an hour late.

Her starter was removed. Her main course, a chicken caesar salad, arrived, along with Nick's. She'd just asked the waitress to take Nick's back for now when her mobile rang again.

'Darling . . .?'

'Yes?' Andie's voice was pure ice.

'Darling, I'm really sorry, I'm not going to be able to make it. Seriously, if I don't do this deal, I'm going to be fired—'

Andie turned off her mobile and sat with her head in her hands. Yes, this had happened in the past from time to time. They'd arranged to meet and then Nick had stood her up. He had a busy job; she understood. But tonight was different. Tonight was the first night they'd arranged to go out in *ages*.

She took a few bites of chicken. It was delicious, though it could have been cardboard for all she cared. She wondered whether she should go home, but she felt too fed up to cope with a bloody bus. She found herself misery-eating her way through the salad, desperate to fill the hollow pain in her stomach. *Now I'm here, I might as well stay*, she thought with tipsy defiance. She had just ordered another glass of wine when she heard a familiar voice. Oh God. She lifted her knife and looked into the reflection: Jonathan, with a gaggle of people.

As he passed, she tried to ignore him but he tapped her lightly on the shoulder. She smiled awkwardly and he gave her a slightly sheepish grin, then hurried on. True to his word, he took a table on the other side of the restaurant, out of sight behind a row of plants. Suddenly Andie felt mean and anti-social, acting as though she barely knew him.

She took a sip of wine and angrily lit up a cigarette, ignoring the cross looks the other diners gave her. Sod her bid to quit smoking. At least she could blame her lapse on bloody Nick.

'Erm, this is the, um, non-smoking section.' The waitress hovered next to the table awkwardly. 'We can move you if you like.'

'It's fine.' Andie ground it out crossly. 'I'll just have the bill, thanks.'

She reached into her handbag for her purse, trickling her fingers through the debris of keys . . . tissues . . . hairbrush . . . eyeshadow . . . where was it? And then horror chilled her. She realised she'd left her purse *in her normal handbag back at school*. She'd been in such a rush to get changed, and besides, Nick was going to pay, and then she'd been in such a strop she'd totally forgotten that she'd left it behind . . .

'I . . . ah . . .' Andie could feel a blush creeping across her cheeks like a forest fire as the waitress reappeared. 'Erm – I've left my purse behind and I'll just . . . have to . . .' *What, Andie; what are you going to do to get out of this one?* 'Erm . . .' she trailed off as Jonathan came loping past, on his way to the Gents.

'We do accept all major credit cards,' the waitress said nervously.

'Everything all right?' Jonathan asked Andie.

'It's fine; well, it's not fine, I've forgotten my purse – but I'm just going to call my husband to come over and pay, so – well,' Andie stammered.

Within seconds, Jonathan had passed over his Visa card and a relieved-looking waitress had been sent on her way.

'Jonathan, you really shouldn't—'

'Don't say another word. You can pay me back tomorrow.' Jonathan sat down in the chair opposite her. He picked up her fork and took a few bites of her leftover salad. 'Mmm, yummy, I might order this myself.' He gave her a reassuring grin. 'So, er, your husband couldn't make it?'

'Oh, he wasn't feeling well,' Andie muttered. 'You know how it is.'

'Hmm.'

As she pulled on her coat, thanked him and said goodbye, Jonathan followed her out into the street. For a moment Andie was worried he'd suddenly decided she was some sort of con-merchant and was going to follow her all the way home in order to get his money back. Then she saw him hail a cab.

'Well, you can't go home in the dark on a smelly bus,' said Jonathan. The cab pulled up on the other side of the road. Cars were roaring past; every time they tried to venture across, they ended up stepping backwards.

'Okay, now!' said Jonathan. Ignoring her protests that they were about to die, he looped his arm through hers and tugged her across the road, ignoring the tooting horns and humming the James Bond theme tune so that Andie forgot to be cross and couldn't help laughing.

'This woman is a VIP so please escort her home safely – if you don't I shall seek you out and personally disembowel you,' Jonathan told the driver as he passed over a twenty, ignoring her hiss of '*Jonathan!*' under her breath.

As the cab rolled away, Andie waved goodbye and then sat back in her seat, overwhelmed by his kindness. She realised she'd totally misjudged him; Jonathan was a sweetie.

As she neared home, however, paranoia started to set in. What if Nick wasn't really in a meeting? Andie pictured Nick and his secretary, arched over his desk, kissing wildly . . . Then, as the taxi screeched to a halt, she blotted

90

it out. She'd promised Nick she wouldn't worry; she promised she'd trust him; she had let it go . . .

As she hurried up the path, she suddenly realised she hadn't worried about Fred all evening; she was starting to trust Cara. Then she thought: *Should I be worrying? I mean, Cara seems all right but what if I'm being lulled into a false sense of security* . . . Then: *Oh, this is silly, now I'm worrying about not worrying. I can't win.*

Andie was about to turn her key in the door when Cara opened it for her. She looked awkward. The way she had the day Fred had emptied the ant's nest over the sofa. Andie felt herself groan inwardly. What had Cara done now? Set fire to the living room? Accidentally fed the dogs arsenic?

'Did you have a nice dinner?' Cara asked nervously, helping Andie with her coat in the manner of an over-anxious maid.

'Lovely,' Andie said defensively, silently thinking: *What business is it of yours?* 'Nick had to go and do a bit of work afterwards, but no, we had a great time. Is Fred okay?'

'Oh, fine. Everything was fine.'

What then? thought Andie.

'There are messages, um, for you, um, on the answerphone. Nick left them.'

So he had.

'*Andie, if you're back, please pick up the phone . . .*'

'*. . . look, I'm really sorry I didn't turn up but it was a massive deal . . .*'

'*. . . Andie, we can go out tomorrow night instead, just please PICK UP . . .*'

Andie quickly pressed delete as Cara edged back into the living room. 'D'you want a hot drink?' she asked gently.

D'you want a smack in the mouth for listening to our private messages? Andie wanted to retort. Then she relented. She could do with a bit of sympathy; the evening's hurt was still coiled inside her and she needed a good old moan. And so they sat down in the kitchen, each sipping a mug of Cara's hot chocolate – a lovely, creamy concoction spiced with cinnamon and nutmeg – and Andie found herself pouring everything out.

'Well, maybe you just need a holiday,' Cara said. 'Maybe it's the only way to get Nick away from his work.'

'That's a good idea,' Andie conceded.

Cara looked so pleased, as if her little suggestion had saved the day, that Andie felt irked again. If only life were that simple; if only a two-week sojourn in Tuscany really could solve everything. Then she sighed. Cara was only trying to help, bless her. Andie had no idea what motivated such kindness but it was very sweet all the same.

They said warm goodnights and went to bed. Upstairs, Andie felt restless. She found herself closing the bedroom door and sliding the lock shut. Opening the wardrobe doors. Nick's suits hung there, a rich array of charcoal and navy and beige and fawn cloth. She went through all the pockets. A dirty tissue. A cinema ticket – for *Monsters Inc*, which they'd taken Fred to see. A receipt for a bottle of orange juice. There was a bang below and she jumped violently with guilt – but she realised it was just one of the dogs scratching the kitchen door. A napkin from Pret A Manger with a butterscotch coffee stain. Nothing.

There, she told herself, *you're just being silly*.

And yet. She sat down on his side of the bed and slowly slid open the top drawer of his bedside cabinet. It was filled with Nick's typical junk. Golf balls, cuff-links, spare chess pieces, a few CDs by David Bowie, a battered copy of *A Hundred Years of Solitude* – Nick's favourite novel. And then she found it. Tucked into the first page of Marquez. Instantly she felt a chill in her heart and a

92

strange desire to laugh. It was a letter. On blue Basildon Bond paper. A letter was serious. It meant business. And all it said was:

Dear Andie, I don't know how to tell you this but
But what?

She reached into the drawer. There were scrunched up balls of paper everywhere, as though he'd been writing draft after draft after draft. Andie swallowed and slowly started to unpeel the first one. A voice in her head kept screaming: *Andie, don't! You don't want to read this! You don't want to see what he has to say* . . . But her fingers moved of their own accord, smoothing it out . . . and *BANG!*

Down below, the front door slammed. Nick was home.

Shit, shit, shit. Andie quickly scrunched the paper up and flung it back into the drawer. Then she realised the letter had to go back in the book. His footsteps were on the stairs – she shoved the letter in the book, slammed the drawer shut, unbolted the door.

As Nick came in, she smiled brightly and asked him how his work had gone.

9
Cara

Tonight I was going out for a drink with Sean and I couldn't wait.

I was starting to feel claustrophobic in the Wilkins' house; it would be good to escape for a bit. Plus, I'd just received my first pay cheque. And though it wasn't a lot, it was enough to do some shopping.

After I'd dropped Fred off at school, I went into Richmond to buy some food for Andie (Nick was serious when he said she couldn't cook – the list was frozen chips, frozen cod, frozen peas – she'd even put 'frozen toilet roll' without thinking). On the way back, I ended up in Top Shop, bundles of jeans and strappy tops slung over my arm. As I tried the clothes on, I glanced around the changing room and felt an odd sense of camaraderie with the other girls. I felt good. I felt *normal*. I was just doing what every other twenty-five-year-old was doing. And as I walked out with a crisp white carrier bag and a shoe-box of chocolate-coloured sandals, a big smile stretched across my face. Okay, so it wasn't a date tonight, but I still wanted to take some pride in my appearance.

I collected Fred from school and spent a couple of exhausting hours trying to prise him away from children's TV and on to his homework; then Andie came home and I spent another exhausting hour answering her interrogation about what I'd been doing with Fred; and then, because I was rapidly growing to hate frozen food, I volunteered to cook dinner.

Andie and Nick both seemed tense. I wondered what was up with them this time. *Maybe Andie knows about the blonde*, I mused, curling spaghetti around my fork.

'Nick, fancy coming out for a drink tonight?' Andie asked. 'Suzanne has organised a little gathering in All Bar One. There'll be loads of people from work, and Suzanne is dying to meet you . . .'

'Nah, I'm knackered. Anyway, I promised Cara another game of chess, didn't I, Cara?'

'Actually, Nick, I think I might have to let you down. Sean asked me out for a drink tonight – I was, erm, going to go after putting Fred to bed, if that's okay?'

Nick looked a little put out; Andie looked pleased. The poor woman probably thinks that over Scholar's Mate and Knight's Defence I'm secretly moving in on her husband, I fretted. Desperate to ease the tension, I cajoled them: 'Why don't you guys go? I mean, you might wake up when you get out, I'm sure it will be good fun. I can look after Fred and see Sean another night.'

Andie and I shot Nick pleading glances but he shook his head, pushing away most of his dinner untouched.

I felt a coil tighten in my stomach. I felt like a teenager watching their parents make their first tottering steps towards divorce.

'Maybe I could stay in,' I suggested desperately. 'Hey, we could all have a game of Trivial Pursuit. I could cancel Sean . . .'

Nick's face beamed. Instantly I felt disappointment flood my stomach. Oh God, why did I say that? I had to let go; I had to leave them to their own lives and start having one of my own.

Then, to my relief, Andie gave me a shrewd glance and said, 'Absolutely not. You go and have a good time, we'll stay in and be old and boring. Coffee, Nick?'

Upstairs, I tried on my clothes: brown corduroy trousers and a V-necked camel-coloured jumper with shimmering sequins threaded into the wool. As I pulled my hair into a ponytail, my palms felt sweaty against my fraying hairband. Did I really look okay? I'd always been a bit tomboyish as a kid and I'd never had much of a feel for clothes that matched, let alone the whole minefield of make-up, handbags and shoes. The only foolproof reasoning I used was: 'If my mother would hate this outfit, it must look normal, and it must look nice.'

I examined myself again in the mirror.

And smiled. My mother would detest it.

I had just swung my bag on to my shoulder jubilantly when Fred called, 'Cara, there's someone for you on the phooone!'

Fred was currently going through a phase where he always had to answer the phone. But I was rather shocked when he added, 'It's your mum.'

'My *mum*? How the hell did she get my number?' I freaked. I'd given it to my grandmother with clear instructions never to give it to Mum; and I'd told Mum the Wilkinses wouldn't allow incoming calls.

And now she had my number. I pictured my future collapsing like a row of dominoes: next time she called Andie would answer it. And my mother would offer her a ten per cent discount on her tea-leaf reading because she knew me. And then it would be goodbye, Cara, we don't want a witch looking after our son, thank you very much.

'Tell her nobody called Cara lives here,' I cried. 'Tell her she's got the wrong number. And that she should bugger off,' I added under my breath.

'Erm, Cara says nobody called Cara lives here,' Fred said loudly into the phone. 'And that you should bugger off.'

Oh God. Oh no.

'Argh!' Fred suddenly cried. He seemed to have got wound up in the telephone cord. Then – to my horror – I realised that the green cord had come to life and was wrapping itself tightly around his neck like a coiled snake, hissing with sadistic pleasure as Fred wheezed for air.

'No!' I cried, 'Mum, no!' I picked up the phone and cried: 'Mum, stop that!'

To my relief, the cord fell slack and poor Fred dropped to the floor, rubbing his sore neck and looking dazed.

'Don't worry,' I patted him with a smile, 'you just got tangled up, that's all.'

Fred gave me a suspicious look and ran off to find Andie. No doubt he'd demand some sweets later to make up for it.

'Cara, it's only me, darling!' my mother fluttered. 'Now, I know you can't have incoming calls but I will just be ever so quick. D'you remember that I sent you a letter saying that Rufus – remember Rufus, darling? He's a wizard . . .'

Yes, mother, you have been trying to set me up with that slimy bastard since I was six years old and we played together.

'. . . I did say in the letter that there's a new nightclub opening in Richmond tonight called the Ritzy and Rufus wants to meet you there . . .'

'Letter?' I asked innocently. 'I didn't get it.' I'd torn it up and thrown it away, more like.

'Now, Cara, I'm sure you have nothing more exciting to do than watch *WestEnders* or whatever it is normal boring people watch. So I'll tell Rufus you'll be at the Ritzy at ten o'clock. I think it will be awfully nice for you two to meet up. It will help you to stay in touch with your witching roots.'

'Look, Mum, I'm going out for a drink,' I confessed at last. 'And he's not a wizard, a warlock, or a nutcase. He's perfectly nice and normal, his name is Sean and he's thirty years old, and I really want to get to know him. So there.'

There was a long silence. I could hear my mother's rapid breathing like some sort of dirty sex caller. Then she burst into a violent rant that lasted at least five minutes: about how I was ruining the family line, how I was poisoning the blood, corrupting the DNA, ending civilisation as we know it. I checked my watch. I was going to be late.

'Mum, I *have* to *go*—'

'Cara,' she said calmly, 'if you dare desert poor darling Rufus to go out with Sean, I will personally put a spell on that Wilkins family that will make you regret ever taking a job there.'

I paused, my heart hammering in shock. I couldn't believe this. I was twenty-five years old. And my mother was still trying to dictate my love life as though I was an errant teenager, threatening spells like a parent suggesting a future loss of pocket money. The only trouble was, spells were a lot more damaging . . .

'Okay, tell Rufus I'll be at the Ritzy, but not until ten-thirty,' I said in a tone of quiet fury. 'I can't get there till then.' I slammed down the phone. God knows how I was going to get out of this one; I'd just have to improvise.

What was it with public transport in London? Why is it that, just when you're in the most desperate of hurries, buses grind to halt, trains derail, tubes get lost in tunnels, entire stations are evacuated because someone has left an empty crisp packet on a bench and it gets mistaken for a bomb . . .

Yes, it would have to be tonight of all nights that I suffered the journey from hell. I waited for twenty minutes for a bus, only to find that the only free seat was next to a smelly drunk. Then we got stuck behind an accident. I tried to call Sean but I hadn't remembered to charge my mobile phone. Finally I got off the bus in Richmond high street, half an hour after I was supposed to have met Sean. A busker who was killing 'Killing Me Softly' not very softly on his mouth organ only exacerbated my blossoming headache. I ran down the road until I finally reached the Goat. I burst in red-faced, sweaty and breathless. It was 8:45 p.m.

My eyes flitted over the swirly brown and orange carpet, filmed with layers of smoke and sweat and spilt beers, over the wonky brown tables filled with chattering office workers and couples on dates, over the heavy, framed pictures on the walls and the flashing jukebox and the dirty snooker table where two spotty teenagers were playing for a wadge of cash.

Oh God. I couldn't see him anywhere. I'd blown it. He'd clearly gone home and I would have to spend the rest of the evening with darling bloody Rufus.

10
Cara

I was about to turn around and walk out when suddenly a voice yelled: 'Cara!'

I turned to see Sean. Oh wow, he looked *gorgeous*. He gave me a huge hug and kissed my cheek.

For a moment I was dumbstruck. Up until now, I'd appreciated Sean's good looks but I'd never been *really* swayed, for every time I'd seen him he'd been grubby: mud caked under his nails, dirt smears over his face, wearing old gardening clothes that smelled of earth and sweat. Tonight he was dressed in a pair of crisp black jeans and a white T-shirt. His St Christopher gleamed at his tanned throat and his hair was damp and newly washed.

Then I realised I was staring speechlessly and quickly shook myself.

'I'm really, really sorry I'm late!' I gabbled. 'I just had one of those journeys from hell – buses and buskers and—'

'Relax,' Sean said warmly, putting his hand on my wrist. 'Don't worry, I was half an hour late myself—' He broke off as Kieran, who was sitting along from him at the bar, snorted into his pint.

'Half an hour late!' Kieran chuckled. 'Sean's been here an hour and he's spent all day preparing. This afternoon I caught him *ironing* his T-shirt. The last time Sean saw an ironing board was way back in a past life. Good Lord, I nearly died of shock.'

There was an awkward silence as I bit back a smile and Sean tried to pretend he wasn't blushing. Hmm, I'd thought Sean liked me just as a friend . . . Still, it was quite flattering to think he might feel more.

'Well,' said Sean, 'thanks for that, Kieran, thanks a lot.'

'My pleasure,' Kieran grinned into his pint. 'Aye, it's such a nice evening, I think I'll have mine in the garden.' And, to Sean's visible relief, he shuffled off.

'So,' said Sean, 'what would you like to drink?'

'Oh, just a mineral water,' I said, still breathless.

'A mineral water?' Sean cried incredulously, giving me a nudge. 'Don't tell me, you're really fifteen?'

'No, I just – don't drink.'

'Oh. Oh, right. A mineral water coming up.' Sean fell silent, drumming his fingers on the bar as he watched for the pretty Italian girl serving the drinks to spot us.

Oh God. I always get this reaction. Why is it people always assume that tee-totallers are boring? As a matter of fact, witches and wizards can't drink. Alcohol affects our subtle powers, eating into them like acid on metal – which was one reason why my mother's powers had started to deteriorate over the years.

Still, I thought, *I'm not supposed to be using magic any more, so* . . .

'Actually, I'll have a Baileys,' I said quickly. 'I mean, water is so dull . . .'

'Well, thank God for that!' said Sean, smiling. 'For a moment I was worried you were one of those boring types

101

and that you'd want to be home by ten. A pint of Guinness and a Baileys, please,' he said proudly to the barmaid.

I might well have to leave you by ten, I thought worriedly, thinking of Rufus. Still, there was a good hour to go.

We found ourselves a table and sat down. I lifted the Baileys and instantly felt ill. To a witch, alcohol smells like faeces. I took a nervous sip and tried not to retch. Then I saw Sean watching me curiously, and smiled brightly.

'Well, it's really nice in here,' I said.

'Yeah, great.' He smiled and took a gulp of his pint.

I raised my Baileys to my lips and pretended to take another sip. Oh God. I was being boring; the ease we'd enjoyed earlier seemed to have vanished.

'So how's it going with the Wilkinses? Are things better now?' Sean asked.

'Much.'

'Oh, by the way, I am so sorry about Kieran the other week,' he continued, 'shouting out of the car like that!'

'Oh, I know! And when Andie called out "Is this the Kieran O'Mara dating agency" I thought I was going to die!'

'Oh God, me too! I mean, I haven't been on a date for ages and I'm not planning to go on one for another millennium. Oh, look, Helen's here.'

Oh. I couldn't help feeling a little disappointed. I hadn't really come out with any expectations, but still . . . Upset, I took a large gulp of Baileys without thinking and then coughed wildly.

Helen, a middle-aged woman with a blonde perm, who was wearing a green shell-suit, came bustling up.

'Hi Helen. Kieran's gone out to the garden,' Sean directed her. He sighed theatrically. 'That's his lady. It's the worst thing about going out with my grandfather – he's fifty years older than me and he's bloody better at pulling than I am.'

102

But you just said you didn't . . . I thought. *Oh I see. You do want a relationship. Just not with me.*

I smiled, feeling relieved. After all, I didn't want a relationship either; friendships were so much easier. And with that thought in mind, I started to relax and the conversation finally started to flow. We discussed Fred, and gossiped about what a flirt Nick was, and talked about *American Beauty*, which we'd both seen on TV recently (Sean loved it for its honesty; I hated it because I thought it was far too cynical). And then we got on to an interesting topic. Sean's marriage. He was due to go to a wedding the following week and he was dreading it, even when I teased him that he could seduce the bridesmaids.

'I just hate weddings,' he said vehemently. 'I've been there, done that, got the T-shirt, seen the movie and, believe me, it was a horror movie with a dire anti-climax ending, the type that flopped at the box office after one week.'

'So, you were married then?' I said, as though I didn't really know.

'Yeah. It didn't last long. Just over a year. Her name was Laura.' He caught himself, quickly picking up his pint and taking a big gulp.

Silence. I sensed Sean wanted to change the subject but I was intrigued. He unwrapped a piece of gum, popping it into his mouth and chewing hard.

'So, d'you get to see her much?' I asked.

'Sometimes.'

'Does she live in England too?'

'Yeah, thank God. She moved over shortly after I did. It means I can see my daughter quite a bit, though I have to say I struggle with the maintenance payments. How about you? I want all the details on your life now,' he said, widening his eyes dangerously. 'Tell me about your ma and pa.'

'My mum is . . .' I floundered. A medium? A madwoman? 'She's a – a secretary. She works . . .' I thought hard, picking a building I used to pass on the way to my old job. 'She works at Reed International.'

'Oh really! God, my cousin Mandy used to work there! Jesus, it's a small world, isn't it?'

'Isn't it?' I wriggled uneasily.

'And your daddy?' he cocked his head, chewing his gum slowly.

I paused. I hated answering that question. Sometimes I just whispered that I didn't know much about him and people gave me a pained look, as though I was hiding the fact that he was a bank robber or something. Or sometimes I'd be brutally honest and say: 'My mother slept with a guy, gave birth to me and that was that.' Only then people just said 'Oh' and gave me a look as though I'd somehow inherited a slut gene and had bastard blood coursing through my veins.

'He died,' I said abruptly.

'I'm . . . I'm sorry . . .' He touched my hand. 'How old were you?'

'Um, it was the day after I was born. He was hit by a . . .' A car? That was a bit of a cliché, wasn't it? A falling piano? Too *Tom and Jerry*. 'A statue.'

'A statue?'

'Yes,' I said, more firmly. 'I'd rather not talk about it, really.'

Sean made a funny noise and for a moment I worried that he was crying. Then I realised he was *laughing*. Were my lies that obvious? He wiped his mouth with the beer mat, holding up his hand like a traffic warden, flushing red and apologising: 'Shit, I'm sorry. I'm *really* sorry. I'm such an insensitive git! It's just – you know how it is when someone tells you something really sad and you know you

104

mustn't, mustn't laugh but somehow you end up cracking up and it's just . . .'

'Really, it's fine.'

'Well, I really am sorry and apologies to you and your dad. Sorry.' And he looked at me so earnestly that I started to laugh too.

'So tell me about Kieran,' I said after we'd recovered. If I couldn't ask about Laura directly, I decided to sidle in through the back door. 'How come you ended up with your grandfather – has he brought you up since birth?'

'Oh no, my parents are alive and well, so I'm afraid you can't get your own back by laughing hysterically at their deaths,' he said, pulling a sheepish face. 'All my family are in Ireland, in Cork. I've got eight brothers and sisters – yeah, eight! – I knew Kieran when I was a kid and – you're not going to believe this –' he leaned in intimately, lowering his voice and touching my wrist – 'he was a priest.'

'Oh my God!' I said.

'God indeed! I'm sure our Good Lord looked down and just thought: "What the fuck is that man doing in one of my sacred churches?" Actually, he was a very different man in those days. He was very austere. When I was six my parents would drag me along to church and Kieran would be in the pulpit and, Jesus, he used to terrify me. He was like an evangelical version of ZZ Top with that beard! I used to piss myself. He told us we shouldn't read comics, we should read the Bible, and I used to worry I was practising satanism by reading *Batman*!'

I smiled, warming to him even more, thinking of all the superstitions I'd inherited from my mother, how as a kid I'd stay awake at night fretting over a ladder I'd walked under or a magpie I'd spotted.

'By the time I was a teenager, Kieran had retired and moved to Richmond. And there were all these stories floating

105

around our village about how London had corrupted him! How he was drinking and smoking and seeing young girls. But that's the thing – if you repress yourself, sooner or later it all has to come out.'

Kieran came back from the garden just then, his arm slung around Helen.

'I'm just going to the loo,' he said. Helen came over and sat opposite us, playing nervously with the poppers on her shell suit.

'D'you think he's all right?' Helen flashed a nervous glance at the door to the toilets.

'I should think so,' said Sean. 'He's not so drunk that he'll go flushing himself down the toilet. Mind you, he did once get his beard caught in a sanitary towel bin. I had to untangle him. You should have been there.'

'What was he doing in the Ladies?'

'Don't ask.'

I started to giggle, but Helen looked flushed and frowned.

'No, I mean *his heart*.'

'Ah, yes – his heart.' Sean looked sober. Helen brightened as Kieran emerged from the Gents, smiling broadly and doing up his flies.

'Is he okay?' I asked Sean under my breath as Kieran and Helen disappeared together.

'He's as right as rain,' Sean grinned, leaning in. 'It's just his standard chat-up line. He drops it into the conversation that he's got a weak heart. Then a few minutes later he'll say he once won the lottery. Of course, he forgets to mention that it was only ten pounds. All the ladies fall for it, thinking they'll be first in his will. They also have vigorous sex with him in the hope it speeds things up . . .'

'The rotten bastard!' I gasped.

'Ah well – you ladies shouldn't be so superficial, thinking about money all the time.' Sean rubbed my shoulder to say 'Only joking' when I pulled an injured face. 'Nah, I'm sure you're not all like that.' He put down his empty pint and eyed my unfinished Baileys. 'Time for another round, I think. Come on, Cara, you're not doing very well!' he teased me. 'I dare you to down it!'

'I can't,' I cried. 'I mean . . .' Suddenly my eyes spotted the clock hanging on the wall. 10:20 p.m. Rufus would be waiting! 'Oh! I have to go!'

'Why? Will you turn into a pumpkin if you stay out late?'

'No – I have to be at the Ritzy . . . It's just that my friend – I – know the woman who, erm, owns the nightclub and, erm, I promised I'd be there, so . . .' I trailed off, resentment curdling in my stomach. I hadn't expected to enjoy my drink with Sean so much; I could have sat and talked to him all night.

'Well, great! We can get free drinks!' He trailed off, seeing my face. 'Sorry, if you don't want me cramping your style, I'll totally understand.'

'No, no, no,' I said, feeling awful. 'I didn't mean that. Of course you can come. Let's go . . . and hit the town . . . and have, erm, a great time . . .'

Sean grinned and pulled on his jacket. I smiled brightly, thinking: *Great, Cara, how the hell are you going to get out of this one?*

The Ritzy looked dreadful from the outside: a huge black building with 'Ritzy' glittering in tacky pink neon at the top. The queue outside – a crocodile of shivering girls in tiny, silky dresses with glamorous streaked hair and pouty lips and blokes hanging off their arms – trailed down Richmond high street. As we joined the end, I checked my watch: 10:40 p.m. Oh God. I could just picture my

107

mother phoning Rufus on his mobile and demanding, 'Has Cara got there yet? If not, the wand's coming out!'

'Can't you use your sway and get us on a special list?' Sean said. 'You do know the owner and everything.'

'Well – erm, yes . . . but she's, um, very Communist,' I said. 'She doesn't believe in giving people special favours.'

'Well, it was very Communist of her to open a nightclub,' he said wryly. 'If the drinks are expensive, I'm complaining!'

Fortunately, the queue was moving quickly. And once inside it wasn't hard to spot Rufus.

It was still too early for anyone to be drunk enough to dance. Except for one guy dressed in a 70s-style mauve suit who was swirling the dance floor, clearly trying to be like John Travolta in *Grease* and looking rather more like a reject on a particularly embarrassing episode of *Pop Idol*. Several girls were sneering and pointing, but he was too busy watching his reflection in the circle of mirrors surrounding the dance floor.

'God, what a wanker,' said Sean, following my gaze.

The wanker turned, looked up and caught my eye. Then he stopped and started to climb the winding staircase towards me.

'Um, Sean, could you get me a drink?' I said, yanking open my purse and wrenching out a ten-pound note.

'Sure,' he said, 'but put that money away, the treat's on me!'

As Sean left to negotiate his way through the throngs of people by the bar, Rufus sidled up.

Suddenly I felt hatred slash through my stomach. How could my mother *possibly* think this guy was right for me? He had greasy black hair laid flat with hair gel. He had huge side-burns. And, yes, he was handsome – technically, he was more handsome than Sean; he had nice checkbones and dark eyes, and soft, sculptured lips. But his personality was like a coat of grime, dirtying his beauty and making his physical perfection repulsive.

'Hi, how are you?' I asked politely.

'Fine,' he said. 'Cool. Usual sort of thing. I'm still working at the bank . . . but I'm hoping to get on to *Masterwizard* next month.'

Poor Rufus. For a moment I really did feel sorry for him. Like me, he'd had a bad time at school and his education had suffered as a result; though he strutted around in the crispest of pinstripe suits, his job at the bank consisted of taking the post round and making endless cups of tea. And as for appearing on *Masterwizard* – I doubted it very much. You had to have an IQ of at least 150 and a specialist knowledge of a wizard subject like The History of the Golden Dawn, the Crowley Years or Merlin's Family Tree; yet every year, his mother kept pushing him to apply, like a proud dog-owner sending their beloved mongrel to Crufts. Rufus was neither a success as a wizard nor a human being.

I looked over at Sean. He was now paying for the drinks. Oh God, what to do, what to do? I couldn't risk any magic. There were people *everywhere*.

'Rufus,' I said slowly, 'look, now really isn't a great time to see you. I'm kind of busy and I came with a friend who turned up at the last minute – why don't I give you my new number and we can meet another time?'

Rufus narrowed his eyes in the manner of a gangster considering getting his gun out.

'That's what you said the last time we met. And the time before that, when we were meant to be seeing *Practical Magic* at the movies. Either you want to see me or you don't . . .'

Out of the corner of my eye I saw Sean pick up the

drinks and start to head in our direction. Oh God. Suddenly inspiration struck. Above us, the glittering lights were swirling. I fixed my eyes on a drink left on the table next to us and, as the lights shimmered over us, I raised the glass and tipped it over, the sparks concealed in the chimera of light. Rufus squealed as he realised his groin was completely soaked. A pair of passing girls tittered.

'You – you bitch!' he hissed. 'Okay. Fine. I'm going. But just wait till your mother hears about this.'

For a moment I paled. Still, what could my mother say? I'd kept my word. I'd turned up. It would be enough to keep her off my back at least for a little while.

'God, was that guy coming on to you?' said Sean, putting down our drinks and sitting. 'Dirty old bugger!' He nodded at my drink; it was a glass of iced mineral water. 'I thought that might suit you better than Baileys.'

I looked up at him and he smiled gently. I sat down beside him and for the first time that evening I felt truly relaxed.

'I'm really glad you came out with me tonight,' he said. 'I've had a really good time.'

'Me too.' We both grinned at each other.

'Here's to the start of a horrible friendship,' he said, chinking my glass.

And that was when it happened. I gazed into his eyes and I don't know quite what ignited the spark – maybe it was the sweet cheekiness of his smile, or the warmth in his eyes, or the way his hair, now dry, was sticking up in boyish, unruly curls like bed-springs – but I felt a wave of chemical reactions surf through my body. Despite my best intentions, I was deeply attracted to him.

Terrified that he could read my mind, I turned away, gulping my water and forcing back my feelings, gaining control of myself.

And then something caught my eye.

I glanced over and did a doubletake. It couldn't be . . . could it?

Just when I'd wanted to forget all about the Wilkins, they had turned up again. For there was Andie. *Andie.* My boss! She was looking unusually glamorous, all sparkling earrings and thin straps. She had an animated look on her face that I'd never seen before. But – most shocking of all – there was a young man sitting next to her. His arm drooped casually around her. He looked somehow familiar.

Oh God, I thought. *First Nick gets a blonde, now Andie gets a toy boy.*

I couldn't quite see who he was . . .

. . . but as the crowds parted, my heart sank.

Mr Yates.

11
Andie

Andie could hardly believe she was in the Ritzy. The whole evening had got out of control; this wasn't what she had planned at all.

Just three hours ago, she'd been sitting on the sofa with Nick. He'd bullied her into sticking with BBC2 and *then*, while Andie got bored stiff watching a zany young presenter transform a young couple's house from a nice cream dwelling into a Feng Shui nightmare, she'd heard loud snoring. Great. She'd hoped that since Cara was out that night they might . . . but clearly Nick didn't even have the energy for so much as a kiss.

She found herself thinking once more abut the note she'd found. It had worried and worried and worried her. Something was clearly up with him, and she wished he would just open up and tell her. All the same, she'd come to the conclusion that Nick wouldn't leave her. She'd realised this the other day when she'd gone to do the washing (since she'd started work as a teacher they'd promised to take it in turns – some joke!). No, Nick would never leave her because he'd have to make the effort to actually *wash his clothes and put them in a suitcase.*

God, with all this worry and washing, no wonder she was tired.

She channel-hopped, the screen glazing before her eyes. She kept thinking about Cara. Andie had caught her just before she'd dashed out of the house, and cried, 'God, you look gorgeous!' And she'd felt jealousy sting her. Why couldn't she go out in a sexy pair of corduroy trousers and have some fun?

Suddenly Andie flipped. *Cara's right*, she thought. *I'm going to go out and if Nick doesn't want to join me, that's his problem.*

Upstairs, she pulled on some jeans and a pink top with spaghetti straps, feeling excitement squiggle in her stomach. She added hoops to her ears and her favourite silver necklace, a present from Nick. She came down ten minutes later to find Nick had woken up. Just about.

'Nick, I think I will go out for that drink, if that's okay.'

'Sure, you go ahead,' Nick yawned.

'Oh. Okay.'

Hang on a minute, Nick, she wanted to point out. I'm wearing make-up; my hair is stiff with spray; I've got a top on that shows my bra straps. Aren't you the slightest bit suspicious? Well, perhaps if I come home at one in the morning drunk, you might just notice something's up.

She decided to call a cab – she was going to drink copious amounts of alcohol, she decided resentfully – and twenty minutes later found herself being dropped off at All Bar One.

Inside, the pub was crowded and foggy with cigarette smoke. Finally, she spotted Suzanne and the rest of the teachers sitting at a table in the corner. They were quite rowdy and, judging from the clutter of empty glasses on the table, quite happy.

'ANDIE!' Suzanne shrieked, bouncing up and giving

her a huge hug. 'Oh, I'm so glad you came, how fantastic; where's your hubby? Is he not coming? Sit down, let me get you a drink!'

'Erm, a glass of white wine, thanks,' said Andie.

Andie grinned at the array of faces. Norman was squashed into the middle of the group, hiding behind a huge cocktail filled with foliage and umbrellas and looking as though he'd much rather be at home watching TV. A large card sat in front of him, scrawled with everyone's signatures, along with a couple of presents: a Boots Gift Voucher from the group and a plastic blow-up doll from Suzanne.

There were about ten other teachers there; even sixty-year-old Mrs Williamson, the school secretary, had turned up. She was sipping a sherry and chatting to Jonathan about her cat sanctuary and the sixty-nine strays she had wandering about her house. Jonathan shot Andie a grin and, spotting a group of people getting up from a nearby table, dragged over a chair next to him.

'Save me,' he whispered in her ear. 'I don't know if I can stand hearing any more about Precious, Tabitha and Twinkle-tail.'

'So,' Andie made an effort to draw him into conversation, 'I see scary Ms Cloones isn't here tonight. Which is just as well, or we'd all be ordering orange juice and sitting here meek and mild.'

'She's probably shaving off her chest hair,' Jonathan grinned as Andie nearly spat her drink out laughing. As Mrs Williamson got up to say goodbye, he turned to her a little sheepishly and kindly promised he'd pop over soon to see her cats, and Andie realised that her emotions had completely flipped over. When she'd first met Jonathan, she'd found him an annoying idiot. Now all she could think was: *I really like him.* It was impossible not to, he was so charming. And Andie loved men who could make her laugh. In a funny sort of way, his teasing manner reminded her of Nick, of the banter they used to share.

Then Jonathan turned to her and said, 'To be honest, when I first met you I found you just as scary as Ms Cloones. You seemed a right old dragon.'

Andie was shocked.

'Me? Everyone says this about me! They say I look so fierce and I'm so abrupt. I don't mean to be, it's just . . . well, me.'

'Yes, but I think you're a real softie underneath,' said Jonathan. 'It's a good combination actually – I'm sure it's what makes you such a great teacher.'

'Oh, you're such a charmer.' Andie rolled her eyes, though she had to admit she was flattered.

They chatted a little longer about the highs and lows of the classroom, until they were interrupted by Suzanne standing up and shouting, 'It's time to sing Norman happy birthday!'

'Sing along everyone!' the barman cried and the whole pub ended up joining in. Norman sat cringeing, his bald pate as red as a tomato.

'Right, guys,' said Suzanne, downing her drink and slamming the glass down on the table with a *thump!*. 'The night is still young. Let's go to the Ritzy! Come on, Norman,' she insisted, 'it'll be a laugh!'

There were only the four of them left by now and they all piled into a black cab, provoking a frown from the surly driver.

'So what's this Ritzy then?' Andie asked.

'It's a new club that's just opened in Richmond,' said Jonathan.

'Clubbing! I thought it was a bar. I can't go clubbing!' Andie shrieked. 'I'm an old married woman. The last time I went clubbing was . . .'

'1938?' Jonathan suggested, laughing as she hit him. 'Relax, I'm sure it will be fun,' he said, sounding rather dubious himself.

It was as bad as she was expecting. If not worse.

Suzanne was out of her head by now. She went boogeying on to the dance floor, dragging Norman with her. Poor Norman, whose dancing consisted of shuffling awkwardly from one foot to the other, left soon after, folding his coat over his arm, putting on his tweed cap and bidding a hasty farewell.

Andie and Jonathan felt equally out of place. They stood above a shiny balcony while girls strolled past in a blur of tiny T-shirts, logos, and pierced body parts. Some of them gave Jonathan appraising glances. He didn't return them.

'God, this place is such a meat market,' he muttered.

'My knickers are bigger than those hot pants,' Andie whispered, eyeing up a Jordan-lookalike. Jonathan laughed and looked more relaxed.

'Her hot pants are probably seriously worried about approaching extinction and are campaigning for their lives as we speak . . . Well, we could sneak out to another pub if you like – or shall we brave a drink?'

A quiet bar would be nicer but Andie felt a little uncomfortable about the thought of splitting away with Jonathan.

'Let's just have a drink to keep Suzanne happy,' she said, 'then we'll make a run for it.'

As Jonathan joined the queue by the bar, Andie stood awkwardly by a pillar covered with mirrors. A group of lads were eyeing her up. Andie was paranoid they were whispering: 'What's that woman doing here? She's so old! Look at her clothes!' She turned away, catching sight of her face in the mirror and giving herself a fright – she had triple chins and cheeks like apples. Then she realised that, no, she didn't look that bad; the club was full of circus mirrors, warping, shrinking and stretching peoples' reflections into strange shapes.

Andie glanced back at the bar. Jonathan was still ordering drinks. Then one of the lads walked up to her. Was he going to tell her to leave?

'Do you have a light?' he asked.

'Um, sure.' Andie fumbled in her bag, squinting in the poor light. Everyone joked that Andie's bag was like Mary Poppins' – she always carried an endless supply of tissues, plasters, creams, pens and essentials; Nick always joked she kept a family of gerbils in its dark depths. Finally she found something hard and long, which she pulled out triumphantly.

Then she looked down and realised she was holding a tampon.

'Oh God, sorry!'

The guy burst into laughter. 'You're sweet,' he smiled as Andie finally retrieved her lighter. 'What's your name?'

'Don't you recognise me? I'm a model,' Andie joked coyly.

'Really? Oh, wow. Yeah, you do look kind of familiar . . .' He squinted at her.

He actually believes me, Andie realised with a thrill of delight. Suddenly she noticed how tense she was, her muscles all twisted into taut knots; now she relaxed, feeling them loosen up. She fitted in. She belonged here. She felt good.

'Excuse me,' Jonathan came back, carrying the drinks. He glanced at the guy, giving Andie a bemused look.

The guy shrugged and walked back to his mates, who booed and gave him sympathetic punches.

'Honestly, Andie, you're such a man-eating flirt,' said Jonathan. 'Now let's go find a seat upstairs.'

117

'I'm not a man-eater—' Andie started to protest, then saw the look on his face and realised he was teasing her. 'Oh, shut up!' she laughed.

Up on the next floor were a variety of chairs and couches in shady corners, where teenagers, spunked up on testosterone and alcohol, were becoming rather intimate. Andie had to try not to stare.

'I didn't realise they gave free sex shows too,' Jonathan joked as they sat down by a balcony overlooking the dance floor.

Still, their cocktails were nice. Andie took a sip of hers and felt a rainbow of flavours fracture deliciously in her mouth.

'So, how is Fred getting on?' she asked, then berated herself silently. She wanted to forget home, forget school. 'I was a bit worried when you said he was playing up, you see,' she finished lamely.

'He's better now,' said Jonathan. 'Most of the time he's fine, but he can be a little . . . awkward. I think sometimes these things start to happen when there are problems at home,' he said delicately, looking sympathetic.

'Things are fine,' Andie snapped, stung. Her home life was none of his bloody business. God, he was making it sound as though Fred was the victim of a broken home.

'So what does your husband do?' Jonathan asked hastily, his tone conciliatory.

Andie stared out at the dance floor, threading her fingers through her necklace. 'He works in computing. What about you? What does your partner do, if you have one?'

'Well, I was engaged a year ago to Rebecca. We'd been childhood sweethearts. We both went to Bristol university together, and then went travelling. She was very adventurous. We went everywhere – all across India, from the north down to the south, then on to Indonesia, Australia, the US. God, it was an amazing time.'

Andie felt a twinge of jealousy. She would have loved to have done all that with Nick.

'So what happened?' Andie frowned.

'She died.' Jonathan glugged back his drink. 'In a climbing accident.'

'I'm sorry.' Andie reached out to touch him, then drew back uncertainly. She was shocked . . . though at the same time, the paradoxes of his personality suddenly made sense. Beneath his boyishness, he seemed older than his years and she'd sensed he glossed over his melancholy with constant joking.

'WHAT ARE YOU GUYS DOING UP HERE?' Suzanne exploded upon them. She collapsed breathlessly onto Jonathan's lap. 'God, all night I've had these disgusting lechs coming on to me. One guy said, "I've got a condom with your name on it." So I said, "I didn't know Durex came in extra small sizes."' Her alcohol-laced laughter sounded more like a hyena than ever. 'Come, come and dance!'

'Well . . .' Jonathan looked pained.

'Oh, go on,' Andie said, starting to get into the spirit of the whole thing. She knew she wouldn't have another evening like this for a long time; tomorrow it would be back to subdued dinners and TV boredom. She wanted to seize the night and run with it and have a ball.

Down on the dance floor, Andie was slightly taken aback by Jonathan's wild dancing style. He was too tall for dancing – arms and legs wiggling everywhere like an octopus.

'Let's tango!' he said.

'Okay,' she cried.

Andie yelled with laughter as Jonathan spun her around at a breathless pace. People were laughing; several teenagers pointed and smirked in an oldies-on-the-dance floor manner but she didn't care. Lights shimmered and swam in

119

a kaleidoscopic blur; happiness fizzed inside her. *I haven't had this much fun in ages*, she thought in a giddy rush.

Jonathan held out his arm and she did a twirl; he swung her back and drew her in tight against him. And then it happened. For one awkward, delicious moment she became unbearably aware of his body: bare skin against warm skin, the sting and tang of his sweat mingling with hers, the pounding of his heart against her ribcage, the closeness of his lips, his brown eyes staring into hers. Then she felt something like a cold snake slither through her breasts, saw something silvery flash to the floor. She pressed her fingers to her throat.

'My necklace.'

They both bent down at the same time. Their heads knocked and they both jerked back, laughing. The necklace was coiled in a silvery puddle on the floor. They both reached for it and his fingers trickled over hers in a caress. Andie looked up at him. Jonathan folded her hand into his like a glove. Andie felt her mind and body press down sharply on the brakes. Suddenly she became acutely aware that the whole evening had left its steady tracks long ago and was hurtling out of control.

She drew away quickly and said, 'I think I should go home.'

'WHAT?' Jonathan shouted over the music.

'Go home.' She tried to smile, tapped her watch. 'I have to get back.'

Jonathan paused. The rainbow lights skipped over his face, highlighting a green hurt; a few seconds later, a pink smile.

'I can walk you home,' Jonathan offered.

'Oh no, it's fine, I can get a taxi,' said Andie. She meant to say it lightly, but it came out sounding like a rebuke.

Jonathan stuffed his hands in his pockets and shrugged. 'Well, bye then.'

They said awkward goodbyes and parted company for the night.

In the taxi home, Andie watched the lights of Richmond sparkle past and tried to sober herself up. What had happened back there in the club? She wasn't sure what Jonathan had been playing at at all – she still didn't know him well enough to judge whether his actions were flirtatious, whether he was some kind of womaniser who tried it on with every girl he met or whether she'd accidentally led him on and was now about to get herself tangled up in some kind of embarrassing situation. Andie didn't want to get into any kind of messy misunderstandings with anyone from work.

Then she thought about the story of his dead girlfriend and felt a little mean. Maybe he was just lonely.

Back home, she checked on Fred, giving him a tender kiss on the forehead. Nick was asleep too. Andie slipped into bed beside him, gazing at his face, the face she knew so well, every nook and cranny and scar and pore of it: his delightfully crooked nose, broken from a school fight aged sixteen; his full lips; his eyelashes, thick as black moths. There were new lines forming on the bridge above his nose and digging themselves into his mouth. The night had released the tension pent up inside her and she was in a mood to be more forgiving. I've been too harsh on him, she realised, he's been having a tough time at work. Suddenly a wave of love passed through her and she leaned over and gave him a gentle kiss.

He carried on snoring.

Sighing, Andie nestled against him and drifted off to sleep, the *thump-thump* echo of dance music still pounding in her head . . .

*

The next day at school, Andie came into the staff room to find everyone looking as wretched as she felt. Suzanne was holding her head in her hands as though it might fall apart if she removed them, and poor Norman's eyes were so red and blurry he hadn't even noticed he was reading his magazine upside down. And Jonathan. She flicked him a glance. Yep, he looked equally rough: grey circles smudged under his eyes, his skin the colour of ash.

She went into the kitchenette and found her mug on the side. Someone had cleaned it so well it looked spanking new.

'I was going to steal your mug again but I thought you might need it for, um, copious quantities of tomato juice this morning,' said Jonathan, coming up.

'Oh, thanks very much,' said Andie awkwardly.

'Oh, that's fine.'

A silence.

'I was completely off my head last night,' said Jonathan, raking his hands through his hair. 'God – the dance floor! My dancing – I was so embarrassing . . .'

The subtext was obvious: *You don't need to worry, Andie. I know you're married. I'm not trying it on and can we just forget anything ever happened?*

'Well, so was I,' Andie laughed, relieved.

'Yeah, but at least you don't have to take assembly this morning,' Jonathan groaned. 'Oh well, I'd best get my nose stuck into the Bible, hey?' He looked her straight in the eye, did his hair-raking thing again and smiled as if to say: *Friends?*

Andie smiled back: *Still friends.*

Well, she thought, everything will go back to normal now, thank God. So why did she feel just a tiny bit disappointed? Pushing the thought away, Andie set about making herself a cup of tea.

122

12

Cara

A week had passed since our trip to the Ritzy and I was still feeling slightly odd about the whole thing. I'd hoped that my attraction for Sean was just the result of drink, but every time I saw him – passing by the window, wearing a pair of shorts, or in the back garden brandishing his shears, or zooming down the road in his Beetle, tooting at me – my heart would whirl about in a little jig. Fortunately, I had enough self-control to hide it well and act as though nothing was different. I wasn't quite sure what to do with my feelings – I was far too scared to ever consider acting on them. I hoped that our friendship solidified, my attraction would quietly evaporate; for the time being, however, I was going to have to live with it in all its squirming embarrassment.

And there was Andie. I still hadn't got over that shock either. First Nick with his blonde; now Andie with Jonathan Yates; and yet, peculiarly, they carried on like any normal couple. Kisses goodbye before they went to work, shopping on Saturday morning at Waitrose, a day out in the park on Sunday. At the same time, they had the air of actors in a long-running sitcom who keep reciting their lines but have an increasingly weary self-consciousness that they are only ever acting.

I couldn't help worrying that I was to blame in some way; I was paranoid that ever since I'd joined them as a nanny, I'd sent their marriage scuttling further downhill. I could tell that I kept invading Andie's privacy – accidentally walking in on their arguments, or picking up the phone when she was in the middle of a call – but unless I tucked myself away in my room, what else could I do? In the end, I tried to compensate by working extra hard. All my nanny colleagues were always warring with bullying employers who treated them like slaves; but I washed up, I cooked, I hoovered, I cleaned the bathroom, but Andie and Nick were too preoccupied to notice.

Nor had they noticed that Fred, who clearly sensed trouble between them, was being increasingly difficult. I definitely felt as though Fred had accepted me, but he was still terribly naughty. The only difference was that now he would give me a hug and say, 'Sorree Cara!' and beg my forgiveness, then, when I granted it, he'd go and be naughty all over again.

The following Tuesday, Fred and I were in the living room playing yet another game of Monopoly (Fred was the banker and his pile of notes seemed to be growing suspiciously quickly) when I had to go up to the toilet.

As I came up the stairs, I froze halfway; I could hear Andie and Nick arguing again. Their bedroom door was slightly ajar and Nick's voice, sharp as nails, floated out . . .

'Andie, we have to economise, okay? We cannot go on holiday this year, and certainly not to Tuscany. Look, Andie, I'm the one who does the accounts. You said so yourself – you're allergic to bank statements. And we cannot afford it.'

'Oh, so you work such long hours you couldn't even make it to dinner but we can't afford to go on holiday,' Andie yelled back. 'I might be crap with money but I'm not an idiot, Nick. You're a bloody workaholic. Come on, that's the real reason, isn't it? You don't want to go on holiday because you can't bear to spend two weeks away from your stupid office. Well, why don't you marry your computer?' She broke off, gulping in air, realising she was ranting.

There was a silence. Then Nick said in a quiet voice: 'This has nothing to do with my work. Something has to go . . .'

At this point, I tried to retreat from the scene but as I took a step backwards, the stairs creaked loudly and I froze, worried I was about to be caught eavesdropping. Fortunately, they were too wrapped up in their arguing to hear.

I was about to go back downstairs, when I heard something that made me freeze again:

'Well, Sean will have to go then,' said Nick.

Sean, go?

'Who will do the gardening? We'll end up with a forest out there, Nick. And don't say you're going to do it because you won't. I know you, I know you'll just end up sitting inside watching the football.'

Good point, Andie, I cheered silently, *good point*.

'Sean doesn't even do it properly. Have you seen the way he shaves off the edges?'

Only by a millimetre, I defended him furiously.

'Okay, fine,' said Andie. 'Sack him. And then maybe we can give Fred a holiday this year?' And with that, she slammed the bedroom door.

Downstairs, I found that Fred had abandoned the Monopoly game: silver pieces and green houses and red hotels and a rainbow spray of money were all scattered across the board in an angry chaos. He had taken his piece – the metal sportscar – and was sullenly tossing it up in the air and catching it. Over and over again.

'But you were winning,' I said in shock. 'You had Mayfair.'

'So?' Fred shrugged sulkily, 'it was a stupid game anyway.'

Clearly I wasn't the only one who'd overheard the row.

Later, Fred went next door to play with (or, more accurately, traumatise) his friend Emma, giving me half an hour's breathing space. I lay down on my bed, watching the wind play with the dreamcatcher hanging from my window, fracturing red and blue and green light across the ceiling.

And that was when I finally decided I had to break my promise.

I was going to have to use magic.

Just a little bit. Just until I'd sorted things out.

This whole mess with the Wilkins is all my fault, I realised with a stab of guilt. *I'd* been the one to suggest the holiday, which had only resulted in a row. *I'd* been the one to push Andie into going back to work. As a result, Andie was now possibly seeing Jonathan and hardly had time to speak to Nick, *which* in turn was no doubt pushing Nick towards his blonde and provoking him into doing mean things like sacking Sean (I was convinced that had nothing to do with money, just Nick's bad temper), which *in turn* was going to cripple Sean's maintenance payments and ruin his already messy relationship with his ex, not to mention possibly cut him off from seeing his daughter.

All I could see was a series of disasters. I had to do something drastic. Magic was the only answer.

I leaped off the bed and pulled out my suitcase, flipping it open. I grabbed a thick pink book filled with clippings, notes, scribbles, dried flowers and leaves. Every witch keeps a Book of Shadows as a daily record of her spells and experiences. Flicking through, I wondered which spell I should try on Andie and Nick. Something for happiness? For binding their marriage?

Then the book fell open at an entry from my previous job:

> *Today I did a spell to help the family. They all complained about suffering from burnout so I wove a little magic to put some zest back in their lives. Now they are all racing about as though they are Julie Andrews on Viagra.*

God, that didn't sound great. It was like something off a magical version of *The Best Home Videos* – wizards performing group spells and accidentally setting their beards alight, or witches' tea parties where the pass-the-parcel-with-a-baby-dragon-in-the-centre caused rather a fracas with the living room curtains. Hmm, I thought, wondering if it was an omen. My magic skills had often been a little up and down and I was very out of practice. Maybe I should start with something small, something simple.

Sean's problem was easier and more urgent – if Nick was going to sack him tomorrow, I had to do something tonight.

Okay, I thought, *Sean it is. Cara Broad is coming to the rescue . . .*

I felt nervous about cooking up the potion so I waited until Fred was safely in bed and Andie and Nick were downstairs watching TV before risking it. The spell was one I'd never used before; all I had to rely on was a torn page Sellotaped into my Book of Shadows from *Witching* magazine's 'Dear Morag' problem page. This letter said:

Dear Morag
I am married to a wizard who is slightly lacking in the manhood department, and my mother-in-law keeps rubbing it in by buying us bonsais. Recently I performed a spell on one of the bonsai trees to try to make it grow into a good size as a symbol of hope to my husband, but unfortunately the spell went wrong and the bonsai shrank to the size of a peanut. My husband thinks I am mocking him and is deeply offended. Please help before it all ends in divorce!
Carol, from Essex.

Beneath it was a photo of Morag looking rather coiffeured and extremely pleased with herself.

Dear Carol
Don't despair – size doesn't matter. Although I guess it's all right for me, with a well-endowed husband and thirty marriage proposals from my wizard fans every week!
*   Anyhow, I don't know what growing spell you used on the bonsai but you ought to try this one on both your trees and your husband – it's cheaper than a sex op, I can tell you. All you need is:*
*   – Several sunbeams (to help the plant become happy – a happy plant grows faster!)*
*   – Some blessed earth (for a union with Mother Nature)*
*   – A few willow leaves (plant of fertility)*
*   Boil all the ingredients in a cauldron and apply as necessary.*

Remember – don't apply too much, else the bonsais may take over the house and lovemaking may become painful! It may interest you to know that I have a new book out next week – How to Make Love to A Wizard for All Your Future Lifetimes *– only £16.99 from all good bookshops.*

Best witchy wishes
Morag

Well, it seemed simple enough. Morag was the magical equivalent of Nigella Lawson – she was always coming up with spells that involved 'ordinary things you'd find in your fridge everyday' which normally sent you flying halfway across the world in search of the leaf of the Amazonian jungle Abracadabra plant. The sun was just setting so I flung open my attic window and muttered an incantation to draw some sunbeams into a jam jar. They flew in and I screwed the lid on tightly, watching them in awe; used to the infinity of the sky, they zig-zagged about in the jar like frustrated lightning. The other ingredients were quite simple. I took some earth from the garden; and in the back of my Book of Shadows I had several pages of dried leaves, forming an exquisite collage of vein and colour. I plucked out two dried willow leaves and then I was ready.

I was about to tip the lot into my miniature cauldron when I remembered that I'd forgotten the period of quietness. Dear me, my skills were getting terribly rusty. A witch should always perform a spell in a state of serenity and calm, so I sat down cross-legged and tried to clear my mind. But all I could think about was poor Sean.

Then I boiled up the mixture, chanting as I did so. Finally, I opened my eyes dreamily to see that I had a nice bubbling blue potion. So far, so good. Now I just needed to test it out.

I poured it into a mug – I figured that if I bumped into Nick or Andie, I could just pretend it was a cup of blueberry tea – and crept down to the landing. Down below, I could hear the blare of the TV – good. This meant they'd be far too preoccupied for a while to come upstairs.

Andie's plants were her pride and joy and one of the reasons why the dogs were banned from coming upstairs (apparently they were always either eating them or knocking them over). The selection sprawling across her window including a large fern, some cacti and a baby spider plant, her latest addition and a present from Nick.

I decided to test out the potion on a small rubbery green cactus sitting at the back of the windowsill. I dribbled a little into its soil and waited.

Five minutes later, I had a result, but it wasn't very dramatic. The cactus was now slightly bigger and its green shoots were curved upwards in the shape of a radiant smile. The cactus was certainly happy, but it wasn't substantially bigger. I'd have to go back to my cauldron and try again, using less sunbeams this time. Without thinking, I went to the toilet and flushed the potion down it.

Instantly, I heard the toilet gurgle loudly as though it was laughing; the water sparkled and splashed with a thousand tiny gold stars; and the wallpaper in the room, which was decorated with suns and moons, suddenly came to life, a dancing chaos of cosmic energy. I froze in panic, wondering whether I would ever be able to let the Wilkins family use their toilet again, but to my relief it settled down after a few minutes. All the same, I couldn't help picturing the potion whooshing down through the drains, sweeping happiness through whatever it encountered: it was a weird thought.

Time for potion number two. I cooked up another concoction in my cauldron, only this time I used less sunbeams and some extra willow leaves. This time I tried it on the spider plant, tipping it gently over its pale green leaves.

A few minutes later, it started to sprout, it leaves unravelling and spilling over the sides. It had worked!

In my excitement, I didn't notice that Fred had come up behind me. He was wearing his pyjamas and looking excited.

'Fred, you should be in bed!' I spluttered, hastily positioning myself in front of the spider plant. It was still growing like mad and I could feel its long leaves shooting out, tickling my back in a playful massage and lightly nipping my waist.

'But I couldn't sleep,' he moaned. 'What are you doooo-ing?'

'Um, I'm just watering the plants,' I said, 'now go back to bed!'

'Oh, can't I help?' Fred moaned. Seeing the living room door open and Nick come up the stairs to go to the loo, he cried, 'Dad, Cara's watering the plants, can I help?'

'That's very kind of you, Cara,' said Nick, giving me a flirtatious smile. 'Well, Fred, I think you could help out with just one, but only if you promise to be good and go to bed afterwards, hey?'

'Cool, Dad,' said Fred.

Cool? No, not cool! The spider plant – thank God – had stopped growing but I couldn't let Fred water a plant. I could just picture their faces when they saw it spurt into a botanical monster – I'd be packing my bags within five minutes.

Nick and Fred gazed at me patiently. Oh God. This was just like the incident at school. I'd done it again; got myself into a real magical mess. *Mind you*, I thought, *if Fred is the only one to see the magic, who would believe him? He is only seven years old . . .*

'Okay, sure,' I said, handing the mug to Fred. 'Come on, let's let Daddy go to the loo.'

'Oh, no, I want Dad to watch,' Fred insisted.

'No, no! I mean . . . I mean . . .' *What did I mean?* Nick was giving me a puzzled look, as though wondering why I wanted to spoil a seven-year-old's innocent fun. 'I mean, let me help you or you'll spill it!' I cried. I curled my hands around his, drawing the mug up to the plant . . . and then, just as we were about to tip the potion in, I knocked him and it all went sloshing over the carpet.

'Shit!' said Nick.

'Shit!' Fred echoed him, then, seeing his father's face, apologised meekly.

For the next five minutes we all panicked as we rubbed the stain out of the carpet and made a pact not to tell Andie – 'She goes bonkers about stuff like this,' Nick said.

Fortunately, we managed to clear it up without leaving any marks. Even so, I was horribly conscious of the fact that some of the potion had splashed on to Nick's shoes. One of his laces had sprawled out like a piece of black spaghetti.

'Well, sorry about that, but I think Freddy ought to be in bed anyway,' I said, firmly pushing Fred back towards his bedroom.

As Nick went down the stairs, he tripped on the lace and nearly went flying, only just catching hold of the bannister in time. He frowned, sat down and retied them, glanced up at me, grinned and said 'It's okay, I'm still alive!' and went back into the living room.

Nice one, Cara, I thought, *just help Nick out by breaking his leg while you're at it.*

Thank God the potion was ready; my nerves had been torn to shreds and I didn't think I could handle the strain of any more deceptions. Even so, the shoelace wasn't the worst of my worries . . .

I went back up into my attic room and climbed into bed, picking up *The Lion, the Witch and the Wardrobe*, my favourite novel. I couldn't take the potion out into the garden until everyone was asleep, so I had to read to keep myself awake. But I found it impossible to escape into the delightful world of Narnia when I could hear the toilet flushing happily of its own accord and Andie's worried voice: 'Nick – what's up with it? I think we're going to have to call a plumber in the morning.'

Well, that's just great, I thought wryly. *Even though all my magic keeps going wrong and I have no idea if this spell is going to work tonight, hey – at least I can say Nick and Andie are the proud owners of the happiest toilet in the world.*

13
Cara

People were giving me funny looks, I was sure of it.

I got on to the bus, fumbling clumsily with my change. I sat down, gazing at my hands encased in black woollen gloves, even though it was a summer's day, so hot my plastic sandals felt as though they would melt into the pavement and my body was bathed in a constant sweat. Behind me, I could feel my plait, now so long that it nearly touched my waist.

How could I have been so stupid? I shouldn't have dabbled with magic – not when I was so out of practice. And now I was suffering the consequences . . .

My grandmother owns the most amazing shop called The Mistress of Magic. It's in one of those Soho streets where the dark shops are all bunched together, lodged incongruously between a strip club and a sex shop. Their shops look so gross beside hers, red and blue neon lights flashing lewdly. Her shop is subtle, mysterious: the window-panes are stained glass, rainbow diamonds held together with lattice piping. Inside is a temple of delights, lit by candles and perfumed with jasmine

incense. The dark walls are lined with shelves filled wɪ.
hundreds of glass-stoppered bottles. Dried herbs hang
from the ceiling in clusters: rosemary, thyme, basil and
marjoram.

As I approached it, I prayed feverishly: *Please don't let
Mum be there, please can I avoid her.* I knew it was mean; I
did want to see her, but not now; I just couldn't face her
crowing over my magical failures.

The doorbell jingled as I entered.

'Grandma!' I called. 'It's me!'

'Hang on,' she called from the kitchen out the back. 'I'll
be out in a second!'

While I waited, I glanced around the shop. I noticed a
new selection of goods; there was a cardboard sign with
big cerise letters screaming THE LOVE RANGE. Hmm,
this looked interesting. I jumped and quickly put the
bottles down as my grandmother entered the room.

'Cara, my darling!' She kissed me, curling her fingers
around my shoulders. 'Ooh, you're tense.' She probed the
knots. 'How are you?' She always had a way of looking into
me, lasering past the layers of social façade into the very
core of my soul.

'I'm fine.'

'No, you're not. What's the matter?'

'I'm terrible,' I said, suddenly feeling close to tears.

'Sit down,' she said, pressing a mug of tea into my
hands.

I tried and failed to lift the cup without spilling the
liquid inside; my gloves were too thick. I stared down into
the tea, too ashamed to look her in the eye.

'I tried some magic and it went wrong,' I said in a small
voice. 'Horribly, horribly wrong.'

She nodded, waiting. So I told her the whole story.
How Andie and Nick had been about to sack Sean and I'd

anted to help him out. How I had waited until everyone had gone to bed and crept downstairs into the garden.

I'd drizzled the potion over the grass, the earth, the flowerbeds. It had trickled over stems and shimmered in rainbow dewdrops on leaves before winding into the earth in glittering paths. I'd put the cork back in the bottle and my hands had been shaking. My grandmother always used to joke that magic was better than sex; afterwards, there is the same feeling of exhilaration, heightened senses. I'd gazed up at the moon, clouds passing over her like two frowning, wispy eyebrows. I'd gone back indoors and barely slept all night, shivering with feverish restlessness . . .

'Did it work?' she asked.

'Yes, it did! Andie and Nick haven't seen it yet, but, boy, their garden is definitely, um, *different*. The trouble was,' I explained, 'I didn't realise it at the time, but I'd spilled a little on to my hands. And I forgot to do the spell for protection.'

'Ah.' My grandmother's eyes glinted with disapproval behind her glasses.

I pulled my gloves off slowly. Even though I'd cut my nails this morning, only an hour ago, they were curling out like witchy talons.

'They won't stop growing! I woke up this morning and they were like quills! And as for my legs – I've broken my bloody shaver, it's so clogged up with hair. Don't laugh! My hair is growing at the speed of Rapunzel's and I feel as if my body is this big sprouting *machine*. I had to tell the Wilkins I had terrible toothache and needed to go to the dentist to get out of the house without them noticing. What am I going to do?'

Besides this, the toilet was now totally out of control. In a permanent state of ecstasy, it kept merrily flushing of its own accord every fifteen minutes. The tinkly toilet paper also exuberantly rattled out 'If You're Happy and You Know It Clap Your Hands' at every available opportunity. I'd had to pretend I'd bought some special new toilet roll, and the Wilkins thought I was insane.

'Well, Cara, I've told you a thousand times. If you play with magic, it will play with you,' she tutted, as though I was a naughty child who'd been messing about with fireworks.

'I know, I know,' I muttered.

'I shall have to work out a paste. We'll need some tea tree oil and some neem leaves and—'

'Neem leaves?' I winced as she pulled out a jar filled with dry green leaves. 'What are they?' I was quite suspicious; her potions often contained all kinds of weird and wonderful ingredients, from frogs' legs to cats' whiskers.

'In India, women rub the oil over their private parts as a contraceptive. It's the secret ingredient of any infertility potion.'

All the same, I found it thrilling to sit there and watch her. Her work apparatus was a mixture of modern science and ancient wisdom, of black cauldrons and teat pipettes, of magical candles and Bunsen burners. My grandmother always argued that both science and religion, though seemingly opposed, reached the same conclusive truths, just from different angles. As she crushed some pomegranate seeds using a pestle and mortar, she gave me a long look.

'And?' she asked. 'I can tell you haven't told me everything.'

'Oh God,' I moaned. She passed me my cup of infertility tea and I took a sip, pulling a face as the bitter chalky taste pinpricked my tongue. Seeing her drink-up-or-else

137

frown, I hastily took a few more sips. 'The problem is, the Wilkins – you won't tell Mum this, will you? – well, they're having marriage problems and I think I've made it all worse . . .'

I poured out the whole story: about Andie and how I'd persuaded her to go back to teaching, how she seemed to be with Jonathan, how Nick was also being disloyal, and how I'd tried to help them without using magic but everything had got out of control . . .

'I don't understand why you're so nervous about using magic. No wonder your skills are rusty!'

'I know, I just . . . I . . .' I trailed off. 'I just wanted to live a normal life for once.'

'Who wants to be like everyone else?' my grandmother demanded. 'If we were all the same, life would be very dull.'

I shrugged uncomfortably, realising that she was right; I was ashamed of magic. I regarded it as a prop; when my life was going well, I forgot about the tarot and just lived; when things were going badly, I clung to my tea leaves and almanac, desperately looking for answers.

I looked down at my nails and let out a cry of relief. They had shrunk back down to their normal size.

'See?' my grandmother said. 'A little magic is a very fine thing. You know, life seems chaotic on one level, Cara. But there is a thread of order running through it. Scientists call it the unified field; religions call it God or fate. You only have to look at the universe to marvel at its miracles – just the fact that the earth was made at all. It's just a case of harnessing that power: that's the secret of magic, pure and simple.'

My grandmother was always so fascinating to listen to. For her, magic wasn't about cheap tricks or showing off; it was a profound philosophy. For a moment I longed for her wisdom; I felt stupid beside her.

138

'Cara, the lesson you need to learn is not to practice magic in haste. You can be a little impetuous at times. *Think* before you cast a spell. *Plan.* Power is responsibility—'

We were interrupted as the shop bell tinkled. A voice cried, 'CARA!'

Oh great. My mother. All the same, I had to admit I was glad to see her. I ran up to her and gave her a hug.

'Careful, darling,' she said, wincing theatrically and holding her side. 'I've been terribly poorly since you left me; oohhh, it does hurt.'

I turned to my grandma and rolled my eyes but she looked worried. God, my mother's hypochondria was so convincing even my grandmother was fooled.

Then my mother rolled her eyes at me. 'Rufus informed me of the little trick you played on him in the Ritzy,' she said icily. 'Honestly, Cara, if you carry on like this you'll end up an old woman surrounded by her cauldrons with nobody to love her.'

'It wasn't my fault! He spilled his drink down himself!' I said, feigning an innocent face. 'I'd love to give him another chance sometime.' Like the next millennium, if at all possible.

'Well, you can give him another chance at the Summer Solstice,' my mother said sharply. Summer Solstice is one of the key festivals in the witching calendar. 'I trust you will be attending this year, rather than coming down with a mysterious dose of flu as you did last time?'

I sighed. As a matter of fact, I really had been ill; but my mother was convinced any illness I contracted was a personal slight, a means of spiting her, because – of course – the whole world revolved around my mother.

'Okay, I'll be there,' I said. It wasn't for a while, which gave me plenty of time to think up excuses. 'Look, I must dash, I've got to get back to work. Bye, Mum. Bye, Grandma!'

As I made a hasty exit, my grandmother came over to hug me and surreptitiously pressed a little bottle into my hand. I looked down at the label. Love Potion. She whispered, 'For the Wilkins!' and gave me a wink. I grinned back and said a warm thanks.

Despite the aggravation of seeing my mother, I came out of The Mistress of Magic feeling a sense of peace I hadn't felt in a long time. My grandmother was right. I *should* be proud to be a witch.

Life is tough, I mused, *and everyone needs something to help them cope with it.* Alcohol to blur reality, drugs to give it more colour, meditation to wash away the scars and stains, astrology to inject a pattern into the chaos. I was only human, I needed a bit of escapism like anybody else, and using magic was a lot more positive than most options.

By the time I reached Leicester Square Tube, I was completely exhilarated. Everything that had seemed fixed now looked malleable; everything that had seemed permanent now sparkled with possibility. I felt as if I could pluck the stars down from the sky; while I waited for a train, I was convinced I could tie the tracks up into knots with the power of my gaze. The world seemed a swirl of vibrating colour and energy that I could mould into any picture using my magical palette.

That evening, I heard loud voices coming from the kitchen. I heard Nick cry, 'Andie, I just can't believe that you've given Sean a *rise*! Fine, don't fire him. But to pay him more – for crying out loud!'

Sean was getting a rise! Fantastic! See, my grandmother was right, I told myself. Magic is the answer to everything.

'Well, who can blame me?' Andie continued. 'The garden has suddenly become a state—' She broke off, looking a little embarrassed as I entered the room. 'Hi, Cara. Last week Nick gave Sean some new kind of genetically engineered fertiliser to use on the garden and it has suddenly taken effect. Nice one, Nick.'

I gazed out of the window. The lawn was a sea of thick grass, the evergreens were ridiculously bushy and the apple trees at the bottom of the garden were positively groaning with fruit.

'I still don't know why we had to give Sean a rise,' Nick started up again.

I couldn't help wondering if Andie had done it to wind Nick up as much as anything.

As their row started to escalate, I quickly backed out of the kitchen, feeling my bubble of happiness and confidence burst. That was the trouble with magic. There were always unexpected side-effects.

Still, I told myself, Andie and Nick *are* going through a bad patch. They looked for things to argue about. God, even if they won the bloody lottery they'd probably still come to blows. No, Andie and Nick were in trouble, and I was going to save them. I'd have to think very carefully about how I used the love potion, but provided I acted carefully and planned it out properly, what could go wrong?

Upstairs in my room, I hid the love potion under my mattress and started to work out what I was going to do . . .

14
Andie

Andie screeched on her brakes. The car skidded to a halt halfway across the zebra crossing, flinging her forwards so that her seatbelt cut into her stomach. An old granny, who was guiding her little grandson across the road, gave Andie a filthy look, as if she felt Andie's license should be torn into pieces. In the back, Beethoven and Mozart, who had been expecting a nice, leisurely walk, not a Hollywood-style car chase, barked chidingly.

She shouldn't have come out. It was crazy. She was in no state to drive, no state to do anything. A chaos of voices chattered in her head like a cage of birds; then a sensible, quiet voice came to the surface: *Andie, slow down. You're seriously going to get yourself killed at this rate. Slow. Down. Stop.* So she pulled over into a car park, put Beethoven and Mozart on their leashes and went for a walk by the river.

The weather was horribly unsympathetic. It was weather for happy couples, for loving and laughing. The sky was a bright forget-me-not blue; little chimney-smoke puffs of clouds gently moving across it. An elderly couple walked past her, hand in hand. The sight of them set her

142

off crying again. She collapsed on to a park bench, sobbing.

She was jerked out of her unhappiness by a little Scottie dog who came yapping around her heels.

'Becks, slow down!' a familiar voice called.

Andie peeked through her blur of tears. Oh God. It couldn't be. No, she didn't want Jonathan to see her in this state . . .

'Andie! Hi! I just came out to get some milk . . .' His eyes widened in alarm when he saw her face.

Andie couldn't help it. She burst into sobs again. Jonathan instantly came and sat beside her. His dog, Becks, continued to dance around her feet.

'Er, are you okay?'

'I just found out that my husband is having an affair,' she burst out. It seemed strange to say it aloud; she half expected the river to fall silent, everyone to freeze, the earth to pause in its motion, the stars to crumble out of the sky.

Then she looked at Jonathan, who had gone very white.

'My flat's just down the road,' he said gently. 'Why don't you come and have some tea and tell me all about it?'

They walked towards his flat in an awkward silence. Every so often Jonathan looked across and gave her a 'cheer-up' smile and Andie forced one in return. Things were made even more strained by Becks and Beethoven deciding they didn't like each other. Beethoven might have been a huge lumbering labrador but he was rather elderly, very soppy and easily scared; Becks was young and made up for his tiny size by being a bully. He danced in between Beethoven's legs with grizzly little barks. Beethoven whined and tried to hide behind Andie, tangling her up in

143

his leash. Mozart then leaped to Beethoven's defence by barking madly.

'Becks!' said Jonathan sternly. '*Behave!*' In the end, he had to scoop him up into his arms and carry him.

Jonathan's flat was situated in a quiet, very expensive-looking block overlooking the Thames. They went into a tasteful, creamy reception, up a spaceship-style lift and got out on the second floor. They were about to go into Jonathan's apartment when a door suddenly opened and a woman craned her neck out. She looked to be about ninety years old and her balding curls were coloured a rose-pink.

'Jonathan, it worked!' she cried, clasping her skeletal hands around his shoulders. 'I tried it on my marigolds and they spurted up overnight!' She kissed each of his cheeks and he smiled and kissed her back and took her hands in his.

'Dear Mrs Williams,' he smiled, looking deep into her eyes and enjoying the soft blush on her face. 'I must come by later and have a look.'

As they entered his flat, Andie momentarily forgot all about Nick, she was so intrigued by this new side to Jonathan, this private side which seemed so different to his work persona: a man who gave tips on growing flowers to OAPs.

'Older women seem to like me,' said Jonathan, grinning rather shyly. 'Now, I'll make some tea and you go and sit in the living room.'

The kitchen was tiny; the living room much larger, with windows that opened out on to a balcony that overlooked the Thames. Instantly Beethoven and Mozart (relieved that Becks had been shut in the kitchen) started to pad around, giving the place a good sniff. Andie did some exploring too.

It wasn't what she had expected at all. She'd envisaged a noisy, laddish pad with crumpled beer cans and dirty underwear sprawled on the floor and pictures of the latest plastically-enhanced babe on the wall. This flat was tasteful, quiet and full of light; the walls were clean and white and the room was filled with squashy leather sofas. There was a bird table on the balcony; judging from the dangling oblong of seed, Jonathan enjoyed regular visitors. His CD selection was mostly classical: Mozart, Rachmaninov, Pacibel. And on the walls were beautiful watercolours of various landscapes: not the twee deer-and-woods scenes that normally turn up in middle-class dwellings, but pictures of mountains and oceans and plains that shouted with energy and colour. Then Andie looked closely.

'Oh,' she said aloud.

The signature said: Rebecca King.

And there, on top of the TV, was a photo which could only be her. A girl with a heart-shaped face, ruler-straight hair the red of a fox's coat, scowling brown eyes and a sulky smile. Then Andie felt very sad. She realised the pictures depicted all the places Jonathan and she had travelled to. For a moment her worries about Nick seemed trivial in comparison, and she suddenly felt silly and selfish.

'D'you like them?' Jonathan asked, making her jump as he re-entered the room carrying two cups of tea. 'Look, I'm in all of them.'

'What?' Andie asked.

'Yes, look.' He put the mugs down and pointed. Then Andie saw: a tall stick-man painted on to the sweep of the Alps. A man in the background of a Delhi bazaar, smiling at a cage of green parrots. A man in a boat on the stormy wind-flecked sea. She was suddenly reminded of her and Nick on their last holiday together, looking just like

145

Jonathan and Rebecca, like a couple so wildly in love nothing else mattered. She found herself starting to cry again.

'Andie, shush.' Jonathan gently pulled her down on to a sofa and squeezed his arm around her. 'Now, tell me about Nick,' he said. 'If you feel comfortable telling me, that is.'

Andie rubbed her eyes, reached for her tea, took a sip and scalded her tongue.

'Okay,' she sighed. 'I don't know where to begin. You probably don't want to hear about this, not really . . .' She trailed off uncertainly. She was so used to maintaining a façade that it felt strange to dismantle it, to admit there were cracks, least of all in a situation where a friendship was so fresh.

'I have a feeling you need someone to talk to,' said Jonathan. 'Look, if you feel funny with me 'cos I'm a bloke we can always call up Suzanne.'

'Suzanne!' Andie laughed. 'Oh yeah, right. Suzanne. God, has she even had a relationship that's lasted longer than five minutes? Make that five seconds.'

'As a matter of fact,' Jonathan informed her, 'Suzanne was once married, when she was eighteen or nineteen.'

'*No!* You're kidding?'

'Yes, really. To a terrible guy who was much older than her and a chauvinist pig who controlled her every move. Eventually she broke free and divorced him. Which is why she is how she is now. She's living her lost teenage years.'

'Oh.' Andie suddenly felt a little bit better; everyone had their problems, she realised.

'So you think he's having an affair?' Jonathan probed gently.

'I don't know. First of all, I found this note in his drawer. It was addressed to me – it didn't really say anything, but . . . it was very, you know, worrying . . .'

'A note. I see.'

'But the worst part is this – a friend, Maggie, called me today. She told me she'd been out to the park and she'd noticed Nick with a blonde woman. She didn't say exactly what they were *doing* . . . but, well, it's pretty obvious. It came as a bit of a shock.' She laughed at her understatement. 'And I know Maggie quite well – she lives in our road and her daughter plays with Fred. I know Maggie wouldn't lie.'

A silence.

'Andie, don't you think you're, um, over-reacting?' Jonathan said at last. 'It could have been anyone.'

'You're not married!' Andie flared up. 'Oh God, sorry, I didn't mean that. It's just – you're, you know, a man . . .'

'Look,' said Jonathan, 'I used to have this all the time with Rebecca. Her dad had cheated on her mother and she was paranoid about me doing the same. We travelled all over the place and I had countless opportunities, but not once did I ever so much as *touch* another woman. Okay, so men are men and we do contain large doses of testosterone,' he said in an acid, irritated voice, 'but, contrary to what you might read in crappy womens' mags, we're not all chained to our dicks. We can be capable of loyalty.'

Andie shook her head fiercely, feeling riled. 'Well, Rebecca was very lucky to be with you. But Nick had an affair – years ago – so that's how I know now. I just *know*.'

Jonathan was so shocked he choked on a gulp of tea. He put down his mug, slopping a pale brown pool of liquid on the table. Then he looked up at her face and muttered, 'Fucking hell.'

'You won't tell anyone, will you?' Despite herself, Andie suddenly felt raw with guilt. She'd promised, absolutely sworn to Nick that she would keep it secret. She hadn't

147

even told her own family, for God's sake. Now she felt she'd betrayed him. 'You won't tell Suzanne or anyone at school?'

'Andie, of course I won't!' Jonathan said.

'So you see,' she said in a hot, trembling voice, 'as much as I love my husband, I'm afraid he is the male cliché. He *is* chained to his dick.'

'Oh Andie.' Jonathan drew open his arms and hugged her tight as she burst into a fresh flood of tears. She buried her face in his jumper, the fuzz of brown cotton comfortingly scratchy against her cheek. His hands were gentle on her hair.

Time passed. Her body stopped heaving; the tears softened and then stopped. Still, they held each other. In the distance, a few geese fought on the Thames; a blue tit pecked at the bird table; they could hear the sound of Becks' claws scuttling on the kitchen lino and Beethoven heaving a long sigh. And still they held each other.

Andie was suddenly aware that her tears had stopped and she pulled back a few inches. Jonathan stared down at her. They were so close she could see the flecks of stubble that he had missed while shaving that morning; a smattering of freckles by his left ear; the black pores on his nose. His breath was like a warm circle on her forehead. She swallowed back tears; they felt cool in her hot throat. Suddenly she felt hot all over. She looked down awkwardly and fiddled with her tissue, ripping a few shreds between her fingers. Then she felt his hand on the small of her back, drawing her in a little closer, and she looked up sharply and his eyes said everything.

He might have kissed her at that moment, but something passed between them that was more intimate than a kiss; so subtle, in fact, that a kiss would have seemed crude.

148

'I ought to go,' Andie said suddenly, getting up.

'Andie, please – I'm sorry – I didn't mean—'

'You've been so kind. Thanks so much for the tea and everything—'

'Andie. Don't.'

And his voice was so pained that she sat down again, feeling mean.

They sat there for a minute, sipping cold tea self-consciously.

Jonathan said: 'I just want to be here for you, Andie. Look, I admit I . . .' he trailed off. 'I don't want anything . . . okay . . . so . . .' He was getting thoroughly tangled up with his words, though Andie felt the pauses said a lot more.

Another pregnant silence formed. Andie finished her tea and said: 'Have you had any girlfriends since Rebecca?'

'No,' said Jonathan. 'I – no. Well, one.'

'Tell me about her.'

'It was just a one-night stand,' he said. He fiddled stiffly with his mug; Andie got the impression he didn't talk much about Rebecca to anyone. 'After she died, I went travelling again, trying to forget her, but it was a stupid mistake; everywhere I went, I had a memory of her – a joke we'd shared, her smile, a restaurant we'd eaten in. And then in Bangkok I had a one-night stand with a Thai prostitute. It had to be – I couldn't have made love to a girl with any real feelings. It had to be base, soulless. I felt terrible afterwards.'

'Jonathan—'

'It's okay. I'm fine. But look – just now – I didn't mean to complicate anything. Okay, I admit – you're gorgeous. I'm going to come out and say it. You're the first woman I've found attractive since Rebecca. God, the day I first saw you in that classroom, looking so wonderfully fierce –

I nearly died. But I'm not about to make a move on you, and I know things are difficult with Nick, so I really hope you sort things out.'

Andie sat there, still and wide-eyed.

'Andie?' he winced. 'Have I been too forward? I just thought . . . I ought to come out and say it. Though I've probably been so obvious you've already guessed.'

'No, no, it's fine,' Andie said. Then she smiled. 'I'm really flattered, actually. You make me feel sexy.' She knew she was fishing but she couldn't help it; her self-esteem was rock-bottom.

'Of course you are!' Jonathan said, so vehemently that she laughed; she really did feel cheered now. 'You are so, so pretty, and smart and funny, so fucking *incredible*.'

'Oh Jonathan,' she said, and she nearly hugged him again, then felt awkward.

'You mustn't worry,' said Jonathan earnestly. 'I know you're married and I totally accept it. I don't want you to think I'm going to be leaping on you at every opportunity. Like trying to grapple your mug off you in a provocative manner.'

'Or offering me a lift home and mistaking my knee for the gear stick,' Andie teased; somehow, by joking about it, it made it much easier to handle.

'Or pushing you up against the photocopier when Cloones isn't looking.'

They both collapsed into laughter.

'Anyway,' said Andie, feeling another rush of anger, 'I should have a bloody affair. Nick would bloody well deserve it.'

'But you love him, don't you?' Jonathan said sharply. 'I know you don't want to give up. Go back and talk to him, Andie. Because if there's one thing I learned from Rebecca, it's that life is too short to waste letting relationships fall to ruin, letting precious things crumble into dust. Otherwise, what's the point of it all?'

Andie suddenly pictured how she would feel if Nick died tomorrow and she stood up.

'You're right,' she said. 'I'll go home.'

When she got home, however, Andie found herself struck dumb. Normally Andie never let anything fester inside her, but she couldn't find the words to say what she needed to.

'Hi, darling.' Nick was standing in the kitchen, making himself a toasted HP sauce and tomato sandwich.

Fred was doing his homework at the table. 'Muu-um,' he said, with a bright smile and that certain ring to his voice that implied he was going to ask for something he wasn't normally allowed.

Andie opened her mouth to tell Fred to go outside, that she needed to talk to his dad for a moment. But the words rasped in her throat. She swallowed; her jaw ached and her mouth hurt, as though she'd been talking for hours and hours.

'What is it?' Andie asked distractedly, watching Nick, who was munching obliviously. He looked so normal, so *innocent*. She suddenly felt a desperate hunger to fill her yawning pain with food. She reached into a cupboard and took down a jar of peanut butter, taking out quivering bites with a spoon.

'Can I have a Twix?' Fred asked.

Andie was so cross she dropped her spoon. Nick jumped. Mozart came bounding forwards, licking the spoon joyously.

'Fred, you had one earlier. You know you're not allowed too many or you'll come up in a rash. Have an apple.'

'I hate apples. They taste like poo.'

151

'No, they don't. They taste nice.' Her voice was harsh, strained.

'Anyway, I didn't have one earlier, I had two earlier,' Fred said sulkily.

'What did you say?'

'I stole one from the cupboard,' Fred admitted defiantly, 'and I don't have a rash and I'm not getting hyper!'

'FRED! You know you're not allowed to steal from the cupboard. How many times have I told you—'

'But Dad caught me and he said it was okay!' Fred cried, close to tears.

'Actually, I thought it wouldn't do him any harm to have a little treat,' said Nick quietly.

Andie glanced at Nick. He was back to reading the *Daily Telegraph*, pretending not to listen, not wanting to get seriously involved except for the occasional flip comment. Suddenly she wanted to tear the paper from his hands, clutch hold of his lapels and demand: *Who is she? Who is she?*

'See?' said Fred, poking out his tongue. 'Dad's much nicer than you.'

'Fred, don't be cheeky with me!'

'Oh come on, Andie, it was only a Twix. A Twix a day helps you work, rest and play and all that. Or is that Mars?' Nick said with a smile.

'Nick, keep out of it. Fred, this conversation is between you and me!'

Nick opened his mouth to speak, but Andie steamrolled over him. 'Daddy shouldn't be letting you have extra chocolate and he won't do so again in the future.' She heard a scratching noise and noticed that Mozart was still licking the spoon, nosing it around the kitchen in a helpless chase. Andie picked it up and threw it into the sink, giving Mozart an angry *thwack!*.

'Don't hit him!' Fred yelled, curling his arms around Mozart protectively. His face was screwed up in frustration.

'Go to your room,' Andie said sharply. 'And you can forget your pocket money this week.'

'But Mum—'

'No buts—'

'Just because you're a stupid cow!'

'Fred, don't you dare use language like that!' Andie was stunned, but Fred had already run out of the kitchen. His footsteps hammered on the stairs, then his bedroom door slammed shut.

Andie gaped at Nick. Her temper snapped. 'You could have bloody well stood by me!' she yelled.

'Well, don't look at me!' Nick snarled back. 'I think you're being completely over the top – sending him to his room over a bloody Twix. But hey, you told me to keep out of it. Because my opinion doesn't count, of course – it never does! And I'm sick to death of it!' Nick stormed out.

'Where are you going?' Andie yelled after him, but he didn't look back.

'COME BACK HERE!' she screamed. How dare he walk out like that when he was the one having a fucking affair.

She was so furious that she whirled around, picked up the peanut butter and lobbed it on the floor with a satisfying crash. For a moment, she stared blankly at the shards and shimmers of glass, tears trickling down her cheeks. Then she collected herself; Mozart was sniffing around; he'd get glass in his paws.

'No, Mozart.' She bent down and felt like crying again when the dog licked her face lovingly, as if trying to cheer her up.

She shut Mozart outside, sweeping up methodically. There was something oddly soothing about the nitty-grittiness of the task, the concentrated attention of checking every coloured square of the lino for every last splinter of glass. By the end she felt calmer. Well, a little, anyway.

She went into the garden, realising that she was waiting for Nick to come back. Oh God, what if he never came back, what if he'd gone off with his blonde mistress? And what about Fred? How could he be so rude to her? She was becoming conscious of changes in him that scared her; one day he was laughing naïvely over willies, the next he was calling her a stupid cow. Should she go up to him, make peace? But she was in no state to talk to him. Suddenly she felt full of theatrical self-pity. Her world seemed to be crumbling around her; she was losing her husband and her son was growing away from her. She had a wild urge to call Jonathan and beg him for more advice. But she mustn't. This was between her and Nick; they had to sort it out themselves.

She went back into the kitchen, splashing water on her face and rubbing it with kitchen paper. Her heart started to beat more quickly when she heard the back door opening again. Nick.

She still couldn't confront him. She just stared at him dumbly.

'Maybe I'd better go and speak to Fred,' he said, adding in a sarcastic tone, 'Man to man, you know. He is upset.'

Andie nodded dully. A few minutes later, she went up to their bedroom, leaving the door ajar, half-listening to Nick chatting to Fred quietly. Twenty minutes later, Nick sought her out.

'I think it's okay,' he said. 'I said we wouldn't take his pocket money away. It is my fault for letting him take the chocolate, after all.'

'Yes, I was probably over-reacting. It was just a Twix.' Andie laced her fingers together. 'I—'

'I—' Nick said at the same time.

'I'm sorry,' Nick blurted out and came and put his arms around her, holding her tight. She wanted to hit him and yet it seemed so natural, so easy, just to let him hold her.

He drew her towards the bed, and they lay together. He tried to kiss her but Andie felt funny and she pulled back, shaking her head and nestling into his shoulder. He smiled and nodded, stroking her hair gently.

As they lay there for a while, Andie felt her anger dissolve into a soft sense of peace. Dusky sunlight came in through the window, lighting up a funnel of dust-motes and highlighting crimson flecks in Nick's dark hair. Andie felt exhausted, emotionally drained. She couldn't think any more. She fell into a short sleep, drifting between dream and memory. The scene reminded her of years back, when they'd lived in their flat and everything had been getting on top of them – the business, the mess, the kids below who played music at 3 a.m. They'd been shouting across the room; then Andie had felt a tight pain in her pregnant stomach and she'd laid down on the futon, panting. Apologising, Nick had come and laid beside her, putting his hand on her stomach, stroking it gently and kissing her. And in that moment before her waters had broken (they'd always joked afterwards that it had been Nick's fault, he'd somehow triggered it), she'd felt a wonderful sense of peace and wholeness.

Andie opened her eyes, drifting back into consciousness, aware that Nick was staring at her here and now. His brown eyes looked so warm and soft, she felt a flicker of pain and thought: *He can't be having an affair. He can't be. Last time he promised me it would never happen again. And he meant it, I know he did.*

'You okay?' Nick asked.

'Fine.' Andie smiled suddenly and felt a sense of relief. Suddenly she knew that she had to be right. He wasn't having an affair; she just knew, intuitively, that she'd over-reacted. It was all a silly misunderstanding.

But the next morning her bubble burst again.

Soothed, Andie had finally had one of those rare and wonderful nights where she'd slept all the way through. Waking at seven o'clock, she felt fresh for once, and thought wistfully: *If only I could sleep like that every night.* Nick was already up and about but Fred came in. He sat on the edge of the bed, curling his hand under the covers and tickling her feet. Andie grinned. They were friends again.

Andie lay back among her pillows, stretching pleasurably, when she suddenly heard noises from downstairs, above the crackle of the radio: Nick and Cara's voices, their laughter entwined together. A sudden realisation struck her – Cara was blonde . . . What if the blonde Maggie had seen was Cara?

Mozart and Beethoven came creeping into the bedroom and bounced on to the bed, wanting to join in with the fun.

'Oh Fred, I told you not to let the dogs in!' Andie moaned, her happy mood waning. 'You know you're supposed to shut the door!'

'Sorry, Mum.'

Andie sighed, drawing Fred up and giving him a big hug. She buried her face in his soft dark hair, breathing in the sweet, innocent smell. But Fred wriggled away, restless and hungry for his breakfast.

Andie got up too, pulling on her dressing gown, her mind still whirring. She realised then that she couldn't just ignore the problem. It was like trying to cover a gaping hole in a wall with paper; winds of fear simply kept tearing through. She couldn't carry on like this, with that sneaky little voice in the back of her head noting down every girl with fair hair and thinking: *What if she's the one?* She was certain Nick was blameless, but all the same, she had to stop being a coward and confront him sooner or later.

15
Cara

Think before you cast a spell. Plan. Power is responsibility.

My grandmother's words: I kept repeating them like a mantra as I twisted the love potion between my fingers, pondering, pondering . . .

To be honest, I was starting to lose my nerve again. My trip to my grandmother's shop already seemed fuzzy and strange, like a memory of a dream. And spells were so risky. I might have saved Sean from getting fired but he had been toiling away in the garden for the last week, cursing as the mower kept getting clogged up with grass, muttering, 'It'll be a decade before I get through this. I've never seen anything like it . . .' Plus, I'd also had to deal with the absurdly happy toilet. I'd given it a dose of Downer Potion, only now it had swung the other way and was deeply depressed; it kept flushing grumpily and getting blocked up all the time.

Okay, I thought. Before I use the love potion on Andie and Nick, I need to get to know more about them. When did their marriage start to go wrong, and why? I needed Andie to open up to me.

The trouble was, Andie had suddenly turned on me.

I just couldn't understand it.

One minute our friendship was starting to blossom, the next she was having a go at me every other second.

To be fair, she seemed to be in a bad mood with everyone. She nagged Nick about *everything* and had reduced Fred to tears by taking away his pocket money for two weeks merely for not finishing his dinner.

By lunchtime on Friday I was seething. The school was closed for a day, so both Fred and Andie were home. Not that I was pleased. *Cara, why don't you do the dishes? Cara, how dare you leave your shoes in the hallway, I nearly tripped on them coming down the stairs.* I mimicked her loud, ringing voice as I made a pizza for lunch. Fred was standing on a stool beside me and helping (although Fred's 'help' consisted of banging a wooden spoon on the worksurface or sticking his thumb in the mixture, licking it and then complaining it tasted 'like poo'). I rubbed together flour and butter into golden crumbs, glued it together with a slop of yoghurt and found myself shaping a clumsy, creamy voodoo doll. I picked up a fork and pronged strands of hair and features.

'A gingerbread man!' Fred peered into the bowl, delighted.

I quickly swirled the dough into a firm ball, stopping myself. It wasn't fair to curse Andie. Something was obviously up with her; I needed to find out what it was.

'ANDIE!' I called half an hour later. 'It's ready . . .'

She entered the kitchen, a frown etched on her forehead.

'I can't eat pizza,' she said. 'Far too fattening. Sorry. I'll just have salad.'

I looked her over. I could have sworn she'd lost about half a stone in the past few weeks and her face had none of its warm plumpness. There were hollows under her eyes and in her cheeks. Just what was the matter with her?

'So, your marking going well?' I asked, making one last attempt to be friendly.

'Not really.'

Silence.

Oh great, so we're all happy then, are we?

'I'm not hungry,' said Fred, eager to reclaim the attention. He pushed his pizza slice away, jumped down off his stool and slid up on to my lap, then proceeded to take food from my plate.

'Fred, you're not a beggar.' Andie gave him a Medusa look. 'Leave Cara alone. Let her finish her meal in peace, okay?' She took him off to watch a video.

But when she came back, things only felt more tense between us. I watched her picking at the edge of her salad, rolling it into a limp green ball and pushing it insipidly into her mouth. And then I noticed a tear slide down her cheek.

I didn't know what to do. I got up and threw the rest of the pizza into the bin. I walked awkwardly to her side, then rubbed her back. She jumped violently, hunching her shoulders. I kept asking her what the matter was, but she shook her head, blowing her nose on a napkin.

'Are you okay?' I asked.

She suddenly looked up, narrowing her swollen eyes into pink slits.

'Are you having an affair with my husband?'

My jaw dropped. 'I . . . I . . .' I was so amazed that I burst into laughter.

'Okay, fine, if you're not willing to own up, I'll ask Nick when he comes home tonight.'

'Andie, of course I'm not, I've only been with you for a month or so—'

'You're obviously a fast mover then,' Andie said acidly.

'Andie,' I said, suddenly remembering a few tit-bits I'd overheard from her telephone call to Suzanne a few days ago. 'Look, I know you probably don't like me and you feel I'm invading your space and trying to come between you and Nick but, honestly, I swear to God, I'm not. I'm just trying to do my job and, I mean, how could I have been with Nick? I hardly see him for more than half an hour a day, he's at work and I'm looking after Fred—'

'Maggie saw you,' Andie cried. 'She saw. I'm not an idiot. You get a lift with him when you do the shopping and then you and Nick go down to the park together and you sit on a bench and – look, d'you think I'm an idiot?' Her voice grew quieter, emotions condensed into a hiss. 'I tried calling him three times on Tuesday and he was 'in a meeting'. His meetings seem to last all day. I know you were with him yesterday. I *know* you were.'

For one terrible moment, I was torn. Did I betray Nick or betray myself? Should I tell Andie that I'd also seen him with a blonde girl? What was better – the raw truth or the cushion of lies?

'Tuesday ... Tuesday I was mostly with you,' I suddenly realised triumphantly. 'Remember? I came to collect Fred and then I stayed to help Suzanne with the finger-painting and we came home together. It was the day before that that I went shopping.'

'I – oh. But Maggie said it looked just like you. I – finger-painting. Wasn't that Wednesday?'

'No. Absolutely not.'

'Oh.' Andie rubbed her temples, unable to meet my eyes.

'Nick was probably just going for a walk with one of his colleagues,' I said gently. 'It was probably just his secretary. Is she blonde?'

'Yes ... she ... yes, she is. I'm sorry,' Andie said, looking dazed. 'I'm terribly sorry.' She was on the verge of tears again, her whole face jerking and contorting to hold them back. Then she turned and hurried out. I went after her, but she fled to the spare bedroom, slamming the door behind her.

'Andie?' I knocked gently on the door. I could hear muffled crying. 'Andie?'

I ought to have just turned the handle and gone in, but I didn't have the guts. And then a brainwave struck me. I hurried upstairs to my room.

The bottles were all there on my window ledge. In the gloom, they seemed to jostle together in their excitement, bouncing up and down lightly on their glass bottoms.

'I need something to lighten Andie up,' I said, gasping for breath. I could almost see their labels splitting into smiles, their voices chorusing, 'Me, me, me!'

Of course, bottles that have been reused are worldly-wise and have seen many things. They've been placed on restaurant tables, kitchen tables, evoked rows, sparked off love affairs. They all have stories to tell, but even so they still get terribly bored sitting on window ledges all day, looking out at the same old view. Sometimes it's nice to twist them a few inches or move them around to give them a little variety in their dull lives, but it's easy to forget . . .

'I'll certainly cheer her up,' cackled a little black jar.

'You're a joke sweet,' I said uncertainly, bending down and inspecting his label, decorated with cartoon bats and a garish little logo. My mum was always sending off for joke sweets from her witching magazines, then offloading them to me. '"A sweet that *looks* like liquorice – give it to your enemy and their mouth will fizz up with black froth and their teeth will go black". I'm sorry, but that's not going to lighten Andie up, it's going to give her a cardiac arrest.'

'That's all I've ever been, just a joke, a clown . . .' The bottle put on a teary voice. 'I always wanted to be a proper bottle with a noble aim; I wanted to sit in Boots and carry paracetamols. Ah yes, I wanted a serious profession but we were born poor, my family, we were made in a cheap factory, we were wrought by rough workers . . .'

In the background, some of the other bottles made sarcastic violin noises.

'I'm very relaxing,' drawled a sexy bottle who sounded as though she ought to be singing in nightclubs. I gazed over at her glossy red shape, her voluptuously curved neck. There were several wolf-whistles of appreciation around her and echoes of, 'I found you very relaxing indeed,' and a reply, 'In your dreams . . .'

Her label flushed pink with embarrassed pride as I inspected her. I couldn't remember what was inside, so I popped off the lid.

'Oh, you're bath salts.' I breathed in the heavenly jasmine scent. 'You smell divine, and I'm sure you're very relaxing, but I don't want to have a bath with Andie –' another saucy wolf-whistle and I pulled a stern face – 'I want to give her something nice to drink.'

'Drink,' a large, grandiose bottle at the back with a Southern Comfort label drawled, 'drink. God, there was a time when I held serious drink. There was a time when I rested in the best bars in Mississippi, where I watched men playing blackjack until the early hours of the morning. I was even in *Gone With the Wind*! I'm a Hollywood star—'

'Oh yes, we've *heard* this story just a few times before,' retorted the joke sweet, letting out a loud yawn.

'What's inside you now?' I picked up the Southern Comfort bottle.

'Oh, some old shit.'

'Language!' I said sharply, eyeing his label. Apricot wine. Special wine. Brewed two summers ago in the kitchen with my mother and grandmother. I remembered spending hours chopping apricots, endlessly slashing the knife through their fleshy orange skins, hitting their grisly stones, their juice running over my fingers until no matter how many times I washed them, they still smelled of fruit and liquor. All wine frees inhibitions. But this wine . . . I unscrewed the lid, eyeing the frothy orange mixture, hearing a faint humming noise, as though the liquid was singing seductively . . . This wine was aching to be sipped, to trickle down a throat and swirl in a stomach and unleash its powers, loosen tensions, free dammed-up emotions. A wine that makes people say what they feel, not what they ought to say. I wanted to see the real Andie. This wine was the solution.

'Oh, you're not going to take me away and execute me, are you?' wailed the Southern Comfort bottle. 'Those bottle banks – they're the worst kind of torture! All my family ended up shattered to pieces. I don't want to die a public death, I want to die quietly, thrown aside into a bin—'

'Darling, I promise not to throw you away, I'll use you again,' I assured him.

'That's even worse; next you'll fill me up with something pathetic like juice,' he sneered.

I turned away, letting my imagination calm down, the bottles settling down as reality asserted.

Downstairs, I knocked gently on the door and went into the spare bedroom. At the far end was a new bed, the tartan mattress still in its cellophane wrapping. Andie was sitting on the edge of it, crying noisily.

'Here,' I said, going over and pouring her a glass of apricot wine.

'I'm not about to drink at this time of day, give me some credit.' Andie looked up in irritation.

'It's not wine, it's a herbal remedy,' I said hastily. 'It's got ginger and cloves and all kinds of things in. It'll soothe you, make you feel better.'

'Well. Thanks,' she said dubiously. I noticed her surreptitiously taking a sniff before taking a sip. I saw an instant result, a faint smile tugging at her lips, the knots in her spine loosening. I took a big gulp too to encourage her. Ooh, it was lovely. Apricots sang sharply on my tongue; the liquid oozed in a bubbling froth down into my stomach. I poured us both another glass. Rather like the chocolates Edmund eats in *The Lion, the Witch and the Wardrobe*, the more of the wine you drink, the more your body craves.

We sat there for five minutes, sipping in silence. Andie kept sniffing and I saw her searching her sleeves for a tissue.

'Here.' I pulled one out of my pocket.

'Thanks.' She blew her nose loudly. 'Look – I'm sorry, really sorry about – what just happened. As you might have guessed,' she went on bitterly, 'things aren't exactly hunky-dory between me and Nick.'

'Oh?' While she was preoccupied, I filled our glasses again, ignoring the Southern Comfort bottle's quiet hiss that there was too much chilly air on his neck and he was getting a crick.

'It's just . . .' Andie spread out her tissue, lacerating it into little shreds with her nails. 'You'll understand this when you're older and you've got married, Cara. Sometimes marriage can feel like a job.'

Tell me something, I thought, *that my mum hasn't already told me a million times.*

'Hmmm.' I widened my eyes, looking naïve, like a child waiting to be enlightened.

'You need to work at it. And I think Nick and I haven't been putting enough hours in, that's all.' Andie let out a deep breath.

'So, d'you think Nick is having an affair?' I took another sip.

'No!' Andie burst out and I bit my lip; the wine was

making me a little too abrupt. 'It's just . . . you know, when you're married to someone who is good-looking, it's hard. Everywhere we go, whether it's a party or shopping or whatever, women look at him. I *feel* them. I *see* them. And I know what they're thinking; they all want to steal him, all of them! I saw it on your face when you started working here!' Andie suddenly recoiled, realising that she was saying things she would only normally think but never voice. 'I—' She flushed pink.

'Andie, I really just don't fancy Nick,' I said, then saw offence scrawled over her face, and added hurriedly: 'and I have a boyfriend. Well, nearly – I'm in love with Sean.'

'Are you?' Andie asked.

Am I? I looked down at the bottle of wine and swore I heard it chuckle mockingly. Clearly I was getting a taste of my own medicine, finding out things about myself as well as Andie.

'Well – he is attractive,' I said carefully. 'Though we're just friends. Anyway – I do understand what you mean about Nick. But it's like that proverb: if you love someone, let them go, and if they're yours they'll come back to you. I know it's a cliché but surely love isn't about being possessive or owning someone?'

Andie gave a sarcastic little snort and downed the rest of her wine.

'What about . . .?' I'd very nearly blurted out, 'How's your sex life?' but just caught the words before they tripped off my tongue, silently rebuking the wine for prompting such crudity. 'So . . . I mean . . . I suppose with Nick working late hours . . . d'you have much time to be alone together?'

'I really don't see that *that* is any of your business.' Andie kept snapping open and shut like an oyster, letting me in, then pushing me out.

'No, of course not, I'm sorry.'

Silence. Then she said, staring into space, in a trembling voice: 'We haven't made love in three months.'

'That's not such a long time—'

'We're both just so *knackered* all the time. I feel like I'm trying to juggle everything – work and Fred—'

'Maybe you shouldn't have gone back to teaching,' I said in alarm.

'Oh no, it's the best thing I ever did,' she said.

Because of Jonathan? I pushed the thought away. There was no way Andie could be having an affair if she was this paranoid about Nick.

'By the time I get home from work, I feel I don't have any energy left to be a wife, to give to Nick. The other night we actually arranged to make love – it was almost comic. We jokingly pencilled it into our diaries. And we both put on some nice underwear and got into bed and within minutes Nick was snoring – but to be honest I was relieved, because all I wanted to do was sleep too.' She let out a long sigh. 'I just feel so *pressured*. Oh dear. I'm supposed to be going out shopping,' she said, checking her watch. 'I'm supposed to be getting Nick a birthday present. And now I'm drunk.' She looked into the glass and suddenly let out an unexpected giggle. 'You shouldn't have given me this, Cara. Herbal remedy indeed.'

I opened my mouth to apologise but then I caught her eye and she smiled at me. Not one of her usual brisk smiles, but a soft, affectionate grin. I found myself warming to her. I liked seeing this other side to her – a more vulnerable, delicate side. It made her seem more human.

'Why don't we both go shopping?' I suggested impulsively. In the past, whenever I'd cheered my mother up after she'd been dumped by yet another lover, a good shopping spree had always been a tonic.

'What?'

'Shopping! Now! Come on, we can go and have a cake or something. Something to cheer you up!'

'But one of us needs to stay to look after Fred,' Andie said uncertainly.

'He can come with us,' I said, getting up before she could change her mind. As she hurried off to get her coat, I scooped up the Southern Comfort bottle and took it back to my room, giving it a little kiss of overwhelming gratitude. As I left, I heard it exhale a blushing little sigh of delight . . .

Our shopping trip was a whirlwind of pleasure and energy. Andie had to look for a present for Nick, as it was his birthday in two weeks' time. We rejected ties and socks as being too boring, mused over watches, gazed at glittering cases of Rolexes. I felt a rush of envy towards Andie; she seemed to have no idea how lucky her financial freedom was. At the same time, it was touching to see just how determined she was to get Nick the perfect present, and I saw a flash of how fiercely she loved him.

After an hour or so, Fred started to get tired so we rounded off the trip by going to Coffee Republic for cappuccinos, scrummy blueberry muffins and a large slab of chocolate cake for Fred.

'So, are you planning a celebration for Nick?' I asked, ripping open a sugar packet.

'Well – a little get-together maybe,' Andie said. 'I was thinking of a few friends . . .'

'Why don't you throw a really big bash?' I suggested. 'Turn it into a special occasion?'

'It would be a lot of work,' Andie said, though she sounded as though she might relish getting her teeth into something.

'Don't worry, I can help out,' I volunteered.

'But the house – I don't want a hundred guests trampling through it—'

'No problem! You could have it in the garden.'

'God, Cara, you're full of great ideas, aren't you?' Andie teased me. She took a pen out of her handbag and started scribbling a list on to a napkin: *Food, drink, guests, invites.*

'I know Sean would love to help,' I mused. *Well, if he ever finishes mowing the lawn.* Still, I *had* got him a pay rise, so he owed me one!

Andie looked up from her napkin, a funny smile spreading across her face.

'I'm sure he would love to help,' she said in a knowing voice. 'So what's going on between you two then? Is it *love?*' She echoed my earlier words.

I flushed, embarrassed. I was normally quite secretive about my emotions; I liked to play my cards close to my chest. Unfortunately, the apricot wine had left them sprayed all over the place.

'Of course not,' I laughed, pronging my fork into a lump of leftover cake and mashing it into a brown paste. 'We've only been out, er, once. I think we're probably just friends. Probably.'

'*But* . . .?' Andie asked, smiling. 'You're obviously attracted to him, and it's obvious he is to you. Oh come on, Cara, I can tell from the way he looks at you!'

'Really?' My cheeks were burning now.

'Yes, really!' she laughed, and patted Fred, who was starting to interject and moan about being bored. 'Yes, we'll leave in a minute, darling. Cara, it sounds to me as though you're at the see-saw point where it could go either way – friendship or . . .'

'Yeah, that's it,' I admitted.

'Well, Sean *is* a sweet guy,' said Andie, 'but—'

'What?' I asked nervously. Oh God. I knew there had to be a catch. Sean was so secretive about his past – was I about to find out he was a bank robber or something?

'Don't look so worried – he doesn't rob banks if that's what you're thinking. No, I just think you could do a lot better. I mean, all Sean does is mow a few lawns and smoke roll-ups. There's nothing but air and marijuana in his brain. He's not exactly a safe bet. Sorry,' she suddenly caught herself, 'I sound like your mother.'

I laughed with a sudden swirl of affection. *Believe me*, I said inwardly, *you most definitely do not sound like my mother. You are a million times nicer.*

'You can always have a sexy fling with him and see how it goes,' said Andie, clicking her pen. 'You're only twenty-five – you're young! Have fun, play the field! You don't want to turn out an old married woman at the age of twenty-nine like me,' she said jokingly, though there was a shade of bitterness beneath the fun. Then she shrugged, wiped Fred's sticky mouth and declared it was time to go home.

On the way back, we discussed the party excitedly, but Andie's words kept churning in my head . . . *we haven't made love in three months . . . there simply isn't time . . . you don't want to end up like me . . .*

I've got to do it, I thought. I have to use that love potion. It would flush away the grey tiredness and leave them zinging with love and energy; I could almost hear Andie now, coming down to breakfast, face flushed and whispering: 'Oh God, Cara – last night with Nick! It was just like the old days again, the spark has suddenly come back . . .'

Then I thought: *the party!* It would be the perfect time to use it. They'd both be in a good mood, both celebrating a decade of being together.

Perfect, I thought, absolutely perfect.

16
Cara

There was a sudden bang as something hit my window.

I jumped violently. It was Friday evening. I'd been sitting cross-legged on the floor, jotting down ideas in my Book of Shadows for a good time to use the love potion on Andie and Nick, though all I'd got down was a willowy sketch of a black cat. Hearing the bang, I got up nervously, wondering if a burglar was about to invade. Then I saw Sean in the bedroom window opposite, waving cheerily, and I realised he'd thrown a pebble. My heart skipped a beat and I opened my window.

He called across: 'Iwangherkiuhercomeoveryoucan?' Or something.

'*What?*' I called back.

The gap between our houses, divided by gravel and hedgerow, was just that bit too far apart.

Sean disappeared for a moment, then popped up and tossed a paper aeroplane over.

I had to lean across the ledge to reach for it and I very nearly fell out. When I stood back up again, catching my breath, Sean rolled his eyes and put his hand on his chest in a 'thank God you're still alive' gesture. I smiled and opened up the message.

> *Hi! As you may know, we're a member of the Neighbourhood Watch Scheme and as you seem a distinctly suspect character, I was wondering if you fancied meeting for another drink? I enjoyed our last soirée, but I think I ought to suss you out in greater depth before I can feel safe sleeping at night with a dubious girl like you next door . . .*
> *Sean*
> *xx*

Me, dubious? Huh!

Laughing, I picked up a pen – God, this was so childish, but so much fun – and scribbled a quick note back.

> *I need to go out on a major shopping spree tomorrow – we are organising a surprise birthday party for Nick. Would you like to help?*

I tossed it back; Sean caught it deftly, read it and then sent back a reply:

> *I could DEFINITELY help.* [He'd drawn a fat picture of a wine bottle.] *I'd love to be the official wine-taster* [there was another picture of him lying on the ground in a stupor, stars around his head]. *P.T.O.* [I turned over.] *But I'm looking after my darling daughter Maeve tomorrow. Is it okay if she comes too? We could pick you up at 10 a.m.?*

Of course! I was quite intrigued to meet Maeve. I nodded yes and he gave me a thumbs-up and we both waved smiley goodnights to each other. And then – *so sweet* – he blew me a kiss.

There is a tradition among witches for finding out the nature of a man's true feelings about you, and I can tell you, it's a lot better than that old maxim of twisting an apple core while saying, 'A . . . B . . . C . . .' for the name of your future husband. The trick is that if a man blows you a kiss, you catch it and feel the vibration of his heart echo in yours. But kisses are slippery things; I caught Sean's kiss in my palm, a pink lip-wisp, and felt just a shimmer of feeling before it trickled through my fingers and dissolved into the air like an ethereal butterfly.

Hmm. That shimmer felt good. Felt warm. Friendly. Sexy.

Andie was right. He liked me.

I lay back on my bed with a silly grin on my face. Then I gave myself a mental slap. This was exactly how I'd felt with my last boyfriend. The day before I'd walked into his flat and heard him saying what a freak I was. *Sean doesn't know you and you don't know him,* I told myself. *You're just in lust with him and you're turning him into a fantasy man. Yes, he seems charming now, but who knows what he's really like? What about his past? What about his marriage and his kid? He could hurt you all over again.*

But . . .

I sat up suddenly, an idea rippling across my mind.

It was a dangerous idea, but . . .

I recalled a spell my grandmother had used some time ago when she had been checking out a man my mother claimed was an IT designer with a 150k salary and trendy flat in Clerkenwell, who had turned out to be a drug dealer. My grandmother had had no idea that I was peeking through the door, watching her conjure up a flock of ethereal women . . .

No, I thought to myself, *don't. You're already playing with fire by performing magic on the Wilkins. Just get to know Sean the normal way.*

And I lay back on the bed, the smile returning irresistibly to my face. A whole day having fun with Sean! I could hardly wait.

Normally I had a lot of free time at the weekends so that Andie and Nick got to spend precious time with Fred. This Saturday, however, Andie was so busy organising Nick's surprise party that she was happy to let me have Fred. As I passed her in the kitchen, I noticed her notebook scribbled with lists, and though she looked tired and was drinking a fat mug of coffee, I sensed she was enjoying getting her teeth into it.

'Here's a list of things to get,' she whispered – for Nick was next door, watching the golf on TV – and passed me a folded piece of paper. Suddenly she winked at me and gave me a little nudge. 'Behave yourself with Sean. And when you get back, I want all the gossip!'

I took Fred over to Sean's. I spotted the battered red Fiesta outside his house, which meant that Laura was there. I probably ought to have backed off and waited until she had gone, but – being the bloody busybody that I am – I banged the knocker. My heart started to thump with anticipation. I kept picturing Laura as a young blonde with a vulnerable air, still madly in love with Sean.

The door was suddenly flung open. A girl of about Fred's age stood in front of me. She had curly hair and Sean's eyes, the colour of the sea.

'Hello,' she said calmly, looking me up and down as though she was interviewing me for a job. 'I'm Maeve. So are you Daddy's new girlfriend?'

'Er – no—' I broke off suddenly as I heard a tirade flowing from upstairs.

'Sean, I just don't know what the FUCK you're thinking of!' An angry female voice was rasping in a strong Irish accent. 'I mean, for fuck's sake, why can't you just get your fucking life together? Why can't you get a PROPER job? How the hell are we supposed to live off this? Your maintenance money is fifty – *fifty* quid short.' Sean said something back, and she flipped. 'No, no, Sean, don't give me that. You're thirty years old and you've got a daughter. When are you going to learn to take some fucking responsibility?'

Laura's voice was growing louder and she started to storm down the stairs. She was absolutely not what I had expected. She wore heavy make-up and her hair was completely shorn. She was wearing jeans and a baggy green cardigan and there was a diamond glittering in her nose. She looked scary.

Then she caught sight of me and broke off from her rant. She put her hands on her hips. 'Oh, I see.'

I opened my mouth to introduce myself, but I was too intimidated to speak. Fred, equally terrified, slipped his hand into mine. Ironically, for a moment I found myself squeezing it as though he was the grown-up.

Sean came down the stairs slowly. He looked completely different from the chirpy guy who had been boyishly tossing me paper aeroplanes last night. There were deep violet bags under his eyes and his skin was a yellowish pallor.

'I see you're taking Maeve out with your new girlfriend?' Laura asked. 'Well, it's not on, Sean. How d'you think Maeve will feel, watching you two drool all over each other? That's it. I'm not letting you have her.'

'Laura,' said Sean in a low voice – as though he'd suffered years of raising it and realised it was a wasted tactic. 'I get one day a fortnight with my daughter and you're not going to take that away from me.'

'Mummy—' Maeve began nervously.

'It's all right, darling, we're going. Sean can see us another day when he's not busy spreading his manly seed about.'

'No, I want to be with Daddy!' Maeve suddenly lost her grown-up composure.

'Look,' I said, 'I'm not his girlfriend, okay? I live next door and I just thought Fred and Maeve might have some fun together.' And Laura gave me such a hard look that, on a complete impulse, I foolishly added, 'As a matter of fact, I'm a lesbian.'

Oops. Sean looked flabbergasted. Laura blinked. Maeve and Fred looked at each other, then asked: 'What's a lesbian?'

'Well,' said Laura. I couldn't believe I'd silenced her. I'd been expecting her to accuse me of corrupting Maeve. 'Well. Fine. I'll go then. I do have a dentist's appointment I have to get to. But I'll be back at six to collect Maeve and you'd better fucking be on time, Sean, okay?' And she gave Maeve a theatrical kiss goodbye, then slammed the door after her.

Phew!

'Okay,' said Sean, 'let's get out of here.'

17
Cara

We all got into Sean's car, strapping the kids firmly into the back seats. Just as we were about to go, Nick suddenly came racing outside. I wound down my window and he pressed a fiver into my hand and whispered, 'While you're out, can you get me a packet of Silk Cut?'

'Nick, I saw you sign the smoking wallchart this morning!' I hissed back.

'I know, I know, but I've very very nearly given up. Don't tell Andie. *Please*,' he added with a sexy, cajoling smile when I gave him a reprimanding look.

'Okay,' I said, tutting.

Nick told Fred to be good, then waved us off. Maeve and Fred were soon chatting away and playing I-Spy together. But Sean was unbelievably moody. Every time I tried to pick up a thread of conversation he replied in monosyllables. I was a little hurt and rather intrigued. What on earth had gone so sour between him and Laura?

I was worried that Sean's bad mood might last the whole day, but to my relief he started to cheer up a little as we strolled along Richmond high street. It was hard not to: it was one of those gorgeous summer days, blue sky, lemon sun, ecstatic birds, happy people. We bought ten packets of balloons and streamers in The Party Shop, then went into a large toy shop for the children's sake. Maeve and Fred were instantly side-tracked by a display of fluffy yapping dogs, which left me a chance to chat to Sean.

'I hope I didn't cause any problems with Laura by dragging you out today,' I said.

'Nah, it's all right,' Sean shrugged, still a bit prickly.

I swallowed, fingering my list, and suddenly felt deflated. Last night I'd been floating around on a cloud of anticipation . . . and now this. *I told you not to be so airy-fairy, Cara*, a sharp voice that sounded like my mother's told me. *Sean is a moody bastard. Just the same as all the rest.*

'God, that assistant's nice, isn't she?' Sean suddenly nudged me, pointing to the girl showing Fred and Maeve the dogs. She had blonde hair in a plait and looked about seventeen.

'Lovely,' I muttered. I hoped Sean wasn't about to spend the rest of the day eyeing up women. He was obviously trying to make a clear point that this wasn't a date of any sort.

'For you, I meant,' Sean continued as I gaped at him. 'I thought you were a LESBIAN?' He said it so loudly that I saw the assistant look up. I flushed and quickly dragged Sean away. 'Well, Cara, you did say—'

'You're so evil,' I laughed, kicking him. 'I thought Laura was going to kill me when I said that.'

'Yeah, well, she's living with a woman called Sarah at the moment, so she can hardly have a go,' said Sean, fingering a jigsaw puzzle. 'She probably did fancy you,' he said with an edge to his voice.

'Oh. Oh right,' I said, taken aback. 'So was that why things fell apart for you?'

'Oh no,' said Sean. 'It wasn't one of those left-me-for-another-woman clichés at all. Though – fuck knows – that might have been nicer compared to what did happen. No, she was thoroughly heterosexual with me. The lesbian thing came later. Clearly I managed to turn her off the entire male sex.'

'Oh Sean!' I laughed, and put my hand on his arm. He shrugged, moody again.

'So what about you and the Wilkinses?' he said, pointedly changing the subject. 'Things going well with them now?'

'Andie's finally being nice to me!' I said. 'We're practically friends.'

'Cool,' said Sean. Then he shot me a sidelong glance. 'And Nick seems to be very *friendly* with you too.'

'Sean!' I hissed, blushing. 'No, it's not like that *at all*! We play chess sometimes in the evenings, that's it. He's been teaching me new positions.' I clamped my hand over my mouth, realising the innuendo too late.

'Ooh, chess?' said Sean. 'Chess. I *see*.' He let out a wild dirty laugh as I nudged him, pointing to Fred who was just a few feet away. He shut up.

'Dad, can you buy me a dog?' Maeve asked, grabbing Sean's hand as he went over to her.

'Maeve, we can't really . . .' Sean broke off, looking awkward. I felt terrible for him and wished I could offer to pay, but my bank account was still recuperating from another recent shopping spree. Then, seeing Maeve's face, Sean hastily took out his wallet and handed over a credit card to the assistant. I had a feeling that, like me, he had quite a few plastic friends with large balances sitting on them.

'I want one too!' Fred moaned, tugging my hand and pointing to the black dog. 'We can't leave him, he's friends with Maeve's one.'

'Fred, you can't,' I said. 'Look, you'll have to come back on Monday with your mum and we'll ask her.'

'Monday's no good; she'll be at school and Dad will be at work,' said Fred in a devastated voice.

'Daddy?' Maeve whispered, looking up at Sean.

'We'll have the black one too,' said Sean.

'Oh, Sean, really you don't have to—' I started.

'It's fine, it's fine,' he fobbed me off.

The assistant wrapped them up and put them into a carrier bag. I saw the look on Sean's face and realised at once why he had done it. He loved his daughter like mad, and seeing her once a fortnight just wasn't enough; he wanted to make it up to her in every possible way he could.

For lunch, we managed to grab a table outside a café and sat down to sip cappuccinos and munch on vegetable panninis crammed full of delicious chunks of spicy roasted peppers and aubergines.

As the waitress returned to clear our table, she shot Sean a surreptitious glance beneath her charcoal-lidded eyes, and Maeve said loudly, 'Dad, she's nice, isn't she?'

The waitress, who clearly thought I was Sean's wife, gave me an apologetic smile. Sean chuckled and tickled Maeve's neck.

'When she's not trying to get me and Laura back together, she's always trying to matchmake me,' Sean confided. 'It's a nightmare.'

'Does it ever work?' I asked.

'God, no,' said Sean viciously. 'I'm never going to get married again as long as I live.'

I was taken aback by his venom. Then I shrugged and said, 'Neither am I.'

'Er?' Sean gave me a puzzled look. 'Why not?'

Because no normal guy would ever want to marry a girl who makes potions out of frogs' legs, I thought. Instead, I blustered: 'Why should I? You don't want to get married; neither do I. So what's the difference?'

'The difference is, I'm a cynical old divorcee and you're a young girl in her prime,' Sean said in a rather brotherly way that made me blush.

'Yes but, you know, I don't think I'm likely to find the right person,' I said. 'I'm, um, not the easiest of people to live with.'

'Fair enough,' said Sean, still looking a little puzzled. Then he shrugged again. 'God, I can't blame you. You know, I'm not like most guys. I've only ever had three proper relationships – don't look so surprised, I might seem like a total lad, but I'm not really. Kate, Vanessa, Laura,' he ticked them off on his fingers. 'Disasters, the lot of them.'

'So now you just have flings?' I asked casually, then, seeing that Maeve was starting to listen in, I quickly changed the subject.

For the rest of the afternoon, we shopped, shopped, shopped. I felt as though I was becoming closer and closer to Sean, and yet I also found him more and more confusing. He kept flirting with me, and yet the vehemence of his words at lunchtime was still stinging. I kept wondering what on earth had gone so wrong between him and Laura.

He had just looped his arm through mine and taken Maeve's hand to cross the road when we saw an accident site. A woman had been hit by a car; ambulances were pulling up, blue lights flashing and sirens squealing. How strange, I thought, just fifteen minutes ago we were walking down this pavement and now fate has flipped its coin; a woman may die, a man may go to jail and the lives of those around them will be irrevocably transformed. I gazed around at the hordes of passers-by who were

181

intrigued by the accident, their ordinary, peaceful Saturday afternoon interrupted by a soap-opera moment of tragedy, and felt ashamed to be one of them.

'Let's go,' I said abruptly.

'I'm so sorry,' said Sean. 'God, I'm sorry. I know it must be hard for you.' He pulled me tightly against him and I walked along in a confused silence. 'Does it remind you?' he said. 'Every time something like this happens, does it put you back there?'

'Where?' I asked, laughing. 'Sean, what the hell are you going on about?'

'Your father,' said Sean, looking rather shocked.

My father. Ah. Of course. I'd told him that lie back in the Goat. Something about my father being killed by a falling . . . what? And now Sean was looking at me as though I was a cold-hearted bitch who couldn't even remember the death of her parent.

'I – I just try to blot it out,' I said, forcing a brave smile, and Sean gave my hand a squeeze. I saw Fred and Maeve nudging and pointing. Sean didn't notice them; he seemed pensive.

'It's terrible, isn't it?' he said, unexpectedly morose, 'how we all die alone, ultimately. I used to think I was looking for love, but then I realised I just want someone who understands me. Now I realise it's impossible to have that either; we just love ideals in our minds. You can be married to someone, breathe the same air as them, sleep with them and then they turn around and show that they never even knew who you were when they were saying those vows . . .' He trailed off, catching himself. 'Sorry, I'm not cheering you up, am I? Let's have another break!'

I smiled, but Sean's words had tunnelled into me. Suddenly I suffered a profound sense of loneliness. I thought of Andie and Nick; of his blonde in the park; of

their secrets and lies. And they'd been married f[or]
decade. *People are such complex creatures,* I thought, *with*
many layers of idiosyncrasy and contradiction, that perhaps [it]
was possible to go through life without really knowing anyone.
And yet, when I looked at Sean, I felt a deep, affectionate
thirst to know him. I wanted to know about his childhood.
When he had lost his virginity; when he had come to judge
his parents. What he had dreamed of becoming, and how
his life had turned out. Why he had married Laura.
Whether he believed in God or life after death. What he
thought about when he woke up in the dead of night or
first thing in the morning; and, most of all, what he really
thought of me.

I bought everything on Andie's list and we had just
arrived back at Sean's when I let out a strangled sigh. Oh
God; I had forgotten to get Nick a present. Bugger, bugger,
bugger.

'I'll have to pop out again tomorrow,' I sighed.

'Nah, don't do that,' said Sean. 'Look, it'll only take me
half an hour if you tell me what to get him. You keep Fred
and Maeve under control, okay?'

'Sure,' I said, forcing a smile. 'Sure.'

And I knew. I knew with a deep sense of foreboding
that I was going to perform the Exs Spell.

It was easy enough leaving Maeve and Fred downstairs.
They were both utterly engrossed in arguing over what to
call their dogs. I left them to it.

Upstairs, I gingerly opened the door to Sean's room. It
was an absolute tip. His blue futon was covered with
crumpled sheets and clothes; the floor was carpeted with
old copies of the *Guardian*, strewn sheets of musical script,
CD cases for Blur and David Gray all muddled up with the
wrong CDs. But amid all the chaos were some charming

nes. Quirky little Sean-type things. A strip of masking
ʋe running down the length of his wall, on which he'd
ʋcribbled all his favourite quotes. A mud ball which he'd
made himself and was sandpapering to perfection, one half
still rough and caked, the other as smooth and black as
ivory. I felt a funny flood of affection, picturing Sean sitting
up here in the evening, a cigarette drooping out of his
mouth, a Blur CD playing in the background, polishing
away at his ball like a little boy with a toy.

Pull yourself together, Cara, I told myself sharply. *Get on
with the task in hand.*

And yet. Guilt was churning in my stomach. This was
a major invasion of his privacy and, after all, Sean and I
were only friends so far.

No, do it, I told myself. *Okay, so you're not going out with
him. But if something IS going to happen with Sean, you need
to find out what he's really like.* I had to protect myself
before I risked getting hurt again.

All I needed was something intimate to Sean to hold.
My eyes fell on a small black diary sitting on his bedside
table. No, too personal. A pair of stripy boxer shorts? No,
too smelly. Then I noticed his St Christopher looped
across his pillow. Aha.

I held the chain in one hand and unfolded a piece of
paper with the other. For a moment I paused, my heart
beating, and cast a nervous glance at the door, paranoid
that Sean was suddenly going to barge in and say: 'Caught
you!' Did I dare do this?

Though intuition told me to stop, I found myself going
ahead. I recited the spell and then said, '*I summon Sean's
first ex, Kate, to appear before me.*'

I was aware of a figure materialising, but I didn't dare
look up. If I stopped, I would never find the courage to
finish the spell; I bowed my head and carried on.

'*I summon Sean's second ex, Vanessa, and his ex-wife Laura . . .*'

Then a deep Irish voice said: 'Just what the hell are we doing here?'

And a fine, cut-glass English accent said: 'I feel terribly dizzy. Have I been kidnapped?'

And a ringing, Irish, all-too-familiar accent said: 'God, this room is such a tip. Couldn't he even bloody clear it up?'

I slowly raised my eyes.

They stood before me like a trio of sirens. Kate: a plump girl with dark hair in a ponytail wearing jeans and a red T-shirt. Vanessa: a slender girl with blonde hair in a sleek chignon who was wearing a smart black trouser-suit and a trendy orange shirt and wafting an expensive lavender scent. And Laura, just as I'd seen her this morning. They all had an ethereal quality, lacking in clear edges and leaving hazes of colour and blurs of limbs.

They all looked me up and down in bewilderment.

'Hi,' I said. 'Um – I'm Cara. I just called you here for a quick chat.'

'Well, I'm busy!' Laura screeched. 'Sarah and I were having a bath together!'

A-ha, so that's what she was really doing. Dentist's appointment indeed.

'Relax,' I said. 'Your real selves are carrying on just as normal in the real world. You're astral projections, splinters of your soul that I've called here because I want to ask you a few questions. I'm a witch, you see, but you needn't worry – the spell I've cast only lasts a few minutes.'

'Great,' said Vanessa crisply, crossing her arms. 'So my normal self is in the middle of a piano recital in Dublin while my astral body is faffing about several hundred miles away in London. If I don't win this competition, my *astral* ody will be coming back to haunt you, you can count on that.'

'I just want to find out about Sean,' I said hastily.

'Oh yeah? And why's that?' Laura put her hands on her hips. 'You his next flavour of the month?'

'No – I—' I chewed my lip; I'd thought these astral projections would be under my control; I hadn't anticipated having to deal with bolshiness. My eyes flitted to the clock; precious time was running out. 'Okay, I admit it. I've met Sean recently and, yes, I'm attracted to him, but I don't want to go any further until I find out more about him. And the most obvious way is to ask you lot – his exs.'

I gave them all a let's-be-girls-together smile. They all stared back dubiously.

'Come on – it'll be fun. A good old girly gossip. You can dish the dirt, you can say anything . . .' I broke off, realising I sounded like a tabloid journalist trying to get a scoop. Maybe this is seedy, I reflected, maybe it is a bad idea.

But Kate, it seemed, had decided she wanted to open up.

'I first met Sean when I was sixteen. He went to St Phillip's Catholic School for boys and I was across the road at St Agnes and I used to see him every day after school. God, all the girls fancied him. He had long blond hair – just about the only guy I've ever met who was good-looking enough to carry off a ponytail. I could hardly believe it when he picked me out at our school dance. We went out for a while; I thought he was the love of my life. Funny – a few years later I ended up marrying Richard and having two kids.'

'So why did it all end?' I asked.

'Sean isn't the type of guy you can marry,' said Kate impatiently, as though I was a bit dim for not realising. 'He'll never settle down and he hates work. He's just not interested in taking responsibility for his life.'

I was silent for a moment, feeling a little worried. Did I really want Sean if he was just going to use me for a fling? But, hey, he'd only been sixteen then; he might have changed. And it wasn't as though I wanted to marry him or anything.

'Believe me, Kate, you have *nothing* to regret,' said Laura savagely.

'Okay, Vanessa, you go next,' I said, purposely winding Laura up – I could tell she was dying to dish the dirt.

'Well,' said Vanessa. 'I met Sean in somewhat unusual circumstances. He was my cleaner. He was about nineteen then and at first I thought he was terribly uncouth. And not a very good cleaner. I think he thought he was too good for the job.'

Bloody snob, I thought.

'But I'd just moved to Ireland with my husband and I'd left all my friends and family back in London. I was very lonely . . .'

Husband! So Sean was an adulterous lech too. I felt sick. Sean and Nick. They were all the same, just like my mother said.

'My husband is gay,' Vanessa faltered, blushing, 'and so I was very lonely. I was giving piano lessons and my husband was playing the saxophone in clubs so he was out most nights. I must say, Sean did cheer me up. He has a way with women . . .'

So I'm finding out, I thought grimly. Suddenly I felt self-conscious and cynical. Was Sean just working his magic over me the way he did with all women? Was I naïve to really think he was picking me out as someone special?

'And he was terribly good in bed,' Vanessa admitted, going even pinker. 'He loved jazz, and after we made love he'd make me laugh by playing my husband's spare sax. Sean loved it but, God, he was terrible. The screeching!

187

he neighbours all heard and one of them mentioned it to my husband . . . he put two and two together and I had to break it off. Yes, my husband wasn't good to me, but I couldn't take the guilt. Poor Sean. He didn't want to let me go. He came to my flat every day for two weeks, crying. He is really very vulnerable beneath his laddish exterior and, like all cynics, deep down he is a romantic, an idealist. He is very sweet.'

I nodded, too touched to speak.

'I missed him. I miss him still. He's one of those people you can just open up to really easily and be yourself – so rare. And then, a while after we'd split, I met him in a bar in Dublin and he told me he was getting married. I was so pleased for him.'

Laura rolled her eyes. We all stared at her, waiting for her confession.

'Well,' Laura said. She picked up Sean's comb and ran her fingers over the serrated edge as though it was a knife. I felt a sudden possessive flare, an urge to rip it away from her. 'As far as I am concerned, Sean is just an evil, selfish, manipulative, lying *bastard*.'

Something snapped inside me. 'As a matter of fact, I'm not interested in your opinion,' I said. My eyes flitted to the clock; Sean would be back soon. 'And though you've been married to Sean, I don't think you really know him. I mean, he's such a lovely, lovely guy and you . . . you . . .'

'Oh yeah? So lovely he managed to get himself arrested only *three days after Maeve was born*?'

'What?' cried Kate.

'*What?*' I cried.

'Oh yes, I did hear about that,' Vanessa sighed.

'Yeah,' said Laura, 'it happened when he—'

'Wait,' I said, standing up. What was that I'd just heard? *Sean's key turning in the lock*. He was home. My heart

almost stopped with fear. And then I heard him sa
'Laura, you're half an hour early! God, this is the one da
I get with Maeve and you can't even let me have that!'

'Yeah, well,' I heard Laura stepping from the driveway
into the house, 'I'm going to the theatre and I've got to get
Maeve to the babysitter, haven't I?'

I stared at Laura. My head spun. One Laura was bad
enough, but *two* . . . This was a total disaster. Then I heard
Sean go into the living room to get Maeve. 'Dad,' Maeve's
voice floated up to me. 'I haven't got my coat . . . I don't
know where it is.'

'Well, darling, where did you leave it? In the car? Oh –
I know – we left it in my room. I'll just run up and get it.'

No! No! I turned frantically to the girls, who all stared
back at me, looking equally nervous.

'You have to hide!' I cried. 'Um – in the wardrobe!'

I swung it open, revealing a chaos of clothes. Sean was
obviously allergic to washing things or folding them up. To
my relief, however, Kate and Vanessa stepped inside –
though Vanessa pinched her nose disdainfully between two
fingers.

'Laura?' I begged her. 'Please.'

'Jesus Christ, you must be kidding,' she said.

Bloody Laura. I knew in despair that there was no point
in even trying to argue with her; the more I cajoled, the
more she'd wind me up by refusing.

I was going to have to brave it out. I swung open the
door to Sean's bedroom, quickly slammed it shut before
Laura could slip out, and stood in front of it.

'Um – hi,' I said.

'You've been in my room?' Sean said edgily. Then he
shrugged and joked. 'Well, I hope you didn't find too
many skeletons in my closet.'

No, just a couple of astral bodies.

'Can I go into my bedroom then?' Sean asked, looking at me oddly.

'Sean, can you get a bloody move on?' Laura called.

For a moment, I thought she was calling from downstairs. Then, in shock, I realised that she was standing in the hallway. *Right next to us!* She must have slid straight through the wall.

Sean did a confused double-take. The spell was starting to wear off and Laura was looking decidedly transparent. In my panic I didn't think, I just grabbed hold of her and yanked her into the bathroom, crying, 'I think we need a girlie chat!' and slamming the door in Sean's amazed face.

'Listen, Laura,' I whispered, 'if you don't stay here I will do a spell to ensure you never return to your body again, okay?'

Despite her sulky expression, she was scared; she sat on the edge of the bath, examining her nails crossly.

I left Laura in the bathroom and rushed back out into the hallway. Sean was in his bedroom: *he was opening the wardrobe door* . . . I ran in, skidded to a halt, closed my eyes in disbelief. Waited for him to say: 'What the fuck is this?' But then I heard him pulling Maeve's coat off a hanger. I opened my eyes. The wardrobe was empty; the spell had worn off. Relief drenched over me like an icy bucket of water; my legs started to wobble and I collapsed on to the futon, feeling deliriously light-headed and making a firm promise to myself that I would never use magic around Sean again. With the Wilkins, yes, but Sean was too special to risk losing.

'You okay, Cara?' Sean gave me a strange look.

'Fine, fine,' I smiled weakly.

Downstairs, you can imagine how shocked Sean was to see Laura back in the living room.

'Finished in the bathroom?' he asked.

'What are you talking about?' she snarled. 'And I'm glad that though you apparently have no money to keep up the maintenance payments, you managed to get Maeve a fluffy dog. Maybe we can eat it next week when we run out of food!'

After Maeve and Laura had gone, Sean stared at the glass diamond panes of his front door for a few minutes, swearing, 'Bitch, bitch, *bitch*!' Then he went back into the living room, burrowed into his jacket pocket and tore out a packet of tobacco. As he rolled a cigarette, spilling lumps of brown tobacco everywhere, I saw his hands were shaking.

'I don't like to feel I'm polluting Maeve,' he explained, breathing in deep, desperate lungfuls, 'so I never smoke in front of her.'

I was so touched that I reached over and gave him a hug. He looked surprised and hugged me back, grinning and murmuring, 'Cara, my sweetie.' *Sod Laura*, I thought suddenly, *whatever's happened in Sean's past, whatever bad times he's been through, I don't care. I'll find out about it all soon enough.*

Back at the Wilkins, Fred and I slipped in through the back door. I quickly said, '*Sssh!*' to Fred and climbed on to a stool, hiding our purchases at the back of the top cupboard.

I grabbed Fred's hand and was about to lead him into the living room when I heard laughter mixed with soft music.

Through the slightly ajar door I saw them together. They'd kicked off their shoes and were dancing slowly on the rug; then Nick whispered something in Andie's ear and she giggled and they kissed, achingly softly, like a pair of teenagers.

I was touched. In a flash I suddenly saw why they had married each other. They looked so good together. The chemistry blasting off them could have set off fireworks.

'Right, Fred, we're going for a walk,' I whispered, yanking him out, ignoring his squeal of protest by clamping my hand over his mouth.

Outside, we wandered by the river playing Poo Sticks. *Thank God for that,* I thought in happy relief. *Andie and Nick have finally made up.* Which meant I wouldn't have to use the love potion at the party after all.

I couldn't help suffering just a sneaky feeling of disappointment. I'd been *so* looking forward to using it . . . Then I reprimanded myself: it was good that everything had worked out of its own accord; it was much better that way.

Wasn't it?

18
Andie

Okay, thought Andie, *everything is ready. I think I've covered everything. I think.*

She slowly uncorked a bottle of sparkling wine and poured herself a glass, enjoying the burning chain of bubbles in her stomach. This was the first bit of peace she'd had all day, the first moment where she could actually pause to *think*, and she became aware of just how exhausted she was. She'd been up since 5 a.m. Her eyes burned red and her body felt heavy, as though it would have liked nothing better than to collapse into bed and sleep for three weeks. But she felt wildly happy as she gazed out into the garden.

It looked gorgeous.

The lilac trees had cables draped over their heavy blossoms that would light up in rainbow lines. Yellow and pink crêpe Chinese lanterns hung from bushes. Trestle tables were set up by the patio; the white paper tablecloths, weighed down with bottles, flapped like bats' wings in the breeze. Sean was helping to set up the DJ equipment; Kieran, declaring he was 'exhausted' from carrying a couple of wine glasses out, was lying on a sun-lounger, sipping a glass of wine to 'test it wasn't corked'.

In one hour's time it would all begin. Nick was currently out with Cara, taking Fred kite-flying in Richmond Park. But at 7 p.m. precisely Cara would bring him back here and then . . . Andie hugged herself. She could hardly wait to see the look on Nick's face.

Ever since Cara had given her that herbal wine and they'd shared a chat, Andie had been feeling much better. She felt as though a knot in her had untied and she could finally be open and honest. The next morning at breakfast she'd casually said to Nick: 'Oh, by the way, Maggie said she saw you with a blonde in the park the other day,' and Nick had shrugged and said, 'So? I was with Carole.' His secretary. It was so ironic. She'd spent ages mentally torturing herself over an imaginary affair and the whole mess had been cleared up in two minutes. *Why do I do this to myself?* Andie wondered. *Why do I create my little whirlpools of worry which all turn out to be about nothing?* Compared to most people my life is paradise, Andie realised. I have a lovely husband. A lovely son. A nice house. A job I enjoy. Friends and family.

From now things are going to change. I'm going to enjoy life, day by day. And I'm going to repair things with Nick.

She'd had to deal with Jonathan, of course. It had been harder than she'd thought. She'd nabbed him one morning in the staff room and they'd gone for a brisk walk over the playing fields.

'It's all fine with Nick,' she'd explained. 'He's not having an affair, nothing's going on . . . so . . . it's all great. I'm sorry I got all silly and teary and rubbishy.'

'Hmm,' Jonathan had said. He'd stuffed his hands in his pockets.

'I mean, things are just so good . . .' she'd trailed off, thinking: *Don't bloody 'hmm' me again or I'll kill you.*

'Are you sure things are all right?' Jonathan had said, staring down at the ground. 'You can't solve everything just because you find out one of you *isn't* being unfaithful.'

Suddenly he'd turned to stare at her, the wind tossing his dark hair into his eyes. He'd looked so handsome that she'd felt a sudden longing for him, a doubt.

Then Andie had felt cross. She was finally piecing her world back together. What right did Jonathan have to try to tear it all apart?

'I'm sorry,' Jonathan had said hurriedly; he was very sensitive to people's feelings and picked up on them quickly. 'It's none of my business. I'm happy for you. And I'd love to come to the party, I'll bring Suzanne if that's okay.'

Bring Suzanne? As in a date? Andie had felt girded. Was he trying to make her jealous?

But then he'd squeezed his arm around her in a little hug and said softly, 'And you don't need to worry about me. I am happy for you, really I am. I think Nick's a very lucky man.'

'Mr Yates. Mrs Wilkins. Do you not have classes to teach?' Cloones had suddenly called across the pitch and they'd scarpered off to lessons like a pair of naughty children who'd just been caught smoking behind the bike sheds.

And despite Jonathan's cynicism, things *had* got better.

It had been amazing, actually, how easy it was to repair things. It had made Andie realise that just lots of little changes here and there could result in something miraculous. Nick had started coming home from work an hour early, and instead of slapping a plate of unfrozen muck down in front of him, she'd made more of an effort to cook him something decent (well, something heated up

195

rom M&S to be precise, but Andie had no illusions about her cooking and figured that giving her husband food-poisoning was hardly going to aid their marriage). He kept buying her little presents: a bottle of her favourite Yves Saint Laurent perfume, a new book. They'd spent a few evenings out to dinner and had made an effort to climb into bed early instead of watching TV so they had enough energy to make love. Really, it was just a question of attitude. A question of *giving*. They'd both been taking too much recently, expecting so much from one other, clawing for time and sympathy and attention.

And she promised herself never to let this happen again, to let their relationship slide into the gutter and rot due to a lack of communication, of worry, of projection and speculation and silliness. Relationships, she reminded herself, were tricky things. In theory, they ought to grow and evolve naturally, of their own accord. But like a plant, they needed tending, needed sunlight and water, spade-work and effort.

Hearing the doorbell ring, Andie smiled. It looked as though the first guest was here.

By 7 p.m., the garden was full of people. She'd pretty much invited everyone Nick knew, except for his work folk; she'd recalled that, a few weeks back, Nick had said, 'I definitely don't want to do anything with *anyone* from work on my birthday. I just want to get away from all that and have some peace.' And Andie had respected this, inviting only his friends, neighbours and close relatives. Hearing a car pull up outside, Andie flapped her hand at Sean.

'Okay, quiet everyone!' Sean ordered.

The crowd fell silent. People grabbed streamers to toss. They listened to the click of shoes on the gravel. Low voices; intimate voices.

Andie could hear Nick flirting with Cara, then giggling together. Jealousy jack-knifed her, bursting her bubble of newfound happiness. Suddenly all her irrational paranoias were back. What if Cara and Nick really were having an affair? What if Nick grabbed Cara in the kitchen and kissed her and everyone saw? Crazy, she told herself, Cara knows about the party.

The key twisted in the front door. They came down the hallway. The back door swung open. Their footsteps clicked on the patio steps and then – *BHAM!*

The party exploded in a chaos of colour and noise as streamers flew and people cheered and balloons bobbed and champagne corks popped.

The noise dimmed and Andie went to Nick's side. Her heart was bursting with love and pride. She waited for him to hug her and tell her she was the best wife in the world and it was the best party she'd ever organised. She waited for him to laugh and clap. She waited for him to at least *smile* or something.

But he couldn't even manage that. Nick swallowed hard and visibly grimaced at everyone.

'Andie, you shouldn't have,' he said flatly. 'I mean, this must have cost a bomb. And I told you I didn't want a party.'

The guests were starting to shift uncomfortably. Andie thought: *I can't believe his ingratitude. He's going to embarrass me in front of everyone and throw one of his moods and tell them all to go home.* She felt tears trammelling up her throat and quickly grabbed hold of his hand, but her palm was coated in sweat and his fingers slipped out of her grip like butter.

'Did you invite anyone from work?' he demanded.

'No,' said Andie, trying to still the angry panic flickering in her voice. 'You said you didn't want anybody, so . . .'

'Good. Well.' Nick finally managed a smile. Then he started to clap and there was a palpable sense of relief. 'Thanks everyone – I mean, sorry, I was just a bit shocked . . . it's great.' He leaned over and kissed her gently.

Great. Great. So glad you appreciated all my efforts.

Soon Nick was sucked away into a swirl of people plying him with presents and cards. Andie watched rather sourly. Then she turned and saw a couple coming through the side gate. Suzanne. And *Jonathan*. They spotted her and came bounding up, hand in hand, looking flustered.

Andie felt flustered herself. She couldn't believe how gorgeous Jonathan was. He was wearing a pair of black trousers and a pastel-striped shirt; he was clean-shaven and his newly washed hair shone. He looked like he belonged in one of those adverts for some stylish Italian clothing firm, driving a flash car with a beautiful raven-haired girl in the passenger seat.

'I'm *so* sorry we're late,' Jonathan said breathlessly. 'We missed the surprise bit, didn't we?'

'What's your excuse?' Andie demanded in her best school marm voice.

'Sorry,' said Jonathan, ducking his head and doing a splendid imitation of a child, 'the cat ate my homework and my mum couldn't give me note because she was caught by an alien.'

They all burst into laughter and Jonathan gently patted her shoulder. Suddenly Andie felt better. There was something amazingly soothing about Jonathan's presence. He was so sensitive that she felt he could penetrate through the layers of social show and see at once exactly how she was really feeling. He made her feel understood.

Jonathan went off to get drinks and Suzanne gave Andie another hug.

'So, what's up with you and Jonathan?' Andie asked, trying to keep her voice light.

'Oh God!' Suzanne beamed. 'Well, you know I've fancied him for ages and ages and ages and ages. But he is a bit hot and cold . . . well, not so much hot and cold . . . just elusive, I suppose . . .'

'Hmm,' said Andie. She realised Suzanne didn't know about Rebecca. Somehow she felt pleased that Jonathan had confided in her and not Suzanne.

'But over the last week he's suddenly got warmer, if you know what I mean!' Suzanne enthused. 'And he was so keen to take me tonight so fingers crossed!' She held up two sets of crossed, scarlet-polished fingers, cackling. Then she turned and caught sight of a man wearing what looked like a gladiator's costume, his white shins covered with a forest of brown hair. Andie did a double-take . . . had Sean or Kieran hired a stripper for a joke? But no, no stripper would have a costume made out of tin foil, bits of painted cornflake boxes, all held together with duct tape, would they?

'Poor old Norman,' said Suzanne, with a barely repressed giggle of glee, 'I told him it was fancy dress! He's going to kill me . . .' And she ran off to greet him with a bear-hug. 'Hi, Norman! God, you look *gorgeous*! Oh don't get in a sulk, you'll have women after you all night.'

Andie smiled, but it faded rather rapidly. *Jonathan was keen to take me out tonight so fingers crossed!* There it was again. That feeling in her stomach. Like a corkscrew was twisting through her gut.

This is so stupid, she thought, shaking her head. *I can't be jealous. I'm married, for God's sake!* She looked back at Nick, flirting with a group of younger girls. Suddenly she felt as though she was looking at him for the first time; not as his wife but as a stranger who barely knew him. He was pouring wine into his guests' glasses, and he looked a little . . . *seedy*. Then she looked back at Jonathan, bounding about in the garden: young, preppy, sweet and intelligent. He caught her stare and smiled at her for a moment: a secret, intimate smile that replaced the corkscrewing in her stomach with butterflies.

Then she turned, aware of someone watching her, and saw Cara staring at her with a funny look on her face. Andie frowned; Cara grinned quickly and asked if she ought to bring out more sausage rolls.

19
Cara

GRANDMA'S LOVE BREW
Ingredients:
Ylang ylang, jasmine, sandalwood powder,
dried gardenia petals, rose water, star anise and
Grandma's own special magic touch!
Instructions:
Put *three drops* into the drink of each individual.
Potion must be drunk quickly or the
effects may be delayed.

I read the label three times over and let out a sigh, slipping the bottle back into my pocket. I was locked in the bathroom, toying with myself over whether I dared use the love potion.

As I went back down to the garden, I fretted on how nothing was going according to plan.

The party was going fabulously well, sure. The garden was a busy swirl of laughter and champagne and bonding. I was certainly enjoying myself; Sean had brought Maeve over and she and Fred were having a great time hiding beneath the curtain of white cloth hanging over the tables, flinging sausage rolls at unsuspecting people's ankles and giggling hysterically. Sean and I had also chatted over sausage rolls, only in a slightly more civilised manner.

But what the hell had happened to Andie and Nick? They were supposed to be holding hands, gazing into each other's eyes. Yes, they were being very jolly. But not together. Nick was chatting to his niece, Jem, a seventeen-year-old with a nose stud, and her circle of adolescent friends, and worse, Andie was chatting to Jonathan, close to the drinks table. And I didn't need to use my body language skills to read the chemistry between them: the way she was angled towards him, tipping her face up to his, twisting a curl of hair around her finger, laughing at his jokes as if they were the funniest things on earth.

I went over to the drinks table, my mind whirring. A woman came up to get a glass of pink champagne. She was wearing huge scarlet spectacles, too much lipstick and looked very familiar. I realised she was Suzanne Hampton, another teacher from Andie's school. A-ha, I thought. Andie must confide in her, surely? Perhaps I might be able to extract a bit of information from her.

'Hi, Suzanne, great party, isn't it?' I grinned at her.

'Hiya.' She was very friendly; she flashed me a huge grin that showed off a pair of slightly buck teeth.

'How's it going?' I said, trying to steamroll over my shyness.

'Oh, okay. There just aren't enough decent men here,' she said, disarming me with her gossipy directness.

'Mr Yates is sexy though, isn't he?' I said slyly, nodding towards him.

'Ooh, so you've noticed Jonathan too!' she cried, elbowing me violently and nearly taking out three of my ribs. 'Can't say I blame you. Nearly every female here's

202

trying it on with him and he's supposed to be with *me, me, ME!* Huh. Men, hey?'

We chatted for a few more minutes as I waited for something to distract her. In my pocket, my fingers fumbled to unscrew the lid on the love potion bottle. Then the perfect opportunity arose. Mozart and Beethoven came dashing by, chasing each other. Jonathan, distracted and amused by them, broke off from chatting to Andie and for a moment he and Suzanne bonded in stroking and petting the dogs.

Now!

I turned and quickly flicked a few drops of the love potion into one glass. Oops, I'd used much too much! The bottle was nearly empty but I managed to shake the last few drops out into the glass beside it. The potion hung in the champagne for a few seconds like a little pink snake, then it diffused and dissolved into the bubbles. I picked one up and gave it to Jonathan, who smiled and said, 'Thanks.' I was just about to give the other one to Suzanne when Nick came strolling up and—

—*picked up the glass!*

Ah. Oh. Argh!

'Cheers!' He raised it at me with a wink, took a glug and then went back to entertaining Jem's crew.

Suzanne and Andie, meanwhile, picked up ordinary glasses and started to sip and gossip.

So . . . so . . . Nick had a love drink, and Jonathan had a love drink . . . and so . . .

This is a complete disaster, Cara, a voice which sounded just like my mother's rasped in my mind. *You have done it yet again. You've made a terrible mess of things.*

No, I argued back fiercely. *There must be a solution. I mean, if I can just prise Andie away from Jonathan and get her with Nick, then Nick will still leap on her. And if I can just gently push Suzanne and Jonathan together, then Jonathan will leap on her.*

'Andie,' I said breathlessly, 'can you come into the kitchen? I think I've burned a whole load of sausage rolls!'

'The oven isn't even on,' Andie said in a cross, mystified voice as she hurried after me into the kitchen to find the rolls sitting neatly on a tray.

'Oh, sorry – I just got muddled up,' I said. Seeing her irritated expression, I feigned a yawn and said, 'My head's all over the place after all this mad organising for the party.'

'Yes, of course,' she said quickly, looking guilty. 'God, I'm just the same.'

When we went back into the garden, I saw Andie do a double-take. It had worked. Jonathan and Suzanne were looking extremely playful together. Jonathan had drooped his arm around her back and was giving her a tickle; Suzanne, shrieking with laughter, was fending him off half-heartedly.

I saw Andie blink and swallow hard. Her jealousy was so palpable that for a moment I felt terribly sorry for her. But then I thought: *It's for her own good, right?* It was better that I severed her link with Jonathan before anything started to happen.

'Erm, isn't it time for the birthday speeches?' I nudged Andie gently.

'Right, right.' She forced a smile. 'Yes.'

She chinked a glass and slowly everyone fell silent. I flicked a glance at Jonathan. He wasn't watching Andie; he was watching Suzanne watch Andie. Good.

'First of all,' Andie said, 'I'd really like to thank everyone for coming tonight. And I'd like to say a very happy birthday to Nick. So cheers.' She raised her glass and everyone echoed her.

Is that it? I fretted. I mean, I knew Andie wasn't Martin Luther King when it came to speech-making, but she could have said something *nice* about Nick . . .

Everyone burst into a rousing chorus of 'Happy Birthday' and Nick looked flushed with pleasure. Then, as I watched him walk over and squeeze Andie's hand, I felt relieved. *It's going to be okay,* I thought.

Everyone went back to mingling, but it appeared the speeches weren't over yet. Kieran had wandered to the front of the throng and everyone murmured in surprise as he called for quiet.

'Since it's Nick's birthday, I was asked to provide a little entertainment this evening for all of you. So I'm just going to give you a little ditty on my mouth organ.'

Behind me, I heard Nick say to Andie under his breath, 'Who agreed to this?' and Andie whispered back with a giggle, 'Not me, I swear!'

'I'd like to raise my glass to Nick,' Kieran continued, 'and echo the words of Dylan Thomas: "There I could marvel; My birthday; Away but the weather turned around".'

'What the hell's that supposed to mean?' Nick pulled a face and then nodded at Kieran, feigning a smile.

And then Kieran started to play.

A few minutes later, everyone was trying very hard to pretend they were deaf. Kieran's playing was awful, and halfway through he seemed to forget the tune (which sounded something like a cross between 'The Grand Old Duke of York' and 'Happy Birthday') and paused, frowning.

Feeling deeply embarrassed for him, I quickly cut in and started to clap.

To our collective relief, Kieran bowed grandly, tucking his trusty organ away and prowled off – no doubt looking for some more young ladies to try to pull.

And then – to my complete shock – *Sean* went up to the front. Carrying a large black case.

'Jesus – another one,' Nick swore with disbelief. 'What is this – *Stars in Your Eyes*?'

Sean saw several people drifting off into the house to escape. 'Don't go,' he cried hastily and then joked, 'I'm about to play the spoons!'

There were ripples of laughter.

'Not really. I've, um, got a sax. I mean, I'm not very good but I thought I'd like to have a go playing "Happy Birthday".'

I froze in horror. What had Sean's ex, Vanessa, said about his saxophone playing? That his screeches had been so appalling the neighbours had complained.

I squirmed with embarrassment for him. Kieran was too thick-skinned to care if people laughed at him. But Sean was sensitive. *Please don't do this, Sean,* I prayed.

Sean picked up his sax, took a deep, shaky breath and played a few false notes. I peered up at the sky, watching some clouds pass across the deepening twilight. Perhaps I ought to do a quick weather spell and shower rain down on us . . .

. . . when suddenly it happened. He started to play properly.

And it was beautiful.

I watched him, my mouth open. He closed his eyes and visibly melted into the music, so that his saxophone seemed not an instrument but a curvaceous woman, dancing and swaying before him in beautifully choreographed notes. It certainly wasn't a normal, chirpy rendition of the song – it was long and slow and sad and achy – but it made the hair on the back of my neck stand up.

Pride filled my heart. Clearly Sean had come a long

206

way since his days with Vanessa. I saw the look of surprise on Andie's face too and I remembered the verdict she'd given on Sean way back in the coffee shop. *I always knew he was more than that*, I thought triumphantly, *I always sensed he was talented*.

As he broke off there was a long silence. Then the guests burst into clapping and cheers.

I went up to him slowly. Sean gazed at me with worried eyes. The music seemed to have stripped away his bravado and left his emotions unmasked. For the first time since I'd known him, I saw beyond his casual laddishness, through to the shyness and insecurity underneath.

'Oh Sean, you were so fantastic!' I cried.

'I was? But nobody really clapped . . .'

'They did!' I said. 'Really, it was so great. You never told me you were so brilliant. Do you have some secret life: gardener by day, star saxophonist by night?'

'Ah, no.' Sean quickly packed up his case. 'I never normally play in public. I'm glad you're impressed . . . I kind of hoped you'd like it . . .'

The DJ took over once more and put on a slow song. As the achy, breathy lyrics floated across the garden, couples oozed into each others' arms and started to dance.

'Come on, let's dance!' said Sean, swallowing.

Suddenly I felt shy. 'Well, I really should be putting Fred to bed . . .' I said. But then I saw that Fred and Maeve were dancing together in a little Irish jig. They looked so sweet.

Sean blushed and ruffled his hair boyishly as though he was no older than Fred himself, playfully tugging me on to the grass. We stood opposite each other, swaying. Every so often our eyes met and we grinned. I twisted my head and surreptitiously checked out Andie. She was dancing with Nick. And Jonathan was dancing with Suzanne. I felt the knot of tension loosen in my heart. It looked as though my plan had worked.

I jumped as I suddenly felt a pair of arms circle my waist and draw me in closer.

'That's better,' Sean whispered, and added unnecessarily, 'I mean, this isn't the Victorian Age, is it? We're friends. We can dance.'

'Oh sure, mmm,' I laughed awkwardly. I became aware of the tension in my body and, determined to show I wasn't a prude, I leaned against Sean, resting my cheek against the cotton of his T-shirt. I could hear the delicious thump-thump of his heart. His skin smelled like vanilla. His hands were at the base of my back, just at the gap between the waistband of my T-shirt and skirt, and then, oh so gently, I felt the tips of his fingers start to circle the bare slit of my skin.

I felt as though an icicle was being dripped down my spine.

I found my eyes slowly travelling up to meet his. Over his neck: hazel skin, Adam's apple. Over his stubbled chin: God, he had a little cleft that was so sweet! Over his lips: they were full and pink and just so kissable—

'CARA! HELP! SHE'S GOING TO GET ME!' Fred suddenly went bumping into my thigh and I was vaguely conscious of something falling down by my feet. Then Fred flew off towards the greenhouse. Maeve chased after him with a handful of ice-cubes.

In a split second, the spell was broken. Sean and I moved apart.

'Maeve, behave!' Sean called after her. Then he looked down. 'You dropped something.'

I looked down. Sure enough, there was something glinting in the grass. My potion bottle! Sean bent down to pick it up and I yelled, 'NO!'

Sean recoiled and I quickly kneeled down, scooped the bottle up and put it back in my pocket. 'I think I'd better just go to the loo ... to ... er ... put this away ...' I said, ignoring the bewildered expression on his face.

'The loo to do what?' he asked slowly.

Oh shit. *He knows,* I thought. *He caught sight of the label.*

Or maybe I was just acting in a suspicious manner. I needed to calm down, keep my cool.

'I just dropped my deodorant,' I explained.

'Right.' Sean stared at me as though I was completely mad. I realised how lame my excuse was. Who carries *deodorant* in their pocket to a party? Hardly the sort of thing you throw in with your lighter and lipstick, is it?

I decided to head for the loo before the hole I was digging for myself threatened to hit the Earth's core.

As I hurried back to the house, I saw Suzanne pull Jonathan in for a kiss, sucking his lips as though she was a Dyson.

'Let's go,' I overheard her say. 'Come back to my place!'

Andie, rigid in Nick's arms, was watching them, her mouth so thin it had nearly disappeared. *Sod it,* I thought. Andie would have to come to terms with it; the whole night had suddenly got way too messy and confusing and I could feel a headache pounding at my temples.

Upstairs in the bathroom, I gazed at my flushed reflection in the mirror. I'd been wondering and hoping and praying that Sean was attracted to me. And now, finally, finally it seemed that he was. The way he'd pulled me close against his chest. The way he'd looked at me. I'd been so close to kissing him, so close ... and then I'd gone and blown the perfect moment ...

And he'd been so close to finding out that I was a witch. I pulled the love potion out of my pocket and tore off the

209

label, tearing it into scraps and throwing it down the toilet. *Bloody, bloody potion,* I thought. *If I hadn't got back into magic then none of this would have happened. I'd be in Sean's arms right now* . . . I tossed the bottle into the bin with an angry chink. Once again I was back to square one: hating myself for being a witch.

By the time I came back downstairs – feeling just as confused as when I'd gone up – I found the party was winding down. People were pulling on coats and a tired-looking Andie and Nick were kissing and hugging their guests goodbye. I spotted Sean. He was carrying Maeve, who had fallen asleep on one of the beds upstairs. There was something so sweet about seeing Sean being all fatherly.

'I hope you had a nice time,' I said to him.

Sean looked up abruptly. ''Night.' His tone was cold. 'Hope you had fun in the bathroom.' I laughed but there wasn't a hint of a smile on his face. He clearly thought that running off and deserting him in the middle of our dance had been completely rude; or worse, that I was a total tease.

I desperately tried to think of an excuse to save the last shreds of our relationship. Perhaps I should explain to him that I had a terrible BO problem and the situation had been desperate . . . but that was hardly going to enhance my attractiveness . . .

But by the time I opened my mouth, Sean had already turned away.

At the same time, I saw Andie pulling away from Nick and saying, 'I'm going to sleep in the spare room, okay? I'm totally knackered. Goodnight.' She turned away, then added lamely, 'Happy Birthday.'

20
Cara

Clang! I tossed the three-hundredth beer can into the black sack and rubbed my aching back, blowing an exhausted breath.

I glanced around the garden. The moonlight shone unicorn light over the chaos: cigarette stubs and crumpled napkins and dented cans and smeared paper plates. At the rate I was going, I'd be here until dawn.

But I didn't feel like going to bed. I knew that it would be a waste of time; I'd only lie there thinking about Sean and dissecting every little painful detail of our conversation.

I carried on picking up the rubbish. Fleecy clouds veiled the moon and a shadow passed over the garden. The black sack wilted in my fingers. *I should just go and tell Sean the truth,* I thought. *I should explain everything.*

'Cara, what the hell are you doing?' a voice called out across the lawn, making me jump. I turned to see Nick standing in the doorway of the kitchen. His hair was tousled, his eyes sleepy and bloodshot. 'God, I can't believe you're clearing up. You are an absolute saint; at this rate we're going to have to burn you at the stake and make a stained-glass window out of you! For God's sake, come and sit on the steps with me and have a beer.'

Nick passed me a beer can, ignoring my protests that I didn't drink, downing back half his can himself.

I smiled, feeling slightly uncomfortable. Why hadn't the love potion worked on him as it had on Jonathan? Why wasn't he upstairs with Andie, behaving like a caveman and tearing off all her clothes? Still, these things were subjective; a spell might work well on one person and draw a blank with another.

'So did you have a good time, birthday boy?' I broke the silence.

To my surprise, he blew out a deep sigh.

'Yes. And no. I just feel as though it's been a bit of an anti-climax. But I don't know what I was expecting – a miracle or something. It's just another day in the year really.' He curled his fist and rested his chin on it, looking pensive.

I was surprised. Nick was normally so flirty and jokey, I'd found it difficult to see what he was really like beneath the surface. Even with his family he had a habit of avoiding confrontation, or indeed any situation that involved emotional depth; if Fred had a problem, he'd tell him to be brave and just get on with it, and if Fred really complained, he'd tell him to discuss it with his mother. Nick seemed the eternal optimist, treating life as if it was one big party. And now, all of a sudden, he was prepared to be serious. Suddenly Sean was forgotten; I sat up straight, sensing that he was holding a confession inside of him like a ball of wool that he was waiting for me to unravel.

'So, what big miracle would you like to happen, if it could? If you could wish for anything, what would it be?' I asked playfully.

'I guess . . . I don't want anything to change. All I want is security – just to pay off the mortgage and that Andie enjoys her job and Fred calms down and does well at school. I'm scared. I've got it all and I don't want to lose it. I was watching the news last night and there was this guy – my age – he'd been killed in a train crash. He was only thirty-two. Married. It could have been me.'

'Well, that's the same for everything in life,' I said, a little taken aback by his morbidity. 'You never know what life will throw at you so you may as well just enjoy what you've got while it lasts.'

'I know,' said Nick, tearing up a blade of grass. 'I know. I – even went to church the other day.'

'You did?' I blinked, wondering if this was all building up to Nick telling me he'd had a spiritual epiphany and was about to go away and spend the rest of his life as a monk, living on nothing but prayer and chickpeas.

'I always used to laugh at religion. I considered it to be the opium of the people. But I went along and I felt a real sense of peace.'

'That's lovely,' I said.

'Are you religious?'

'Erm, kind of, in my own way.' Which wasn't a complete lie: I did regard Wicca as a religion.

'Maybe you could come with me to church next week,' he said eagerly.

'Uh, maybe,' I said.

'Anyway, you seemed to be having fun with Sean.' Nick suddenly flipped back to his usual jaunty self.

'Hmm,' I said, refusing to give away any further details. 'Mmm. Hmmm.'

'Mmmm hmmm, that's interesting,' Nick teased me. 'Well, he gave me a shit present. A ratty old black comb.

He'd even left the price tag on. He'd bought it in the pound shop and it had been reduced to fifty pence.'

'Well, that's because you pay him so little,' I reprimanded him, giving him a little poke. I refused to collude with Nick against Sean. 'What else did you get?'

'Well – Andie got me a tie and some socks, blah, blah, blah, but she says she's also got me a big present that's coming next week. Fred gave me a box of nicotine patches and, er, a chewed green monster which I found in a cereal packet last week. In fact, the only person I haven't had a present from—'

'Oh, Nick!' I realised, clamping my hand over my mouth. Shit. 'I'm so, so sorry. I've got it upstairs.' I'd been so busy dashing about all over the place, I'd clean forgotten his present. 'Wait here!' I ordered.

By the time I came racing back down, Nick had downed his beer and started on another. I noticed a tiny white ring at the back of his dark head: the seed of a bald patch. Suddenly I was overwhelmed with affection for him and I thought: *I wish I'd had him as a father.* Crouching down, I crept up behind him and clamped one hand over his eyes, thrusting the present into his lap.

'I haven't had time to wrap it either,' I apologised, 'so you have to guess what it is.'

'Er . . . it's quite hard. It feels like a book?'

'No,' I giggled over his shoulder.

'It feels like some kind of big cigar case.'

'No.'

'A block of wood?'

'Nope.' I removed my hand and he gazed down. I'd been too broke to buy him something really expensive, but Sean had remembered seeing a beautifully carved box when we were shopping together. 'It's from India,' I said.

'I thought you could keep your chess pieces in it.' I paused, worried. 'D'you like it?'

'Like it!' Nick cried. 'I'm completely bowled over. It's fantastic. Just what I need. Oh come here and give me a kiss, you lovely girl.'

It looked as if the love potion was finally working.

I leaned over gingerly and suddenly his arms were around me, tight. Our lips touched; I tasted alcohol on his breath, flowing sharply on to my tongue. I tried to pull away but he held on, lost in desire, his breathing fast and excited. I curled up my hand; I wanted to slap him yet, even in my panic, I couldn't quite bring myself to do it; it seemed too harsh. Instead, I did something even more crazy: I picked up the beer next to him and splashed it all over his head.

He recoiled backwards like a little boy who'd just been slapped, brown foam sliding down his face. I got up, my skirt wet with beer.

'You're drunk,' I said in a shaky voice, 'go to bed.'

Then I turned and hurried quickly up the stairs, running into my bedroom and pushing the door shut.

The next day I felt too scared to come out of my room and face Nick. I consulted the Tarot twice. The first time I got the Ruined Tower so I shuffled again but the result was even worse: The Hanged Man. So, it was going to be a great day.

To bolster my courage and confidence, I decided to wear a new dress. I pulled it on but then worried it was too low-cut and showed off just a bit too much leg. I pictured Nick looking me up and down and shuddered. I'd have to change.

Is this how it's going to be from now on? I thought wretchedly, smashing through the coathangers in my

215

wardrobe, *constantly terrified he's going to leap on me?* Finally I settled on a black T-shirt and black floor-length skirt, though it was ridiculously hot for summer. I covered my face in make-up, circling my eyes with kohl, practising freezing-Nick glances in the mirror. Oh God, did I look like a goth? Never mind, Fred was wailing . . .

Downstairs, Fred was wearing only the top half of his pyjamas and was clutching a decapitated Barbie doll.

'Can I have a kiss good morning?' he asked sweetly. I gave him one and we both laughed.

'Time for your bath!'

Apart from taking a worrying delight in playing at drowning Barbie, Fred was good for once. He didn't even complain when I washed his hair. *What a shame, I'm really making progress with him,* I thought with a pang as I rubbed his hair dry. Then I thought: *Calm down, you won't have to leave. Nick was just drunk and love-potioned-up. It was his birthday, he and Andie have been having problems, things are tough for him, he just wanted female company and took it too far. He'll have forgotten all about it.*

But Nick clearly hadn't forgotten about it.

By the time I took Fred downstairs again it was 10 a.m. Nick looked very hungover and grey-faced. Andie must still have been in bed.

'Hi,' I said with a cautious smile.

Nick grimaced but said nothing. Fred pottered outside to play in the debris of the party.

'Nick,' I began, 'about last night—'

'Forget it.' He waved his hand.

'But . . . I just thought it might be better to talk about it.' I felt anger curdling inside me. For crying out loud, I could bloody do him for sexual harassment, I thought – he could at least apologise. 'I just think—'

'Look!' Nick slammed down his mug, making me

216

jump. 'I've had enough, right? You can pack your bags and go.'

'What?' For one blurry moment I thought he meant go shopping.

'You heard me!' Nick stood up, his eyes blazing like coals, and perversely I felt an unexpected flicker, a *frisson* I hadn't felt last night. 'Pack your bags. Get out. You're fired.'

My jaw dropped.

And so I packed my bags.

'Cara . . .' Nick appeared in the doorway just as I was walking down the drive. He looked tired and confused. 'I didn't mean . . . Christ . . .' He rubbed his bleary eyes. 'I don't know what I meant . . .'

He looked as if he wasn't sure whether he wanted to apologise or tell me to fuck off.

I left.

I could only think of one place to go.

Please be in, please be in, I prayed silently. The front door had a silver knocker on it in the shape of a nude nymph; I knocked it so hard I was terrified I was going to break her. To my relief, Sean finally appeared, looking very bleary-eyed and very grumpy and not at all pleased to see me.

'Nick's just sacked me,' I blurted out. I was still so shocked I could hardly believe it myself. 'He bloody well tried it on with me last night and then, when I wouldn't shag him, he sacked me! Sacked me!'

Sean blinked. For one scared moment I thought he wasn't going to forgive me for last night, was just going to send me packing. Then, to my relief, he drew me into a tight hug, whispering, 'The absolute *bastard*!'

He sat me down in the living room and made me tell him every detail. 'God, he is such a git,' he said finally. 'This doesn't surprise me at all, actually. You can tell he's the type from the way he leches over women.'

In the past, I had always felt that Sean was perhaps a tiny bit jealous of Nick's natural magnetism and ability to attract women. Now I was utterly on Sean's side.

Sean got up to make me a cup of hot, sweet tea. I felt tears oozing into my eyes and blinked them back fiercely. I hated crying in front of other people. But by the time Sean came back, I was in floods.

Sean was wonderful. He just sat there and patted my shoulder, and told me silly anecdotes about how he hated the Wilkins because they'd always been such snobbish neighbours. He told me a story about when he and his grandfather had first moved in. The Wilkins had invited them next door for a welcoming drink and they'd all made stiff, self-conscious chit-chat. Andie had had a bowl of pot pourri on the coffee table and his grandfather had slowly eaten his way through it while the conversation dwindled to silence and they all watched him with cool astonishment as he complained that the 'nuts' tasted a bit weird . . .

'Sean, don't!' I cried. Now I was laughing instead of crying.

'Seriously,' said Sean, 'now you've cheered up – where on earth are you going to stay?'

'I don't know,' I said. 'I can't go back to my mum's. She's got a lodger in my room now.'

'Then you'll have to stay here,' said Sean. 'No, really, it's fine. We've got masses of room; we'll just have to clean out some of my grandfather's junk.'

I felt so overwhelmed by his kindness that my laughter turned into tears once more. Sean smiled and patted me on the back, and said: 'Don't worry – I promise that staying with us won't be that bad. Okay, so my grandfather farts all the time and he sings Abba songs in the bath – don't say I didn't warn you – and I smoke too much and the place is a tip – but other than that, it'll be okay, I promise.'

Sean showed me to the spare room and left me on my own to sort myself out, but I only started to feel much worse. Slowly the implications of what had happened started to crawl across my consciousness.

I'd been fired. Soon another nanny would be staying there, and I'd be forgotten. I'd be stuck at my mother's, my future in tatters. Even with magical assistance, it would be hard to get another job so soon; I would have a black mark on my CV, suggesting I was either fickle or trouble.

Oh God, it was so unfair. Okay, so I'd given Nick a love potion. But so what? Jonathan had also had the potion and he hadn't grabbed every girl in sight. It was up to Nick to control his desires and send them in the right direction.

Maybe I should ring Andie and tell her the whole story. But then what? Divorce? And what about Fred? I couldn't do that to him.

My anger for Nick kept boiling up to the surface, steam-rolling over my conscience and reason. My mother was right. All men were the same. No matter how charming they were on the outside, they were rotten inside, bastards to the core.

Don't Cara, no, I told myself, but I found myself flinging open my suitcase, my fingers spidering through my folded clothes until I found some black candles. I lit one in a saucer and melted the other slightly, until the wax was soft and pliable.

And then I started to mould it. I smoothed it into a banana-shaped oblong, circling rings around the top for a foreskin and grooves down the side. I carved NICK into the wax penis and caressed it playfully, teasingly . . . then I suddenly thrust it into the candle until it slowly melted into runny wax, dripping into pools like ink blots. *There Nick,* I thought, *next time you'll think twice before you ever try it on with a girl again.* Slowly, the melted wax hardened, leaving a shape like a black plastic bat.

My anger, melted into the spell, had gone, leaving me feeling tired and hollow.

I bit my lip.

I had broken Wiccan law.

Modern witches never practice black magic. There is actually a law in Wicca called the Threefold Law: if you cause harm or curse another being, it will return to you Threefold.

Well, so what? I tried to convince myself. Maybe I'll lose my libido. Or maybe men will shun me. I don't care. I don't want a man anyway.

21
Cara

My first night in Sean's house was terrible. Sean was so lovely and did everything he could to make my stay comfortable; but sleeping in a foreign bed always felt strange. My sleep was restless and clouded with nightmares. I dreamed that Nick was a green demon with pointy eyes who chased me through the house demanding a kiss so that he could suck my soul out of my body. I finally dropped off, only to be woken by giggling, footsteps, the sound of Abba throbbing above me and the unmistakable noise of a couple having extremely vigorous sex. Great. It looked as if Kieran was enjoying himself.

I woke up again around 6 a.m. The world was silent. I lay watching pale gold bars of sunlight creep across the window. And then I remembered with a jolt: *The spell on Nick with the black candle . . . for his . . .*

Oh Cara, what have you done? I thought.

Now that my anger had died down, I was starting to suffer severe guilt pangs. Nick had been out of order, but it was a very mean thing to do. What if I'd made a mistake? What if his penis had *shrunk*? I burst into a

221

nervous explosion of giggles, then berated myself. It wasn't funny; I had to undo it before the damage began. I got up and flicked through my Book of Shadows, drinking in the spell. Right. Now all I needed was a white candle, a bottle of fertility potion, a bathroom and a bar of soap.

Sean's bathroom was dreadfully messy. I picked up a hard yellow scrap which had presumably once been a healthy bar of soap. I rubbed it over the white candle, dripped fertility oil on to it and started to murmur a reversal chant when there was a sudden sharp bang at the door.

'Er, yes?' I called back.

'Cara, it's me! What are you doing in there?'

What did he think I was doing? It was a *bathroom*. Unless . . . unless he'd heard me?

There was another sharp bang on the door. It was like being back at the bloody Wilkinses.

'I'm *coming*,' I said. I quickly hid the candle behind the toilet. As I unlocked the door and brushed past him, I slipped the fertility bottle back into my pocket.

Then I did a double-take. Sean was looking absolutely thunderous.

'I'm sorry,' I repeated. 'I was just washing my hands.' I laughed awkwardly. 'The soap you have is, ah, lovely—'

'Lovely soap?' Sean echoed sarcastically and folded his arms in a very knowing manner, like a nightclub bouncer about to turn away a gaggle of underage kids. 'Well, I'm so glad you enjoyed yourself in there.'

He glared at me as though he'd like nothing better than to beat me to a pulp. Suddenly I felt scared. My grandmother was right. This was a side to Sean I hadn't seen before. Maybe he had an obsession with soap; maybe a fern handwash would send him over the edge.

Fear pin-pricked me. 'Well . . . I'm really, really sorry.' I edged towards the stairs, keen to flee. There was a pay-phone a few roads away; I could go there and call my grandmother and beg her to come and pick me up. 'I'm just popping down to the newsagents; d'you want a paper or anything? No? Okay, fine, I'll just be off—'

'You're not going anywhere,' Sean said, suddenly grabbing hold of my wrist. I yelped, terrified. What had happened to my lovely boy-next-door? He was now possessed by the spirit of a psycho.

'Sean, stop it!' I hissed, trying to stay calm. 'You're scaring me.'

'Well, you're scaring me! Just what kind of a druggie are you?'

'*What?*' I barely had time to register before he had reached into my pocket and pulled out the little bottle. He dropped my wrist and it hung limply by my side as I watched him in complete confusion. He unscrewed the bottle and peeped inside. He sniffed it heavily. He frowned. Then looked up, utterly mystified.

'What is this?' he asked.

'It's a herbal remedy from The Body Shop,' I improvised. 'To help me wake up in the mornings.'

'Oh.'

'Yes, oh,' I said, snatching it back before he could read the label. 'God, Sean, what the hell was all that about? Drugs? I've never taken them in my life!'

Sean suddenly burst into embarrassed laughter. He blushed a violent plum shade and buried his face in his hands. I started to chuckle too, realising some sort of bizarre cross-purposes had just taken place. Then Sean pulled me into a tight, apologetic hug. I tensed, still jittery; then he whispered, 'I'm so sorry, honey, I'm so sorry,' and I relaxed into him, hugging him back.

'I'm so sorry,' he repeated. 'God, Cara, you look terrified of me. Look, I just over-reacted . . . it's just that . . . Laura was into all that . . . Oh, fuck it, come down to breakfast and I'll explain.'

Down in the kitchen, I started to feel better as Sean made some fat mugs of tea and a heap of thickly buttered toast. He slathered his with peanut butter, wrinkling his nose in disgust as I opted for Marmite.

'So,' Sean said quizzically, 'you're not a drug dealer?'

'Sean, do I look like a drug dealer?' I laughed. 'Where on earth did you get that half-backed idea from?'

'Because you have a strange habit of disappearing into bathrooms at odd moments, that's why!' he retorted, as though the whole mess was entirely my fault. 'Like last night at Nick's birthday party. One minute we were dancing and the next you were running off to the bathroom and mysterious things were dropping out of your pocket.'

'God – so that's why you were so moody with me when you left,' I realised, though I was slightly disappointed; I'd hoped it had been motivated by something stronger.

'And then this morning – I just thought – look, I know this sounds rude, Cara, but sometimes you seem . . . I don't know . . . a bit far away. And at other times you do seem all kind of secretive . . . as though you're hiding something . . . so . . .' he trailed off, holding out his palms in an apologetic gesture. 'On one hand I had you as being slightly bonkers. On the other hand I had you disappearing into toilets. I put two and two together and made you a druggie. And I hate druggies. Especially druggie women – one of my friends back in Ireland married one and the hell she gave him . . . Anyway, does that sound so bad now?'

I laughed, shaking my head. 'It's not that at all. Firstly,

I'm not bloody bonkers. And secondly, I like going to the toilet because . . .' *Why, Cara, why? What excuse can you make up?* 'Because I'm really . . . really . . .' *Maybe I should just say it. It would be so easy for the word to pop out.* 'A . . . w—'

'Supergirl?' said Sean. 'That's it, isn't it? You go to the toilet to change into your sexy uniform?'

'That's me!' I laughed shakily. 'No – seriously, I'm a bit of a compulsive handwasher.'

'Oh,' said Sean, pulling a boyish face. 'For a moment there you really had me; I thought you really were Supergirl. So tell Uncle Sean why you're a compulsive handwasher? Sounds very weird to me.'

'Oh – I just have this thing about dirt,' I laughed. 'Everyone has their own little neuroses, don't they?'

'Are you a Catholic?' Sean asked.

'Er, no, why?'

'Well, it all sounds very puritanical to me,' said Sean, looking at me closely. 'You *are* a secretive madam, that's what you are! But,' he added, suddenly leaning over and digging his fingers into my rib-cage for a tickle, 'I'm going to find out what your little secret is, you see if I don't!' and he laughed as I screamed for mercy.

'Don't you think you should tell Andie about this kiss with Nick?' Sean asked. We were sitting on the sofa, eating a takeaway pizza piled high with lashings of cheese, tomato and little squidgy triangles of pineapple, the TV murmuring in the background.

'What about your sax career?' I asked, changing the subject. 'Sean, I just couldn't *believe* how good you were at the party. Why aren't you playing professionally?'

Or are you being held back by this mysterious occasion when you managed to get yourself arrested?

'Ah, you know me, I'm not ambitious,' he laughed. 'Anyway, don't change the subject: don't you think you should tell Andie?'

'Er, no.'

'But aside from your job, I thought you were the best of friends now? Doesn't she deserve to know?'

'It's not quite as black and white as that,' I said uneasily. How could I explain that I'd got caught in the sticky threads of a magical web? 'Sometimes these things just happen and look, it was only a kiss—' I broke off as I descended into purple prose.

'A kiss is a kiss,' said Sean stubbornly. 'God, if I kissed a girl I wouldn't leave her in any doubt of it.'

'Oh *really*?' I smiled, unable to resist flicking a glance at his lips. 'So how would you kiss her then?' I was trying to flirt with casual cool, but you could have struck a match on my cheeks.

Sean put down his plate; I did the same. Suddenly the air rippled with tension.

'When I kiss a woman, I always kiss her lightly at first,' he said. I widened my eyes, tendrils of desire whispering all over my body. 'Just a few little butterfly kisses. And them something a bit stronger, a bit harder. I'll run my hands through her hair – I love women's hair, the silky texture, the curls and the kinks and the lovely curve of the head. And then I'll open her mouth with mine and feel—' He broke off, suddenly self-conscious. 'Sorry, I'm sounding a bit like a porno movie, aren't I?' he laughed.

No, please carry on! I wailed inside.

Sean picked up his plate. Oh, so we're going back to eating again. Fine. Cool. I reached over to pick mine up too but just as I reached out he put his back with a clatter and I turned, hovering, my hand stretched out in mid-air.

He shuffled up a few inches on the sofa and gave me a

funny little smile. I was so embarrassed I smiled back: a huge, inane grin.

He reached out as though to put his arm around me, but at the last minute he seemed to lose his nerve and drummed his fingers on the coffee table instead. I gulped – was he going to bloody well kiss me or not?

He was. He leaned in. He smelled delicious. I knitted my fingers in my lap and felt my breath fluttering in my throat like a baby bird.

Brrrrrrring! The doorbell rang.

Sean jumped up quickly, ran his hands through his curls, stuffed his hands in his pockets, did a funny little jig, looked at me and muttered, 'Won't be a sec,' and then hurried out.

I sat on the sofa, dazed, cursing the God of Doorbells.

'Well, as a matter of fact,' I heard Sean saying in the hall, 'she is here.'

Was that Andie? There was *no way* I was going back to work next door, they'd have to *beg* me . . .

'Oh good, she hasn't been in touch with me for ages. I was wondering where she was.'

I recognised that voice. Oh God. No way. It couldn't *be*—

My mother came waltzing into the room. She was wearing a long black dress with a ra-ra skirt and a grotty patchwork shawl. She looked like a wannabe flamenco dancer who'd been hauled backwards through a wool factory.

'*Cara!*' she cried, sweeping on to the sofa and scooping me against her bosom like Madonna with child. 'And how nice it is to meet your lovely friend Sean! Who I've heard so much about.'

My mother turned back to me and confided in a low voice, 'I went next door and they told me you were staying here. What *has* happened?'

Immediately alarm bells and warning signals started flashing in my brain. Next door! I had an awful picture of her trying to sell white feathers and heathers wrapped up with pink twine, just as she had done when I was five years old and we were going through an especially poverty-stricken patch. The feathers had been stolen from my favourite toy; when I'd found its plucked carcass I'd cried myself sick all day, until my mother came upstairs, wrapped me in her arms and cried too, saying, 'I'm sorry Cara, but life is terribly hard now, we just have to do our best . . .'

Only it hadn't been her best. Most mums would have got jobs cleaning or something, not torn their daughter's favourite toy to bits in order to harangue strangers on doorsteps.

'Would you like some tea?' Sean asked.

'I have my own special bat-win—' My mother blinked crossly as I nudged her. 'I have my own special tea bag.' She unclasped her handbag grandly and passed it to Sean.

'Normal tea is fine for me,' I beamed up at Sean.

The moment Sean had left, I turned to her. 'Mum, you didn't say anything to the Wilkins, did you?'

'Say? Of course I said something. I couldn't stand on their doorstep and pretend to be mute, could I? Don't worry, Cara, I didn't tell them. But you're going to have to tell Sean, aren't you? I mean, if you choose Sean over darling Rufus then you must be taking him very seriously indeed,' she sniffed.

My heart was beating. In less than ten seconds she was about to reveal I was a witch and I was about to lose the first guy I'd liked in a long, long time. I couldn't let her do it. I *wouldn't* let her do it. The only solution was to be brutal. Rude. Cold. As she took hold of my hand affectionately, I pressed my fingers firmly into her palm, feeling the knarled knots of veins, stared her straight in the eye and hissed, 'Mum, if you dare say anything to Sean about me being a witch, I will never, ever, *ever* come home and I will never, *ever* speak to you again, all right?'

'Cara, I don't know what you're talking about,' she said lightly, though to my relief my words appeared to have had an effect; she looked a tad unnerved.

Our conversation was cut short as Sean entered the room holding a tray. As he laid it on the coffee table, he banged it gently and sploshs of tea ended up in brown pools all over the tray.

'Sorry, sorry,' he muttered. I felt anxious for him; he seemed nervous – and who wouldn't be with my mum in the room? 'I'll just go into the kitchen and get a cloth.'

As Sean hurried out, my mother reached out, muttered an incantation and all the tea-puddles hovered in the air and then flew back into the cups.

'Mum, you can't do that, he'll notice!' I cried. I pointed at the cups, muttered an incantation in retaliation and replaced the puddles just as Sean came back into the room. Unfortunately, my anger had heightened the spell. One of the mugs shook violently, turned on its side and flooded a sea of tea across the tray.

'I'm so sorry, Sean, I just knocked it—'

'It's fine,' he laughed, waving his dishcloth. 'We are a clumsy lot, aren't we?'

'Sean,' my mother interrupted loudly, as though he was a servant that needed dismissing, 'the reason I've come here is because I'd like a little chat with my daughter. Perhaps you could give us a moment?'

'Sure, sure,' said Sean, backing out. 'I'll leave the tea, shall I?'

I heard the stairs creak as he retreated to his bedroom.

'Honestly, Mum – this is Sean's house, you can't send him off upstairs,' I began.

'Cara, darling, listen. I'm only trying to do what's best for you,' she said, in such a tender voice that, despite everything, I found myself listening to her. 'You know this can't possibly work. It just won't. It's the same with any religion. D'you remember that girl who lived a couple of doors down from us – the odd Buddhist one who shaved her hair and smelled of chickpeas all the time?'

I rolled my eyes; my mother was so un-PC.

'Well, she married a Jew. Against her parents' wishes, against his parents' wishes. They got divorced within a year. I mean, how could it work when she was aiming for Nirvana and he thought their second album wasn't as good as their first; when she gave his copy of the Torah away to a jumble sale because she thought it was an old sex manual?'

'Mum, I don't think this is quite the same—'

'Oh, but it is. Yes, it seems nice with Sean now when you're all starry-eyed. But when the lust burns itself out, you're left with friendship, and once that crumbles, with companionship. The simple foundation of compatibility. It's the little things, you know, as much as the big things, that matter – yes, love and lust and trust and all those big ideals are important. But so are routines and tastes and eccentricities. And how will it work? What will he say when you're off celebrating Yule and he wants to drag you down the pub for a drink? When you're performing rites to the moon goddess in the back garden and he wants to hold a barbeque for his mates?'

Oh, what would you know? I thought sourly. *You've spent the last twenty years shagging anything with a wand.*

But deep down I knew she was right. That was the odd thing about my mother; beneath her haphazard air, she had a good deal of wisdom, and though her own life was a mess, she was rather good at seeing how to straighten other people's out. That was how she managed to get by in life; intuition and perceptiveness saved her. Then I suffered a flicker of suspicion: my mother knew me too well. Was she manipulating me, as she did her customers when she read their palms or their tea leaves?

'I can be normal,' I insisted in a weak voice. 'I've stopped using magic. Well, except for . . .' Except for the growth potion on the garden, the love potion on Jonathan and Nick, summoning up Sean's exs and cursing Nick's penis. 'I could try . . .' I trailed off.

My mother gently smoothed back a strand of hair from my forehead; she did this sort of maternal gesture with an unconvincing air of self-consciousness, like an actress playing at being a mother.

'Darling, magic is in your blood,' she said softly.

I twisted away from her with a heavy heart, not wanting to accept the truth.

'Well, it's up to you,' she sighed, getting up. 'I should go.'

After she'd gone, Sean said brightly, 'Well, she seemed nice.'

'You're very polite.' I forced a smile.

'Anyway, why don't I play a bit of sax for you? I've got some Haagen Dazs in the fridge which you can eat while you're listening,' he said with a glint in his eye.

'Oh, no, I don't think so,' I said, stretching and forcing a yawn. 'I think I should go to bed.'

'Oh come on, Cara, don't be boring!' he cajoled.

But it was no good. My mother had changed my mood, broken the spell.

'No, really,' I snapped. 'I want to go to bed.'

Sean looked bewildered for a moment. Then he took the hint. He slumped down on the sofa, picked up the remote control and folded his arms.

'Well, goodnight,' I said brightly. As I walked out, he muttered a limp echo.

Upstairs in my room, I told myself it was for the best. I got changed into my pyjamas and went into the bathroom for a wash. But as I brushed my teeth, I saw his toothbrush and for some reason it brought tears oozing out of my eyes, mingling with the skeins of white foam. It wasn't just having to give up Sean that cut me so deeply, it was the whole unfairness of it all. If I couldn't have Sean, would I ever be able to have any man? And though I'd told him I never wanted to marry, secretly I did harbour fantasies of a husband and two happy children. Now I replaced those with a more realistic picture: me as an old woman, spending all day dusting her collection of three hundred china cats.

I went back to my room and slid into bed. I could hear the canned laughter from the TV below. Then the flick of the TV being clicked off. Silence. And then the sound of Sean playing his saxophone. Quietly but painfully. I could hear the misery in the long soulful notes, the anger as he jumped abruptly from key to key. I felt as though every note arrowed into my heart and trembled there. And I knew that somewhere in those notes lay a question. An invitation. To go down and undo the damage.

Go on, Cara, I told myself. *Go to him! Just go and pluck that sax from his hands and bloody well kiss him!*

But my body lay hunched under the covers, refusing to obey.

Why? Why let your mother ruin everything? Why live the rest of your life being her puppet? How do you know it won't work! Not until you've tried . . .

I rolled back the covers. I got out of bed. I tiptoed to my door . . .

. . . but at the last minute I lost my nerve and went scuttling back under the covers, pulling them high above my head. Below, I heard Sean's playing soften into a melancholy drizzle of notes and then fade out altogether.

CARA, GO! the voice exploded.

Suddenly a fierce resolve gripped me. I got out of bed. Yes, I was going. But just as I reached the door, I heard his footsteps on the stairs. And in those precious seconds, I lost my nerve again. I heard the footsteps trudge up the next flight of stairs and then felt the dejected slam of his bedroom door. Too late now; I'd lost my chance. So I went back to bed and cried myself to sleep.

22
Andie

Andie was furious to hear that Nick had sacked Cara for no apparent reason. But she was even more incensed to find a message on her answerphone from Suzanne the following morning in her typical exclamation mark-peppered speech: 'Hi, Andie, sweetie, how are you? Great party! Thanks so much for the invite, Nick! Jonathan and I would love to come over next weekend for dinner! Call me, big kiss to you and Nick, Suzanne!'

'I didn't even know you knew Jonathan,' said Andie, suddenly paranoid.

'Andie, I told you before. We invited them last night as they were leaving, remember? God, you complain all the time that we never do anything interesting, then you throw a strop because they're coming over.'

Good point, thought Andie frantically. But she *had* to get out of this. She couldn't face a dinner with Jonathan.

'Well, since you've kicked out Cara for no reason whatsoever, who's going to look after poor Fred?' Andie snapped.

'We can get Maggie to babysit and get a takeaway.'

'No,' said Andie sharply. 'Fred can stay upstairs. And

I'm definitely doing the cooking.' She gave him one of her hawkish glares, challenging him to disagree.

Nick didn't dare.

A week later Andie was standing in the kitchen in her dressing gown, face flushed and hair damp from a hot bath, nervously clicking a ballpoint pen on and off, on and off against her mouth as she frowned at her menu: *Melon, Risotto, Chocolate mousse.*

Tonight, there would be no ready meals. Andie was determined to cook. Deep down, she knew the reason was perfectly childish and silly: she wanted Jonathan to see her – a vision of feminine loveliness – dishing out a sumptuous meal while her husband stared up at her adoringly. She wanted him to see what he was missing; and she wanted him to go home with a lingering feeling of regret.

Since the party, she'd tried to quash the jealousy she felt over Suzanne and Jonathan but it kept springing back up like a jack-in-a-box. How had they got together so quickly? As she watched them at school she felt she hated him; how could he have transferred his emotions so easily? God, to think she'd been on the verge of an affair with this guy . . . But, in quieter moments of reflection, she told herself she was being unreasonable. She was married; she couldn't expect Jonathan to hang around like a knight in shining armour, a suitor adoring an icy Petrarchan mistress who would never fulfil his desires.

For the next hour, Andie dealt with the main course: slicing and dicing tomatoes, green peppers, aubergines, all mingling in an autumn medley of colours in her pan. The recipe said six large chillies but she hadn't been able to find any big ones, so she'd made it using small ones, only twice as many. Every so often Fred would venture in and moan that he wanted to 'lick the chocolate bowl' and she would ruffle his head and say, 'Soon, darling.'

'I wish Cara was here,' he said sadly, hugging the Monopoly board to his chest. 'She was the only one who would play with me properly.'

Andie, who had been measuring out cream for the mousse into a Pyrex mixing jug, froze, barely noticing as it slid past the blue 'quarter pint' lozenge to the 'half'.

'I can play with you,' said Andie quickly. 'Or Daddy can.'

'Yes, but it's not the same.'

Andie swallowed and unseeingly slopped the cream into the mixing bowl. She'd been planning to make the chocolate mousse without Fred's interfering sticky fingers but now she said: 'Go and tell Daddy to lay the table, and then come back and we'll make a mousse together, okay?'

And we'll have a lot more fun than bloody Cara, she thought crossly.

They had just finished working on the chocolate mousse when she heard the doorbell ring.

Andie turned to the clock. It was only 6:45 p.m. *No,* she thought, *it can't be.*

It was.

She heard the click of the front door and Jonathan's cheery, 'HI!' and Suzanne's squeal of 'NICK! So lovely to see you!' and the suckered sounds of her French-kissing his cheeks four times over.

Andie looked down at her now-grubby dressing gown and chipped cerise toenail polish in horror.

'Freddy,' Andie dragged him back before he could launch himself on the guests, 'I want you to tell them I'll be ready in ten minutes, can you do that, darling? But nobody is allowed in the kitchen because I'm busy cooking, okay?'

Andie had just bent down and put the chocolate mousse in the fridge when Nick came in to take the wine out.

'Nick, you told me they'd be here at seven-thirty!' Andie hissed.

'Well, I meant seven-thirty to start; I kind of said they could come a bit earlier for drinks.'

'Nick, you bastard! Look at me! I've been cooking all afternoon and all you've had to do is lay the frigging table!' Seeing his face, she clenched her nails into her palms. 'Nick, you have laid the table, haven't you? Right. Well. How would you like me to kill you? I can do it any way you like.'

'Okay, okay, okay,' Nick backed off, brandishing the wine in front of him, 'I'll just give them something to drink first – I don't want to be *rude*.'

Andie waited until she could hear them all safely in the living room before she dared sidle down the hall and rush up the stairs to their bedroom. On the way she heard Fred yelling at Jonathan, 'Mr Yates, can you do tick-tock on me like my Dad does, please, Mr Yates?' Then, from Fred's ecstatic yelps, it sounded as though Jonathan had obliged.

Upstairs in her room, Andie ran a brush through her hair – thank God she'd bathed earlier. Her curls had gone frizzy, so she put some spray on them in the faint hope that they might be persuaded into thinking they were soft ringlets. And now for the dress.

Her heart beating, Andie slid it out of the bag. She'd been so nervous buying it that she still hadn't cut the price-tag off.

Yes, it was a gorgeous dress. It was a white silky thin-strapped thing that looked as though it could double up as underwear; at mid-thigh, it was the shortest thing she'd worn in a long time, and she had a suspicion that in the wrong light it was dangerously see-through. She'd bought it on a whim in a sale. Now she wasn't sure if she had the guts to pull it off. She suddenly had a vision of Jonathan exchanging appalled glances with Suzanne and trying not to laugh into his risotto; them driving home together and whispering, 'God – did you see that dress? Does she think she's still sixteen? What did she think she was doing, auditioning for *Playboy*?'

No, thought Andie, *this is no good. I cannot possibly wear this.*

Andie was about to tear the damned thing off when there was the sound of footsteps on the landing and a cautious knock on the door.

'Yes?' she snapped, wondering what Nick had done now to annoy her.

'Oh – it's—' Jonathan stood in the doorway, his eyes mooning at her. 'I was just looking for the toilet and I couldn't remember which door it was. . .' He paused, eyes roving.

Andie was about to make a quick excuse about trying on her new nightdress when Jonathan spluttered: 'You look gorgeous. Totally and utterly gorgeous. God, you should dress like that every day.'

'I do? I mean, thanks.' Andie glowed at her reflection in the mirror, like an ugly duckling realising it might be a swan after all. 'Thanks. I'll just . . . well . . . go down . . .'

She paused awkwardly; Jonathan was still barring the doorway, staring at her, and she had to make a pointed *ahem*.

'Sorry!' Jonathan quickly bounded out of the way. Then, as she was going down the stairs, he said, 'By the way, thanks very much for going to all this trouble. It's very kind of you . . . when . . . well . . . you know . . .'

'Oh, it's no trouble.' Andie waved her hand gaily. 'I

love cooking. Really. Nick and I have people over all the time.'

'Right.' Jonathan nodded as though that wasn't what he had meant; though they both knew that she had deliberately misunderstood his words. 'Well. Thanks anyway.' He shrugged and disappeared into the loo. Andie paused for a while on the stairs, caught in a moment's regret. Then she shrugged and went downstairs. She could hear Nick and Suzanne chatting; Nick was telling a joke and his voice had deepened in that way it always did when he was trying to impress a woman. Despite the fact that she'd seen Nick flirt a thousand times over the last ten years, she still felt a jack-knife of jealousy in her stomach.

'Oh my God! ANDIE! You look so SEXY!' Suzanne shrieked as Andie entered the room.

Nick, meanwhile, nearly choked on his wine.

Fred looked puzzled. 'Mum, I can see right up your skirt,' he said.

'Oh, you naughty boy,' Suzanne laughed, though she looked a little taken aback too. Next to Andie, Suzanne looked a little lame in her sparkling jeans and neon pink top. Suzanne wasn't used to being in situations where she was the more conservatively dressed person.

Andie, feeling foolish again, hurriedly laid the table, while Nick went back to flirting with Suzanne. She checked on the chocolate mousse. It still hadn't set. She checked the risotto – it was bubbling away nicely. Good.

Just before they sat down to eat, Nick got another bottle of wine from the fridge and whispered, 'Andie, what the fuck are you wearing? You look ridiculous!'

'Oh fuck off,' Andie shot back, 'Jonathan said it was lovely—' She broke off as Jonathan entered the kitchen. From the look on his face, it seemed as though he'd heard everything.

'I just came in to see if you needed any help,' he offered politely.

'Here – have the plates,' said Andie, with a shaky, grateful smile.

'God,' Nick whispered again as Jonathan left. 'And Suzanne is so intelligent and steady. What's she doing with that git?'

Andie was flabbergasted. Could Nick possibly be such a dreadful judge of character? Then she realised he was probably just jealous: here was Jonathan, young, free and potentially single – with a pretty blonde he could dump tomorrow if he liked; and here was Nick, stuck in a marriage he wanted to wriggle his way out of so that he could start dating fresh young things again.

Suddenly she felt like dropping the risotto to the floor, seeing it flood across the perfect lino, and saying, '*Why? Why bother to pretend? Why not just call up the bloody solicitor right now and call it a day?*'

'Andie, are you okay? You've been staring into space for the last few seconds . . .' Nick asked, his tone soft, genuinely worried.

'Fine,' she said blankly. 'Can you put Fred to bed while I dish up?'

Finally, they sat down to eat. The mood at the table, however, was still a little odd.

Over the melon, Jonathan attempted to ingratiate himself with Nick. 'So, what job d'you do again?' he asked.

'Oh, I'm a manager at a computer firm,' said Nick, his voice laced with pride. 'It's very long hours and I hate the commuting – but, you know, the money's not bad . . .'

Jonathan took a small bite of melon and Andie saw something flash in his eyes.

'I worked in the City for a year,' said Jonathan dismissively. 'It was piss-boring – there just wasn't any *soul*

240

to the job. That's why I got into teaching. The pay might be crap but I swear there is nothing like the feeling of coming home and knowing you've got a difficult kid to learn their alphabet, knowing you've created the foundation for their life to come.'

Nick looked stung. He was used to people being deeply impressed with his job. And although part of her wanted to burst into applause at Jonathan's speech, Andie found herself defending Nick: 'Well, computing might not be so inspiring but someone has to pay the mortgage. Anyway, we're all suited to different things.'

'Oh, but teaching is so cool,' Suzanne chimed in, oblivious to the tension. 'I mean, you get paid for dipping your fingers into pot-paint with thirty kids!'

Nick looked murderous; then, suddenly, he broke into a grin. 'Obviously I'm missing out,' he grinned. 'I guess making finger-paintings is much more fun than sitting behind a desk all day.'

Andie felt like hugging him. Then, as Nick asked for Suzanne to pass the salt and let his fingers linger on her wrist, she felt like slapping him instead.

A brief silence fell. Suzanne filled it quickly: 'By the way, Andie, I've got that Jackie Collins you lent me in the car. Remind me to give it back to you.'

'Jackie Collins – ooh, Pulitzer Prize stuff, eh?' Nick teased them.

'Actually, I'm reading *Captain Corelli* now,' said Andie, desperate not to look a philistine in front of Jonathan.

'God, it's so boring,' said Nick. 'I gave up after ten pages.' He smiled at Suzanne.

'Actually, I think it's the best book I've ever read,' said Jonathan.

'Really? Well, I did give it another go,' Nick said quickly, 'and on the second read I thought it was very profound and well written, sure, but I read in the *Times* that much of the war description is historically inaccurate, which I felt weakened it as a whole.'

Andie could almost see Nick licking his finger and drawing a point in the air.

'Yes, but I find that sort of criticism trivial,' said Jonathan. 'After all, fiction and fact blur all the time. Governments supposedly talk facts, but most of it is spin and propaganda; newspapers supposedly deliver objective viewpoints but much of it is subjective opinion. History is constantly being rewritten; it's really rather naïve to classify anything as fact or fiction, real or unreal.'

What? What the fuck was this? Nick didn't even like reading.

'Well—' Nick began pompously.

'Well,' Suzanne intervened in a bored voice, 'I think we should dissect the complex post-modern rhyming structure in *The Cat in the Hat*.'

She looked at Andie and they burst into laughter. Jonathan and Nick looked confused.

'Anyway,' Nick carried on, totally failing to take the hint, 'if you like heavy reading, maybe you ought to try Proust. You might find him a bit hard-going but . . .'

Men, thought Andie, shaking her head and going off to get the risotto.

In the kitchen, she looked out through the window and caught a sudden glimpse of Cara in next door's kitchen. Andie was surprised to feel a pang; she missed her. She missed her laughter, her ability to diffuse the tension in the house; *recently Cara's been looking after me and Nick as much as Fred,* Andie realised. Now that Suzanne was coupled with Jonathan, Andie missed having a female ally, someone to gossip and joke with. If Cara had been here

242

she would have helped with the cooking and told Andie not to wear such a stupid dress.

Back in the dining room, Andie dished up and waited for them all to say how divine her cooking was. But Nick and Jonathan were too busy arguing over whether Al Pacino or Marlon Brando was the greatest film star of the last hundred years; whether the war on Iraq was justified or just a spin-slick attempt to get our hands on their oil; whether Manchester United or Arsenal was the better football team.

'. . . yes, but if one applies a Derridan analysis to Beckham's goals then . . .' Nick was saying, when he suddenly broke off. 'Suzanne? Suzanne? Are you okay?'

Suzanne had suddenly turned a worrying shade of puce and was gasping, '*Water! Water!*'

Quickly Jonathan dashed into the kitchen to get some. Andie had a funny feeling in her tummy. A sense that, despite everything, her culinary ship was about to strike an iceberg. The feeling got even more funny when she took a bite herself. Her tongue felt as though it was on fire; her nose stung and water streamed from her eyes in icy, shocked floods.

'It's lovely,' said Suzanne quickly, trying to smooth things over. 'It's just a bit *hot.*'

'You baby,' Nick teased her, putting on a Northern accent. 'Now I'm a man who can handle me curry.'

'No, Nick,' Andie said quietly, '*Don't*—' From the way Nick's eyes bulged, she realised she was a little too late.

Five minutes later, Nick had recovered. 'Jesus, Andie, what the fuck did you put in it?'

'Just chillies,' she said in a sulky, girlish voice. 'I couldn't get any big ones so I put in twice as many small ones . . . *what?*' she asked as they all fell about laughing.

243

She was being made to look a complete and utter idiot, right in front of Jonathan. When Nick explained that the smaller the chilli the hotter it was, she wanted the ground to swallow her.

'Come on,' said Jonathan gently, 'sod the main course, Suzanne and I aren't that hungry anyway. Let's go get some dessert.'

In the kitchen Andie and Jonathan surveyed the un-set chocolate mousse. Andie suddenly burst into tears.

'Look,' she found herself saying. She knew she was being ridiculous, crying over a mousse, but this was the last straw in an evening that absolutely stank. 'It's . . . like . . . *slop* . . . it hasn't set *one bit* . . .'

Jonathan dipped a finger in and licked it.

'It tastes lovely,' he said in a light, cajoling tone, as though she was an upset pupil he was comforting. 'You can say it's chocolate milkshake. Here.' He dipped his finger and Andie sucked it. It did taste good. So did Jonathan's finger. Suddenly she smiled, blushing. Jonathan smiled too and, curling his fingers around her chin in a fatherly manner, he whispered, 'Chin up.' Andie gazed at him. A pulse beat between them. Jonathan slowly brushed his finger around the outline of her cupid-shaped lips. His hazel eyes were all pupil, liquid with desire.

Andie was lost. She thought in a daze: *Is this how Nick felt when he was tempted by that girl on the business trip?* For the first time, she understood how he'd felt; the thrill of temptation, that moment when reality starts to slip away, when all your labels – mother, wife, teacher – disappear and there is nothing left but naked emotion. She reached up; Jonathan leaned down . . .

From the dining room, Nick and Suzanne sang mockingly: '*Why are we waiting?*'

IT'S COMING!' Andie called, turning and throwing

the mousse down the sink. Jonathan shuffled backwards, blushing.

'Sorry,' he said.

'It's fine.' She couldn't look at him. Then she burst out: 'What the hell are we going to give them?'

Jonathan was ransacking the cupboards for her. 'I can only find one thing,' he said in despair.

'What?'

He held up four of Fred's Twix bars.

Two hours later, Andie watched Jonathan and Suzanne drive off together. Then she slowly padded upstairs and pulled out her earrings; her ears, which had never seemed to like being pierced, were bleeding as usual.

The rest of the evening had got rapidly worse. Jonathan and Nick had nearly come to blows over chess. For the first time *ever*, Nick had been beaten. Nick had been stunned and muttered something about the wine blurring his brain. Andie had felt pleased at first. It served Nick right for taking the piss out of her cooking. But when Nick became withdrawn and sullen Andie had felt exasperated by his childishness.

Nick entered the bedroom. She didn't turn around. She waited for him to make some feeble joke about the risotto or the Twix bars again.

But he came up behind her and suddenly slipped his arms around her waist. Andie bristled, but as he licked her ear she found herself responding. He had taken off his shirt and was wearing nothing but his jeans; despite his slightly swollen belly, he looked gorgeous.

Strange, thought Andie, as they kissed, *even when we don't really like each other, we can still go to bed together. And enjoy it.*

'This dress is truly fabulous; you should wear it more often,' Nick murmured, running his hands over it, savouring its silky texture and the familiar feel of her curves underneath.

She felt aroused again, desire lapping at her worries and dissolving them; she reached down and unbuttoned his jeans. Nick groaned with pleasure. She carried on, vaguely aware that he was unusually limp. She thought: *What if he's lying there thinking of Suzanne?*

'You stopped,' said Nick.

'Sorry.' Feeling guilty and suddenly determined to please him, she slipped her dress over her head, smiling at his groan of appreciation . . .

Half an hour, they lay in the darkness, staring up at the ceiling. Andie couldn't believe it. How had everything gone so wrong?

Nick had been impotent. It was almost *funny*. For the first time in his life, he hadn't been able to get it up.

Maybe I can't satisfy him any more, thought Andie. *Maybe he doesn't find me attractive. Maybe that groan wasn't 'Oh you're so sexy' but 'I can't believe I have to go to bed with this old thing'.*

Maybe that blonde girl in the park has changed his tastes.

Maybe that's what he wanted to say to me in the note I found in his drawer.

She glanced over at Nick. His eyes were closed but she knew he wasn't sleeping. She felt that familiar ugly feeling in her stomach again; how could it have returned so soon? She felt helpless. What was it with life? You could have the best intentions, work as hard as you could to solve things and heal things and make them work but sometimes it just wasn't enough; sometimes it was as though life had its own stubborn plan that it was going to carry out whether you liked it or not.

Maybe that was the way it was supposed to be with her

and Nick. Maybe they were meant to slowly grow apart, limp into a divorce and a pact of friendship and sharing Fred on Saturday afternoons. Suddenly she felt tears in her eyes. She rolled over quickly and smothered them in her pillow, feeling the cotton absorb the wet droplets. She flinched as she suddenly felt Nick's hand on her back.

'Andie, are you okay?' he whispered.

'I want you to bring Cara back,' she found herself saying, and realised with a sparkle of hope that Cara could help her. 'It's too much without her, I can't cope with Fred and everything, I need help. I need more time, *we* need more time, time for us, time to . . .' She swallowed hard, looking at his worried face. 'No buts, Nick. I don't know why you fired her but I want her back.'

23
Cara

I was lounging in Sean's living room reading a copy of the *Guardian*, half-heartedly lassoing job possibilities, when the doorbell rang. I was expecting Sean back from Safeways and I just prayed that he'd remembered to get me the big bar of Fruit 'n' Nut I'd asked for. Since that embarrassing night when we had spectacularly failed to kiss, I'd offered to move out, worrying that Sean would hold a grudge against me. But, much to my relief, Sean had refused to let me.

All in all, Sean had been really sweet. He'd offered to get me a job working behind the bar of the Goat, but with my problem with alcohol it would be worse than working in a sewer's. Though I kept up a cheerful I'll-get-something-soon front, I was starting to feel a bit depressed. I couldn't help wondering if I was cursed, if every job I attempted would end in a magical mess. Or maybe my mother was the one doing the cursing?

The doorbell shrilled again; I threw down the paper with a defeated sigh and hurried to the door.

To my amazement, it was Nick. His hair was damp and raindrops slithered over his face. He looked dreadful, dark crescents under his eyes, his mouth down-turned at the corners.

'Cara. Hi.' To my surprise, his tone was gentle, conciliatory. 'Could I come in?'

'Look, I know my contract states that you have to give me a month's pay but it's fine, you don't need to,' I said quietly.

'Well, actually, I was hoping to – kind of – unfire you, but it's pretty wet out here and if I could just come in . . .' He glanced over my shoulder into the hallway.

Come in? With Sean about to arrive back in five minutes? Sean, who would probably sock him one?

'Um, it's a bit tricky at the moment . . .'

'We could go for a drive?'

I left a hasty note for Sean and slammed the door, hurrying into Nick's car.

We drove through the wet suburban streets, the windscreen wipers whirring loudly in our silence. Nick circled awkwardly a few times; all the roads in Richmond have double yellow lines, or are permit only. Eventually we ended up in the car park by Tesco's. He switched off the engine and we sat there, watching the rain drum down, people milling in and out of the revolving doors.

'Look,' said Nick, staring straight ahead, 'I'm sorry about firing you. I really didn't mean it . . . I just . . . I'm just pretty stressed at the moment.' He held his head in his hands, his fingers furrowing his dark hair.

Suddenly my anger started to slip away. I could feel his sadness clouding around him. I almost knew what he was going to say before he said it.

'Something pretty awful happened to me a few months ago. You know I've been working at Carlton Heist . . . well . . .'

The blonde girl, I thought in alarm. *He's going to confess he's been having an affair.* In the distance, I watched a child throwing a tantrum. The mother slapped him, exacerbating his screams, and I winced, thinking of Fred. *Please don't say it,* I willed Nick, *please don't say you're going to leave Andie and Fred and go off with some dumb blonde.*

'. . . and so I lost my job.'

'*What?*'

'I was fired,' he said weakly.

'But why?'

'I made a mess of a deal with a Japanese client at the worst possible time – when my company were downsizing. I knew they were going to fire me so I offered to accept a redundancy package. That's what's kept us going for the last few months, but it's not going to last for ever.' Nick shrugged. I don't think I'd ever seen him so ashamed, hardly able to look at me, fingering his car keys as if he wanted to tear them from the silver ring.

'Shit! God, when did this happen?'

'The night I was supposed to have dinner with Andie and I didn't turn up.' He laughed bitterly. 'She was so furious with me about not coming to the bloody meal I didn't dare tell her that things were actually rather worse than that . . .'

'Don't you think you should maybe mention it?' I cried.

'No, Cara!' He suddenly flared up. 'And I don't want you to tell her either, okay?'

'But Nick, she has to know—'

'The mortgage is fine for now,' he carried on, as if barely listening to me, engrossed in arranging his own thoughts. 'I opened up my own account and took out a loan. I feed the money into our main account and Andie thinks it's my wage. She hasn't even noticed there's no PAYE code, but she's never been any good with money.

I've always been the one to do the accounts.' He smiled bitterly.

'But why don't you just say something to her?'

'Because you don't know Andie. She's got used to having everything – designer clothes, a nice holiday. I'm trying to save every bloody penny at the moment and she's ringing up her grandmother in New Zealand – the BT bill is *hundreds*.'

'But Nick, it's not her fault. She doesn't know.'

'I will tell her, but I can't right now . . . our marriage is in a total state and if I tell her this it'll be the final straw. I know I can get another job soon; I'm going to start applying.'

Start? I thought.

'For the last couple of months, I've been pretending to go to work. You'd think it would be nice having so much time on my hands, but I haven't really known what to do with it. I've been going to the park quite a bit. My old secretary's been sweet – she's even kept covering for me if Andie calls at work. She doesn't think I should have been fired; she hates her new boss.'

So that explained the blonde in the park and the all-day meetings . . .

'I can't keep this up much longer though. Yesterday I was wandering around town and I saw Andie – she nearly caught me.'

'Oh, Nick, you poor thing,' I said. 'Look, I swear I won't say anything to Andie. I'll do anything I can to help you – we can go through the papers together . . .'

'Oh thanks, Cara. Thanks.'

He smiled, looking like his old boyish self again, and spread open his arms charmingly. I leaned into him gingerly, sharing a warm hug. His hair smelled of rain-water and smoke. Then a moment of self-consciousness passed between us and we drew apart, suddenly embarrassed and awkward.

'I don't want you to accuse me of molesting you again,' Nick said. 'I sincerely apologise for that too. I was drunk. As you may have guessed. You . . . you won't tell Andie, will you?'

'Well, no . . .'

'I mean, there's really nothing to tell, is there? I just tried to kiss you, and you stopped me – it wasn't even a kiss. Oh God.'

'Nick, it's fine, I promise I won't say anything,' I said, though I couldn't help recalling that it had most definitely been a kiss . . .

'I love her, you know, I love her so much. I wouldn't want to . . . You see, I once made a mistake, years ago . . . Oh, it doesn't matter,' he shook his head, 'I'm sorry. I don't know why I threw myself at you, but it was very stupid.'

'You're stressed,' I said soothingly. 'I understand. But if you've lost your job, I can't really come back, can I? Surely you can't afford it?'

'We can't,' Nick admitted. 'But if I don't re-hire you, Andie will anyway. She's been moaning at me ever since you went. So you see, you must come back, or else I'll soon be divorced as well as unemployed. Please, please, come back.'

'Okay then.' I smiled, touched. Though Andie had been more friendly with me recently, deep down I'd still been paranoid that she didn't really like me.

'Though I guess if I don't get a job,' he admitted, 'we will have to let you go . . .'

'Well, we'll have to make sure you do get a job then, won't we?'

'Oh Cara, thank God for you!' Nick laughed, looking a lot better. 'Yes, I'm going to get a new job and it's all going to be all right.' Though, it had to be said, he didn't sound entirely convinced.

Back at Sean's house, I clambered up the stairs two-at-a-time. I realised that, despite everything, I had missed the Wilkinses, missed their troubles, missed my paltry attempts at trying to sort them out. I started packing things up, then went to the window. I saw Sean in the garden and I felt a wave of passionate affection for him, an urge to run down and kiss the living daylights out of him . . .

But it was no good. If I stayed here with Sean any longer, he was going to find out who I really was; my mother was bound to come back and start stirring again. I had to go.

But as I heard the bang of the back door, I felt my heart shrink nervously behind my rib-cage. How was I going to say it?

I went downstairs and into the living room.

Sean had a huge grin on his face. 'Look, this is my David Blaine chocolate trick,' he said, rather clumsily 'magicking' a Twix from his pocket. 'And here's another.' He pulled out a Mars Bar from behind my ear. 'Oops, where did this Fruit 'n' Nut come from?' He ended up spreading about twenty or so chocolate bars out on the table. All for me. Oh, he was so sweet.

'Cara, what is it?' He looked worried. 'What?'

'Well . . .' I said, drawing him down on to the sofa. 'I'm sorry but I'm going to have to desert you . . .'

24
Cara

Though it was horrible leaving Sean's house, I had to admit that I was overwhelmed by the warmth I received from the Wilkins family on my return.

Andie actually gave me a warm hug and dragged me into the kitchen for a cup of coffee. 'Look,' she said, pushing handfuls of curly hair behind her ear, 'I don't know why the hell Nick fired you, but it's fucking outrageous. I mean – you're a brilliant nanny.'

I laughed uneasily. Despite my promise to Nick, my conscience was still nagging at me. Didn't Andie deserve to know that Nick had kissed me? Sean had said I should tell her. And yet . . .

'Look,' she said again, taking down a fresh jar of coffee from the cupboard and tugging to unscrew the stubborn lid, 'if there is ever anything wrong, I want you to tell me. Anytime. I mean, I know you're supposed to have weekends off and we've thrown Fred on you, and I know you shouldn't be cooking and cleaning for all of us . . .'

'It's okay, I *like* cooking,' I said, taking the jar off her and having a go myself.

'But all the same, I think we should give you a pay rise.'

'No!' I cried, thinking of Nick.

Andie gazed at me wide-eyed. I realised I sounded insane. Next I would be begging her *never* to give me a company car and benefits.

'No, I insist,' said Andie, finally unscrewing the lid with a no-nonsense twist. 'It's the least we can do. I'll speak to the agency.'

Well, I guess I can always take it out of my wages and give it back to Nick, I reflected.

'And,' said Andie, suddenly grabbing my hand conspiratorially, 'I've got something else you should see. I finally bought Nick a *proper* birthday present.' She cast a nervous glance towards the living room, but Nick was watching TV. Then she opened a drawer and pulled something out. My jaw dropped. It was a Rolex.

'When are you going to, erm, show him his surprise?' I asked, trying to keep my voice steady.

'Well, it's our wedding anniversary soon,' she said, 'so I thought then. Make sure you don't tell him.'

'Believe me, I won't.'

Despite the watch shock, I had to admit I had a lovely evening with the Wilkins family. I'd really enjoyed staying with Sean but I'd missed a clean house, hot running water and not being woken early in the morning by Kieran singing Abba in the bath. And I was so touched when Fred burst into the kitchen, jumped on to my lap and cried, 'CARA, YOU'RE BACK!' And though Andie went red and shot me a slightly jealous glance, I could tell she was pleased.

Later that evening, we all made popcorn together and then sat down to watch a video. As the sun went down and Nick switched on the lamps, filling the cosy living room with a golden glow, I felt an incredible sense of happiness and acceptance. I felt as if they'd adopted me. At last, I felt as though I belonged somewhere.

I still look back and remember that night with a kind of nostalgic sadness, because it was their last night of peace before all the problems simmering beneath the surface finally came to the boil and tore them all apart.

Nick's job-hunt became our secret conspiracy. Every morning Nick would change into his suit and pretend to go off to work. I would drop Fred off at school and then go out to the park, armed with bundles of newspapers. Nick and I would sit by the Thames, sharing sandwiches and chocolate bars, going through the jobs pages, circling possibilities. Sometimes, if Andie was busy marking, we worked together in the evenings, updating his CV or typing out letters. It was awkward though; sometimes Fred would storm in and demand to be entertained. When Nick told him to leave us in peace for a while, Fred would let out a Tarzan yell, fling himself on to Nick's back and evoke a play-fight, thus wasting a whole evening of precious time. I realised that Fred was jealous of our growing intimacy, and also slightly suspicious.

But Nick, at least, was grateful. 'Thank God for you, Cara,' he kept saying. 'I needed someone to give me a bit of a slap and tell me to get on with my life instead of wallowing in my own self-pity. I just felt so daunted . . . you know . . .'

'It's fine,' I smiled at him, 'you just have to be positive. If you think you're going to fail, you will; if you think you're going to succeed, you will.'

Nick smiled, though I couldn't help sensing that his heart wasn't really in it. Something was wrong, though when I pressed him, he reacted with guilty vehemence, denying anything else was the matter.

The next morning, I was downstairs in the living room when I picked up the phone and heard something I shouldn't have.

I'd been meaning to call my mother – I hadn't spoken to her in ages and I had just about forgiven her for turning up at Sean's. But when I picked up the phone, I realised Andie was on the extension upstairs.

'We haven't made love for weeks,' Andie was saying. 'We were watching *Reservoir Dogs* last night and I joked to Nick that he'd be called Mr Floppy – it was a *joke*, y'know, to bring the subject up without getting all serious about it. Nick wasn't amused though.'

'I'm not surprised,' a familiar female voice retorted (Suzanne?). 'Men get very sensitive about these things . . .'

I gently put the receiver back in its cradle, wracked with guilt. An hour later, when Andie finally got off the phone, I hastily called up my grandmother and relayed the story to her.

'. . . so I did a spell for impotency with this penis-shaped candle and it actually worked. I'd forgotten all about it; I'd assumed it wouldn't work. So many of my spells produce no effect, or go wrong, and now I finally do one I don't want to work and it *does*.'

'Were you angry when you cast the spell?' my grandmother interjected.

'Very,' I admitted.

'Well, you know as well as I do that the success of a spell isn't about ritual, it's about the power of intention behind it. Why do people go around saying "Be careful what you wish for or it might come true"?' Thoughts are powerful, and thoughts fanned by anger even more so. The poor man

257

probably hasn't got a willy left.' Her voice was hushed with excitement. 'It's probably the size of a peanut—'

'Grandma, *please!*' I cried. 'Between you and me, the wife is having an affair. With a much younger man. I swear it's partly my fault.'

'Well, you'll just have to do a spell to undo it,' she said calmly.

And so here I was, standing in the kitchen, aproned, flour on my fingers, my ammunition spread out on the work-surface before me.

I'd caught Nick and Andie at breakfast this morning. They'd both been rather stressed and busy; Andie was dealing with an imminent Ofsted inspection and a parents' evening and Nick was going for a job interview. But I'd pinned them both down and asked them to be home by seven so that they could share a meal. I'd dropped Fred off earlier to play at his friend Gavin's house. Now the coast was finally clear.

A magical seduction meal has to be cooked in three stages, mirroring the seduction and consummation of two lovers. The starter symbolises flirtation and foreplay; it should open up the taste-buds gently without blunting them with anything too heavy – just a light, teasing taste. I split open a watermelon, licking off the sweet, sticky juice from my fingers. Then I placed a cherry on the top of each segment which shone like nipples in the juicy flesh. Finally, I sprinkled a little rose powder on top, chanting the love spell under my breath.

The main course should always be substantial. If the starter sparks lust, the main course should fan the flames as high as they can go, using heavy spices. So I sprinkled in garlic, and cloves, and scarlet paprika powder.

As I prepared the vegetables, I kept chanting under my breath until I slid into a dizzy, intoxicated trance. I felt the magic pulse through my fingertips as I chopped tomatoes, their hot red mouths splitting open, squirting seeds of lust, sliding my knife through green peppers to form taut slithers. I cooked them in a frying pan over a hot heat, taking care to keep the lid on, so they simmered together claustrophobically; this would ensure that the two lovers eating the meal would sit and stare dreamily at each other, locked in their own world. Every so often, the lid of the pan would puff up with a gust of steam and a little orgasmic wail as the vegetables kissed and melted into each other to form a rich red sauce.

Dessert symbolises the post-coital chat. It should be tender, sweet and a little sleepy. I chose some rich, meaty dates, figs and currants and blended them together with rose petals. I added whipped cream on the side.

My grandmother's recipe recommended adding a tear as a final seal of emotion. I was so happy with my cooking that I couldn't summon tears. I had to slice an onion to make my eyes water.

There.

I glanced up at the clock: six-thirty. In half an hour they'd be home. I pictured the surprised delight lighting up their faces when they saw that they were going to finish a hard day with some unexpected pleasure . . .

I sat down on a stool, feeling suddenly drained, but excited. The magic was still dancing in my brain, the syllables slurring into each other. Steam had filled the kitchen with whirling shapes like an ethereal Cupid dancing around. I gazed down at the nearby goldfish bowl, a present for Fred, where the steam had left beads of condensation on the glass. The goldfish had certainly woken up! They were squiggling through the water, fins flying in a game of tag. I leaned towards the bowl, fancying that I could hear them seducing each other . . .

By seven o'clock, everything was ready.

I had cleared all the junk off the kitchen table and had smoothed a white tablecloth over it (there was a brown stain, like a birthmark, on it so I covered it up with a few roses in a vase).

I lit two candles – red, for love – and placed them in a saucer in the centre.

My heart was beating in excitement; everything looked wonderful, just as I had planned. *Eat your heart out, Nigella,* I smiled triumphantly.

Hearing the front door open, I danced down the hallway; the dogs, indignant at being usurped of their positions as guards, followed, yapping at my heels.

Nick came in, briefcase swinging, his face bright.

'Did your interview go well?' I asked.

'Yes, it did. It went *really* well, in fact. I think it could be in the bag.' Suddenly he pulled me into a tight hug. 'Oh, thanks for your pep-talk, Cara. It really helped. You are an angel.'

I disentangled myself, smiling.

'You should have heard Andie this morning – moan, moan, moan about going to bloody Tuscany this year. I know where my first month's wages will be going.'

I chewed my lip. Suddenly my vision of Andie and Nick sitting with dreamy eyes and fingers entwined vanished in a puff of smoke, to be replaced by Andie and Nick flinging bread rolls at each other and snarling insults.

But the magic will overcome any negativity, that's the point, I reassured myself.

As Nick followed me into the kitchen, he gasped with surprise. 'Oh, Cara, you shouldn't have. Shit.'

Shit? What kind of a reaction was that?

'So that's why you were asking at breakfast . . . Oh Cara, don't kill me, but Andie will be home late. She's got to prepare for a parents' evening . . .'

Andie wasn't coming? But . . . but . . . but . . .

Sean suddenly came barging into the kitchen via the back door.

'Cara, darling! I could smell gorgeous things from next door and wondered if you had any free grub going spare for a hungry man . . .' He trailed off when he saw the intimate table laid for two. 'Oh sorry, are you . . . and Nick . . .?' He shot us a quizzical, irritated glance.

'Of course not!' I said, suddenly feeling cross. One minute ago everything had been perfect; now Fate, like a spoilt child smashing up a neatly laid jigsaw puzzle, was ruining all my plans. I had lost control and I didn't like it. 'Look, Nick, why don't you stay here and enjoy it, and save some for Andie when she gets back? I'm sure she'd really appreciate it if you put some in the oven.'

'Sure,' said Nick, 'but you and Sean go ahead and take some too. There's loads here.'

'Ah— erm . . .'

'Thanks, Nick,' said Sean, picking up a plate and shovelling food on to it.

As Nick sat down to eat, Mozart put a paw on his knee and looked up with mournful eyes. Nick threw him a few scraps. A minute later, Mozart popped back up, paws dangling, as if to say, 'Please, sir, can I have some more?'

Next Beethoven joined in, yowling as if to say, 'If he's having some, why can't I?'

'Erm, Nick, maybe you shouldn't feed them at the table,' I snapped.

'It's just a few scraps,' said Nick, looking surprised.

'Sure. Right. Well, have fun.' I shrugged and followed Sean out through the back door. Though I doubted that magic would work on animals, I was miffed; it seemed a complete waste. I was convinced that by the time Andie got back there would be none left for her. Damn, damn, damn.

25
Cara

Now what? I couldn't let Sean eat the food, I couldn't! As I searched about for clean knives and forks, I frantically tried to formulate excuses in my mind.

'Sean,' I said, clearing my throat, 'I think maybe we should, er, throw this food away. I mean, come on, wouldn't it be nice to have a McDonalds? Yes, a McDonalds! God, I'm dying for a Big Mac.'

Sean looked at me as though I was crazy. 'But this – this looks great.'

'Yes, but—'

'But what?' he demanded.

'I think we might get food poisoning!' I cried, laying down the knives and forks in a silver clatter.

'*What?*'

'I used some raw eggs and I've just realised that the sell-by-date had passed . . . so . . .'

'Well, maybe you should go next door and tell Nick.'

'Yes, but Nick will be all right, won't he?' I realised I wasn't making any sense, implying it was fine to poison Nick but not us. 'Oh, I'm sure it's fine.' I waved my hand weakly. 'Carry on.'

Sean gave me a long look. 'I mean this with affection,' he said, 'but sometimes I do think you're nuts.'

Charming, I thought crossly. *I'm not nuts, nor am I stupid, I'm just caught in a web of lies. Just you wait till you eat that and feel so desperate you'd shag the TV set. Just you wait.*

'Any food for me?' Kieran came in, putting his arm around both of us.

'No,' said Sean, 'piss off.'

'Come on, guys, I'm starved,' said Kieran.

Oh great, I thought. Great. Why don't we all stock up on the aphrodisiacs and have one great big orgy?

Sean put a few courgettes on a plate. He handed the plate to Kieran. 'Here you go,' he said.

'Is that all? I'm a growing lad.'

'Stop messing about, you two!' I laughed, caving in and giving Kieran a generous helping. At least that meant less for Sean.

In the living room, we all slumped in front of the TV. Sean and Kieran tucked in ravenously. I was determined not to eat a bite, so I kept pushing the fork towards my mouth and then putting it back on my plate.

'That was delicious, Cara,' said Kieran. He patted my shoulder with a knarled hand, the dirty old goat, and I shuddered. 'Well, I'd best be off. I have a date. And not with Helen, I may add.'

'Oh, who's the mystery woman?' Sean asked.

'Never you mind,' said Kieran with a wink. 'She's a younger woman, so I'm dressed to impress tonight. Take a look at this.' He pulled off his jumper, revealing a white T-shirt with large red letters that shouted: NOT JUST A PRETTY FACE . . . Then he turned around to show off the back: . . . I'VE GOT A BIG KNOB TOO.

'Er, great, that'll do the trick,' said Sean, looking at me and trying not to laugh.

264

Kieran shook his head and stormed out.

After Kieran had gone, we rolled about laughing.

'Deary me,' said Sean, wiping his eyes as he calmed down. He eyed up my plate hungrily. 'You've barely taken a bite.'

'Oh, I'm just a slow eater, you know me,' I laughed.

Sean had polished his food off. One thing was for sure: the potion was definitely working. Sean, unable to help himself, kept undressing me with his eyes; then, when I caught him doing it, he blushed and looked away. Then I noticed him surreptitiously placing a cushion over his lap. Those shorts he was wearing were dangerously tight, and I bit back an embarrassed smile.

Though I was excited by his attention, I was also nervous. Yes, I wanted Sean to make a move on me, but the magic factor made me uneasy. Performing spells to find out what Sean was really like was one thing. But if we were going to get it together, I wanted it to be natural; I didn't want him to seduce me and then wake up the next morning wondering what on earth he'd done.

Knowing this, I should have left the room there and then. But a naughty part of me made me stay. It's like watching a horror movie; however messy it gets, you have to keep going, compelled by an excited shiver at the bottom of your spine, to see how it all pans out.

Trying to cool things down, I changed channels on the TV. *Wildlife On One* was being repeated over on BBC2. *Great*, I thought in relief. *Something innocent and sweet*.

The programme's theme was underwater creatures. We watched in fascination as a whale rolled and lolled gracefully through the water. Several men swam along beside it, tiny as ants next to its enormous body.

'Wow, it's so incredible,' Sean sighed.

'And now,' said David Attenborough, 'watch this footage of whales mating . . .'

The atmosphere quickly became way too heated. I picked up the remote control to change the channel again when Sean reached across and stopped me, his hand on mine. Currents of sexual energy were fizzing and pulsating up my arm. I shuddered, gazing down at Sean's hand. His long square fingers. The gauze of blond hair on the backs of his freckled hands. Slowly, Sean drew away.

'I, er, was enjoying it,' he whispered awkwardly.

'Okay, fine,' I said, my eyes fixed firmly on the TV, the colour building in my cheeks.

So we sat and watched them mate. Despite their huge size, the whales never appeared clumsy; they lolled gracefully through the waves, kings and queens of the ocean. Entranced, I lost my guard. Without thinking, I picked up a forkful of food and started to chew.

'Glad to see you're finally tucking in,' said Sean as the credits started to roll.

'Shit!' I dropped my fork with a clatter, wrapping my hand over my mouth. Oh God, how many mouthfuls had I taken? I resisted an impolite urge to spit it all out and swallowed thickly, giving Sean a bright smile. At this rate he was going to think I was anorexic or something.

Right, I thought, *I have to go. I fancy him enough as it is, but with the potion inside me I'll start having loud and embarrassing orgasms the next time he so much as touches me. This is too much.*

'I think maybe I should be getting back,' I said, getting up.

'Oh, don't go!' Sean wailed. 'Why don't we play a game? Why don't we play strip poker?'

'How about Monopoly?' I suggested blandly.

'Strip Monopoly?'

'Sean, you've got a one-track mind!' I poked him and he laughed.

'I don't have a one-track mind,' Sean protested vehemently. We sat and channel-hopped for a few minutes; then Sean said, 'Let's play The Truth Game, only a compulsory sex version.'

'What – if I don't tell the truth, we have to have sex?' I asked wryly.

'God, that's a good idea, I hadn't thought of that—' Sean broke off hastily as I lifted a cushion to bash him. 'No, what I meant was, all questions have to relate to sex, because, let's face it, that's the point of The Truth Game; let's not waste time asking all that crap about what your favourite colour is or whether you believe in life after death.' Sean paused, swinging his feet up onto the sofa and stuffing some cushions behind his back; his toes just brushed my thigh. He lit a cigarette and stared at me. He seemed to be enjoying making me blush.

'We'll start off with gentle questions, don't worry,' said Sean. 'Okay, when did you lose your virginity?'

I paused, wondering whether to confess.

'You're still a virgin, aren't you?' Sean said. 'I can tell.'

'Oh, how?' I rolled my eyes.

'Your compulsory handwashing thing,' he said.

My *what*? Sean must be muddling me up with another girl, I thought indignantly. Then it clicked. Yes, I had told Sean that – when I'd been defending myself against his drugs-in-bathrooms charge. God, the trouble with telling all these lies was trying to remember them. They were threatening to come back and devour me.

'So,' said Sean, 'am I right or am I right?'

'No,' I retorted, 'I'm not a virgin. Anyway, tell me your story first. I assume you're not a virgin?'

'Ha ha. I lost my virginity when I was seventeen in the back of a car. End of story. You?'

Poor Kate, I thought, remembering his astral ex. I think she remembers you with a good deal more affection. Suddenly I felt cagey again.

'It was this guy . . .' I leaned forwards, knitting my fingers together, frowning. 'I was pretty young and naïve. I fell in love with him, but it all went wrong when . . .'

'When what?' Suddenly Sean had a serious look on his face; he stared at me very intently and repeated gently, 'What?'

'I . . . he . . .' Dare I tell him? Dare I tell him the whole story of how he'd found out I was a witch and called me a freak? 'I found out he was married,' I blurted.

'Jesus, the bastard!' Sean cursed. 'Tell me who he is and I'll go and smash his teeth in.'

'Sean, calm down!' I said, though I was quite touched by his passion. 'It was years ago. I have recovered, though to be honest, I haven't really been out with anyone seriously since.'

Sean looked shocked. 'But Cara – that's really sad.'

'Oh, thanks very much!' I cried.

'No, sorry, that came out wrong. I didn't mean sad in the pathetic sense of the word. I mean it's a terrible waste. You're beautiful, and intelligent . . . and . . . it's a bit weird, that's all.'

'Well.' I couldn't look at him now: I was addressing all my replies to the coffee table. 'To be honest, I'm not really interested in men.' I paused, glanced at Sean and guessed the mechanics of his thoughts. 'Or women.'

'Animals?' Sean roared with laughter as I swatted him with a cushion. 'Ow, ow,' he moaned sarcastically. Huffing, I threw down the cushion and grabbed hold of his feet, trying to tickle them, but he shrugged infuriatingly, explaining that he wasn't ticklish.

'Seriously,' he continued when we'd calmed down. 'Tell me what your ideal man would be like.'

'Oh God – what a question.'

'I thought you'd like it. You're very idealistic, aren't you?'

'I am?' I feigned surprise, though I knew he was right. 'Well, there's nothing wrong with that, I'm just a wild optimist. I like seeing the good in people. I can't help having high hopes for everyone around me, even when things are looking grim . . . D'you think I'm naïve?' I asked, a question that had been troubling me a lot since I'd moved to the Wilkinses.

'No, I think you're very positive. But stop psychoanalysing and answer the question.'

'Okay.' I pondered; the glib answers were easy – good looks, intelligence, a nice car. And yet it was a formula that never worked in real life; I'd met countless handsome men with decent IQs and flashy wheels and I'd never felt tempted. 'I think . . . someone who could understand me, very deeply – who could look into me and see who I am.' Suddenly the words came and my blurry thoughts crystallised. 'Someone,' I said excitedly, 'who could accept me for who I am, who could love me for me.'

'Hmm,' said Sean, looking slightly wary.

'Maybe I should go,' I said, feeling suddenly deflated.

'No,' said Sean. 'You can't go!' His eyes wandered to the drinks cabinet behind the TV. 'We've got to make some crazy cocktails first. Come on, I know you don't like drinking much but just try.'

I rolled my eyes as Sean scooped up the bottles. But in the kitchen, I couldn't help getting into the swing of it. We sloshed vodka and Baileys into a mixer jug, adding a little juice from a tin of canned peaches. I even found a shrivelled lime at the back of the fridge and chopped it up into slices.

'Okay, this cocktail shall be named A Long Slow Screw Against A Bicycle Wheel. Let's see who can down it first,' said Sean, handing me a glass.

'Sean, we're not students, you know,' I said.

'I know, I know,' said Sean. He had clearly decided to appeal to my competitive spirit. 'Come on! I bet I can beat you at drinking.'

'Oh, that's not fair, I'm such a lightweight,' I complained doubtfully. I still hadn't learned to like alcohol and I worried that my magical skills would be fuzzy for the next few days. Then I thought: *Just go with the flow! Enjoy yourself, capture the night!* And Sean was right – I couldn't resist a challenge.

So I lifted my glass and we downed them. I slammed my glass on the table victoriously, eyes watering, tongue burning, belly on fire.

'Best of three?' said Sean with a grin.

26
Andie

Andie was having a very strange day.

It had started that morning in the staff room.

'I've got some gossip about Jonathan to tell you!' Suzanne hissed excitedly.

'Oh?' Andie said lamely. She wasn't sure if she really wanted to hear it.

'Oh God, it's—' Suzanne was cut off by the abrasive shrill of the school bell. Time for lessons. 'Okay, I'll tell you later.'

Andie shrugged and picked up her books, but she had to admit, she *was* intrigued. She was wondering what Jonathan had been up to. Since that awkward moment in the kitchen at her dinner party they'd kept a nervous distance from each other, and though she felt it was for the best, she did miss the intimacy of their friendship.

Speak of the devil. As she rounded the corridor, she passed Jonathan. He was holding a giant cuddly giraffe – presumably for another of his drama projects? Over the past few weeks, whenever they'd passed each other they'd exchanged awkward glances. But today, to her surprise, he flattened down the fluffy ears and flashed her a broad grin, crying: 'Mrs Wilkins – my favourite teacher!'

'Well, you're in a good mood.'

'Yep – I'm on the up. I've got some news about Suzanne – shit, I'll tell you later,' he added, seeing Cloones striding round the corner.

Suzanne and Jonathan. Both in a great mood. *Suzanne and Jonathan.* Andie knew it was silly to jump to conclusions, but surely it could only mean one thing?

Don't be silly, it's too soon, way too soon, she told herself. They've been seeing each other – what? – less than a month?

But then she remembered that, after all, she and Nick hadn't been going out for long when he'd proposed.

They'd been having dinner in a Chinese restaurant when he'd suddenly leaned across their little ceramic dishes of wriggly noodles and spicy chicken and plucked open a blue-velvet box. Andie had been so stunned she'd choked on her mouthful of food and had had to swallow a glass of water; when she'd recovered, red eyes streaming, deeply embarrassed, her heart had been doing a crazy little dance and screaming, 'Oh my God! He's *proposed*! Oh yes, say YES, say YES, YES, YES!'

But her brain had thought otherwise. 'Nick, I'm sorry . . .' she'd found herself stuttering.

He'd quickly snapped the ring away, laugh-shrugging as if, hey, it had all been a joke anyway, picking up his chopsticks and stuffing himself with noodles. She remembered how, in the taxi home, they'd barely spoken to each other, and when she'd been dropped off at her flat he'd given her a cool, chaste kiss on the cheek that said it all.

Back in her flat, Andie had suffered the longest, longest night of her life. She'd been convinced that she'd lost him. She'd played herself long horror movies about other girls

Nick had his eye on, and would start dating from dawn tomorrow, so that in six months' time she'd hear the rumours: 'Oh, did you hear Nick and Angela are getting married? Don't they make *such* a sweet couple?' And she'd have to go to the wedding and try not to tear the bride's lacy veil off and pummel her to the floor when the priest asked if anyone had any objections to the union. In the end she'd given up on sleep, just sat and watched the orange dawn rising and the hands dragging round the clock. How early could she call him?

But she hadn't needed to. There had been a knock on her door. Nick, who clearly hadn't slept either, was standing there. She'd flung herself into his arms and cried, 'Yes, I meant yes . . .'

Andie smiled as she recalled how they'd made such hearty love on her sofa that the deaf woman below had banged on her ceiling.

So why shouldn't it be the same for Suzanne and Jonathan?

Still, she thought savagely, *it might be all rosy now but it won't last. In ten years' time they'll find themselves just like me and Nick.*

Or maybe they wouldn't. Maybe in ten years' time they'd have three kids and be absolute soul-mates. She felt like crying at the thought, but since she was in the middle of teaching her class about Queen Victoria she thought it was best that she didn't.

So when the bell rang for the end of school she found herself copying the children. For once she was the first out of the door, sprinting to the staff room. Suzanne was waiting for her, making a cup of tea.

'We've split up,' said Suzanne cheerfully.

'*What?*'

'Yeah it was –' Suzanne broke off as Jonathan came in – 'that bastard who dumped me!' She laughed as Jonathan came up and gave her a hug from behind.

'So glad to see you're still friends,' said Andie.

'Oh, we hate each other,' said Jonathan. 'I'm only being nice to her because she's still got six of my favourite CDs!' Then he laughed as Suzanne hit him and told him she'd given them all to charity.

As a result, Andie drove home in a good mood, despite the traffic and the extra work she'd had to do for the parents' evening. *Andie, you are so vile,* she kept telling herself. *Everything's died down with Jonathan now anyway; how can you be such a bitch?*

Maybe it was just because it was nice to know someone else had failed at a relationship, Andie mused. Because her marriage was definitely looking as though it wasn't going to pass its end of term exam. Even their sex life had been affected. Nick had become impotent.

At first they'd just laughed it off. It had never happened to them before, and oddly enough, Andie had almost found it touching that Nick could have a sexual weakness. But then it had happened twice, and then three times, and then it wasn't funny any more.

She'd never considered sex that important after their years together but it was; removing it was like taking the spinal cord out of their marriage, leaving it limp and sprawling. Nick had started sleeping in the spare room, complaining her insomnia kept him awake. And he didn't kiss her goodnight properly any more – just nervous little pecks, as though he was worried she might try to drag him into bed, leading to the inevitable failure and embarrassment. Even his hugs were stiff and jerky. And – worst of all – as if to make up for his failure and

274

prove he was still a man, he was flirting with Cara more than ever.

The moment Andie came home from work, Nick came racing out of the kitchen to say an exuberant hello. Beethoven and Mozart also had the same idea. They beat Nick to it, dashing out in front of him. As a surprised Andie wriggled out of her coat, Beethoven tried to lick her face while Mozart insisted on burying his nose into her groin.

'Mozart, don't!' Andie chided. Since Andie was the only person who really scared him, Mozart backed off. Then he turned suddenly and went galloping down the hallway, letting out a nerve-twanging howl; Beethoven followed, his tail frisking all over the place like a frenetic question mark.

'What's up with the dogs?' Andie enquired. She looked rather grumpy and there were make-up smudges under her eyes. 'Have you fed them?'

'I certainly have,' said Nick, drawing her into his arms and trying to waltz her up and down the hallway. 'Cara made this *amazing* meal and I just feel so horny. Let's go to bed.'

Andie let him tug her up the stairs. What was going on? Nick had barely laid a finger on her for weeks and now he'd turned into Casanova. And although she pretended to laugh with Nick and look excited, in truth she felt far too tired to make love, or kiss, or even talk. All she wanted to do was kick off her shoes and have a hot chocolate, unwind with a long bath and then sink into bed – she'd just put new sheets on this morning so they'd be so lovely and crisp. She was at the point of exhaustion where she knew she could steamroll over her insomnia and crash out for ten hours, at least.

Upstairs on the landing, Nick was about to pick Andie up in his arms and carry her into the bedroom when Fred appeared in the hallway, crying and saying that he'd had a nightmare and was terrified there were some Teletubbies under his bed.

'Oh Fred!' Nick rolled his eyes at the unbelievable timing. 'For goodness sake, Teletubbies are *nice*. They're not like werewolves or vampires. I don't see how you can be scared of them, you silly thing?' He picked Fred up in his arms, rubbing his nose against his son's wet cheeks.

'Can I sleep in Mummy's bed?' Fred wailed.

'Look, I'll tuck you into your bed and leave the bedroom door open so the light shines in. I want you to try and sleep and if you get really scared, then you can come in. Are you going to try for me, Fred?'

Fred nodded sulkily, rubbing his eyes.

Andie gave Fred a reassuring kiss and then went into the bedroom, feeling relieved. Then Nick came in after her, curling his arms around her.

'Oh Nick – I need to—'

'Don't,' Nick groaned. 'Come on, before Fred wakes up again.'

Andie reluctantly crawled on to the bed, opening her legs and looking rather like a patient being forced to have an examination by a gynaecologist.

'We should close the curtains,' she muttered, squeezing back a yawn.

'I can't be bothered,' said Nick, advancing on her. He wanted her so badly. God, he hadn't felt like this for *weeks*.

He couldn't understand why he'd been impotent. It had been awful and humiliating and made him feel like a confused teenager again. Not tonight though. Tonight, suddenly, as though he'd snapped his fingers, it had all changed. Desire raged inside him. He had an erection like a steeple. Andie, lying beneath him, suddenly looked so beautiful. Part of him wanted to make love to her all at once and the other half wanted to stretch it out into hours of excruciating pleasure. He held her hips between his knees and bent down on her, teasing with nearly-but-not-quite kisses until she was arching her head in frustration. Nick smiled; then he leaned in and kissed her properly, his tongue exploring her mouth. Happy pride flooded through him. He wanted to give his penis a pat and say: 'We're back, boy; we're back in business!' Thrilled now, he ran his kisses over her neck, lightly biting the soft skin, moaning, his head cloudy—

—when suddenly there was a crash and the door burst open.

'Fred!' Nick groaned. Then something heavy bounced on to the bed and Nick realised it wasn't Fred but the dogs. They were chasing each other and cut a path straight over Nick and Andie, bouncing off the bed and on to the rug.

'What the hell?' Nick cried. Normally the dogs were in their baskets at this time of night. So why was Beethoven trying to pin Mozart down and jump on top of him?

'It looks as if they're trying to mate,' Andie laughed.

'This isn't funny! The dogs are neutered and they're both boys. Since when were dogs ever gay?'

'We'll have to rename them Graham and Norton!'

'Ha ha. Come on, you two, out!'

Nick took them both by their collars and hauled them out.

'Daaad,' Fred called from his bedroom. 'Can I come and see what's going on?'

'No, you can't! Go to sleep!' Nick slammed the bedroom door shut with a thunderous clap. He stormed to the window and started to yank the curtains shut. He was about to close the window when a neighbour, an old man who always wore a tweed cap, rain or shine, and was one of the more crochety people on their road, caught sight of him, pushed up his cap and called out: 'Can't you keep those dogs quiet? They're driving me mad.'

Nick lost his temper. 'You mad! They're driving *me* mad. Can't I – for just half an hour – have enough peace and quiet to have sex with my wife?' Then he banged the window shut.

Andie burst into laughter as Nick came and sat down on the bed. Smiling, he gazed down at her. She had a sexy smile on her face and she was twisting a strand of curly hair around her finger and teasing the end against her lips like a schoolgirl; the effect was an unintended combination of innocence and wantonness that reignited his desire instantly.

He leaned down and kissed her.

The kiss went on and on and Andie suddenly found her desire passing away like a shower, clouds of tiredness seeping back. *Just get on with it, will you?* she thought. Then: *What a terrible thing to think.*

Suddenly Andie found herself thinking of Jonathan. Back in the kitchen. His fingers on her lips. Her eyes flew open and she looked at Nick, but his were closed; his face was hungry, engrossed in the kiss. She closed her eyes again. *I didn't do anything,* she told herself, *I didn't kiss him.*

Nick pushed a finger into her mouth. She didn't bite it or respond. He caressed the scratchy-soft surface of her tongue with its tip. Andie winced as though it tasted rather unpleasant. They gazed at each other. Something unspoken passed between them. Nick slowly drew his finger out.

'Nick? Nick—'

'What?' Nick suddenly felt all his desire seep away from him. Something was wrong; something was very wrong.

Andie took the back of his hand and kissed it

apologetically. 'I'm really tired. I'm sorry. Can't I just have a bath first and then . . . we can see . . .' she trailed off.

Nick gazed down at her. He was shocked to realise that although she was genuinely sorry, she really had no desire to sleep with him.

'Okay, fine.' He got up abruptly, taking his pillow from the bed.

'Nick!' Andie sat up. 'Where are you going?'

The slam of the door indicated that it was obvious where he was going: the spare room. Andie lay back and burst into unexpected tears. She let them flow, then blew her nose and got ready for bed, feeling guilty and confused. What had just happened? It was strange; no matter how much tension there was between them, they'd always been able to make love. But tonight she'd felt something angry and resentful coiled up inside her, something that refused to let itself translate into passion. She'd felt herself *fighting* him.

Neither of them slept well that night; partly due to anxiety and partly because of their two dogs, who persisted in trying to mate each other all night long, their long, painful howls echoing down the road.

Andie had finally managed to drop off by stuffing her ears with foam earplugs when she was woken up by a door slamming. She yanked out an earplug – couldn't Nick do something about those bloody dogs – when she suddenly heard someone cursing and realised it was *Cara*. Andie listened to her stumbling up the stairs, shaking her head and laughing despite herself. Cara – drunk! Back from Sean's in the early hours of morning! And she seemed such a goody-goody. Andie put her earplugs back in. Oh well, she thought miserably, at least someone's been having some fun tonight . . .

27
Cara

I woke up the next morning feeling as though the Light Brigade were charging into my head, exploding cannons and giant puffs of black smoke. My eyes felt so raw it seemed as though they'd been hollowed out. As I opened them a peep, horrible yellow sleepydust clogged them up and I brushed it away, and then I remembered.

I remembered it all.

Last night . . . Sean . . . the cocktails . . . *kissing* . . . and . . . a row . . . and hating each other . . .

Quickly, I dammed up my memories. I didn't want to think about them.

There was a knock on my door and a small head popped through. Fred emerged, giggling.

'Dad told me to come and wake you up!' he said, clambering on to my bed. 'So I brought you breakfast in bed.'

He held out a sweaty biscuit. I nearly nibbled it, but the pungent whiff coming off it made me want to puke. I examined it closely: it was bone-shaped. Fred couldn't reach the biscuit tin in the far corner of the top cupboard, so he'd obviously raided the dogs' bowls instead.

'Er, thanks, Fred, that's lovely,' I said. 'I think I'll save it for later, if you don't mind.'

Fred smiled and nestled against me under the covers. We lay there for a while, watching my dreamcatcher spin and whirl in the gentle morning breeze. My throbbing head calmed to a peaceful ache and, despite last night, I felt a sense of fulfilment warm over me. Fred had stopped fighting me. We were finally friends.

Then my eyes slid to the clock.

'AHHHHHH! It's eight-thirty!' I cried. 'Your mum – oh God – she had to go in early; I'm supposed to be taking you and you – you have to be at school in *five minutes*!'

Fred seemed to think it was all very amusing. I sent him to get dressed and dragged on some clothes. My head hurt more than ever. I filled a mug with water and downed it, hoping it might dilute the pain. It didn't.

Oh God. I couldn't even use a potion to clear my head; I dragged out my altar cloth and sat crossed-legged on the floor, hastily trying to bless one; I felt my magic creeping feebly through my veins like cement. I had paid the price for my drinking: I was human, and therefore I suffered.

I was just dragging Fred down the stairs while filling his schoolbag and helping him tie his laces when I heard voices in the porch.

Sean! Nick was chatting to Sean.

I quickly dragged Fred into the living room. The voices lulled. Then, through the net curtains, I saw Sean weeding the front beds outside. Oh great. How was I supposed to avoid him?

'Cara!' Nick came into the living room, looking cross. 'You're supposed to be taking Fred to school!'

'We're going!' I cried. As Nick strode out, I bent down in front of Fred and said in an insistent voice: 'Fred, we're going to go outside into the garden and we're *not* going to talk to Sean – we're going to run past him, okay?'

'Why?' Fred asked.

'Because he's a bastard and I hate him,' I burst out without thinking. 'I mean – he's very nice, but we're in a rush, right?'

'Right!' Fred looked pleased, as though it was all an exciting game.

I clutched his hand and led him up to the front door as though we were entering a war zone; 'Okay, we're going in!'

We raced down the garden path, all flurried and self-important. Out of the corner of my eye, I saw Sean glancing at me. Then he swallowed, grinned and said, 'All right, Fred?'

Fred? Hang on, what about me? Was I the invisible woman? Suddenly I felt deeply cross. It was okay for me to ignore Sean, but not for him to ignore me.

'Come on, Fred,' I said sharply.

'Yeah, we don't like you and we're not talking to you 'cos you're a bastard,' said Fred to Sean.

Oh God. *Fred!* I saw the hurt on Sean's face. As he turned away, I also caught sight of the bruise on his cheek: a red welt laced with purple. I'd done that to him last night, I suddenly remembered, cringeing with shame.

I hurried Fred off to school. As I dropped him off, Fred turned to me, eyes mooning in worry, and said: 'Did I say the right thing?'

'Sure, Fred,' I lied gently.

'Look, I can beat him up for you if you want me to,' he said, doubling up his fists fiercely.

'Oh Freddy!' Suddenly I laughed and felt tears in my eyes. 'It's fine. Don't worry about it. It's fine.'

But it wasn't fine.

As I walked home slowly, I lingered over the whole night, piece by piece.

The cocktails: all four of them. A Long Slow Screw Against A Bicycle Wheel had been followed by A Long Slow Screw In An Asda Shopping Trolley (vodka, orange juice and a few Asda glacé cherries) followed by A Long Slow Screw In A Bouncy Castle (vodka, orange juice and whisky) followed by An Abrupt Screw Because He Couldn't Get It Up (I can't remember what went into this one; we were too busy giggling our heads off because we thought the name was *hilarious* – which shows just how drunk we were).

All in all, I was having a good time. Over the course of the evening I slowly got over the alcohol – as my magical antennae drooped, I became less sensitive to the demons in the drink, and I even started to enjoy the taste. In turn, however, the drink seemed to heighten the effect of the aphrodisiac. We couldn't stop tickling and sharing sips and feeding each other cherries and threading little cocktail umbrellas in our hair and sharing lingering glances. I had a fluttery feeling in the pit of my stomach. We were in exactly the same situation we'd been in last time I was over at Sean's, that feeling of tension in the air, the sense of inevitability that sooner or later one of us was going to cross the line . . . But this time it was a little different. Sean could see it. I wasn't going to be held back by my mother.

I was fed up with being 'Miss Uptight Compulsive Handwasher', as Sean put it. I was taking this whole magic thing way too seriously. Andie's words echoed in my mind: *you're only twenty-five, you're young, enjoy yourself!* Just because Sean and I were from different worlds, it didn't mean to say we couldn't *try* dating. Okay, so it might not work out between us, but at least we could have a go. And have some fun while we were at it . . .

But things didn't turn out quite as I had expected.

We had just gone into the kitchen to make cocktail number five (not yet christened) when the light bulb went out with a yellow flash and a fizzle.

'Okay, you make the cocktail, I'll change the bulb,' Sean said, rummaging in the cupboard for a spare. Humming merrily, I took the lid off the mixer.

'Sean, what's your ideal woman?' I asked suddenly.

'Hmm?' He looked up and banged his head against the cupboard door laughing and rubbing it better.

'Well, you asked me, now it's my turn to ask. Come on, your Miss Totally and Utterly Perfect?'

'Oh, I don't really have one, to be honest,' he said vaguely.

'Oh, so you just do one-night stands, do you?' I asked cheekily.

'No!' he protested, extracting a bulb and standing up, the alcohol exaggerating the rather indignant expression on his face. 'I'm just too old for that crap now. I did all that when I was younger, and it was fun, but I got fed up of waking up in strange beds feeling empty. So I guess I am looking for Miss Right, though I can't say I really know how to describe her . . . I just think that when I meet her, I'll know.'

I felt a warm glow spread over me. So if we did get together, it was going to last more than one night . . .

'Come on, girl, get on with that cocktail!' he laughed, quickly changing the subject.

In the dim light I could barely see the labels on the bottles but hey, what the hell, it was all good stuff! I thought blurrily. I switched it on and—

—*WHAM!* There was a huge explosion. I felt something cold and wet splatter across my face, heard *phat*

phat! sounds as it hit the walls and ceiling. I turned the mixer off and looked at Sean. He slowly wiped off the blobs that had splashed across his face.

'Oops,' I said in a small voice, 'I forgot to put the lid on.'

Sean ran his eyes over me. I was literally dripping with alcohol. I thought he was going to tell me off, but he collapsed into laughter.

'Sean, this is NOT funny!' I growled, a smile twitching at my lips.

'It is, it is! Oh God, Cara, I'm *so* glad I got you drunk. You – you're just hysterical . . .'

'Oh great . . . I'm hystyrical . . . I mean . . . hysterectomy . . . I mean . . .'

'You are absolutely classic. Come on, we'd better get you into the shower, honey.' As Sean led me out into the hallway, I ricocheted against the wall. 'God, you *are* pissed, aren't you? You girly lightweight!'

'Piss off! You're the one who force-fed me!' I cried. I winced as I noticed that I'd left rather a nasty red stain on the cream wallpaper.

'Whoops, sorreee,' I slurred.

'S'alright,' said Sean. 'It needs a splash of colour to brighten it up. Hey,' he grabbed my waist in a playful tickle, 'maybe I should pretend you're a paint-roller and rub you up and down the walls.'

'*Sean!* Remember that I'm covered in gunk and if you start being mean to me, I'm going to give you a hug.'

'Okay, okay. Now – watch it – here's the stairs.'

As he dragged me up, I suddenly felt the effects of the aphrodisiac returning. I could feel a pleasurable tingle of excitement at the bottom of my spine. *It's going to happen,* I thought excitedly, *we're finally going to get together and I'm completely drunk but I don't care, I want him to take advantage of me, oh yes please.*

Up in the bathroom, I climbed clumsily into the bath and sat down with all my clothes on.

'Er – it might help if you take your clothes off,' said Sean.

Well, that was a come on!

I started to tug at my jumper when, through the wool, I heard him cry, 'I meant – when I'd left the room – oh God, now you're stuck!'

The jumper had caught around my face and I flailed my arms about, my mouth full of wool. Sean came over and helped me tug it off. I gazed down, relieved to see I was wearing a decent bra: creamy and lacy. Sean had a quick glance too.

'You're staring at my breasts, aren't you?' I demanded, giggling.

'No!' Though he was drunk, he wasn't beyond blushing.

'Liar!' I poked out my tongue at him and he cracked up again.

'Look at you – sitting in the bath, pulling faces!' He shook his head. 'All right, I don't think you're going to manage to handle the shower so just sit tight and I'll hose you down.'

Sean had just turned away to fiddle with the taps when – oh –

I stood up and shyly slid my arms around his waist and gently kissed the back of his neck. I felt him stiffen and draw in a deep, shuddering breath; I felt his heart speed up and reverberate through his rib-cage. He slowly turned to face me. I saw wonder in his bloodshot eyes. He smiled and leaned over and kissed me on the lips – a sweet, vodka-flavoured kiss – and then whispered in my ear, 'When you came over tonight, I definitely wasn't expecting this to happen.'

I smiled. Neither was I. Well, not really . . .

We kissed lusciously and then he let out a yelp as I got over-excited and yanked him forwards. He lost his balance and we half-fell, half-collapsed into the bath. I banged my head on the tiles; Sean grazed his forehead against the taps.

For a moment, we lay groaning and nursing our wounds. Then we smiled at each other, rubbing our noses in a gentle Eskimo kiss. Then we started giggling. Then kissing. Again and again and again.

I felt something leap in my stomach and I pulled away, groaning.

'What?' Sean touched my cheek.

'I feel a bit sick.' I rubbed my tummy, then smiled, dazed. 'No, I think I'm okay.'

'Are you sure?' Sean asked. Suddenly he sat up, looking all serious and worried. 'Cara, maybe this isn't a good thing. I think it might be best if you went home.'

'I don't want to go home,' I said sulkily. 'I want you.' I reached up to hug him and one of my bra straps fell down my shoulder. In the manner of a reproving parent, Sean pulled it back up. Then he got out of the bath and picked up my jumper.

Suddenly I felt stone cold sober. I realised I was not only behaving like a brazen hussy but making a complete fool of myself. I got up and slowly took my jumper from him, pulling it back on despite the fact it was still covered in gunk.

'Come on,' he said, trying to sound jovial. 'I think it's time you were in bed, young lady. Why don't we have a cup of coffee and then you can shower back home?'

'But I want to be with you,' I moaned unhappily.

'Cara – I'm sorry. I really shouldn't have kissed you. It was a mistake, the timing was crap and I just feel . . .'

And on and on he went. I can't remember precisely what he said; it was like a radio station a few degrees off

287

frequency, a mixture of the odd clear phrase and high-pitched fuzziness. I remember stuff like 'Don't want to take advantage' and 'Not the right time' and 'When you're sober' and 'Unsuitable'. I stood there, his words pouring over me, feeling more and more insulted. *What was this crap?* Basically, his waffle could be encapsulated in one sentence: Sean did not fancy me. He might have been tempted in the past with our near-kisses but when it came to the crunch I obviously didn't do it for him. He was simply too bloody polite to say so.

And that was when I did the awful thing. I don't know where the urge came from; all the alcohol seemed to have congregated in my right hand, which flew up with an inebriated mind of its own and – *wham!* – slapped him.

Sean recoiled in shock.

'Goodnight,' I said and flounced out.

And that was how the evening ended.

So now you see why I never drink: aside from ruining my magical skills, I turn into my mother.

He was still there.

I had dawdled home for a good half-hour but Sean was still in the front garden. I hesitated, wondering if I could go shopping. But this was silly – I couldn't hide from him for ever. And then suddenly his voice made me jump.

'Cara,' he said through the hedge. 'Can we talk?'

I came into the garden and crossed my arms, my heart beating.

'Look, I'm sorry about last night. Can we just forget all about it and be friends? It seems silly and childish to worry about it . . .'

Friendship. He drove the final nail home in my coffin of hope.

288

'I mean – I'm sorry – I just got drunk and I was way out of line getting you so drunk – it was all so messy . . . and . . .'

Messy. A messy mistake, that's how he saw it. I gazed into his lovely eyes and thought wildly: *I can't bear this. I'm going to cast a spell on him. I'm going to make him fall in love with me the way I'm falling in love with him.*

And then I realised with a sickening thud I'd already performed a spell. Last night he'd eaten bewitched food and it hadn't worked.

My eyes fell to the grass and I felt sadness seep into me. I realised then that even magic had its limits. Love was like alchemy – you could try fancy tricks and manipulations and magical chemical reactions but in the end, if the passion wasn't genuine, you were still left with a lump of useless lead. I couldn't make Sean love me and nothing could change that.

'Cara?' Sean stepped forwards, rubbing my arm. 'Please don't be mad at me. Everything in my life is so crappy right now, and being friends with you over the last few months has been so fabulous . . . I really value our friendship so much and I'd hate to lose it.'

'No, it's fine.' I managed to trammel my tears back down my throat. I tossed back my hair and smiled. 'Of course we're still friends. I love being friends with you too; you're lovely!'

'Oh, thank God for that!'

And then he did something awful. He pulled me into a hug and held me with such deep affection I felt my heart would break. It was obvious that Sean did care for me, but only as a friend, a sister, somebody he could never really feel any passion for.

28
Cara

Over the next few days, I desperately wanted to avoid
Sean, but I felt it would then look obvious that I fancied
him. So I put on my best act. Every time we exchanged
banter over the garden fence, I teased him carelessly when
really I wanted to grab hold of him and shout, 'Why don't
you fancy me? What's *wrong* with me? Do you secretly
think I'm a freak too?' He was so sweet to me – horribly,
infuriatingly sweet. Every day he left me a different
chocolate bar in the porch; the chocolate tasted
simultaneously gorgeous and horrible. And nearly every
night after Fred had gone to bed, he called me up or
tossed me a paper aeroplane through my window saying:
Come and watch TV with me and Kieran! We discovered we
shared a love for sci-fi videos and stayed up late renting all
our favourites, from *Alien* to *The Man Who Fell To Earth*;
we went out for kite-flying expeditions with Maeve and
Fred; we played cards and Sean taught me how to cheat at
poker; we swapped our favourite books and I taught him
to love all my favourites; and sometimes we just sat about
talking for hours about nothing very much. Ironically,
we'd never been closer.

One night we lit a bonfire in his back garden and toasted marshmallows and made up stories about the stars.

'Now we've got the "relationship thing" out of the way, it's so much easier between us, isn't it?' Sean sighed, putting his arm around me and dropping a kiss on my head. 'The thing is, relationships never last. If we had gone out, we'd only end up getting bored, falling out, making demands and three months later never speaking to each other. But friendship . . . friendship lasts for ever.'

'Oh yes,' I lied with a wide grin, cuddled up against him.

I kept reminding myself that it could never have worked: I was a witch and he was a human. But you know how it is: no matter how much your head berates you like a world-weary parent, your heart acts like a spoiled kid who just goes ahead and does their own thing.

Laura was away on holiday for a week and she had left Sean to look after Maeve. Maeve and Fred were now best of buddies. Fred was practising frantically for his school concert; Maeve, with astonishing patience, would sit and listen for hours while he scraped his bow over the strings, and then clap her hands and cry, 'Wow, Fred, you're *so* good!' Several times, Sean remarked grimly under his breath, 'I'm worried Maeve's showing signs of early hearing problems!'

The night before Maeve was due to go home, she begged us to let her come along to Fred's concert. Sean was devastated not to be able to come too but he was now doing some shifts at the Goat to help pay for Maeve's school fees. I tried not to linger too much on images of Sean pulling pints and flirting with sexy barmaids.

That night, however, twenty minutes before we were due to leave, something disastrous happened. I had called my grandmother for a chat when I noticed Nick walking through the kitchen, opening a drawer, and going pale. Oh God, it was the drawer containing his present from Andie. I hastily hung up the phone.

'That . . . that . . . *thing* . . . in the drawer,' he said faintly. He hadn't got the job he'd been interviewed for and it had knocked his confidence slightly.

'The watch. Yes,' I winced. 'It is an anniversary present, from Andie to, um, you.'

'You let her buy it?'

'Nick, it's not my fault! She only bought it to show you how much she cares and—'

Nick heard the tread of Andie's footsteps on the stairs. She was humming carelessly, happily, and broke off to say, 'Fred, are you nearly ready yet?'

Nick stared at me, looking helpless.

'Nick, you have to tell her you still haven't got a job. Now.'

Nick nodded and left the room. I heard him say to Andie quietly, 'Could we just have a chat upstairs?'

I took a nervous sip of tea and tried to study a magazine on the table. *Okay, Dionysius,* I prayed, *please can it not be too horrible. Please can Andie be forgiving, please can she see the bright side of the situation—*

'WHAT DO YOU MEAN, YOU LOST YOUR JOB MONTHS AGO!' Andie's voice reverberated through the ceiling and the house seemed to shake in its very foundations.

The row carried on for a good fifteen minutes. Fred came into the kitchen and rolled his eyes sullenly at the ceiling. Somehow, the gesture struck me as being worse than him bursting into tears as he might have done a month or two ago; his air of weary, resigned cynicism made him suddenly seem like an adult, not a child.

'If we don't go, we're going to miss it,' he moaned.

'Okay, let me see if I can sort them out,' I said, going upstairs and gingerly entering The War Zone.

'Oh yes – the concert,' said Nick, glad to be extracted from the argument. 'We'd better get going.'

'We can't go!' Andie cried. 'We've got to sort this out!' 'We can't let Fred down.'

For a moment they glared at each other intently. 'Okay, fine,' said Andie, snatching up her bag. 'We'll go.'

We all climbed into the car; Fred, Maeve and I in the back, Andie and Nick in the front. We'd only been going for five minutes when Fred said that he felt sick. Then we hit a traffic jam.

'Mum, we're going to be late,' Fred said edgily.

'Well, I told your father to get ready ages ago.'

'I was ready,' Nick retorted. 'If you hadn't been having such a go at me—'

'Oh, and how terrible that was of me. You've only gone and lost your job and, strangely enough, I'm annoyed. What did you expect me to do, give you a massage?'

And they were off, playing the blame game, throwing insults at each other like a ball. In the back, Fred and Maeve and I sat in silence. Finally, thankfully, we reached the school gates. There was a large banner saying SCHOOL CONCERT on the gates; some cheeky pupil had scrawled over it in pink neon *Britney Spears LIVE!*

The concert was being held in the school hall. It was nearly full by the time we arrived, so we had to make do with seats at the back. Fred went to the front while Maeve sat down next to me, reading the programme with a slight frown on her face as though she was a music critic about to dissect a rendition of Rachmaninov. Sophie West, one of Andie's pupils, came running up, banging her trumpet case against the seat.

'Mrs Wilkins, I'm going to play "Land of Hope and Horny",' she said with a giggle. Andie forced a smile and said she couldn't wait, but as Sophie was whisked away by her overbearing parents, Andie got up abruptly. 'I need the toilet,' she snapped, shoving past Nick.

An awkward silence fell. Beside me, Nick was folding his programme into squares.

'Don't worry,' I said to him gently. 'It'll be okay.' Though I wasn't convinced it would be.

He did his Nick thing, his Nick way of coping; he just shrugged his shoulders and laughed, as if it was all a minor tiff and he didn't care. Though the look in his eyes suggested he did.

I gave his shoulder a gentle rub. Various teachers were sitting at the front of the hall, including Jonathan. A number of female staff were flirting with him; one of them brought him a mug of tea, and he said, 'Cheers' but sipped it distractedly. I noticed him looking up and down the rows as though he was searching for someone.

Then the headteacher appeared next to us, saying how pleased she was with Fred's musical progress.

'When's Britney Spears going to be on?' Nick asked innocently. Unfortunately, Ms Cloones took him seriously and explained the problems of graffiti at length.

'So I'm afraid she won't be here,' she concluded, as though Britney had very nearly been persuaded, had it not been for another pressing engagement.

Nick and I nearly exploded into giggles. Somehow, behaving like naughty children relieved the tension.

'Cara, do you need to go to the toilet?' Maeve interrupted rather disapprovingly, as though I was a child that she needed to supervise.

'Yes, Maeve,' I teased her, 'I need you to show me where it is.'

In the toilets, Maeve washed her hands very carefully with soap and water and dried them on a paper towel. I examined my reflection in the mirror. God, I looked a state. My roots were showing a good inch now, but as Sean wasn't interested in me I just couldn't be bothered to get them done. I suddenly became aware of Maeve watching me intently, copying my gestures and combing her fingers through her hair like me. I hid a smile.

'You're pretty,' she said, also smiling. 'Dad says so, anyway.'

'Does he?' I jumped violently.

'Yeah. Just last night he was saying so to Granddad.'

'I . . .' Then I caught myself. Maeve did like matchmaking; she could be making it all up and she was such a little minx that I knew I'd never get the real truth out of her.

'Cara,' she said as we left the toilets, 'are you thirsty?'

'What?' I muttered, my mind still reeling. 'Oh. I see. Would you like some water? You wait here, I'll just pop into the staff room.'

It was then that I saw her. As I approached the door I saw Andie in the shadows, passionately kissing a young man. I was so shocked I scurried on. It was only a few minutes later, back in the hall as the orchestra started up, that I realised who he was. Jonathan.

I sat there, listening to the cacophony of the orchestra warming up, feeling a cold sweat crawling over me like bugs. I couldn't believe it. Yes, I'd been suspicious of Jonathan and Andie ever since seeing them in the Ritzy together but deep down I'd never really believed it was anything more than a flirtation. Now all my worst fears were confirmed. Just how long had it been going on? Why and how?

And what the hell was I supposed to do now? Go running out there after them and tell them off like a schoolteacher? Fred, who was practicising his violin at the front, kept glancing over the rows of heads, looking worried, wondering where his mum was.

'Have you seen Andie?' Nick leaned over and asked me.

'No!' I jumped and he looked slightly taken aback. 'I didn't see her in the loos . . . maybe she, er, took a walk or something.'

'Don't worry, she's probably just faffing about with her hair as per usual,' he sighed.

I noticed that at the front of the hall, several teachers were chatting and looking worried. I couldn't help feeling paranoid that perhaps someone else had also spotted Andie and Jonathan. I mean, how could they be so *obvious*? It was as if Andie *wanted* to get caught out.

The audience quietened down as Fred and two other violinists started a scratchy rendition of Pacibel. I closed my eyes, searching for a vision, trying to see them . . . running across the empty playground together, giggling nervously. For a moment I caught a taste of Andie's lust, a hollow yearning in her stomach as though she hadn't eaten for weeks. Their sharp prickles of fear as they spotted someone coming. They quickly slid behind a tree, avoiding a passing teacher. They laughed with relief when she'd gone, hurrying out into the core of the dark woods, crashing through bushes and branches . . .

I opened my eyes. There was polite applause as the violinists took their bows. Fred looked edgy. As the orchestra plunged into 'Land of Hope and Glory', I noticed him lifting his bow a millimetre from the strings and pretending to play. He'd lost his confidence; his chin was quivering against his neck-rest. My panic started to mount again and I looked out of the window, the last dying embers of the sunset in the sky. And in a flash of relief the answer came to me. A distraction.

It had been a long time since I'd practised any weather magic. My mother practised it all the time; she was always telling me about the storms she whipped up, the rain she calmed. It was just a question of will. I closed my eyes, rolling together all my worry and fear into a quivering peak of determination. I could feel the air, hot and dry, start to tremble around me, a sudden moistness in the air molecules. My mind arrowed through the sky, searching for floating, carefree clouds, calling them, gathering a jostling grey cumulus mass above the school. I remembered with a smile a story I'd told Fred a few days ago about how rain came from old women who lived in the clouds, washing out their clothes with their knarled hands. A few drops of water spat against the windows, a few on the playground. I felt triumphant excitement ballooning inside me, my mind expanding, my soul stretching upwards like a giant. I reached out with a huge invisible hand, tickling my fingertips like a harpist along the blue ribbons of sky. I pictured Andie and Jonathan lying in the woods, on a bed of bark and moss, kissing hotly ... The sky moaned with delicious pleasure; I dipped my fingers into the clouds and there was a groan of painful thunder, a quiver of lightning zig-zagging down like a boomerang, whirling back into the sky. The clouds erupted. Suddenly the rain fell in huge sheets, hammering against the windows in diagonal droves.

'Cara,' Maeve moaned, slipping her hand into mine.

I opened my eyes, coming to. Her eyes were round with fear and I gave her a little cuddle, whispering: 'It's all right, darling, it's just a little storm.'

Beside me, Nick joked into my ear: 'Did you fall asleep? If only I could.'

297

I looked back at the orchestra with a wince. The storm was distracting them; they kept looking up at the ceiling and missing notes. As a gust of wind suddenly tore in through the doors, a few sheets of music went sailing on to the floor.

I suddenly jumped as Jonathan sidled in. He was holding hands with Sophie West, who was looking rather tearful. I frowned in confusion. Andie was nowhere to be seen. What on earth was going on? Had I got it all wrong?

As the orchestra swept into a dire finale, Sophie wove her way to her seat and joined in. Her enthusiasm for her trumpet was tremendous; she blew great snorting notes like a mating elephant. Nick was trying so hard not to laugh his body shook. I bit back a smile as Sophie's mother turned and gave us both an icy glance. As 'Land of Hope and Glory' roused to an unrecognisable end, she was the first to break the appalled silence with loud clapping. Nick blew a few sarcastic wolf-whistles, catching my reproving glance.

'You are naughty,' I hissed at him, and we both laughed again.

'I didn't know you could play heavy metal on the trumpet,' I overheard one parent saying.

'Where's Mummy?' Fred asked, running up with his violin, his face tense again. 'How did I sound?'

'Sensational wasn't the word,' Nick said but I frowned at him and said warmly: 'You were great, Fred, really great.'

'I don't care what you think, I want to know what Mum thinks,' Fred retorted sulkily. But his face softened when Maeve flew at him with a hug and told him he was the best violin player ever.

Nick sensibly suggested that Andie had probably gone back to the car. I knew she wouldn't be there and I kept telling him that we ought to look around for her.

'Come on, Cara, we hardly need to send out a search party,' he said, giving me a weird look. As Nick went to get the car, Fred, Maeve and I huddled outside against a wall, shivering. Water sluiced in a stream from the gutter; rain splished and splashed against my face, Nature inviting me to come and play. I shook my head, whispering: 'It's time to stop now . . .'

As Nick pulled up, I was surprised to see Andie sitting in the front seat. We all climbed into the back.

'Are you okay, Andie?' I asked, my voice high.

'We just had a bit of trouble with one of the girls, Sophie,' said Andie. 'She had last-minute nerves and we had to sort her out.' Seeing our faces, she added quickly, 'I couldn't come back in, I started getting a migraine.' She curled her hand against her temple, hiding her expression. 'I'm so sorry, Fred, I'm so sorry I missed you.'

Fred gave her a look that suggested it would be a long time before she was forgiven.

The sky was angry now, angry that I'd used and abused her, that I was refusing to continue playing our game. She sent a gale whistling after us, leaves flying against the windscreen, the wind hammering its fists against the windows. I surreptitiously opened the window a fraction, breathed in a gulp of wild air, held it in my throat, murmuring soothing words, opened my mouth and let it fly back out: my peace offering to the sky. The wind calmed a little; the rain slowed to a damp, melancholy trickle.

'Oh well,' said Nick, pulling into the drive and switching off the engine. 'The forecasts predicted a gale so we've probably got off lightly. Feeling better now, darling?' He rubbed Andie's shoulder.

'A little.' She couldn't even look at him. 'I think I'll just go to bed.'

'We can talk about everything in the morning,' said Nick with a broad smile. He tried to kiss her goodnight but she turned her head.

Nick insisted on taking Fred up to bed and reading him his story.

'But Cara normally reads it,' said Fred.

'Tonight it's going to me, okay?' said Nick.

'Now you're fired you can read to me every night,' Fred reflected cheerfully.

Afterwards, standing in the shadows of the kitchen, I saw Nick come down the stairs, his face haggard. I heard the creak of the living room door, the chink of the whisky bottle, and I swore to myself that I would try to help them, to weave some magic that would bind them back into a happy family again . . .

29
Andie

Hummus? No. *Sun-dried tomatoes?* No. *Smoked salmon?* Definitely not.

Andie stood in the middle of the supermarket, a wire basket in her hand, and felt like screaming.

She was only just realising how much she'd enjoyed shopping now that she couldn't do it any more. She loved returning home with shiny, brand new carrier bags laden with delicious food, and a new pair of shoes, or something for the house like a lampshade or a cushion cover. It wasn't so much what she bought, just the process of buying, the deliciousness of something new.

And now, *now*, all thanks to Nick, they couldn't bloody well afford anything.

'Mum, can I have a packet of chocolate raisins?' Fred asked in a tired, whiny voice. His hair was mussed up; she'd been dragging him around the shops for two hours, the poor thing.

'Well, we can't really afford treats like chocolate raisins any more,' Andie said gently.

Seeing the look on his face, anger flared up inside her again. She wanted to conjure Nick up and put him here, and have him see what it felt like to tell his son he couldn't even have a box of raisins.

'Okay, I'll put them back,' said Fred.

'No, it's fine,' Andie said sharply. 'Bugger it, let's just stick it all on the Barclaycard.'

On the way home, Fred fell asleep in the back of the car. Andie looked at him in the mirror and thought of *Jonathan kissing her, his tongue in her mouth*—

No, don't think of that, she told herself.

But she couldn't help it. All week her mind had been sliding back to that night. The school concert. When she and Jonathan had . . .

The hall had been hot and claustrophobic, children's voices kniving her ears. Her head throbbed. She was still shocked from Nick's revelation. She wanted to shake him and yell, 'Why did you lie to me? Okay, fine – you lost your job – but why lie? If I'd lost mine, I would have just cried on your shoulder and told you the truth and tried to work something out. Doesn't my opinion or my feelings count at all? We're meant to be a team but you act as if you're a one-man band and the rest of your family are just the audience, just people who watch and don't really count . . .'

Suddenly she couldn't even bear to be next to him. Muttering that she needed the loo, she shoved past him and stormed out. She needed space; quiet. The staff room was empty; a cup of coffee would help too. Jonathan had been using her mug again. Tonight she didn't care. She poured an extra large scoop of coffee granules on top of Jonathan's watery, poorly washed-out dregs and added hot water. As she took a sip she was shocked that, beneath the sting of coffee, she could taste him: his mouth, his saliva, his Jonathanness, and the caffeine rush mingled with an unexpected surge of desire.

I should have bloody well had an affair, she thought mutinously, *considering the way Nick's treated me.* Her mind was nothing but a series of question marks: why had he been fired; when, how, what? And if he had been fired – *what the fuck had he been doing hanging out in the park with his blonde secretary?*

She still couldn't face going back into the concert. She tried to soothe herself, examined the childish pictures tacked to the cupboards. Jonathan had got his class to draw all the teachers; the results were a set of wonderful caricatures. There she was, red-crayon hair frizzing out as though she'd had an electric shock. Charming.

'I can see a certain influence of Picasso in that face, can't you?' said a voice behind her. Andie jumped. It was Jonathan. He had his hands in his pockets and he was smiling.

Suddenly something clicked. Later on, she reflected that it must have been the stress. Or revenge on Nick. Or both. But anyhow – Andie put down her mug, yanked Jonathan towards her and kissed him. She saw Jonathan's pupils dilate in shock. Then he let out a deep sigh that thickened into a groan. He wound his arms around her waist and pushed her up against a cupboard. Hard. She felt a picture crumple behind her head but didn't care. She was conscious that this was utterly insane but she drank in his kisses, drowning in them: Nick and all her worries faded to the periphery of her consciousness; Jonathan tasted lovely, he smelled lovely, he was a real man and he was making everything all right again.

'Oh God, what are we doing?' Jonathan murmured as he bruised a line of kisses down her neck.

Suddenly the spell was broken. She looked down and saw the furrows of his dark hair and felt sick. What were they doing?

Jonathan, unaware of the change in her mood, started to slide his fingers up her blouse, teasing the lace of her bra. She closed her eyes, desire fluttering and fighting with her reason, when—

Bang!

They both sprang apart violently. Jonathan only just had time to tuck his shirt into his jeans and Andie to do up a stray button on her blouse before Norman appeared. He looked worried. He did a sharp double-take at the two of them. Andie quickly attempted a smile, but she was convinced her face was a loudspeaker of shame.

'What's going on?' he barked.

'We were just having a quick cuppa before it starts,' Jonathan said calmly. He was an amazingly good actor, Andie registered in relief. Norman seemed to buy it, for he relaxed visibly.

'Well, Sophie West from Year Six – one of yours, Andie – has thrown a fit. She's supposed to be playing the trumpet for 'Land of Hope and Glory' but she's run off.'

'What d'you mean, run off?' Jonathan demanded.

'I mean, run off,' Norman said pompously. 'Into the woods. She must still be in them – the fencing is too high for her to climb over.'

'But Mr and Mrs West—' Andie began, thinking of Sophie's parents.

'I've told them she's practising,' Norman said quickly. 'I didn't want to cause any unnecessary trouble.'

Andie and Jonathan didn't need to be told. Over the past week, Andie had noticed the dark circles under Sophie's eyes; the way she had been knawing her lip until it bled; the way she'd been bullying other kids. Her parents were behaving as though the school concert was the Royal Philharmonic Orchestra performing at the Albert Hall. Sophie was expected to shine, just as Mrs West repeatedly stopped by after school and interrogated Andie as to why Sophie hadn't come top of her class, or why Sophie hadn't been selected for the netball team when she'd never scored a goal in her life.

If the Wests found out that Sophie had run away they'd call the police and expect helicopters to scour the grounds. The concert would be completely ruined for all the other children.

'All right,' said Jonathan, 'Norman, you go back and placate the Wests and Andie and I'll go out to look for her.' And, as Norman turned away, Jonathan reached out and gently trailed his little finger across the back of Andie's neck and she shivered.

The 'woods' were really just a tiny copse at the back of the playing fields. Children were not allowed to play in them; thankfully the playground rumour, passed down from one generation to the next, of the ghost of a cantankerous old caretaker who gobbled children for breakfast, was a far better deterrent than any school rules. The last time Andie had been there was a few weeks ago, when they had taken tree-rubbings for art. Which must have planted a seed in Sophie's mind.

As they ran across the playing fields, it started to rain.

'Oh God!' Andie moaned, heels pegging in the mud.

'Here.' Jonathan grabbed her hand. His grip was so warm and strong that she felt that sense of relief again; as though she had been standing on the edge of a dizzying precipice and Jonathan had gently pulled her back.

In the woods, they called out, 'Sophie!' over and over. They pushed aside bushes, wet summer leaves brushing their hair and faces. Every so often they stopped, ears straining, but all they could hear was the sound of cars on the road outside and the distant sound of music. Once or

305

twice lightning tore the sky into electric blue pieces and the pitter-patter of raindrops intensified. But there was still no Sophie. They both looked at each other in despair.

'Nick's lost his job,' Andie suddenly blurted out. 'He lost it two months ago and he didn't even bother to tell me.'

'What?' Jonathan stared at her. 'Oh my God. You poor thing. No wonder . . .' He pulled her into a tight hug, nestling his cheek against hers. Then he clasped her cheeks in his slender fingers and somehow they were kissing again. Hot hungry kisses while the rain wet their hair and trickled in rivulets down their faces. They stumbled back against a tree-stump; a branch snapped and a frightened blackbird suddenly flew up in a fire of black wings, bringing them to their senses.

Jonathan broke away and called shakily: 'Sophie, It's Mr Yates Here. I'm Not Here To Tell You Off, I've Brought You A Present!'

Silence.

Andie, still dazed from the kiss, pulled herself together. A vague worry was sharpening into real fear. What if Sophie really had run away? She was just picturing her swift dismissal, the headlines in the newspapers, the fraught reports on TV, when: 'Mr Yates?'

'She's here—' Andie cried.

'Did you hear—' Jonathan broke off. 'SOPHIE, WHERE ARE YOU?'

'I'm up here!' a pathetic voice called out.

They hurried through the woods: where was she where was she? Then Jonathan nudged Andie and pointed. Andie nearly burst out laughing. Sophie had climbed a tree; she was perched up at the top, legs dangling, like a frightened kitten. Her trumpet case, which she had dropped on the way up, lay in a bush with a large dent in the side. Her eyes were wide and frightened tears streaked her cheeks.

'I don't want to play my trumpet,' she said in a choked voice.

'Sophie, it's all right. You don't have to do anything you don't want to do,' said Jonathan softly. 'I just want to help you down.'

'Don't want to come down.'

'If you come down, you don't have to play. You can just come and sit in the staff room with us and watch the rain. Whatever you like.'

A pause as Sophie considered his terms. Then she nodded.

Andie watched Jonathan slowly climb the tree, hug Sophie and then patiently bring her back down, step by step, and felt an unexpected wave of love for him. She had never fully appreciated until tonight just how kind he was.

Andie released the emotion by giving Sophie a warm hug.

'Well done, Sophie, well done,' she said, looking up at Jonathan and sharing a smile.

'Miss?' Sophie asked as they walked back in the soft rain. 'Are you and Mr Yates going to get married?'

'Er, Mrs Wilkins already has a husband,' Jonathan intervened, seeing Andie was too taken aback to reply.

'But I saw you holding hands.'

'You saw us holding hands, did you? You saw us . . .' Jonathan trailed off. And? Anything else?

'Yes – when you were running across the field.'

Clearly she hadn't seen any more than that. Andie and Jonathan tried not to let out violent sighs of relief.

'I was just comforting Mrs Wilkins because she was so upset at losing you,' said Jonathan.

'Oh,' said Sophie.

'God, that was close,' Jonathan whispered in the corridor after he had quietly persuaded Sophie to go back to the hall (Andie definitely couldn't face Nick now). 'I thought I was going to have to have her killed.'

Andie burst into nervous laughter and Jonathan opened his mouth to kiss her again when they were interrupted by Norman once more.

And that was the last they saw of each other that night, though they took each other home in their memories and spent much of the night lying awake thinking of the other.

And yes, she'd missed Fred's performance. She hadn't been able to face going back into the hall. So she'd got into the car and sat there, listening to Sophie's dreadful trumpeting from a distance and crying softly.

Ironically, her guilt had softened the metallic coil of anger twisted inside her over Nick's betrayal. The night after the concert, after Fred had gone to bed, she cleaned her teeth and went into the bedroom to find Nick sitting up in bed, covers rumpled across his thighs, looking devastated. The veil of anger and antipathy lifted for a moment; they both stared at each other in mutual shock and dismay and he opened his arms slightly to say: *I'm sorry.* Andie heard herself say, 'Oh Nick,' in a voice of both irritation and compassion and slid into his arms. They curled up into a ball together; he buried his head in her shoulder and she stroked his hair while he tried to explain: 'Andie . . . I'm sorry I didn't tell you . . . I tried to write it all down . . . I've just been such a stupid bastard . . .'

But the next morning she woke up feeling angry again. Down at breakfast, she was suddenly aware of the stash of bills piling up on the worktop. Nick followed her gaze and suddenly picked up the lot, chucked them into the bin and slammed the lid down.

'There.' He laughed rather wildly and Fred, who was eating cornflakes, laughed back.

'How can you be so stupid? D'you think that's going to solve anything?' Andie cried. She went to the bin and pulled them out. They were covered with bits of lettuce, baked beans and tomato ketchup; she cleaned them tersely with a piece of kitchen roll and then slammed them back on the worktop.

'And what about Cara?' she demanded. 'What are we going to do about her?'

'I've got another interview next week. I'll get the job. I promise,' Nick said quietly.

She hated seeing him like this. Like a frightened little boy. She wanted him to argue back. It was as though the shock of losing his job had sucked all the spine out of him, all the spunk and *joie de vivre*, all his fighting spirit.

'Well, good,' she found herself snapping. 'Good.'

Back at school, she had sat in assembly listening to Cloones read a passage from Revelations to a hall full of bemused, restless kids and felt Jonathan's eyes on her.

Don't look at him, she told herself fiercely. *Don't give him any signals. You'll have to talk to him later. Say you were stressed, say it was just a mistake.*

She tried to focus on glaring at Sophie West, who was surreptitiously making a cat's cradle with her friend. When Sophie didn't take any notice, she shifted her gaze to the criss-cross of beige oblongs patterning the floor. She watched dust motes slowly drifting through funnels of sunlight; her eyes strained with the concentration.

Jonathan's stare burned into her like a laser, begging her to respond.

She tried to busy her brain with thoughts of the future. She must be strong for Nick. She must support him through his interview. Then there were her frantic preparations for the school trip. Jonathan had organised to take Years 5 and 6 to The Kids' Mountain Centre in Snowdonia, Wales, for five days of rock-climbing, white-water rafting, abseiling and various other activities Andie would normally rather slit her wrists than do. But because most of her class were going, she'd been drafted in to help. She had a mountain of ridiculous paperwork to cover. Due to pernickety insurance rules, she had to write to every single parent and ask permission to use a plaster or anything remotely sensible from the First Aid box in the event of their child suffering even the tiniest of scratches.

As the morning sun shifted, Andie suddenly felt a glare in her eyes. She shifted uncomfortably and turned and lost control. She looked over at Jonathan. He smiled at her. She looked away quickly. She thought about the fact that she was going to be spending five days on a remote mountain with him. She thought of the awful bills sitting on the kitchen worktop. Then she looked back at him. They sat, and stared.

30
Cara

Nick had to get this job.

Had to.

I had just about got over the shock of seeing Andie and Jonathan together. *Okay*, I thought, *it's just a fling. A shock reaction to Nick being fired. If he can get more work, everything will sort itself out.*

I hoped.

All the same, every time I saw Andie kiss Nick, I felt my stomach turn at her hypocrisy. How could she just carry on as if everything was hunky dory? I couldn't help wondering if Nick sensed something was up because he seemed to be sliding downhill fast. Though he was jokey and casual during the day, he seemed to have caught Andie's insomnia and I was woken by the creak of the stairs during the night when he got up to make snacks. I dotted his pillow with lavender to soothe him, but it only helped a little. He was also drinking and smoking far too much; despite signing the 'stop smoking' chart daily, every time he took the dogs for a walk he came back stinking of tobacco fumes. When I nagged him, he either laughed or crossly muttered, 'Stop moaning – you're as bad as Andie.'

I also noticed the level in the whisky bottle falling by degrees. It wasn't that I feared Nick was an alcoholic, but I did feel he was losing his motivation, wallowing in self-pity in the evenings, smoking his anxieties away instead of channelling them into positivity and deciding to get his life together.

So one evening when Nick had taken the dogs out, I removed the cigarette packet from his jacket pocket and pulled out the remaining cigarettes. Every witch knows that each cigarette contains a demon: demons that burrow into human hearts, creating a painful addiction, paving the way for the tar to eat into their lungs and liver, hopefully resulting in the bounty of death. I flashed my hands over the cigarettes in a quick and simple spell. One by one, the demons wriggled out of the cigarettes, until I had eight black dancing demons with pointed ears jumping up and down on the coffee table.

'I want you to leave now,' I said firmly.

'Why should we?' one piped up.

'Yeah, why should we?' the others echoed him.

Cigarette demons aren't terribly intelligent; they have the collective IQ of a rowdy football crowd.

'Because there's a newsagents just around the corner from here. If you go there, you'll be able to slip into some heavy tars.'

All demons love hanging out in heavy tar cigarettes because the low tar ones are seen as a bit girly. They gave a cheer of delight and scampered out through the window. I smiled and picked up the cigarettes, which still looked perfectly normal, and put them back into Nick's jacket pocket.

Then I turned my attention to the fat decanter of whisky on the sideboard. If you hold any bottle of alcohol to the light, you'll see a murky black shadow inside, a horned form, half-man, half-goat, with hooved feet and a muscly chest: Dionysius. However, Dionysius is an elusive and complex fellow, far too intelligent to be cajoled out with fake offerings. But, like everyone and everything, he does have one weakness, and I knew what that was.

I took out the glass cork and leaned over the bottle, whispering seductively: 'Darling Dionysius, come out and you can kiss me. I'm one of your followers and I'm aching for you . . .'

There was a pause, then the dark whisky churned and slowly, like a genie emerging from a bottle, a shadow uncurled and took shape. He hovered before me, a black cloudy form, as large as a human, waving his hooves. He looked so dangerous and powerful that for a moment I suffered a flicker of fear, then I pushed it away. Humans are stronger than demons or spirits. I thrust the glass stopper back into the whisky bottle triumphantly.

'You won't be going back in there, I'm afraid,' I said. 'And I'm afraid the kiss is off too.'

'Is that so?' he said, his voice hoarse, whisky-soaked.

'I'm afraid so. And don't bother fighting me. I know enough magic to obliterate you entirely,' I bluffed.

For a moment we glared at each other. He narrowed his almond-shaped eyes into thin slits of fury. I swallowed uncertainly.

Then, with a snarl, he whirled away, disappearing under the door.

There. Nick could drink as much as he liked now, but he wouldn't be able to get drunk.

Then I heard footsteps in the hallway; the sounds of the dogs scampering into the kitchen. Quickly, I pushed the decanter back in its place behind the sherry just in time – Nick entered the room.

313

I quickly sat down on the sofa, picking the threads on a cushion and trying to look innocent. Nick stood in front of me, hands on his hips, a half-smile crooked on his lips.

'Ooh, that innocent face isn't going to wash with me, I'm afraid,' he said, shaking his head.

What! Had Nick seen Dionysius? My heart started to thump madly.

'I know what you were doing,' he continued.

'No, it wasn't – um, what you think – you see I was just talking on the phone, that was the voice you heard and—'

'Talking on the phone?' Nick blinked. 'Well, that's a good one.'

Oh shit, I panicked. He's found me out. He knows I'm a witch. In a minute he'll be telling me to pack my bags and—

'You've been taking sneaky little sips from my whisky, haven't you?'

'Ohhhh,' I laughed. 'Yes, well . . . I just thought I . . . erm . . . I should, you know, test it . . . ah . . .' Actually, was this a good excuse? I fretted. Admitting to nicking your boss's booze was possibly a sackable offence too.

But to my relief, Nick seemed to find the whole thing amusing. 'Don't worry, it's our secret,' he grinned, and then sloshed out two glasses.

'Oh, not for me, I don't drink—'

'Oh yeah, I'm sure.' Nick handed me a glass and sat down on the sofa next to me.

I forced a smile and took a sip. I've always loathed whisky, and even with the alcohol taken out it still burned my mouth like an unpleasant cough medicine. In fact, it tasted even worse without Dionysius's rich fruity threads in it: watery *and* disgusting.

'So, are you all ready for your interview tomorrow?'

My remark completely wiped the smile off Nick's face.

He downed his whisky, put the glass on the table and buried his head in his hands.

'Nick, please don't worry,' I said, patting him on the shoulder. 'I'm sure you'll be fine. You only have to believe in yourself and they will.'

Nick let out a sigh, picked up his jacket, pulled out his cigarettes and lit up.

'You won't tell Andie?' he asked, kicking the door shut and opening the window like a nervous teenager hiding his habit from his parents.

'Sure.' I hid a smile. I couldn't help worrying what would happen when he tried to smoke them. I pretended to be staring hard at my lap, flicking little glances at him out of the corner of my eye.

He blew out. *And no smoke came out.* Just the tiniest little will-'o'-the-wisp of grey nothingness.

Luckily, Nick seemed too preoccupied to notice. Not yet, anyway.

'Cara, I just don't know what to do. I'm going to the interview and I don't want the job. There. I've said it. I have no fucking desire to work in computing any more, to get up in the mornings and get on to a hot sweaty tube filled with men in suits, to spend all my hours in an office that's like a prison with only a glimpse of blue sky and get home so late I have no time to spend with my son. I don't want this interview and I don't want this job.'

'Oh.'

Oh. The understatement of the century. What the hell was Nick talking about? I'd rallied behind him! I'd typed out CVs! I'd ironed his bloody tie! If he didn't take the job, then what . . .?

'So what *do* you want to do?' I asked tentatively, trying to repress a nervous giggle as Nick sucked ferociously on his cigarette.

315

'God, I'd love to travel. You know, I'd love to do a TEFL course and go to Thailand! Yeah, that'd be cool.'

'But Nick . . .' How could I put it? 'Nick, that's the sort of stuff that, well, students do. Not, um, men with kids.'

'I know,' said Nick sullenly, pouring out some more whisky. 'God. I know. I really don't know why I'm telling you all this, Cara. I must be drunk. I don't feel it but I must be.'

I hid another smile. 'Okay, that might be the ultimate fantasy of what you want to do,' I said, 'but why don't you think of something in-between? Something sensible, something do-able.'

'I guess . . .' Nick sighed. 'I guess I'd like to set up my own business again. Be my own boss. I did that when I first married Andie – then I sold it, then I got employed. I'd like to set up my own company, then I can be the one who hires and fires.'

'So why don't you?' I asked.

'Because it's a risk, isn't it? I'd have to get a loan, or remortgage the house. When I was twenty, I wasn't scared of risks . . . I am now. God, this cigarette is weird.' Nick peered at it, eyes narrowed, then cocked his head to one side in bemusement. 'It . . . it doesn't seem to be *smoking*. Weird.'

'Um, maybe it's gone stale,' I said.

'I didn't think cigarettes could go off,' he frowned. 'That's the last time I buy from that cruddy newsagent down the road. Well, anyway. I can't do this interview.'

I pictured the look on Andie's face when she found out. This wasn't going to be good. I couldn't work out why he was behaving like this. There was something self-destructive lurking in him. It was as though he deliberately wanted to hurt Andie, as if she had somehow forced him into the situation.

'Nick, wouldn't it be better if you just tell Andie you're going to the interview, and don't go and then just say you didn't get the job . . .' I trailed off, reading his thoughts: Nick had already lied to Andie once before and look where that had got him.

'Don't you worry about me,' said Nick, patting my shoulder and taking my glass from me. 'It's just something I've got to work out for myself. I'm sorry that I'm burdening you with my problems, I really shouldn't. You're supposed to be looking after Fred and here you are sorting us all out. You're like Mary Poppins – practically perfect in every way!'

'Oh, yeah, right!' I laughed, though I had to admit I was flattered.

'You go off to bed,' said Nick, waving his glass. 'You look exhausted – all this perfection must be tiring!'

'Okay,' I said, getting up reluctantly. I paused, torn between wanting to beg him to reconsider going to the interview and not wanting to lecture him. 'Look, if you want to do well at this interview, maybe you should get an early night too.'

'Hmm . . .' Nick rolled his eyes. 'I'll just have another glass of whisky and one more fag.'

Just let it go, Cara, I thought sadly, *Nick's life is his and his choices are his own.*

I left him to it; as I walked out, however, I saw him puffing so hard on his cigarette that it broke into two halves and I had to swallow back a bubble of nervous laughter.

Upstairs, a slight breeze rippled white wavelets across my duvet; I'd left my window open. It was a habit now, for Sean and I loved our childish aeroplane game.

Sure enough, there was a plane lying on the floor. The

message inside said: *Hmm, you looked sexy in that dress today, I hope you wear it tomorrow when we go out for a drink!* I smiled. Naughty boy!

I looked at Sean's window, but his room was empty; he was probably downstairs watching TV with Kieran.

I lay back on my bed, using idle magic from a fingertip to propel the plane around the room, twirling and dipping and diving. This whole Sean situation was just getting weirder and weirder. I did love the warmth of our friendship but I couldn't help wanting more. And while my feelings were constant, his were as unpredictable as the weather. He seemed to be playing some sort of emotional tango. One day he'd be all flirty and tell me how yummy I was looking; the next he'd be moody and frosty and complain that women were all the same and he was never going to marry again. I noticed that when I acted cool, he took a flirty step forward; but when I turned up the heat, he backed off again. It was tempting to start manipulating the situation and play hard to get. But I didn't want to do that; I didn't want to get tangled up in games. If anything was going to happen between me and Sean, I wanted him to feel ready for it, otherwise I'd only end up getting hurt.

I heard a sigh from Andie in the bedroom below. I wondered if she was lying there thinking about Jonathan. Oh God, I just prayed that Nick got his act together and got this job tomorrow.

I waited for a bit longer to see if Sean was going to come up to his room but I got too tired, so I went to bed and let the aeroplane drop to the floor, fluttering gently on the boards like a dying butterfly.

31
Andie

Andie got up early the next morning, in a furious mood. Nick hadn't come up to bed until gone midnight, and judging by the empty decanter of whisky in the living room he'd sloshed the lot. *And* he'd left an empty cigarette packet on the coffee table – here she was, making all this effort to give up, and he wasn't even trying. He was now lying in bed, snoring, and when Andie prodded him, hissing, '*Interview,*' he merely groaned.

Andie lost her temper. She pulled the duvet off the bed so that the cold air crawled over him. Nick reached out for the covers, clawing thin air.

'*No,*' she said. 'Nick, just get up, okay? You have a few hours to cure your hangover.'

'I don't have a hangover,' he groaned, sitting up in bewilderment. 'I guess I couldn't have had that much.'

Andie stared at him with narrowed eyes. So now he was starting to lie about his alcohol quantities? Wasn't that the first sign of alcoholism?

'Nick, I don't have time for this – in a couple of hours I have to be on a coach escorting thirty children across the country, so just get it together, okay?'

319

'Okay, *okay!*' Nick rolled his hairy legs out of bed. 'I'm up. Satisfied?'

Anyone would think he was a schoolboy being dragged to school, Andie thought, shaking her head. But then she forgot Nick for the next two hours, caught up in a whirlwind of packing and preparing. Finally she had her coat on, make-up on, cases by the door and was ready to go. She'd tried to say goodbye to Fred but he was in a sulk at her for leaving him for five days and was sitting in front of the TV, breaking her already guilty heart by ignoring her.

Shit, I need some mineral water for the coach journey, Andie realised, and hurried into the kitchen.

Nick was sitting there. Still in his dressing gown. His face a shadowy criss-cross of lines. And Andie knew then that something was very wrong.

'Nick, are you ready for your interview?'

'I'm not going.'

'Not going. Right.' Her face was blank, her voice level. She resisted the urge to tear out her hair, scream at the top of her voice and throw Nick's bowl of cornflakes across the room.

'I want to set up my own company again,' he said. 'I don't want to work in computing.'

'Nick, we've discussed this before—'

'*We* haven't discussed it. *You've* told me what I have to do, and I don't want to and . . .'

Suddenly Andie gave up. She felt as though she was talking to a complete stranger. It was all useless, hopeless.

'Fine, well, have fun,' she said. 'Bye.'

And with that she left the house, slamming the door and getting into the car. As she drove away, Fred, guilty at his sulking, pressed his face to the living room window, waving frantically and silently calling her name through the glass.

Andie was dying to confide in Jonathan, to let it all spill out, but the coach trip kept her fully occupied. Firstly, Henry was sick and had to be sat at the front with a Tesco's bag. It then took another twenty miles to reach a service station to dispose of it, and the poor boy had to put up with everyone squealing, 'Urgh, sicky smell!' and pretending to faint.

The kids were playing up a lot more than usual; they seemed to sense Andie's fragile mood. Worst of all were the troublesome trio, as Andie had nicknamed Sophie, Katie and Chloe. They ended up having a huge squabble over a Walkman, which Andie had to confiscate.

Down at the front, she collapsed into a seat next to Jonathan and tested the Walkman out. Seeing the look on her face, Jonathan laughed and said, 'What?'

'Listen,' said Andie, passing the Walkman over.

'"*Hey, bitch, I want your lovin', you're the girl I wanna be shaggin'*",' Jonathan burst into laughter. 'Well, rap's nice for them to listen to, isn't it? I guess it helps them learn how to rhyme.'

Things got rather ugly, however, when Sophie came storming up to Andie and demanded her tape and Walkman back. Sophie was one of those kids who too often crossed the line between being amusingly cheeky and downright nasty. As Sophie complained away, Andie found herself losing focus, thinking of Nick. Was he still sitting at the kitchen table? Suddenly she lost her temper. Without thinking, she yelled, 'SOPHIE, JUST GO BACK TO YOUR SEAT, OKAY?' and gave her a small, frustrated shake.

The coach fell silent. Andie drew back, shocked. If there was one rule of teaching, it was never, *ever* touch a kid. Not even with your fingernail. Not unless you wanted to end up in court.

'I'll tell my parents you hit me,' Sophie hissed. 'I'll get them to sue.'

Jesus. Andie swallowed, seeing her entire teaching career flashing before her.

'Look, Sophie,' said Jonathan, pushing past. His voice was dangerously calm; when Jonathan got angry, it was genuinely scary. 'I saw Mrs Wilkins and she didn't touch you. She shouted at you because you deserved to be told off. Now, we're going to keep this Walkman and when we get to Wales we're going to ring your parents and see if you're allowed to listen to this tape. If so, perhaps they can discuss court proceedings then.'

Sophie chewed her lip, silenced. To their huge and concealed relief, she muttered meekly, 'Okay, sorry, Mr Yates,' and went back to her seat.

Andie and Jonathan sat back down.

'Sorry,' said Jonathan, realising Andie didn't like to be usurped. 'I didn't mean—'

'No, it's fine. I need all the help I can get today. Thanks, really, you saved me.'

'Are you okay?' he asked, his eyes caressing her face softly. 'We can talk later on, if you like?' He reached out and gently threaded his fingers through hers, giving her hand a squeeze; then, as Henry came up for another sick bag, he quickly pulled away.

The Kids' Mountain Centre was a lovely wooden building on the north side of the bracingly cold mountain.

Andie switched on to auto-pilot that evening. They met Janine, Sally and the rest of the team; they had dinner; then there was the rigmarole of getting the kids into their dorms, preventing a toothpaste fight, comforting Nigel

322

who'd been locked out by his roommates. She collapsed into bed at eleven o'clock without bothering to clean her teeth. *Only seven hours till I get up and swim in a freezing cold lake with thirty errant kids trying to drown each other,* she thought numbly.

She woke up early in the morning, tears on her cheeks. A horrible thought that had been crawling through her subconscious like a maggot knawed its way to the surface: *What if Nick wants to set up his own company with his blonde from the park? What if they were making plans together; what if that was why he'd messed up the interview?*

After all, what other reason could there be? Nick's actions were, quite blatantly, those of a single, independent man who was arranging life to suit himself, not his family . . .

She was relieved to escape from the nightmare of her churning imagination when there was a gentle tap on the door. It was Sophie. She was crying. She explained in choky fits that she'd just started bleeding and she didn't know what to do. Andie hugged her and gave her some sanitary pads and a rather blush-blundering lecture on periods, and somehow, by cheering Sophie up, she cheered herself up.

But later that day, things dived again. In the morning they went abseiling and Jonathan descended into a bad mood that she'd never seen him in before. Every time she said something to him he looked blank and answered in edgy monosyllables.

Hurt, Andie was pleased to be split off from him for the afternoon activities. He was taking one group orienteering through the forest while she was helping to supervise the white-water rafting with Sally. Andie had done it before during a holiday in Canada with Nick's uncle and she'd loved it. She and Sally firmly buckled life-jackets on to eight children, took paddles and climbed on to the raft. God, it was fantastic! As the white spray foamed and tossed and whirled around them, she felt all her problems shaken out of her in a flurry. Water slapped her face; the crisp air stung her lungs; she'd never felt more alive.

They ought to have seen the warning signal: a couple of angry bees trickling upstream. Then a few more. There were a few overhanging branches ahead and they all ducked, but it was no use: they'd paddled straight into a great big fat nest of angry bees. Andie screamed, 'Duck!' and felt one buzz straight into her shocked mouth, then fly out again. She reached instinctively for the other kids, pushing them down flat, ignoring the crawl of insects across her face, the stings embedding themselves in her cheeks. A second later, it was all over: they came out the other side and the water flung them spectacularly towards the bottom of the stream, the children crying in fear.

Fortunately, Andie had saved most of them from being stung, despite their wailing. But she and Sally had a good ten stings each on their face and neck.

The orienteering group returned, the kids full of envy and excitement that they'd missed a piece of the action. Andie tried to fob them away, biting back the pain in her cheeks.

'Andie, are you okay?' Jonathan's bad mood had evaporated; he looked shocked and upset at the sight of her.

'I'm fine.'

'No, you're not.' Ignoring her brave show, he insisted that they must sort her out too and dragged her into his room. She gazed at her reflection in his mirror. She looked as though she was suffering simultaneously from mumps and measles.

'Sit down, Dr Yates will attend to you,' said Jonathan in a stern voice.

Andie giggled and sat down on the edge of the bed. Jonathan dipped some cotton wool pads in water and washed her face. He was so sensitive, it was almost unbearable. Andie stared straight ahead at a patch of off-white wall; Jonathan stared at her chin. He swabbed on some TCP and she winced at the sting. 'There, there, darling, it's all right,' he whispered, curling his fingers around the back of her neck and pulling her towards him. *Darling.* Andie felt as though she was about to melt. Suddenly his loveliness overwhelmed her. She leaned in to kiss him.

And then he drew back.

He emptied the water, flushed the cotton wool pads down the toilet and snapped up the first aid kit.

'Coming to dinner?' He couldn't even look her in the eye.

Andie felt shocked and confused. Why had he rejected her? After chasing her for the last few months, had he suddenly changed his mind?

Dinner was even worse.

Downstairs in the wooden dining hall, she'd planned to sit at the opposite end of the room to Jonathan. But she was late and she ended up taking the only spare place – right next to him. Every time Andie tried to eat, her swollen mouth wobbled like a jelly. She ended up with most of the food greasing down her chin and slopping on to her favourite white jumper. Soon the kids were in hoots of laughter.

They were even more amused when Mr Yates offered to feed her. He did it so attentively – sawing up her chicken and chips into little chunks, slotting them into her mouth, gently wiping her lips – that Andie wanted to hit him. He was behaving like a parent with a difficult child. If he really cared for her, he wouldn't be able to bear touching her.

You're not being fair on him, Andie told herself in her room later that night. *It must be hard for him too, with the Rebecca situation.*

Then she thought: *But God, I need help right now. He could at least be sympathetic.*

And then: *This is crazy. He has been sweet to me. He's bathed my face and chopped up my food. What more do I want from him; should I want from him?*

Suddenly she couldn't bear it any longer. She had to see him; to explain, to apologise. She marched up to Jonathan's room and banged on his door. He opened it and she faltered.

'Tomorrow we have to be half an hour earlier for abseiling,' she said. Despite her good intentions, her voice was edgy, admonitory.

'Andie, come in,' Jonathan sighed.

Andie entered his room. Her sea of calm was becoming seriously choppy. She couldn't help bursting out: 'I don't want you to think I've come here with any expectations, by the way.'

'Andie—'

'You've just been so hot and cold with me all week and I'm sick of it—'

'Look,' he burst out, 'I'm scared of heights, okay? This whole trip has been completely hellish.'

Scared of heights? Suddenly it all made sense. Suddenly he looked like a frightened little boy and she wanted to hug him.

'But you . . . and Rebecca . . . you climbed all the time before she . . .' Andie trailed off.

'After she died, that's when it happened,' said Jonathan. 'I think it was just a reaction, and . . .'

'But if you're scared of heights, why the hell did you organise an adventure holiday on Mount Snowdon?' Andie burst out. 'Is that why you asked me to volunteer? To get you out of the tough jobs?'

'There was another reason,' he said, wincing and chewing on a nail, looking up at her from under his lids. Slowly realisation dawned on her. Suddenly she felt wildly happy. She went pink. She smiled shyly. She opened her mouth to say something but Jonathan had already stepped forwards and was kissing her.

32
Andie

Five minutes later, they were hot and breathless with kisses. At this rate, Andie felt that her swollen mouth was going to get better very quickly.

'I don't have any condoms,' Jonathan whispered, kissing her neck.

'Neither do I,' Andie licked his lips.

'I'll have to go the loos, I saw some in there. Wait here, okay?'

The moment he had gone, Andie hurried to his bathroom and locked the door, checking her appearance. As the minutes went by, her desire ebbed away. She started to lose her nerve.

I've been fantasising about this for weeks, she thought. *Last night I was practically weeping because I thought it wasn't going to happen.*

But the reality was different.

The reality was scary.

She couldn't back out of it now, could she? She stared at her reflection in the mirror and gave herself a pep talk. *Andie, you're twenty-nine years old. You're a grown woman. You don't have to do anything. Jonathan is the one who picked*

328

you and brought you here. You can walk out and say NO.
Besides, you can't have sex. You haven't shaved your legs.

She heard the click of the door.

Jonathan was back.

'You okay in there?' he called.

'Sure,' she said. She'd better make her mind up and come out soon or he'd think she was suffering from an embarrassing bowel complaint or something.

She quickly sped into action. She splashed some water over her face and dried it thoroughly. She lifted the bottom of her trousers, inspecting the growth on her legs. Oh God. A veritable jungle. She lifted up her top, inspecting her armpits. Oh dear – even worse. Still, Julia Roberts had made that fashionable, hadn't she? Well, kind of. She stared at her reflection, failing to notice the soft voluptuousness of her flesh or the curve of her breasts, seeing only the bands of fat around her waist, the white tentacles of cellulite at the top of her thighs. Suddenly, irrationally, she wished he was Nick. Nick didn't mind about her body – after all, he might be a looker, but he wasn't in such great shape himself these days, with his slight weight-gain and a few premature grey streaks in his hair. But Jonathan was only twenty-five. He was used to ripe young girls with jutting breasts and thighs like matchsticks and tiny little bottoms.

I can't do this, she realised, and then felt awful. What a reason to turn adultery down – not because of any moral principle, but because she had cellulite.

She unlocked the bathroom door with shaking hands.

Jonathan came over to her, his eyes quizzical.

'I've locked the door.' He pointed; he'd even put his suitcase against it, just to be sure Henry or Sophie couldn't negotiate their way past the lock. 'Erm, you okay in there?'

'Uh huh.'

'I thought I'd lost you. I thought you might have fallen in love with the toilet or something.'

'No . . . I—'

'Sorry – stupid thing to say. I'm just a bit nervous. I got some . . . you know . . .' He emptied his pockets. Andie resisted a hysterical urge to laugh. It looked as though he'd emptied the entire condom machine too.

'Well, that might just not be enough,' said Andie wryly. She took a deep breath. 'Look, I don't think I can do this.'

'Oh.'

She felt irrational, irritated. Couldn't he at least make an effort, beg her to stay?

'Well, you'd better go then, hadn't you?' he said, walking up to her; she moved backwards against the wall. He kissed her feverishly and she gasped, feeling desire squiggle through her.

'I should go,' she protested weakly.

'Mmm, go in a minute,' he said, kissing her neck, gently biting the skin. She found her hands flying up to his head and curling in his hair. He ran his hands down her back, over her backside and then started to edge his way up her T-shirt, caressing her skin with the tips of his fingers in feathery, circular motions. She thought of her reflection in the mirror again and suddenly stopped him.

'No.' She tried to push him away but he put an arm on either side of her, pinning her against the wall.

'Why not?'

'Because I'm married and I've got cellulite and stretch marks,' Andie said in a small, shaky voice. 'I'm just not cut out for this sort of thing.'

Jonathan burst into laughter and planted a loving kiss on her forehead.

'Oh, Andie, you're so funny. *Fat!* That's the most ridiculous thing I've ever heard. Of course you're not.'

'If I'd have known I was going to commit adultery six months ago, I could have joined a gym or gone to Weight Watchers . . .' Andie, realising what a dreadful thing she'd said, clapped her hand over her mouth as Jonathan burst into laughter. Then she started to laugh too and for a moment they laughed together, releasing all their pent-up nerves.

'Okay, I have a solution,' said Jonathan. He went over to the window and dragged the long floral curtains shut. Then he clicked off the lights. All she could see was his dark silhouette and the gleam of his eye whites and teeth.

'Now,' he whispered, 'why don't you take off all your clothes and hide under the covers?'

'So you do think I'm fat.'

'I think you're gorgeous. But I want you to be happy.'

Andie swallowed. She lifted her hand, half-pulled up her top, and then paused, the material clenched in her fingers. *Here's your chance now, Andie. You can leave.* But she found herself slowly pulling it over her head. Then she unclasped her bra. She could hear his breathing growing shaky and she felt excited, half-wishing she had let him keep the light on, that she could feel his eyes on her. She pulled off her trousers, kicked off her knickers and dived for the covers, shivering under the cool, crisp cotton. Jonathan came closer and he too pulled off his T-shirt, and she heard the *zip* of his jeans as he tugged them off. The noise, unexpectedly erotic, ripped through her. He lifted the covers, letting in a blast of cold air, his body shockingly and gloriously warm. He was thinner than she'd expected; though he had a broad back, his stomach was skinny and his rib-cage stuck out like piano keys. He put his arms around her and said, 'Oh, it's so lovely just to hold you.'

I've wanted to do this for so long,' and she forgot all her worries and melted into him.

'We're going to have to be quiet,' she whispered.

'I know,' Jonathan smiled and put a finger over her lips.

Then his finger edged down. He smoothed a palm over her breasts, but she tensed again, realising that him feeling her fat was nearly as bad as him seeing it. He pulled her arms apart roughly.

'Look, I *love* your body, okay? You're a real woman, all curves . . . mmm.' He flicked his tongue over a nipple. Andie chewed her lip, torn between vanity and desire.

Then, with a sigh of exasperation, he suddenly dived under the covers. What was he doing? Andie had a horrible moment where she worried he might have some sort of mad foot-fetish. Then she felt him part her thighs and his tongue slithering up the skin and then telling her how delicious she tasted, and she gasped, her worries disappearing, as a silent orgasm tore through her . . .

The Kids' Mountain Centre mattresses were very thin and the bedsteads somewhat old. The bed creaked so much they kept having to stop, then, just as they were nearly there, Suzanne knocked on the door, asking if Jonathan had any spare chocolate. They lay frozen, eye to eye, frantic, sighing with relief as she disappeared.

'Maybe we should give up,' Andie whispered nervously.

'No,' Jonathan smiled, 'you're going to come whether you like it or not.'

Ten minutes later, Jonathan kept his word.

Afterwards, he didn't roll over but held her tightly, whispering how much he adored her. Andie felt dazed.

It was all so strange, she thought. It didn't feel as she'd expected it to. Now and again, during the final ecstasy of their lovemaking, a thought had flickered across her mind, bringing her up to the surface again: *I should feel guilty right now,* or, *I shouldn't be enjoying this.* Somehow she felt the whole thing should be more complicated, more messy, more extreme. More sleazy. This was *sex.* In a *seedy little room.* And yet it didn't meet any of her preconceived expectations. It felt simple, natural and easy.

Andie glanced at Jonathan. He wasn't looking at her. Suddenly he seemed horribly distant. Perhaps he was thinking of Rebecca, she fretted. And then she remembered the Thai prostitute. He'd slept with her because it was soulless. No strings attached.

He's just used me, she thought, and the hollow, dirty feeling she'd been waiting to feel finally came. *He told me he adored me just to get me into bed, to prove he could get a married woman. And now he has, I'll never hear from him again.*

'You won't tell anyone about this, will you?' she said abruptly.

'Oh sure. I'll be on my mobile tonight, telling the world—'

'Don't joke,' Andie said, her forehead creased in pain. 'Don't.'

She rolled over. Jonathan surveyed the wall of her back in amazement. He reached for her but she flicked him away, getting up, turning on the lamp and gathering up her clothes, bunching them up in a bundle against her chest.

'Well, this was just a one-night stand anyway, right?' she said, pulling on her knickers. Jonathan didn't like to point out that she'd put them on inside-out. 'We won't see each other again now, will we?'

'If that's what you want,' Jonathan said, after a long pause.

'Well, it's what you want, isn't it?'

'I don't know; what about you?'

'We were talking about you, not me. Oh God!' She yanked on her trousers, zipping them up angrily. She could still feel the echo of his hands on her body and she had a sudden urge to shower, to scrub his caresses away, remove his film of sweat and saliva from her body. As Jonathan came out of bed and up to her, she shook her jumper irritably, holding it between them like a cloth between a matador and a bull. Jonathan took a step back. 'Well, Mr Smoothie, you did a very slick job on me, I have to say. I'm impressed.'

'Mr Smoothie? Why the fuck am I Mr Smoothie?' he demanded, his voice edged with anger now.

'That "close the curtains' little number – your obviously used to dealing with neurotic older women—'

'Andie, you seem to think I—'

'And I fell for it, didn't I—?'

'You think I'm smooth? Andie, I forgot to get any condoms, then I bought about twenty packets, then I asked you when you came out of the bathroom whether you'd fallen in love with the toilet. And you think I'm smooth? After what's happened in my life . . . Andie, I'm mad about you. I couldn't be smooth around you to save my life.'

Andie swallowed, staring down at his feet. His toes were slightly misshapen and somehow she found them terribly sweet. She put the nub of her palm against her eye and rubbed away a stray tear.

'Well, I guess the toilet comment was a little lacking in finesse,' she said, with a fragile smile.

He drew her into a hug and pulled her back into bed. 'Look,' he said, nuzzling his nose against hers, 'of course I want to see you again. I just . . . I didn't want you to feel I was taking advantage. I guess I was starting to feel guilty . . . since I teach Fred and all . . .' Seeing her face, he winced too. 'Sorry, I know you don't want to be reminded—'

'Things are going badly between me and Nick.' Andie tried to assuage her guilt. And then she told him all about the interview, about Nick letting her down, about her worries that they would lose the house, lose everything. He held her tightly as, sobbing, she poured out all her pent-up emotions.

'I don't understand why Nick isn't getting his act together,' said Jonathan. 'I mean, if he is such a successful businessman, why is he falling apart now?'

'Oh, Nick's just endlessly ambitious. He comes from one of those families where everything is about proving yourself. He can't bear to lose at anything.'

'Oh God, no wonder he was so pissed off when I beat him at chess,' Jonathan laughed softly.

'Exactly. Nick is good at what he does but there's a lot of insecurity underneath his joking . . . But even so, why didn't he tell me? Five years ago we had money and everything was so fantastic. I felt as though I was *in control* of everything, and now I've realised it was just an illusion. Life can throw anything it likes at us, any time. I feel lost, I feel like a little kid – I want to jump up and down and yell "It's not fair!" instead of being mature and accepting and finding solutions. But . . .' She took off her wedding ring and rolled it in her palm. 'I don't know if our marriage will survive this, so . . .'

'Oh, don't worry, Andie, everything will sort itself out,' Jonathan said, and somehow, as he hugged her, she almost believed that it would.

The next few days were a strange cocktail of pleasure and pain.

In between rock-climbing, canoeing and swimming, Andie and Jonathan couldn't keep their hands off each other. They couldn't help it. They were like a pair of lovesick teenagers at the mercy of their first rush of uncontrollable hormones. Andie was terrified that the children would be able to sense it, that every time Jonathan looked at her they would see into her stomach, see the fizz of chemical reactions, the lust dancing a dizzy path to her thighs. Every night she found herself sidling into his room, and every time they made love she felt as though he took away a piece of the pain. Somehow it was easy not to feel guilty; they were so far away from Richmond, from the cramped confines of suburbia. Here, deep in the unbounded wilderness of the mountains, without TV, without the restrictions of a city skyline, without the constant reminder of society and its codes, it was easy to pretend she was in another time, another world. But she couldn't face phoning home and talking to Nick, which meant missing out on talking to Fred, which ate a hole of worry and neglect in her heart.

On the journey home, Andie found her mood darkening again. As the coach headed towards London, the apple air became cloudy, the clear sky smoggy. She gazed at the lines of tooting traffic, the imposing tower blocks, and felt her heart sink like a stone.

Before she went home, Jonathan managed to steal a kiss and whisper, 'Call me. Call me tonight.'

Andie nodded.

As she walked up the path to her house, she felt like turning back and running away. She took ages to find her keys in her bag. Then, the moment she opened the door, they surrounded her.

At first she couldn't take in what Cara was saying. The house was bubbling with excitement. Fred was yelling,

'Dad said we could go to Pizza Express!' and Cara was saying in a quiet, happy voice, 'He got it, Andie!' and the dogs, not wanting to miss out on whatever the excitement was, were running about yapping and trying to nip each others' tails and hoping this might mean they got some chicken tonight as a special treat.

Then Nick came into the hallway, a massive smile plastered across his face. He spread open his arms and yelled, 'I GOT THE JOB!'

'What – how?' Andie couldn't quite take it all in. She put down her bags and tried to digest Nick's news.

'You were right,' said Nick. 'I realised I was being completely selfish. I gave it my best shot – you know I'm good at interviews – and they gave me the job on the spot. Plus, I got them to agree to pay me more, because of my experience.' He pulled her into a big hug. Fred joined in too and Cara, on the sidelines, smiled and looked rather tearful.

Andie felt in a total daze. It was only later, when she went into the toilets at Pizza Express, that she noticed the blank white mark on the fourth finger of her left hand and realised she'd left her wedding ring lying in Jonathan's bed at the Kids' Mountain Centre.

33
Cara

Well, thank God for that. Finally, Nick and Andie seemed to have got it together. Finally, they were a happy family.

The morning of Nick's job interview, I had resorted to magic.

The magic of sheer bloody bullying. I'd watched Andie roar away in her car in an angry cloud of smoke and I'd marched downstairs in sheer exasperation and told Nick not to be so bloody stupid, just to grow up, be a man, be a father, be a husband, and *go to the interview*. I'd been quite worried he might sock me one, but to my amazement some of my words had trickled in. He'd got up, gone upstairs and slowly put his suit on, looking rather dazed. Thank God!

And despite Nick's whingeing about setting up his own business, he seemed to be enjoying his new job. Work had put the spine back into his life. In the mornings I heard him singing in the shower; in the evenings he came back looking snazzy in his suit, overflowing with anecdotes and funny stories about characters from his new office. In turn, his happiness seeped by osmosis into Fred. He stopped throwing tantrums and even let me win at Monopoly once or twice.

Andie was different too. The day after she'd got back from Wales, she'd gone to the hairdressers and swapped her straggling curls for a layered, sleeker look. She'd also invested in a whole new wardrobe that made her look about five years younger. Something had clearly changed inside her. Her tired face was now luminous; there was a new sparkle in her eyes and a blush to her cheeks. She was also much more tactile around Nick. She gave him a luscious kiss every day before he went to work, grabbing him back for a second and third offering until he almost had to prise her away. When they watched TV together in the evenings, she practically sat on his lap. And she laughed a lot more – in fact, all the time. Often at nothing remotely funny, until Nick looked slightly puzzled.

And yet beneath her happiness I could also sense a layer of worry. At night I was woken by the bedroom door creaking and the sigh of her slippers going down the stairs. I figured she was worried that fate might be about to whisk their newfound happiness away at the last minute; she'd been walking on a tightrope for so long that even though she'd reached the other side she was still giddy with fear of falling.

Then, on Saturday morning, I went into the kitchen and found her staring out of the window in a haze, fiddling with her wedding ring.

'Cheer up,' I said. 'You found your ring then?'

She jumped violently, then laughed. It struck me then that, day by day, her laughter was moving up an octave, starting to sound a touch hysterical.

'Yes!' she said, twirling a curl around her finger, 'Sorry, I'm just day-dreaming. What are you doing today? It's Midsummer's Day so we might go down to the green, they've got a fete there.'

'Oh God, I didn't realise it was Midsummer's Day!' I cried.

'What?' Andie asked.

'Oh, nothing . . . I just . . . there's some stuff I've got to take care of.'

Just how much damage would my mother do if I didn't turn up to the Summer Solstice tonight? I mused back upstairs in my attic room. It wasn't a pleasant thought; my mother's magic was unpredictable. *There was no doubt about it,* I thought sulkily, *I had to go.* Which meant having to spend the whole evening with Rufus. Yet again.

The day dragged by. I started to flick grumpily through my wardrobe for something to wear. Traditionally we wore green to celebrate the longest day but I decided to deliberately wind my mother up by picking out the most ugly outfit I could find: a black lycra dress that had been hauled through the washing machine so many times it had faded to the ugly grey of a British summer sky. Ha! I could just hear the other witches muttering, 'Black! She's wearing *black!* What was she thinking . . . *so* unsuitable . . . who did you say her mother was again . . .?'

Below, I heard the front door slam and a babble of voices in the downstairs hall.

'SOMEONE FOR YOUUUU, CARA! IT'S A SURPRISE!' Fred called up. 'AND HE SAYS YOU HAVE TO SHUT YOUR EYES!'

A surprise! Wow. I heard footsteps on the stairs and I closed my eyes obediently, wondering if this was one of Fred's pranks and any minute I'd feel the slap of a water-bomb against the back of my head.

Then I felt two hands cover my eyes and a familiar scent that I recognised at once. And another scent: sweet and elegant. He took his hands away and I looked down to see a rose in my lap.

'Sean,' I said, laughing, 'what are you doing here?'

'Oh, do I have to make an appointment to see you now?' he asked.

'No – I – just—'

'Relax,' he said nervously. 'I was wondering if you, erm, wanted to come to dinner tonight?'

'As long as it's not cheese on toast again,' I said, poking him in the ribs. He looked a little offended.

'Actually, I've got three courses planned,' he said, swallowing. 'I've spent all morning reading Jamie Oliver, would you believe it?'

He's asking me out on a date, I realised. But . . .

'Oh no, oh God! My mum – I absolutely swore to her that I'd go to Summer. . .'

'To *what?*'

'Um, to, to, a summer party – to celebrate my mother's birthday.'

'Well, you can't miss that,' said Sean, his face falling.

'It's fine, I can just drop by for half an hour and then come back, if you wouldn't mind starting dinner a bit late – say eight?'

'Great,' said Sean, looking deep into my eyes and causing a minor earthquake in my stomach. Then he frowned, running his eyes over my yucky dress. 'But could you wear something a bit more sexy?'

'What's wrong with this? It's designer!' I feigned indignation. 'I was just, er, throwing some clothes out.'

'Well, I'd *definitely* throw that out,' said Sean, laughing as I hit him.

'Well, if I'm going to bloody well dress up, you can too,' I said, eyeing his paint-splattered, grass-stained jeans, and he grinned, looking a little embarrassed.

After he'd gone, I stood there smiling, a wild horse of happiness galloping through my veins. Just when I'd finally

341

resigned myself to friendship, he was playing the romantic card.

I rushed off to meet my mother as fast as I could. Sean let me borrow his car. It felt strangely intimate, sitting in the leather seat shaped by his body, rifling through his eclectic tape collection. There was a dog-eared photograph of Maeve blue-tacked to the dashboard. Every time I looked at it, I pictured Sean in a traffic jam or tired at the end of a long day's work, leaning over and gently stroking his finger against the photo, and my heart leaped fondly.

There are eight key festivals, or *sabbats*, in the witching calendar. The Summer Solstice has always been my favourite because it's such a joyous affair. It's funny how Christianity has borrowed and stolen so much from the heathen tradition it despises so much; as well as building churches on our sacred sites, they turned Samhain into Harvest Festival, Yule into Christmas, Ostara into Easter and Beltane into May Day celebrations. Even as a child I remember getting dressed up in a pink crêpe paper outfit to dance around the May Pole in a flurry of flying ribbons.

Tonight's celebration, however, was going to be a little more adult. I just wanted to get the whole thing over as quickly as possible. If I was going to celebrate the longest day I wanted it to be safely indoors at Sean's house. I'd made up my mind.

As with most witching festivals, I found myself enjoying it a whole lot more than I'd expected.

The coven had gathered in a select clearing in Richmond Park, hidden from the world and unlikely to be interrupted by anything except the odd deer. I kissed my mother and grandmother hello, and then stood watching as the celebrations began.

It was a beautiful evening: the sky was streaked with tongues of red sunset and the air was sweet with the scent of oak and flowers. A circle of girls danced around a bonfire, chanting, while several men banged drums. A pretty girl with a candyfloss mane of dark hair dressed in a beautiful medieval dress stood out among the other girls.

'Who is she?' I whispered to my mother.

'Artemisia,' my mother whispered in reply, an edge to her voice. 'She's the daughter of Morgan Le Fay. She won the 2003 Most Beautiful Witch Contest, but we all know she cheated by magically enhancing her breasts.'

I stood on tiptoes in curiosity, and watched her dance around a group of men, one of whom was Rufus. Even I had to admit that he looked rather stylish in his costume, and he was obviously enjoying the attention.

The celebrations continued. A small group of musicians played in the background; some elderly witches ladled out a summer punch; the air was filled with laughter and chatter. A gaggle of thirteen-year-old witches huddled past, whispering with red faces, 'Did you see Rufus? Wasn't he *gorgeous*! I wonder how big his wand is . . .' I smiled. There was no accounting for taste.

I turned back to my mother and cringed as she beckoned for Rufus to come over. He shrugged and flapped his hand at her, as if to say *in a minute*. Clearly he hadn't forgotten or forgiven the Coke-over-his-trousers-incident.

'Oh darling, can you at least go and say sorry to Rufus?' she wheedled.

'As a matter of fact, I really need to get going . . .'

'What? But you've only just got here!'

'Look, Mum,' I said gently. 'I'm really sorry but I can't stay for long tonight. No—' I stopped her before she could bulldoze over me. 'Mum, I don't want you to bully me, okay? I want you to try to understand me. Look . . . I know you mean well with Rufus, but he just isn't my type.'

'But why?' she asked, her eyes all big and doeish.

'Because I find him physically repulsive, his conversation banal and don't feel the slightest spark or connection with him in any way,' I attempted politely.

'Well, can't you get over those little obstacles?'

'Look, Mum—' I felt impatience rising in my throat and swallowed it back. 'I thought about what you said about me not suiting a non-wizard. And I know it will be hard with Sean but I just want to try. I'm going to go there tonight and tell him the truth and talk it all through with him. I can't just go out with someone because you tell me to, don't you see that? Love and attraction have to come from inside. If I did go out with Rufus, it would only be to please you, and I'd end up unhappy in the end. I know it upsets you and I don't want to hurt you because I do . . .' *Love you*, I wanted to say.

But I couldn't, somehow. I'd never ever told my mother I loved her. The gulf between us was too big.

My mother pursed her lips and shook her head several times. Then, to my complete amazement, she gave me a hug. An awkward one, but a hug all the same. Then she reached into her handbag and drew out a large, juicy-looking apple. She pressed it into my palm surreptitiously.

'Darling, have this. I was going to give it to you for Rufus's sake, but Sean may as well benefit. It's been blessed. All you need to do is take a few bites and you will shine and shimmer with irresistibility.'

'Oh, Mum, thanks so much,' I said. I wasn't sure if I fancied trying it, but I was deeply touched by the gesture.

I hung around for a few more minutes. My mother continued to be amazingly sweet; she didn't even blink when Rufus, shooting me a filthy, triumphant glance, put his arm around Artemisia and disappeared with her into the woods, saying loudly, 'Come on, Artemisia, let's go and study some plants.'

By the time I'd said goodbye to my mum and my grandmother, and driven back to Sean's, however, it was 8:30 p.m.

'Sorry I'm late,' I gabbled, feeling nervous. Sean was looking smart again, dressed in a pair of tan-coloured chinos and a chunky cream-coloured V-necked T-shirt. His Saint Christopher gleamed at his throat; he looked preppy and rather grown-up. I was glad I'd taken some clothes to change into; I would have looked awful next to him in my black dress.

'It's fine, don't worry,' said Sean. 'You're always late anyway. I was expecting it.'

'I am *not*,' I protested unconvincingly, walking into the living room.

Instantly I shut up. My heart gasped. Sean had filled the room with candles. Tall white candles lining the mantelpiece; fat pastel-coloured ones on the windowsill; slender black ones on the TV and red ones in a gothic candelabra on the table, all winking in a choir of soft light. He'd cleaned the room and removed all the rubbish from the coffee table, replacing it with clean plates and tall champagne glasses.

It was simply magical.

'I hate champagne,' Sean admitted, 'so I got Baileys instead. I thought you'd prefer that. But if you're feeling teetotal, you can have Ame.'

'It's beautiful,' I kept saying. 'I mean – thanks for making it look so lovely – it's so sweet – so . . .'

'Oh well,' he shrugged.

'Do you mind if I just use the bathroom?' I asked. If he

had gone to all this effort for me, I could at least make an effort to look good for him.

'Sure,' he said, then shot me a wicked grin. 'I expect you're off taking your drugs again?'

'Oh, well, you know I can't dine without a line of cocaine first,' I joked back.

Okay, I thought, this is it. Time to tell Sean the truth. By lying I was placing a wedge between us; we could never properly know each other. Then I pictured the look on his face, the anger in his voice: 'Thanks for not telling me you were a freak earlier, Cara.'

Don't be silly, Cara, I told myself, *you're blowing things out of proportion.* Besides, I could break it to him gently, in stages. I didn't have to tell him I was a real witch; I could pretend I was one of those flaky New Age-style ones who got weird symbolic tattoos and lit strange-smelling incense to 'chill out the vibes, man'.

As I fumbled in my handbag for my hairbrush, my hand knocked against the apple my mother had given me. The fruit that would Make Me Irresistible. I weighed it in my palm, glossy and still: rosy on one side, smudging into lemony-green on the other. Temptation tickled the lining of my stomach . . . Okay, so it was cheating, technically . . . but I was about to confess something major to Sean, I needed all the help I could get . . .

Before I could change my mind and start moralising, I took a huge bite out of it. It was the most delicious apple I'd ever tasted: crisp and sweet, laced with a bittersweet tang. I took another bite and another and another, letting the juice flow over my tongue and sting my saliva. Yum yum yum!

I ate it all and tossed the core into the bin, my stomach gurgling with pleasure. As I brushed out my hair, I felt a wave of gratitude towards my mother.

Grandma's right, I realised with a pang of guilt, *I really should make an effort to be nicer to her. She might be bonkers, but she's got a good heart—*

Hang on. I suddenly realised something was wrong. I was, er, running my brush through thin air. Because . . . I turned back to the mirror, gawping . . . my hair had fallen out!

No. No, it hadn't fallen out. It had *shrunk*. It was now short and spruce and dark, my natural colour.

I let out a yelp and Sean called from the hallway: 'Cara, are you all right in there?'

'Fine, fine,' I called back, then broke off. What had happened to my voice? I sounded all deep and hoarse and croaky . . .

'I expect you're up to your compulsory handwashing tricks again, hmm?'

Suddenly my brush fell to the floor with a clatter. I could feel prickly sensations dancing over my hands like pins and needles. And then they crept down my legs. I rolled up my jeans frantically. Hairs were shooting from my shins in a mat of black silk. It could only mean one thing: *My mother had turned me into a werewolf.*

Thankfully, Sean didn't get to hear my second cry of fury, for I was so shocked I half-sank, half-collapsed on to the floor, knocking my elbow against the toilet, which saved me with a loud flush.

I closed my eyes in disbelief, a sharp knot of hatred twisting inside me. *I can't believe it,* I thought. *I shall never, ever, EVER talk to her again. She is SUCH a bitch, a witch, a . . .*

And so I went on, for the next five minutes, silently calling her every insult I could think of until I could nearly feel sparks flying from my brain and steam hissing from my ears. Finally, I managed to drag myself towards the mirror. I'll count back from three, I told myself – it was the only way I could muster up the courage to peek . . .

Three . . . *Oh God, I'm going to open my eyes and see myself covered with hair like Michael J Fox in* TeenWolf.

Two . . . *I don't ever plan to be a basketball star, so this is of no comfort to me . . .*

One . . . *What if the moon's full? Is it? Will I suffer an urge to yowl and tackle Sean to the ground for dinner?*

I would have gladly started again and counted back from one hundred but I forced my eyes open.

Oh. It wasn't so bad. I wasn't a werewolf . . . Actually, it was bad. I was worse than a werewolf.

I was a man.

I looked a little like my brother – if I'd had a brother. I was taller, I had a goatee beard and bushy eyebrows like black caterpillars. And – I felt my chest – my breasts had gone! And – I felt my trousers – I had . . . Oh, God – it moved! It had a mind of its own!

'Cara, are you going to carry on teasing me like this all night?' Sean called through the door, his voice maniacally cheerful.

Sean? Now what? What excuse could I make? 'Sean, I've suddenly had a sex-change operation, so why don't you become a girl and change your name to Sheila?' No, no good. I looked at the window.

'Sean,' I said, shocked again by my deep voice. I quickly tried to speak in a higher, girly one: 'I'm just coming – I'm feeling a bit ill!'

'Are you okay? Why do you sound as though you're on helium? I hope you haven't taken too many of those drugs again,' he joked, though there was a note of genuine worry and suspicion in his voice.

There was only one thing I could do.

I was going to have to leg it. Through the bathroom window.

Unfortunately, I was halfway through the bathroom window when I realised that either it was too thin or I was too fat. I got stuck, arms hanging out into mid-air, feet back in the bathroom.

Great, I thought. *Not only have I turned into a man but now I need to be surgically removed from a toilet window.* It was the sort of scenario Jeremy Beadle would have died for.

Okay, I thought, either go in or out. Out, I decided, was the better option. I just needed to find something to push against. I felt about with my foot and kicked off against the toilet, knocking the handle. As it flushed, I grasped the guttering outside, stepped on to the windowsill, closed my eyes and jumped. I landed in a heap on the gravel, letting out a cry as I suffered a nasty scrape on my arm. I got up, wiped away the blood on my jeans and slowly sauntered down Sean's path, whistling casually.

I nearly made it. I had just reached the gate when I heard the front door open.

'Um, hi?' Sean eyed me suspiciously, clearly wondering what this stranger was doing in his garden.

I turned uneasily. The easiest thing would be to run for it. But then Sean would be left there, his food spoiling, wondering why I hadn't come out of the bathroom. He'd probably conclude that I had fainted and eventually break down the door, only to find I'd scarpered without even having the grace to tell him. I couldn't do that to Sean, it was too mean.

'My name's Ralph,' I said, shaking his hand vigorously. 'I'm Cara's brother.'

'Cara's brother? She told me she was an only child . . .'

Sean trailed off, shaking his head in bewilderment. 'And Cara . . . where is she? One minute she was in the toilet, the next she'd disappeared . . .'

'She had to leave,' I said quickly. 'It was an emergency . . . with her . . . her mother. She wasn't in next door so I called her on her mobile. I'm really sorry but she won't be back this evening.'

'But—'

'She went out through the window and—'

'The *window*?'

Swallow. 'Yes. I know it sounds slightly weird, but . . .' I tried to think up a plausible excuse as to why squeezing through a bathroom window was preferable to going out through the front door. Unsurprisingly, I couldn't come up with one.

'No, it doesn't sound weird,' Sean sighed, 'it sounds just like Cara. I do love her, but she is bats. I expect I'll catch up with her tomorrow.'

Love her. I shone inside.

'To be honest, I've kind of lost my appetite,' Sean said. 'I feel like drowning my sorrows in a nice pint. Fancy one, Ralph?'

'Um, sure,' I said. 'Why not?'

It was surely the strangest situation I'd ever been in. Here I was, strolling down the road with the man I adored, who thought I was the brother of the woman he (hopefully) adored, when I was really myself trapped in a masculine shell due to a spell cast by a wicked witch of a mother. Elizabeth Bennet and Bridget Jones had it positively easy in comparison, I mused.

I sat down on the bar stool in the Goat and crossed my legs, reaching up to fiddle with an absent earring. Then I noticed Sean giving me another odd look and I caught myself again. I swept my eyes over the bar, pretending to eye up some girls sitting on a table by the jukebox.

'God, they're fit, aren't they?' I said in a laddish voice, giving him a nudge and nearly causing him to spill his pint.

'Well, they look about twelve,' said Sean in a worried voice. 'I think their parents are about to take them into the beer garden. Where *children* are allowed.'

Oh. I took a closer look. So they did. Oops.

'I meant fit as in . . . athletic,' I said hastily. 'As if they go to the gym a lot. I like a girl who's a bit, you know . . . my favourite Spice Girl was always Sporty.' I broke off, sweat trembling at my hairline. How much longer could I keep this up? I felt acutely conscious of every tiny ripple of my body language. I was convinced that any minute someone was going to stand up and yell, 'He's a she, can't you tell!'

Don't be silly, I told myself. *We're a superficial race. We all judge each other by our appearances. Nobody is giving you a second glance.*

A glum look passed over Sean's face and I suddenly realised just how much effort he was making to hide his disappointment over our failed dinner. I felt guilt slash through me; how I ached to be able to lean over and hug him and explain everything.

As he searched around for an ashtray, I turned to the blokes on the next table, shot them a sexy smile and took the spare one off their table, expecting them to grin back. Instead they shot me faintly menacing glances.

'Hey, thanks for asking,' one said.

'I'm sorry – I – can I borrow this?' I asked politely, and then they shot me looks as though I was a complete nerd.

Being a man was harder than I realised. There was a

whole new set of rules, etiquette and interaction. I was never going to learn it all in the space of an evening. *Maybe I should just make up an excuse and get home before I cause any more trouble,* I fretted.

'So what about Cara's emergency?' Sean asked. 'I keep worrying about her. Is it serious?'

'Um, I think so . . . It's our mother, you see – she's rather ill.' I realised that my tone was far too cheerful and so I feigned an upset face.

'God!' said Sean, going white. 'Cara never told me! She never tells me anything, mind you. Don't you think you should be with her now? I mean – you're her brother . . .'

'We're not very close,' I said hastily. 'To be honest, Cara's always been her favourite.'

'Really?' Sean looked fascinated. 'I met Cara's mother and she didn't seem to like me very much – but I sensed a bit of friction between her and Cara. Mind you, I don't know what's going on in Cara's head half the time. I've known her for months and sometimes I feel like she's my best friend and sometimes she feels like a total stranger.'

I felt hurt. Up until now, I'd regarded my friendship with Sean as exquisitely intimate. But perhaps it wasn't by ordinary standards; it was merely as deep as I could go without letting him find out my true nature.

'So, what's going on between you and Cara?' I asked casually, stroking my goatee.

Sean lit a cigarette, narrowing his eyes and blowing out a stream of smoke. 'What does Cara say is going on?' he asked jumpily.

'She confided in me the other week that she doesn't really know what's going on with you. She said she finds you a bit hot and cold.'

'Did she?' Sean looked rather shocked. 'Well, yeah, I guess she's right. In fact, I'm lucky she puts up with me; most girls wouldn't. Look, don't get me wrong. I've always fancied Cara. I mean, who wouldn't, with that lovely hair and her eyes and those . . .' He broke off, suddenly realising who he was talking to. 'And as I got to know her, I realised she was intelligent and funny and kind and sweet. At first, I was all for it. I mean, one night she stayed over at my house and something nearly happened between us and I spent *all* night with a raging hard-on – it was *painful*.'

Oh my God. This was *SO* fantastic. I wasn't ugly. He fancied me! Hallelujah! So what had gone wrong?

'But then another night she came over and we made these crazy cocktails and got very drunk and it all went wrong, somehow.'

'You went off her?' I asked in dismay.

'Yes,' Sean reflected. 'Yes, I suppose I did. I felt . . . I felt I was taking advantage of her . . . but, you see, the thing is . . .' He circled his fingers around the rim of his pint glass, trying to find the right words.

'Yes?' I was nearly on the edge of my seat now, fingers digging into my palm . . . when I suddenly noticed that my nails felt different. I looked down and gasped. They were no longer short and square. They were now long and smooth and oval. *I was turning back into a woman.*

'You see . . .' said Sean, 'life is very complicated and . . . I'm a bit complicated right now . . .'

Hurry up, hurry up!

'She just isn't my type,' he said quietly, rolling up a beermat. 'I don't think it would work out.'

I felt as though I wanted to melt on to the floor in a puddle of misery. I decided I'd heard enough. I checked my watch ostentatiously in a look-at-the-time-gasp and made quick apologies about needing to meet a friend in Camden.

'Okay, sure,' said Sean. 'Well, nice to meet you, Ralph. Hope Cara sorts it all out with her mum.'

Without thinking, I leaned across and gave him a tight hug and kissed the edge of his mouth. Sean froze in shock. I drew back. The lads at the next table were giving us strange looks. *Homophobic bastards,* I thought, standing up and adopting a defiant expression. All the same, I walked out of that pub pretty quickly.

All the way home, I felt as though my heart was breaking. Sean had said it. Man to man. I wasn't his type. There was nothing there.

But if there was nothing there, why cook me a romantic dinner and buy a hundred bloody candles? And Sean complained that *women* were confusing. Oh God, I hated being in love with him so much, stuck in this yo-yo of emotions all the time.

Back home, I had to sidle into the Wilkinses' house through the back door and dash up the stairs, ignoring Andie who called, 'Cara, are you okay?' after me in a mystified voice. Upstairs, I braced myself and looked in the mirror.

Oh. I was still a man. I had slightly longer fingernails and the vague seedlings of returning breasts, but the change back seemed to have lost momentum and fizzled out.

Oh God, what if the spell took ages to wear off? What if it didn't wear off at all? What if I got stuck in between, a magical hermaphrodite? Whenever I filled in credit card applications, I'd have to tick both the 'Mr' and 'Ms' boxes and people would have to address all letters to me as 'Dear Sir/Madam'.

I slumped down on to my bed. I didn't dare come out of my room for fear of bumping into Andie.

This, I thought, *is a total nightmare. If I'm ever able to get out of my room again, I am going to kill my mother.*

And then the answer came to me.

Around 5 a.m. the following morning, I crept downstairs and went outside. The garden was still and serene: birds cooing softly; a startled fox picking his way delicately through the undergrowth, tail swishing; sleepy flowers uncurling their buds; everything veiled in a cobweb of white morning mist.

According to tradition, the morning dew is sacred and healing. I trailed my fingers over the grass, the flowers, disturbing insects and rousing plants, collecting the clean drops and running them over my face. Gradually, I felt the transformation beneath my fingertips: the stubble returning to smooth skin, strong jawline to a soft one. I lifted up my nightie, pouring the dew into my palms and splashing it over me. I felt my breasts swell and my hips curve and my waist contract. I felt my scalp prickle as my hair grew out. Finally, I looked at my reflection in the window. I had never been so relieved to see my face again; snub nose and long eyelashes and full lips. I laughed out loud and fell back into the grass and lay there, not caring about the damp seeping into my clothes, savouring my previous body and feeling glad to be a woman again.

Then I looked up at Sean's house, gently wreathed in the morning mist. The curtained windows stared back at me like blank eyes. I felt my smile slowly fade.

34
Andie

Andie felt sweat trickle down her neck, slither down her spine and collect in a damp pool in the small of her back. She was wearing a black dress for the party and she realised it was a mistake: it was far too hot for this weather, she ought to have worn something light and floaty.

She wasn't enjoying the party much. The crowded room was musky with the scent of hot bodies. She felt bored, and glanced across the room, spotting Jonathan. He looked equally uncomfortable in his heavy tuxedo. He started to push through the crowd towards her. Andie pretended not to notice and carried on talking to a dull-looking man with a grizzly beard. Andie went rigid with shock as she felt Jonathan behind her. He started to run his hands over her back in possessive, massaging strokes; then he unzipped her dress, yanking it down angrily. For a moment desire clouded over her and she arched against him, feeling his kisses in her hair. Then she became horribly aware that the whole room had gone silent and everyone was looking at them. Her dress was on the floor and she was naked and they had been found out. Whispers buzzed around the room: 'They're having an affair . . .

didn't you see them at the concert . . . she's five years older than him . . . she's married, with a child . . .'

Andie sat up in shock, her heart pounding. She realised she'd cried 'Jonathan!' as she woke, but to her relief Nick was still asleep. Her nightdress was soaked in sweat. She slid out of bed and padded downstairs to the kitchen for some water, pressing the cool glass against her hot forehead.

Her dream lingered in her mind. She was seeing Jonathan tomorrow; she hoped the nightmare wasn't some kind of bad omen. Oh God – ever since their affair had started, she'd become so superstitious. At this rate she'd be worse than Cara.

I can't believe it, she thought. *I can't believe I'm doing this. It should have ended with Wales; I can't believe it's still going on.*

I'm having an affair.

But tomorrow it would all be over. She was going to tell Jonathan it was over.

But it was a promise she'd made the last five times she'd seen him, and she wasn't very good at keeping it.

The moment she woke up the next morning, Andie's heart did a backflip and she thought: *Jonathan! I'm seeing him today!*

Nick was already up – good. She liked to ponder over what to wear in her own time and space, to hear Jonathan's voice in her head as she tried something on: *Yes, that looks gorgeous, try it with the black skirt*, to run her hands over the fabrics in echo of his hands on her body. She'd only just started to realise how much Nick had corroded her confidence in her looks over the years. Yes, he said that she was beautiful, but five minutes later he'd be eyeing up Cara or his secretary. Or someone. Because, let's face it, there would always be someone prettier than her, and Andie had resigned herself to accepting that this was the fate of a woman who married a husband more handsome than her.

But not any more. Jonathan had finally started to convince her that she was beautiful. She pulled on a short red cashmere skirt with a tartan check and a sexy silk white top with a scooped neck, carefully applied make-up and then smiled at her reflection.

'Wow, Andie, you look lovely,' Nick said as she went out on to the landing.

Andie jumped violently. Nick was looking her up and down with genuine appreciation. *Oh God,* she thought, *this is punishment. I'm so evil. I say my husband doesn't appreciate me and you go and show me he does.*

'Why don't we go out to dinner tonight?' said Nick, curling her into his arms and ballroom dancing her up and down the landing.

'I can't,' she said quickly. 'I've got to go over to Suzanne's, we have to run through sports' day together.'

'Oh come on, surely your intense negotiations on the official length of the egg and spoon race can wait?'

'No, it can't. Sorry.' Andie stepped back out of his arms. 'Let's go tomorrow night.'

'I can't go tomorrow night,' Nick said sarcastically. 'I've got a meeting to discuss the official length of office paperclips in line with EU regulations.'

'Look, Nick, it's not my fault, I have to do this thing,' Andie cried, guilt making her angry.

'Andie, relax,' said Nick in an amazed voice. 'I was joking, okay? Tomorrow night is fine.'

'Oh, good.' Andie managed a smile. 'Good.'

On her way to work, her mind chugged it all over. Logically speaking, her affair with Jonathan should have finished as soon as they left Wales. Nick had a job now. They could pay the mortgage. They could keep Cara. Fred was happy. Everything was hunky dory. So why did she keep going back to Jonathan?

Besides, she argued to herself, *Nick doesn't seem to be enjoying his new job that much. I think he's putting on a bit of an act. I wouldn't be surprised if he walked out of this one in a few weeks' time.*

But she was being unfair. Nick had merely gone through a tough patch and come out the other side. She was nit-picking. Nick's faults had always been there, only at the start of their marriage they'd been 'loveable eccentricities' and now they were 'niggling irritations'. Even so, she could live with them. The point was . . . the point was . . . there was no point. There was nothing really *wrong*.

Andie found this revelation slightly disconcerting. Ten years ago, when she'd married Nick, she'd been so idealistic. She'd had the notion that love lasted for ever. Consequently, she had always thought that marriages had to end with a firework explosion too: violence and custody battles. Not discovering that love could slowly dilute over the years into a sense of companionship that was survivable but ultimately unsatisfying; that she did love her husband, but not as deeply as she thought she did.

Maybe they would have carried on like that, maybe it would have been enough. But Nick losing his job had hit their tidy life like a meteor, tearing cracks through the seams of their very existence, and Andie, losing her balance, had clung on to Jonathan for dear life as she waited for the trembling aftershocks to subside. And now she found she didn't want to let go.

It was crazy, because she was lost in the same cloudy, dizzy joy with Jonathan that she'd first had with Nick.

During school hours, they were very strict, playing their roles of Mrs Wilkins and Mr Yates. Andie told Nick she had 'meetings' after school finished and so the slot between four and seven, when school was over and before Andie sat down to a family dinner at home, was hers and Jonathan's. It wasn't a terribly romantic time of day; it was commuter time, winding down time, lacking the dark danger of the night, of candlelit dinners and secret trysts in the twilight. And yet for Andie those hours were like a secret garden in her daily routine, a time when she let go and wandered in flower beds of pleasure, when she loved and was loved.

Andie didn't want to admit it to herself but deep down she knew it was happening: she was starting to fall in love.

Andie spent the whole day yo-yoing between emotions. At 10 a.m., she decided she absolutely could *not* go; she couldn't face another night of nightmares. At midday, she saw Jonathan pass by the classroom window – he turned and gave her a cheeky, surreptitious wink and she felt herself melt and ache for him with such hunger that she thought: *I have to go.* At 3 p.m., one of her kids, James, whose parents had recently got divorced, started playing up so badly she had to send him out of the class. *Imagine what would happen to Fred if Nick found out,* she thought. *You cannot go.*

Yet at 4 p.m. she got into Jonathan's car. She felt as though she was watching herself swim out into a warm sea; the further she went the more out of her depth she was but the feel of the water on her skin was so delicious she just kept going, letting the current take her.

She slid into the car, waiting for Jonathan to comment on her outfit. But he ran his eyes over her in an awkward flick – like a schoolboy casting a nervous glance over a

360

porn mag before slapping it back on a newsagent's shelf – and then looked away moodily. He drove angrily, grinding gears and cursing drivers; and as they screeched to a halt by some traffic lights, he let out a deep sigh that reminded her of Nick.

Andie felt her bubble of bliss start to deflate. *What is this?* she thought. *I could be at home with Fred. I don't need to sit in a traffic jam with a man sighing at me.*

Then Jonathan drummed his fingers on the steering wheel and said, 'We shouldn't be doing this.'

Andie was shocked to the core. *Hang on, I'm the married woman,* she wanted to yell. *I'm the one who's supposed to be feeling guilty. I'm the one calling the shots. I give up. This is it, it's too much stress, too much pain. It's over. I'm going. Dear God, you can stop punishing me now. You can be nice to me. Because I'm going to end it.*

She tried to open the car door at the same time as the lights changed and Jonathan put his foot down. As she recoiled, her handbag slid down her arm, upending its contents into the road. Jonathan cried 'What are you doing?', screeched on the brakes, narrowly avoiding causing a pile-up as cars swerved and beeped around him. Andie jumped out of the car, stuffing everything back into her handbag, tears burning the back of her throat.

'I'm going,' she said. 'I'm fucking going.'

'Andie, don't.'

She shook her head, slammed the door, and started to walk off.

Jonathan flung the door back open and reached across, clawing thin air. 'Andie, please—'

Andie turned back to face him, arms folded.

'*Please.*'

She slid into the car haughtily, chin up. If he wanted her, he had to apologise.

'I'm not your mistress, you know,' she said. 'I want you to take me home.'

'Andie,' he said softly.

She turned to face him. His face was boyish and hurt. He drew her into his arms and they hugged tightly.

'I just feel guilty,' he explained. 'I feel like I'm ruining your life . . . messing up your family . . . and making you lie to everyone . . .'

Andie didn't know what to say, so she silenced him with a kiss.

They lay in Jonathan's bed, the late afternoon sunlight draped over them, breathless and trembling. Andie could feel post-orgasmic shivers rippling all over her body, a flower of bliss sparkling in her heart. Their lovemaking had soothed her, untied the tension knotted inside. She could hear the lap of the Thames outside like a lullaby. She nestled her head into the pillow, feeling sleep leak into her mind, tug her down into peaceful oblivion . . .

Her eyes fluttered open as Jonathan turned and kissed her. He said, 'Andie, there's something we should talk about . . .'

Andie felt tense again. *He's going to end it,* she thought in paranoid shock. The thought of life without Jonathan suddenly seemed colourless, boring, horrible.

They were interrupted by Becks jumping on to the bed, bouncing around and barking and dissolving the tension as they burst into laughter.

Finally he settled down into a ball between them. They smiled over him in the manner of two parents smiling over their newborn child, fingers touching in his fuzzy fur.

'Look, Andie,' Jonathan said, 'I think—'

'I'm thirsty,' Andie said suddenly, her heart pounding. She sat up. 'Why don't I make a cup of tea?'

'Andie, listen to me. Wait.'

She paused, dreading it. 'Look, I know what you're going to say,' she said, 'and I know it's up to you, but I don't want to. I don't.'

'I know it's a big decision. I know you love Fred and I wouldn't want to ruin that. But it could work, Andie. Fred could live with us, he could spend weekends with Nick, we could make it work. You could live here! You could bring the dogs; I know Becks would grow to love them. It could work, couldn't it?' Jonathan rubbed his hand up and down her arm.

Andie froze in shock, completely and utterly lost for words.

35
Cara

Sean was surprisingly sweet about my escape from the bathroom window.

'Look, Cara, it's fine,' he assured me as I apologised, red-faced, for the thirty-ninth time. 'I realise it was an emergency and anyway, your brother was, um, a nice bloke,' he said, looking very uneasy.

'He said the same about you,' I said wickedly, trying not to laugh as I saw the nervous look on his face.

Even so, my anger towards my mother had not cooled. On Saturday afternoon I set off to my grandmother's shop to tell her just what I thought of her.

On the way, I was vaguely aware that someone was following me. You know what it's like when you get that itchy feeling; you're convinced someone is on your trail and images from *Crimewatch* flash across your mind, but when you look back nervously all you can see are crowds of normal people and you feel stupid and paranoid?

Unfortunately, once I got into Soho, every time I looked back I saw an elderly gentleman walking a pug dog who, on my third glance, winked at me hopefully. I cringed and hurried into The Mistress of Magic.

Instantly, my heart twisted into a knot of fury.

My mother was there, sitting behind the counter, theatrically sipping from a cup as though it was a magical elixir, though I could see and smell that it was only hot chocolate.

I knew at once she was guilty. She flicked a quick smile at me and then pretended to be concentrating on her magazine.

'Mother,' I said, nodding hello as my grandmother came into the room, looking as neat and petite as ever – good, I wanted her to hear this. 'The apple you gave me at the Summer Solstice was supposed to make me irresistible. Instead I found myself turning into a man. I was locked in Sean's bathroom at the time. It was most embarrassing.'

I was trying to sound cool and calm, like a prosecuting lawyer, but I could hear my voice shaking slightly.

'Oh, you didn't, did you?' My grandmother stared at my mother, appalled.

'I haven't a clue what you're talking about it. Now, how would you answer this quiz? "If you were being harassed at a party by an ugly wizard who wants to drag you into bed, would you: (a) perform a quick spell to turn his penis into a ten-foot marrow – that'll teach him! (b) offer to set him up with your best friend (without mentioning that she is a warlock) (c) act in a dignified manner, calmly and politely reject his advances, thank the hostess and leave early – after all, magic is for higher purposes." I think (c),' my mother concluded.

Liar, I thought, acidly – she was only going for (c) to obtain the conclusion: 'You are the Audrey Hepburn of witches'.

'Mum, I know it was you,' I persisted.

Finally, she put down her quiz. 'It was Morgan Le Fay. I bought the apple from her stall, she tricked me, the wicked hussy—'

'Oh, Morgan Le Fay my foot! Mum, you cannot go around doing things like that!' I was close to tears. 'It might never have worn off!'

'Cara, I am sorry,' she admitted at last. 'When you said you were seeing Sean, I panicked. It will never work out with him, darling. He just isn't right for you. I know best – I'm your mother.'

Before I could think of a comeback, the shop door pinged and a young man came strolling in. I did a double-take.

'Hello, can I help you?' My grandmother enquired, perking up.

'I just wanted to look around,' he shrugged, blushing.

I sat on my stool, agape. *Sean*. What was he doing here? I'd *known* someone was following me. I felt my whole body tense with embarrassment. I was just about to take him aside when he turned and grinned at me (as though he'd only just noticed me!) and said, 'Hi, Cara!'

'Sean—' I started.

'Oh – he's *Sean*,' my grandmother said and then turned back to my mother with a knowing glance. '*Sean*.'

My mother got up and went over to him, looking him up and down as though she was in Battersea Dogs' Home and he was a stray dog she was contemplating buying.

'Of course, I met you before,' she said slowly. 'I came to your house.'

'Are you feeling better?' he asked.

I froze in horror. Oh God, I'd told Sean I'd escaped through the bathroom window because of an emergency ... But to my relief, my mother's hypochondria saved the say.

'Well,' my mother moaned, 'I am in rather a lot of pain but, you know, I try to survive.'

Then I saw the evil glimmer in her eye. It was revenge time.

She insisted on getting out photographs of me as a baby: me being christened at Stonehenge; then she offered to read Sean's palm.

'*MUM!*' I exploded. My mother made an innocent face. 'Sean, I think we should go—'

'Cara, darling, why don't you come round the back and look at the spirit collection?' my grandmother said, as though I was a little girl needing to be appeased with something charming to play with.

'Er . . . *spirit collection?*' Sean asked in a dazed voice. He gave me a I'm-totally-freaked-out look. I gave him a reassuring look back that said: My family are totally deranged; please just humour them.

'Spirits as in wine,' I said, grinning. 'Er, vintage liqueurs, that sort of thing.' Seeing his eyes light up – Sean liked a good drink – I added hastily, 'You just stay with Mum for now, I'm sure she's got lots more nice photos to show you.'

Photos were embarrassing but they were a lot safer than spirits.

My grandmother tucked her arm through mine and led me to a large dark bookcase, its sides carved with cupids dancing among swirling clouds and ivy. I imagined that it had once held battered first edition books behind its elegant glass, but now it was filled with rows and rows of bottles. The spirits were like transparent jelly. Some hung in the jars like silent sea creatures; others thrashed about wildly as if desperate to escape.

'Grandma,' I hissed, trying to get away from her, 'I have to get Sean out of here.'

'Cara, he has to find out sooner or later,' she said firmly. 'Just let him take his time and have a look around. Leave him be for now; let it sink in.'

I knew she was right. I'd been waiting for this moment to come; I'd known it was going to happen one day. I couldn't help panicking: *It's too soon, I'm going to lose him* . . .

My grandmother started to blather on about her collection; I didn't want to look, I didn't want to know. I'd had it up to here with magic. Why couldn't she collect something *normal*, like shells or china pigs, like proper OAPs did?

My grandmother went back to offer Sean a cup of tea. *I'll just give them five minutes and then I'm going to drag him out,* I told myself. Yes, he had to find out, but he didn't need an overdose.

Then, suddenly, I heard Sean *laugh*. And say, 'Well, I always thought Cara was nuts; now I know where she gets it from! No, I'm only joking. This is all very interesting . . .'

I felt a tiny trickle of relief cool my panic. Maybe my grandmother was right; maybe I should let them have a good old natter . . .

But as their conversation trickled into my consciousness, I suddenly realised they were charting dangerous territory.

'Don't you have any photos of Cara's brother?' Sean asked.

'Her *what*!?' my mother asked.

Oh my God. No, no – stop –

'Yeah, I met Cara's brother last week,' Sean said cheerfully. 'He's a lovely guy.'

I quickly raced around the bookcase to Sean's side, grabbing his arm violently. My mother gazed at us, wide-eyed, a funny little smile playing at her lips. She knew she had me.

'Um, we have to go,' I cried breathlessly. 'I'm so sorry—'

'Cara doesn't have a brother,' my mother cut in. 'I think you must be mistaken.'

'But . . .' I tried to forcibly drag him out but he gently shook me off, a frown indenting his forehead. 'I don't understand.'

I signalled desperately to my mother to cover for me, miming crunching the apple she'd given me. But she pretended not to notice.

'Clearly Cara has been keeping secrets from us,' my mother said in a gay voice. 'I expect she has a boyfriend she's not telling us about, hmm, Cara? Come on, tell us all the juicy gossip! Gosh, to think she was two-timing poor old Rufus too.'

'Rufus?' Sean shrilled. 'Who's Rufus?'

'Oh, you haven't heard of Rufus?' My mother was on a roll now. She gave me a motherly, reproving glance. 'She's been leading him a fine old dance. She asked him to meet her in the Ritzy a few months' back. Then at the last minute she said she was going for a drink with another guy . . . I simply can't think who it was . . .'

'That was me!' Sean said slowly. 'I took her for a drink and then we went to the Ritzy . . . Cara asked to go . . .' He trailed off.

'Oh – it *was* you!' My mother bit her lip. 'Sorry, I didn't realise. I shouldn't have said anything. I'm not trying to cause a stir, now am I?'

'No, Mother,' I said, hardly able to speak I was so angry and embarrassed. 'I'm sure you wouldn't dream of it.'

'Well, it was terribly embarrassing for you, wasn't it? Having to play off Sean and Rufus. Dear me, you really ought to just stop shilly-shallying around and make your mind up.'

'Okay, we're going.' I gave Sean a pleading glance and, despite the fact that he now clearly thought I was the biggest slapper on earth, he took pity on me and nodded.

We were just about to leave when my mother threw her bullseye.

'Before you go, Cara, I forgot to tell you that I saw your father the other day. He's living in Brighton with his nice new family.' She sounded rather cross, as if the laws of Karma had clearly messed up. 'I can pass on a message to him if you like.'

Sean turned and looked at me incredulously.

'My mother's really into mediumship, aren't you?' I said hastily, hoping to sidetrack her on to some sort of waffle about her recent communication with Elvis.

But – oh the irony – for once in her life my mother was actually being sincere. Perhaps feeling guilty about Sean, she was trying to repair the damage by attempting to be considerate.

'As much as I dislike your father, I do think you ought to be able to speak to him,' she said softly. 'And he would like to speak to you. We discussed it and I think it's a terrible idea, but if you'd like to meet him, we can arrange it. His new wife has given her blessing.'

I opened my mouth, too shocked to even digest the implications of this; then snapped it shut. I felt it was better that I just didn't speak.

'Well, Cara, I'm glad to hear that he recovered from the falling *statue*,' Sean said, his voice thick with sarcasm and hurt.

'Well, thanks Mum, that's great. Let me think it over. Okay, we're going now, byeee.'

Unfortunately, Sean was out of the door before me.

'Sean – stop,' I cried as he hurried away. 'Look,' I called after him desperately, 'yes, I lied, but I'm not the only one around here who's not being totally straight! What about you and the fact you were arrested?'

Sean froze and spun around, looking shocked. 'How the hell did you know about that!' he cried. 'Have you been going behind my back and talking to Laura?'

'No . . . I just . . . I . . .'

'Fine. Well, nice to know you trust me. It's none of your bloody business. Just leave me alone, okay!' he spat out. I tried to chase after him but he crossed the road just before the lights changed. As a fresh flood of traffic swept up the road, I was left on the other side, and there was nothing I could do but stand there and watch him walk away.

36
Cara

The bell of my grandmother's shop tinkled as I stormed back inside.

I didn't mince my words. 'JUST WHAT THE HELL DID YOU THINK YOU WERE DOING!'

My mother and grandmother looked up in surprise. My mother, for some bizarre reason, was sitting on the stool with her jumper rolled up and my grandmother was gently prodding her stomach like an anxious doctor testing for a baby. *She's probably done a spell to give birth to the Anti-Christ*, I thought savagely. She'd be the ideal candidate, for sure.

'Oh darling, I'm so sorry about Seany,' my mother cooed.

'Sorry isn't good enough!' I raged. 'You've ruined my life, ruined everything!' I was aware that I sounded like a fourteen-year-old throwing a tantrum but I didn't care; or perhaps it was precisely because I hadn't thrown enough tantrums at the age of fourteen that it was all coming out now. 'Why couldn't you just drop it? Why did you have to tell Sean everything and make it so obvious! I could have told him myself – but no, you had to spoil everything.'

'Cara, please keep your voice down,' said my

grandmother, gently patting me on the shoulder. 'We know you're upset, but if you just come and sit down and have a nice cup of tea—'

'*No!*' I shook her off so violently that she recoiled, her eyes owlish with surprise behind her glasses. 'You're *not* going to placate me with a cup of fucking bat-wing tea!'

'We have some PK tips or whatever it is normal people drink,' my mother sighed sarcastically.

'Don't you understand, you pair of stupid witches, this isn't about tea! Look, I've got something to say to you and you're not going to like it but I am going to say it—'

'Cara, really, I don't think—' my grandmother began.

'No,' my mother interrupted her, her voice curiously flat and metallic. 'Let her say it. Go on, Cara. Tell me I ought to be burned at the stake, hmm?'

'Sounds like a good idea to me,' I spat out. 'Don't think I don't know what you've been doing. For the first time in my life I've met a guy I like, and you can't stand it. And you know what? I don't think the problem is just that he's not a wizard. I think you're jealous. Jealous that nobody loves you except maybe your own mother, and she does it with a *great* sense of weariness, and – oh, who else is there – me? You've never done anything to earn my love – you've always wanted to just take it and suffocate me and keep me by your side with your silly lies about being oh-so-ill and not being able to cope. Bullshit you're ill! I think you're just jealous because you say you hate men but secretly you too want to find someone special . . . and then I had something, something you wanted, and so you decided to screw it all up . . .' It was all falling into place now; I could see it clearly. 'You've been practising black magic against me all along, haven't you?' I concluded.

'*Cara!*' my grandmother shrieked. 'As if she would against her own *daughter*—'

'No, she has! It all makes sense! Why is it that on my very first date with Sean the buses went crazy? Why is it that every single time we tried to get together something went wrong, or she turned up? Every time I've tried to cast a spell over the last few months she's been weaving her own magic in the background.' I shook my head and looked straight at my mother, seeing it all: sometimes my magic had won through, sometimes hers had; and many a time it had clashed with mixed results. 'Everything is all your fault! I've tried to cast good spells, you know, and not just for Sean. Spells for Nick and Andie, for everyone . . . and they've all gone wrong because you've been undermining me. Well, I'm not your daughter any more and I don't want to know you . . .' I broke off, my voice lacerated with tears.

My grandmother looked aghast. 'Cara, how can you come out with such rubbish?' she said briskly, though there was an uneasy edge to her voice. 'Those spells went wrong because you're an amateur. You're blaming your mother for your own mistakes and being utterly paranoid.'

I stared at my mother. She stared back, her eyes acidic with indignation. 'Okay, you're right,' she admitted. 'You're right.'

'I am?' I could hardly believe she was confessing to it all so calmly.

'Well – what did you expect? All I ever wanted was a normal daughter who would grow up to be a nice witch and all I've ever had from you is ingratitude. You're behaving like some fucking princess from a fairytale who has been brought up by a wicked stepmother who isn't good enough for her. Well, I'm sorry that you're so ashamed of me, but I got sick and tired of it. I haven't been jealous of you and Sean; I think your relationship is perfectly ridiculous and so, yes, I interfered. But it was for your own good.'

374

'You bitch!' I hissed. 'Don't you see what you've done? You've hurt me, and Sean, and the Wilkins . . . they're probably going to get divorced because of the spells I've cast.'

'Oh, grow up, Cara!' she snapped irritably. 'Everyone gets divorced sooner or later. Love is an illusion. You had no business casting spells on them anyway. You seem to have this fairytale idea about happy endings too, but I warned you that they never happen. And yes, I am a bitch. A silly old bitch. I'm glad I've proved you right and lived up to your expectations.' She slid off her stool and started to walk towards the back room, shoulders drooping, head bowed like some bloody Shakespearean actress at the height of a tragedy. Then she turned with a melodramatic sniff. 'You're not my daughter any more.'

My mother always has to have the last word – and the word in the style of an Australian soap opera character.

'Oh, for God's sake!' My tears had dried up now, my anger had turned to a pale heat. I realised that it was useless. Nothing was ever going to change. My mother was just going to carry on treating me like a puppet unless I cut the strings.

'Okay,' I said, 'I'm going.'

I stared at her retreating back and, despite myself, I felt an urge to run after her and hug her and say all was forgiven . . .

'Cara,' my grandmother began. 'Look, I do know what's been going on over the last few months and it's not as simple as you think. You haven't heard the whole story.'

My dear old grandmother. She was the most respectable woman I knew and yet even she was reduced to telling silly lies and excuses; that was what my mother had done to her. I wasn't going to end up the same way.

'I don't want to hear it,' I said, and I walked out before I could change my mind.

37
Cara

On the way back home, I churned over what had happened. How, in the space of half an hour, had my mother managed to screw up my *entire life*? I had to hand it to her. In one swift blow she'd ruined both my love life and my career. And whatever self-esteem I had left was now squashed flatter than a hedgehog on a motorway.

And yet. I knew deep down that I was as much to blame, that the acidic feeling in my stomach was mingled with hatred for myself as much as for her. When I'd first joined the Wilkinses, my desire had been simple. I wanted to belong to a happy family. And instead of patiently letting myself settle in, I'd rushed headlong into magic like a child with a new toy. Magic, I realised, was an addiction as nasty as gambling or drink. Because it was the easy way out. I could have helped Andie and Nick by gently building up a friendship, by earning their confidence, or perhaps even by bloody well leaving them alone. Instead I'd used the Wilkins family like guinea pigs; the flaw in my mother – that irresistible desire to play God with other people's lives – was the same flaw that drove me.

As I went up the Wilkinses' path, I felt tears blur my

eyes again. No doubt Sean was in there right now, telling Andie everything. I wheeled around and, started to hurry back down the path when something made me stop. Their driveway was empty.

I turned back, swallowing, and went up to the door. I took out my keys with shaking hands. The door was double-bolted; they weren't in.

As I went inside, however, paranoia started to flit through my mind again like a bat. Maybe they were with a solicitor; maybe they were at the police station informing a policeman that I was the mystic equivalent of *Single White Female*.

But there was a note on the kitchen table from Andie: *Cara, we've gone to McDonald's. Will bring some back for you! Andie x.* And Fred had signed his own name in childish scrawl with a smiley face underneath.

I screwed the note up into a tight ball and nearly threw it in the bin. Then I put it in my pocket. I'd keep it as a memento.

I ran upstairs to my room and went to the window, gazing over at Sean's room. For the first time since I'd lived there, his curtains were closed.

And then it happened. Suddenly the emotion that had been surging inside me erupted. I ran downstairs to the kitchen and yanked a black sack from the drawer. I ran all the way back up, panting by now. I threw it all in in a red rage. My cauldron, my altar cloth, my Book of Shadows. Bottles smashed; books tore; potions gurgled and split and stained. My athame, my pentacle, my chalice. It all went in. There.

I looked at my windowsill, now bare and lonely, circles of white printed in the dust. From my sack, one of my talking bottles let out a little squeal of protest, saying: '*Do you have to do this to us? Really?*'

'Yes, I do!' I cried out loud. I had to wipe out all temptation so that I could never, ever do another spell again.

I took the black sack outside. Nick occasionally made a bonfire in the back garden and behind the greenhouse there was a pile of black ashes from the last time. I built a fire from some branches he'd pruned, then dumped my stuff into the middle. I lit a match and watched the red flames lick and eat it all up. I stood so close my cheeks grew hot and my eyes watered from the smoke. I waited for the relief to come but it didn't. As I looked down and saw my Book of Shadows crumble to ash, I felt as though my heart was breaking.

Instinct made me look up, across the fence, at Sean's house. He was standing there, watching me; then he drew the curtains quickly.

No doubt he'd be talking to Nick and Andie when they got back.

Upstairs in my room, after the fire had gone out, I lay on my bed feeling tired and hollow. I knew I needed to sort out a place to stay tonight. But all I could think about was Sean. I was starting to become more and more indignant. Okay, so I'd lied, but could he blame me? After all, my last boyfriend had accused me of being a freak; and now Sean blamed me for not coming out of my witchy closet sooner. Men! They were so bloody inconsistent!

Down below, I suddenly heard the bang of the front door. The Wilkins were home.

I heard footsteps creaking up the stairs and rubbed my eyes quickly. It was Nick. For the first time in a long while, he actually looked happy.

'We went to the park, sorry we missed you!' he grinned. 'Look, we've bought a McDonalds and rented out *The Matrix* to watch later, come and join us?'

I thought: *Why not?* I might as well treasure my last hours with them. 'I'll just get changed.'

Dinner was a nightmare.

Everyone was in a fantastic mood and I found my cheeks hurting as I tried to smile and pretend everything was fine. Fred had brought back a free Ronald McDonald sticker which he gleefully pressed to my chest with a giggle; I scooped him up in my arms in a tight hug, not wanting to let them go.

Halfway through the meal, I excused myself to go to the loo. On the way back down the stairs, the phone shrilled and I picked it up. A man said in a low voice, '*Andie?*'

'Er – no.'

'Oh, it's Jonathan Yates here,' he said, suddenly switching to a brisk, charming tone. 'I have some paperwork regarding our trip to Wales which urgently needs to be done – I'm so sorry to bother you on a Saturday but is Andie around?'

She certainly was. Andie, who had clearly jumped up the moment she'd heard the phone ring, came skidding into the hallway. She grabbed the phone off me – she didn't even need to ask who it was – and shooed me away with a breathless, smiley wave.

I walked back into the dining room. Nick was eating voraciously as though filling an empty hole inside him. Fred was bending and twisting his chips and laying them out on his plate as swear words, gleefully waiting for Daddy to notice. I didn't feel capable of making normal conversation so I quickly picked up my glass and went into the kitchen. Jonathan's voice kept echoing in my head; it was amazing just how much intimacy and passion he had managed to squeeze into those two syllables. I wondered how long it had been going on. Since the school concert? Since Wales?

This is unbearable, I thought. *I don't want to leave the Wilkinses like this. I want them to be a happy family; I want to solve everything . . .*

I realised now how obvious it had been. This was why Andie was so insanely happy one minute and then guilt-ridden the next. It was amazing that Nick hadn't noticed, but I suspected that he, like me, hadn't wanted to see the truth. It's always easier to believe in fantasy, to tell yourself lies . . .

'Oh God, this is so awful!' I said out loud. Then, as Andie entered the kitchen, I quickly smiled. 'I was just . . . talking to myself . . .'

'Oh, don't we all?' she said merrily. 'Cara, are you okay? You seem a bit funny tonight.'

I tried to smile but I could feel tears welling up in my eyes. 'I'm fine. I just wanted to say how much I've enjoyed working here over the last few months and . . . and . . . if I ever do go, then I'll really miss you all. Really.'

'Well, I hope that won't be for ages,' said Andie, smiling warmly. Then she pulled me into an impulsive hug. 'What is it, man trouble?' she asked, pulling back. 'You can tell me, come on, spill the beans.'

I opened my mouth to speak when suddenly there was a rap on the back door and it swung open. It was Sean.

I stared at him, speechless, waiting for him to drop his bombshell.

'Oh Sean, I'm glad you came,' said Andie.

Wait? What? What was this all about?

'Sean is going to take a look at our boiler,' said Andie. 'The last time we had to have it fixed it cost two hundred pounds! Sean, if you can sort it out, I will give you a massive bonus next week, darling.'

Here was my chance. A chance to make amends and stop him talking. Nick asked me if I wanted to come and

380

watch the video with them but I declined, saying I should do the washing up leftover from lunchtime.

'I bet you do,' said Nick, giving me a cheeky wink. 'Don't let me get in the way of true love . . .'

'Nick!' I hissed, terrified of Sean overhearing. If only Nick knew the truth, I thought miserably.

In the kitchen, Sean had spread his tools on the worksurface. He frowned and huffed as I squeezed past him to get to the sink. We both worked in silence for a few minutes, the slosh of the water and the squeaking of his tools magnified to an embarrassing volume.

'I want you to know,' said Sean suddenly.

'Uh – yes?' I turned round, smiling.

'Me being arrested,' he said, unsmiling. 'It's not what you think.'

'Oh, right,' I said. I went back to the washing up, watching his reflection in the window. He carried on fiddling and tweaking, speaking in a quiet, intense voice.

'I went through a bit of a rough patch in my early twenties. I started hanging out with a group of dropouts, although I thought they were so cool at the time. And then I got arrested.'

'For . . .?'

'Burglary. I ended up with a suspended sentence. Once you've been in trouble . . . well, it's hard to go back. I felt that life had cheated me. For ages I went about resenting everyone and everything. But I'm fine now – I'm not angry any more. So you see, it's not something I'm proud of.'

'I know that, Sean,' I said, turning to face him.

I watched him fiddling and I couldn't help thinking: *Why on earth is he messing about with a boiler and getting himself covered with grease when he could be playing a sax every night? Or doing a real job?* He reminded me somehow of Andie and a sudden sadness passed over me: *Why is growing up all about giving up? Why is adulthood all about replacing fantasy and dreams with reality, and hope with cynicism?*

'You know, you could always go back to studying,' I said suddenly. 'Or you could play the sax . . . you could go and audition . . . I could set something up for you!'

'Look, Cara,' Sean said, cold again, 'I don't need you to sort out my life for me, Little Miss-Fix-It. Just drop it.'

'Look, I'm sorry about lying to you—'

'I'm not going to say anything to Nick and Andie if that's what you're worried about,' he said. 'I don't care if you want to carry on lying. It's really up to you.'

'But—'

'I said, just drop it, okay?' he said roughly. 'I want you to leave me alone.'

38
Andie

Ah. Caught red-handed.

Andie quickly rolled up a mauve jumper and threw it into the case on top of several sets of rather sexy peach silk underwear with the 'Secrets' price tags still on them as Cara came into the room.

'I'm going to stay with my parents for a few days,' she said brightly. 'Just for the weekend.' Swallow. 'It's great because it gives Nick some time to be with Fred; he hasn't seen much of him with the new job.' Swallow. 'I was actually just going to come and chat to you to see if you wouldn't mind helping out if necessary.'

Cara just stood there dumbly, undoing and doing up buttons on her white cardigan. She shrugged and nodded, turned to leave, then suddenly swung back, catching the edge of her cardigan in twitchy fingers.

'I know you're going to see Jonathan,' she burst out.

What! How the *hell* did she know? Was it really so obvious to everyone? *And I thought I'd put on a good act. If she knows, does Nick?*

'Please don't do it,' Cara pleaded. 'Please don't leave Fred and Nick . . . they both love you so much. And you hardly know Jonathan, why throw it all away for him? God, I'm sorry, I know this is none of my business, but—'

'You're right that it's none of your business,' said Andie. 'Anyway, I'm going to see my mo—' She broke off as the full weight of Cara's words sank in. Cara thought she was . . . 'Cara, I'm not *leaving*, okay?' She laughed incredulously and flung down the blue shirt she'd been about to fold. 'Yes, I am going to see Jonathan. But not like that. We're close, we're very good friends, and things are a bit tough at the moment. I just need some time out to be with someone who knows me, who understands me, okay?' She shook her head, her brain ticking away. How had Cara found out? 'Cara, have you been listening in on my private calls?'

'Of course I haven't.'

Guilt made Andie retaliate with harsh anger. 'God, doesn't anyone have any privacy in this house? I mean, you're the nanny, you're supposed to be looking after Fred, I don't need you censoring our phone calls and telling me what I should be doing at the weekends. It really is none of your business.'

'Andie, I haven't – I honestly didn't – I just . . .' Cara trailed off. 'Sorry. You're right. It is none of my business.'

She took a step backwards, but didn't leave.

Andie let out a large sigh and slumped down on the bed. She looked up at Cara, hovering in the doorway, her dark eyes sad and suspicious. She looked down at her half-packed suitcase. *Can I really go through with this?* she wondered.

Jonathan had been the one who'd suggested they go away for the weekend. To give them a chance to have the Proper Talk she'd been avoiding: the talk about where their relationship was going.

Cara came and sat down next to her on the bed. 'I'm sorry,' she said. 'And I haven't been listening in on your

384

phone calls, really. I saw you and Jonathan together ages ago at the school concert.'

Andie was stunned. How could they have been so stupid, canoodling in a public place, in the school of all places?

'And did you tell anyone?' Andie asked in a measured voice. What if Cara had said something to Nick? But Nick couldn't know . . . could he?

'I haven't told anyone,' said Cara, 'honestly. I thought that should be up to you . . .' she trailed off awkwardly.

'Yes, it is up to me,' Andie retorted hotly. 'It's between me and Nick.' Inwardly, she was swearing like mad. What if Cara wasn't telling the truth, what if she'd let it slip to someone?

'I can understand why,' said Cara. 'I mean, Jonathan is really good-looking.'

She was clearly trying to sound light-hearted but her voice was loaded with reproach.

'Look,' Andie burst out in guilty retaliation, 'this isn't all my fault, you know. Nick's had an affair too. It's not as if I'm doing anything he hasn't already done.'

'He *what*!' Cara was genuinely shocked.

'Yes. He did. We were perfectly happily married at the time. There was no reason . . .' Andie swallowed at the memory.

'But what happened?' Cara pushed. 'I don't understand.'

'Nick was travelling a lot with his business and he was tempted.'

'Go on,' said Cara.

'Well, one night he was flying back from Madrid. I drove to pick him up.'

Andie could remember every detail of that night. The leather seat of the car, the glacier mints she'd sucked on the way. She'd spent an hour waiting in the airport lounge, flicking through magazines. His flight was delayed but Nick wasn't on it. She'd watched crowds flow into the airport. She'd seen couples hug and families reunite. She'd seen lone businessmen being collected by people carrying cards. But no Nick. She'd panicked and called his hotel, who'd told her he'd checked out. She'd waited another hour.

'When he didn't turn up, I was convinced he'd been kidnapped or something,' Andie said. 'So I called home and found he was there.'

'But why on earth did he go home? When you'd gone all that way to pick him up?'

'To be honest, I think he just couldn't face me. But he had to, eventually . . . In the end, he told me everything.'

She'd come home to find Nick sitting in the living room. A mug of undrunk tea with swirls of congealing cream sat on the coffee table. She'd thrown down her car keys.

'Nick, where were you?' she'd demanded.

'My flight was delayed . . .'

'But I've been waiting THREE HOURS!' Andie had suddenly felt close to tears.

'I'm sorry. I can't believe I missed you,' Nick had apologised. He'd looked tired; his eyes rimmed with purple crescents, as though they were sinking into his face. 'I just assumed you'd gone and I hopped into a taxi . . .'

Andie had looked at him. And she'd just known.

'You've been with another girl, haven't you?' she'd said.

'How did you know?' Nick had been so shocked that he hadn't even denied it.

Silence. Andie had picked up her keys, running her fingers over the serrated edges.

'Andie, I'm really sorry –' Nick had begun.

She'd stood up and he had too. She'd come towards him and he'd opened his arms in apology. Then she'd whammed her fists into his face, his head, his shoulders. He'd grabbed her wrists and tried to push her away. They'd knocked against the table. The cup had flown off, soaking their legs in lukewarm liquid and hitting the carpet. Andie had kicked him and he had stumbled and they'd both half tripped, with awful clumsiness, on to the floor. Andie had been lying on her front, crying into the wet carpet. Nick had reached out with trembling fingers, running them softly over her hair, and she hadn't hit him again.

'So . . . who was it?' Cara asked. 'Who was the girl he'd been with?'

Just a one-night stand. A silly mistake. That night, after rowing themselves hoarse, they had laid down on their bed in the dark, still fully clothed, and she'd tortured him by making him tell her every detail. How he'd got drunk and gone to a dinner. How the blonde had come on to him and followed him up to his hotel room, pretending she'd lost her key. How in a moment of madness it had all got out of control. How afterwards he had lain there feeling sick with regret and self-loathing.

'And . . . what did you say?' Cara asked.

'Well, we didn't get much sleep that night. And he did say he was sorry,' Andie said. How could she possibly put into words what it had felt like that night? Andie hadn't slept *a wink*. She'd wondered if it was all over between them. It seemed impossible to digest. She'd finally sunk into a weak sleep when Nick had woken her up again, crying and clinging to her, suddenly as vulnerable as a child, begging her not to leave him. And she'd kissed away his tears and told her she'd forgive him and that, no, she could never leave him.

'Anyway, Nick made me promise not to tell anyone about it, though I did tell a few friends. They told me I was mad for taking him back, they thought I was a complete pushover and that he'd do it again . . .'

Cara suddenly went white and dropped her eyes; Andie frowned uneasily. 'What?'

'Nothing.'

'Anyway, back then I didn't want to give up on our marriage. All my friends were single and it was easy for them to say just toss it aside, but marriage isn't something you throw away like an old dress that's gone out of fashion.'

'So you got over it,' said Cara.

'Kind of,' said Andie. 'To be honest, it wasn't easy. I was paranoid . . . the first few months were awful . . . I just felt I couldn't trust him. Every time I saw him talking to a woman I felt all panicky inside; every time I picked up the phone and talked to his secretary I thought I could hear something in her voice. I kept checking his collars for lipstick, his coat pockets for notes, his wallet for credit card bills, his drawers for new underwear. And Nick, in his own way, was bogged down with the most awful guilt. But one day I just stepped back from it all and thought: *This is crazy.* I realised I had to let go. *Life is too short,* I thought, *I've got to enjoy it!* So I did. I moved on. And it worked. We gelled back together. Or I thought we did.'

'So d'you think maybe . . . maybe you haven't quite forgiven Nick?' Cara asked.

'No! What d'you mean by that?' Andie sighed; she couldn't expect Cara, who was twenty-five, virginal and looked as if she belonged in a nunnery, to understand. 'What's happened with Jonathan has just happened. But I'm not going to go off with him.'

I don't think, a tiny voice added inside her.

388

'Well, I guess when you're just dating someone they always seem ideal, don't they?' Cara said. 'I mean, being married to someone is bound to be harder, because you've got to live with them every day, whereas if you have an affair you just get the nice bits. But it's all an illusion, isn't it?'

'I'm sure you've experienced this, having been married three times,' Andie teased her, though she had to admit, these were the thoughts that had been floating around her own mind. Then she suddenly felt embarrassed. She hadn't meant to splurge all this stuff out – as far as she was concerned, it was all in the past. That was the nice – and the dangerous – thing about Cara; she was such a good listener. Andie always felt better after talking to her. Maybe it was because she didn't judge.

After Cara had gone, Andie carried on trying to pack. But five minutes later she realised she'd absent-mindedly swung into auto-pilot and packed three of Nick's shirts and five pairs of his socks. She took them out with a sigh. Her chat with Cara had left her feeling deflated. Not long ago she'd been all revved up for a lazy, hedonistic weekend of lovemaking and sunbathing and cream teas and pottering around charming cobbled Cotswolds villages and old stone churches. Now she felt guilty, seedy, evil: a selfish adulteress leaving her son and husband to fend for themselves with food from the freezer while she ran around with a toyboy.

Maybe I should call Jonathan and tell him I'm ill, she thought. But that would be so obvious.

Because, let's face it, their weekend wasn't just going to be about scones and sex. Ever since Jonathan had suggested she might leave Nick for him, a subtle strain had entered their relationship. Andie had told him that she felt it was much too soon, and Jonathan had quickly back-tracked saying of course, of course, she should take as long as she liked. But it made her feel uncomfortable. Sooner or later she was going to have to make a choice – whether it was in a month's time, six months' time, longer. All that deception. It was a terrible thought.

Downstairs, she found Nick reading the paper. 'Off now?' he asked.

Andie nodded. 'I bought some fish fingers,' she said. 'And there's some frozen chicken pieces and bags of chips and peas. They shouldn't be too hard to cook.'

'Great, we'll put some on now. I'm famished!' Nick smiled. He paused for a moment and she stood there, unable to look him in the eye, staring at his blue T-shirt. Then he pulled her in for a sudden kiss – not a marital peck but a *real* kiss, like two lovers kissing for the first time: his hand cupped around her chin, his lips sweet, his tongue softly probing hers. Andie was surprised to feel a ripple of love scuttling down her spine. He drew back and for a moment they stood close together, lips brushing, breath intermingling; a moment that was so unexpectedly intimate that it took Andie's breath away.

Then she smiled and stepped back. It was time to go.

Halfway to Jonathan's house, Andie got a call on her mobile. It was Nick. Suddenly paranoia gripped her. What if Cara had told him? With sweating hands, she answered the call.

'Andie?' Nick said, his voice crackly, 'how do you cook the chicken pieces again?'

'Nick!' she laughed with relief and he laughed too. 'You put them in the oven. Gas Mark six. Middle shelf. I wrote it all down on the shopping list. Okay?'

'Think I've got that!'

She paused, not wanting to hang up, enjoying the giggle they were having.

'Bye, darling.'

'Bye, honey.'

As she pulled up outside Jonathan's flat, she was suddenly gripped by an inexplicable urge to go home. To be in the kitchen, Radio 4 in the background and Fred getting under her feet and Nick pottering about reading bits from the *Telegraph*. She tooted her horn, thinking irrationally: *Please don't be in. Please be ill. Please say you don't fancy going away.*

But, of course, a few minutes later Jonathan came bounding down the steps like an overjoyed labrador greeting his master.

As Jonathan slid into the car and leaned over, she turned her head away so that his kiss landed on her cheek.

Jonathan pretended not to notice. 'How are you?' he smiled. Then he went back into his flat and came down with a large rucksack and what looked like some metal sticks wrapped in blue neon waterproof cloths. Andie frowned. What on earth were they for?

'I was thinking,' Jonathan explained as he got back into the car, 'that we could maybe try camping rather than the B&B.'

'Camping!' Andie cried.

'Don't be like that!' Jonathan laughed, 'Becca and I did it all the time. Honestly, Andie, I swear you'll love it – it's so gorgeous falling asleep under the stars. You sleep so deeply.'

'Jonathan!' Andie practically yelled. 'I don't want to go camping! I don't want to lie on the grass with insects crawling all over me. I just want to stay in a nice hotel and have a good time, okay?'

'Sure,' said Jonathan, wide-eyed. 'Look, Andie, it was only a suggestion.'

'Well, good.'

They drove in a tense silence for some time. Andie felt horrible. She knew she had overreacted ridiculously, and that her anger had had nothing to do with the camping. She searched for the real cause and found that underneath it all she was disappointed. She realised what she had been sensing for the last few weeks: that things had changed between her and Jonathan. The honeymoon period was over.

Their silence was broken by her mobile ringing. It was Nick, asking her why, since he'd followed her instructions so carefully, the chicken pieces were charred black lumps.

39
Cara

Looking back, I'm not entirely sure why I decided to tell Andie about the kiss with Nick. It had happened ages ago; it was insignificant, forgotten-about, buried and kicked under the sand. It was partly the recent chat I'd had with Andie. I couldn't help thinking that after all she'd been through with Nick, she ought to know about the kiss as soon as possible. What if it came out in five years or something? Andie would never forgive him for not telling her.

And I think it was partly to do with Sean's attack on me, the way he'd chided me for all my lies and cover-ups. I felt guilty about lying to the Wilkinses but every time I tried to even begin telling Andie I was a witch, I felt ridiculous. I mean, when could I say it? 'I'm going to the shops, d'you want anything? Oh, by the way, if you look under my bed you'll find a lot more than just incense.' What would she do? Andie was a very practical person; she laughed at her stars in the newspapers and had often remarked that she thought Mystic Meg needed a lobotomy. She'd probably just send me off to the local mental hospital. Besides, I'd given up being a witch now;

I'd got rid of all my magic stuff and, despite my odd pangs of regret, I was going to have to be normal now whether I liked it or not. But I think that was the underlying reason. I wanted to stop lying; I couldn't tell Andie I was a witch, so through perverse logic I decided to tell her I'd kissed her husband instead.

Not a wise move.

It happened the night that Andie broke up with Jonathan.

I was in the kitchen, cooking up some fish and chips for her and Fred; Nick had called to say he was working late. Andie had been behaving strangely all day and I wondered if now was a good time to mention the kiss.

'Hi!' Andie came in. 'Oh, thanks for cooking – *yet again* – that does smell good. We're going to have to pay you double for being a cook and a nanny.'

I grinned and shrugged.

Andie stole a few chocolate flakes off the dessert and then let out a sigh. I turned back to the chips, checking the temperature.

'Well, I did it,' she said.

'What?'

'I broke up with Jonathan.'

'*Did you?*' I swung round to face her. 'Oh wow. Oh my God! Well done . . . that's great . . . I mean, is it great?' I thought it was wonderful but Andie looked very confused.

'I think it's for the best,' she said, though I sensed a flicker of regret. 'I must put Fred first, and if Nick and I are going to sort things out . . .'

Oh God. What was that supposed to mean? She was going to ask Nick for a divorce and *then* get back with Jonathan? That was even worse. But then, to my relief, she said, 'To be honest, I don't think it would have worked out anyway. We're not really that compatible. He's a lot younger than me. Though he is very mature . . .' She zig-zagged between pros and cons, looking torn. 'But anyway. There you go. It's over. So . . .'

So it was a start, I thought. A chance for her and Nick to get some breathing space, to focus on each other. I wondered then if maybe it wasn't the best time to tell her about the kiss, not when things were so fragile. Then again, didn't she deserve to know?

'So what's going on with you and Sean?' Andie asked. 'I've noticed he's stopped coming over to see you.'

'Sean isn't speaking to me,' I sighed.

'Men, hey?' Andie rolled her eyes. Then she looked me up and down critically. 'Maybe you ought to borrow one of my summer dresses. You can look in my wardrobe if you want. It's amazing how men will suddenly start talking to you again when they can see your legs. It's worked on Nick many a time.'

I laughed uneasily. 'Look, Andie, there's something I've been wanting to tell you.'

Andie, who was pouring lemon concentrate and water into a glass for Fred, turned and gave me a warm smile. I felt a sudden moment of awful doubt; finally, finally, we'd woven together a friendship . . . and now I was about to tear it to shreds. But I'd been building up to saying it all day; the words tipped out of my mouth before I could stop them: 'I kissed Nick.'

Andie promptly dropped the glass. The plastic didn't break, but lemony pools stained the lino. Andie reached for the kitchen paper and I grabbed a cloth.

'No, I can do it,' she said sharply. She ripped off sheets vehemently, methodically laying them out in neat squares that soaked up the mess.

'Look . . .' I twisted the cloth around my fingers. 'I'm not – I'm not about to confess that Nick and I are having a raging affair and we're about to run off together *at all*, what I mean is, we had a little accident . . . and . . .'

I saw tension clawing Andie's shoulders. Oh God, this was coming out all wrong. I sounded like a classic case of the lady doth protest too much.

'What I mean is – at his birthday party, he got a bit drunk and—' I jabbered.

'Okay, fine, you've told me, now forget it,' said Andie, standing up.

'But—'

'Cara!' She flung the sopping towels into the bin. 'I really don't want to hear the details. I realise it was just a one-off and that's fine.'

'But, yes – it was just a one-off and—'

'It's fine,' she insisted, though the bright rosy spots on her cheeks and the flash in her eyes suggested it was far from fine at all.

'But—' *But, but, but.*

'Look, just drop it, okay?'

I noticed a few puddles she'd missed on the floor and bent down to mop them up. I felt very strange. I'd expected cutlery to be smashed, shouting, dismissal. How could she just shrug it off like that? It wasn't healthy; Andie *should* be angry. Maybe it was another sign that she was completely resigned to Nick's infidelities and flirtations; or maybe he had actually told her ages back and she already knew?

All in all, I couldn't work it out.

As I rinsed out the cloth, I gazed through the window at Sean. He was hoeing and he looked up briefly. I was aching to confide in him, but too proud to go outside and make up. Then he turned away and carried on tearing up the grass.

Anyhow, I sighed, *at least Andie's accepted it. At least things are fine.*

But, of course, they weren't; there was a lot worse to come.

Andie was funny with me for the rest of the evening. Slowly but surely storm clouds started to gather: pale tendrils at first ('Cara, would you mind doing the washing up too, I'm a bit tired?'), amassing into grey cumulus ('You're not reading Fred a bedtime story tonight – I don't want you going near him!'). Sean's words echoed uneasily in my mind: *Cara, if you think Andie is just going to forgive and forget, you're being incredibly naïve. Sometimes a kiss can cut just as deeply as a full blown affair . . .*

But it had just been a kiss; it wasn't an affair; and if only Andie would just give me a chance to *explain*.

During dinner, Andie had opened a bottle of red wine and drunk three glasses. She'd sent Fred off to bed an hour early, and then I knew the trouble was about to begin.

As I put the dishes in the sink, I felt the hostility of her gaze like knuckles pressed between my shoulder blades.

'So, what the fuck did you think you were doing, trying it on with my husband?' she said suddenly.

'Andie, I wasn't trying it on—'

'Oh, sure you weren't. Oh no. Ever since you entered this house you've had your eye on him, haven't you? You looked at me and I thought I was the boring old wife who would just sit back and take it. You know – I'm not stupid. I did guess.' I kept trying to interrupt but she ranted on, her voice both sharp and slurred with alcohol.

Shit. In the intervening hours since my confession I could see her mind had been ticking away, unpicking memories, assembling evidence. She'd been reinterpreting everything I'd said or done, recalling every joke I'd shared with Nick, every chess game, seeing them all as secret signs and codes.

'. . . and I just think it's a total fucking cheek.' A gulp of wine, a cigarette. 'Your agency didn't mention this in their recommendation. Maybe I should call them up now and ask if it's part of the package?'

I sat there, silent, letting her words sting me. I figured it was best to let her get everything out, then tell my side of the story.

'. . . I know all that stuff about you being in *lurve* with Sean was just a cover-up . . .'

'. . . and you were the blonde in the park, I've no doubt . . .'

'. . . don't think you're going to get him . . . I'm not giving him up . . .'

'. . . I mean, how could you . . . didn't you think about Fred?'

'Look, I'd never do anything to hurt Fred!' I cried in disbelief.

Andie glared at me but didn't say anything. Finally, she'd run out of steam. Because she was starting to cry. I wanted to give her a hug, but I knew that if I tried she'd probably garrotte me. I passed her a piece of kitchen paper; she snatched it and dried her eyes.

'So,' she said, crossing her arms, 'I want you to tell me everything. And I don't want any crap, okay?'

'Andie, it was just a *kiss*, that's *all* . . .'

'Look, darling, you're about to be fired, okay? And I might just give you a vaguely nice reference if you tell me the truth.'

This was hopeless. I tried desperately to think of a spell but my mind was a fraught blank. And from the look on Andie's face, I had a feeling that magic wouldn't have been strong enough to make a difference.

'Well?' Andie snapped. 'I'm waiting.'

'It happened on Nick's birthday party. It was partly my fault . . . the wine . . . it had some aphrodisiacs in it . . . I didn't realise when I ordered it . . .' Andie was looking at me incredulously so I quickly skipped over any mention of witchcraft. 'Anyway, Nick was really, really, really drunk. And we were sitting on the steps and I think he was feeling lonely because it was his birthday and things weren't going well between you and him. The thing is, it's really all about you, not me. It was just a tiny kiss and then I hit him and he came round and realised how idiotic he was being. And later, when he explained about losing his job and everything, I realised it was just the pressure that had made him act so stupidly. And Nick said later that I should just forget it, that it was just a kiss, but I couldn't – not since we became friends, because our friendship means a lot to me—' I broke off, close to tears myself, but Andie raised her eyes to the ceiling with icy sarcasm. 'I don't expect friendship from you now. But I don't think it's fair to fire me.'

'Oh?' Andie waved her arm dramatically, accidentally sploshing wine on to the table. 'So you just expect me to sit back and smile and pretend it's all great? And while I'm at it, maybe we can move a double bed into your room and you can have free condoms as a bonus for good work?'

'It. Was. Just. A. Kiss.'

' "*It was just a kiss,*" ' she mimicked me and suddenly I snapped and burst out, 'Well come on, Andie, you're not so pure yourself – you've been doing a lot more than kissing Jonathan.'

There was a blazing silence. *That's it*, I thought, *I've blown it now.*

Andie buried her face in her hands, red curls falling over the table. Then she looked up, her expression suddenly fragile, confused.

'Nick will be home in fifteen minutes and I'd like to discuss it with him. In the meantime, I'd appreciate it if you could go to your room and allow us some privacy.'

40
Andie

A kiss. *Just a kiss.* Andie snorted and tried to refill her glass with wine, but for some reason nothing came out. What sort of kiss? A kiss on the cheek? On the forehead? The lips? She tried to picture it. Cara and Nick, slowly leaning into each other, pupils bright. They made such a good-looking couple: Cara blonde and voluptuous, Nick dark and thin. She banged the wine bottle as though it was a bottle of ketchup – then realised it was empty.

As she got up and went to the fridge for another bottle, she was vaguely aware that she was drunk – a hot, flushed, bloodshot drunk, everything tinted with a hazy veil of anger. But behind her muzziness was a sharp clarity of thought, a strange sense of calm. Almost a sense of pleasure. Andie realised that she'd been waiting for this for ages – an event, a reason, something to give her the guts to lift the lid on their marriage. After tonight, nothing would be the same; and though it frightened her, it was also a relief.

She looked up at the clock. Half past nine. Where the fuck was he?

She took another glug of wine. Lit another cigarette. After her break from smoking, it was a shock to her system: her throat ached and the smell was doubly toxic. Opposite her, Cara's pink cardigan was hanging on the chair, all little buttons and dainty sleeves, and Andie suddenly felt an urge to rip it to shreds. God, how dare Cara presume to tell her what to do? She was such a busybody. Ever since she'd arrived she'd been sticking her nose in, meddling, wanting to be in on everything. Pathetic really. Andie had worked out long ago that Cara obviously lacked a family; the way she sat down to dinner with a kind of Enid Blyton enthusiasm, as though they were all folks having clean family fun together. And her urge to make them adopt her had gone too far; her substitute daddy had become her lover.

Just a kiss. Yeah, right. And what if Fred had seen them? Andie suddenly felt the wine trickling down her throat turn to ice in her stomach. Maybe Fred was in on this too? She pictured Cara and Nick taking him out to the park, looking like a pair of newly weds; Cara giving Fred sweets, Nick giving him extra pocket money – 'Just don't mention it to Mummy, okay? It's our secret . . .' What if Cara had her plans to . . .

No, Andie thought in a tearful rage. *I won't let them take Fred away from me.*

She suffered a strong urge to get up and run to Fred's room and hold him, to know he was hers, that he loved her more. To ask him what he knew. But she held back; she didn't want Fred to be awake when Nick came home, to witness their row.

She drank another glass of wine and her panic faded a little as she churned things over. She was being silly. Cara wouldn't do that to her. Cara was just too nice.

That was the most sickening, infuriating thing. Because even as Andie had sat there, even while Cara had admitted to the kiss, Andie had still found herself liking her. Feeling

401

sorry for her. Perhaps because it all reminded her too much of Jonathan, of the guilt she'd suffered herself, the urge to confess.

Come on, Andie, you're not so pure yourself – you've been doing a lot more than kissing Jonathan.

For a moment her anger fizzled. Cara was spot-on; what right did she have to accuse him? And yet while she knew it was irrational and unfair, her anger surged back. Nick had made a promise all those years ago that he'd never cheat on her again and where was it *ever* going to *end*—

She froze, hearing the sound of a key in the front door. The door slamming. Nick humming lightly – great, Nick, glad you're in such a good mood, looking forward to coming home and being with Cara, are you? Footsteps in the hallway. As they came closer, she was unnerved to feel a rush of butterflies in her stomach. She wanted to be cool and tough, but even as he entered the kitchen, despite everything, she felt relieved he was home.

'God, I've had such a crap day,' said Nick. 'The bloody new computer system went down *three* times. I see you're smoking, you naughty woman . . . what?' he asked, suddenly noticing the wine bottles, sensing her mood.

'I've got a bit of a bone to pick with you.'

'Great. What have I done now, eh, Mozart?' He sat and ruffled the dog's fur. 'I'm in the doghouse with you.' He sniffed, frowning. 'Are you drunk?'

Suddenly Andie flipped. 'Yes! Yes, I am! And the reason I am is because I've found out that you're fucking the nanny!'

Nick froze. 'What?'

'Cara told me,' said Andie, staring hard at him. 'So don't start lying.'

'She's making it up,' said Nick. 'Look, Cara's a lovely

girl, but I'm no way having an affair with her. She's terribly wacky. I was in her room yesterday and I found a pack of Tarot cards.'

'Oh, and what were you doing in her room?' Andie asked.

'I was fixing her window. The latch was broken.'

'And when you kissed her at your birthday party – when you were sitting on the kitchen steps – what was that about?'

'Oh that.' Nick was caught off guard. 'I didn't realise she meant that. I was drunk . . . I'd lost my job . . . and I was freaked out over the party . . . and yes, we kissed, but it was just a kiss. She slapped me, knocked some sense into me, and that was that. Look, I was drunk.'

For a moment Andie was flummoxed. Their stories matched. Maybe it really had been nothing more than a drunken mistake. But then her fury came back; a fury that had been building up over a long time.

'You know, when you told me you weren't going to stray again, I believed you,' she said, curls falling in her eyes, her fingers twisting her wedding ring. Nick stared at her horrified. 'I really did. I thought it was just a one-off, a silly drunken mistake. And now . . .' She rubbed her eye with the nub of her palm.

'Look, Andie, I'm really sorry. I'm so sorry, I know it's been hard for you—'

'Oh, you'd love that, wouldn't you? You'd love to think that while you've been fucking Cara, I've been sitting about worrying and now I'm just going to cry a bit and then say all's forgiven. You may as well know that I've been having an affair too.' She smiled viciously.

But her smile faded as she saw Nick's face. The hurt in his eyes. Suddenly revenge didn't seem quite so sweet.

'Right.' Nick sounded calm. 'Okay.'

Her emotions, zig-zagging like lightning, flicked back

from fierce love to hate again. Why did he have to be so smooth? Why couldn't he jump up and shout and actually show his love for her?

'So, I guess you wanted to get back at me,' he said.

'Get back at you? Nick, how could you be so stupid—'

'Keep your voice down, Fred's upstairs—'

'I don't care!' Andie cried, but she lowered her voice all the same. 'Look, Nick, do you think I did this just to get back at you? I did it because you don't love me any more and our marriage is a sham. You work all hours of the day and night, you lose your job and you don't even tell me, your wife – but you tell the nanny. You don't even talk to me! I might as well be married to a stranger! What's the point – just what's the point in it all?'

'Who is he?'

'Who is he?' He hadn't even bothered to address the love point. *To say he still loved her,* she thought hazily, feeling sobs rising in her throat.

'He's a teacher,' she said finally, swallowing them back. 'Someone I work with.'

'And what was it?' Nick spread open his palms, his eyes flashing. 'Just a snog? A one-night stand?'

'A bit more than that.' She bit her lip.

'So we're talking a full-blown affair here, basically?'

Suddenly the tables had turned; suddenly she was the one filled with shame. She nodded.

'So I walk in here and you attack me for one little kiss while the whole time you've been shagging some teacher from your school. I do think there's a slight difference between the two, don't you, Andie?'

'Nick, how dare you lecture me, when you're the one who started this? You had the first fling, you started it—'

'*I started it!* Andie, this isn't primary school, we're not children, for crying out loud—'

'No, Nick, you did start it, and you ruined our marriage.' She was crying now, sobs tearing down her face. 'I loved you and I wanted to be with you for ever – and then you had to go and ruin everything with one stupid one-night stand. D'you know what it's been like for me over the past few years? Every time you come home late, wondering if it's happening again. Feeling jittery every time you get a new secretary in case she might be prettier than me. Everyone gets jealous, everyone's afraid of losing the one they love, but you . . . you made me feel as though I had to tie a noose around your neck in case you drifted off again. And I just haven't got the energy any more. And then I met Jonathan and it . . . just happened—'

'*Jonathan!* That little bastard! Jonathan! God, I'll kill him!'

Andie laughed through her tears. 'Oh yes, why don't you! Why don't you go and get all macho. That will solve everything, won't it! Nick, you're pathetic, you clearly haven't been listening to a word I've been saying. You don't understand me! We've been married for ten fucking years and you don't understand me at all!'

'Andie, you're very drunk, you're getting hysterical—'

'Look, I just want you to go, okay?'

The words were out of her mouth before she knew it. They both fell silent, staring at each other in shock.

Nick chewed his lip. He glanced around the kitchen with bewildered eyes. She knew exactly what he was thinking: *I didn't expect this. I can't believe that in the space of half an hour my whole life has changed. I've spent all day at work looking forward to coming home and now this.* She knew it because she'd felt it all herself, the night he'd come home and confessed his affair.

'You don't mean that,' he said at last. 'You're throwing me out?'

'Yes. Yes,' she said uncertainly.

'You're the one who's having an affair and you're throwing me out?' He broke off, shielding his face with his hands, crying silently for a while.

Suddenly she felt tired. Drained of anger.

'Nick, I'm not suggesting you go permanently, I'm just suggesting we need a bit of space, don't we?' she heard herself saying, her voice surprisingly calm and clear.

Silence. Then he nodded. 'I'll go and pack.'

What are you doing Andie? a little voice inside her kept screeching. *You're throwing him out. What the hell are you doing?*

Upstairs in their bedroom, Andie stared down at the suitcase and suddenly felt sick. *This is all wrong. I don't want him to go.*

'I've got some stuff in the dirty washing basket but I can come back and get that in a few days, if you don't mind,' said Nick, coming back into the bedroom with his navy blue towel from the bathroom.

'It's fine. I'll wash it,' she managed to smile.

'And I'm going to leave my suits behind – they'll all get creased. I'll come by tomorrow and collect them if that's okay.'

Tell him not to go. Tell him to stay.

She went to his suitcase and saw that he'd scrunched up his shirts. Nick had always been useless at packing; whenever he went abroad she always did it for him. On auto-pilot, she took them out and started to refold them.

'Don't bother,' he said behind her. 'Really.'

Andie stepped backwards awkwardly. She watched him bung in a jumper and zip up his case.

'Well, I guess I should say goodbye to Fred,' he said.

Andie watched from the doorway, watched Fred

waking up blearily, rubbing his eyes while Nick fed him a story about a business trip, a holiday, about presents he would bring back and postcards he'd send. But Fred knew, as children always do. As Nick got up to go, Fred clung to him and started to cry. Nick, soothing him gently back into bed, looked crucified.

Downstairs, Nick went into the living room and came back with his chess set. Andie felt her heart break. Suddenly reality struck her like a guillotine – no more Nick in her bed in the mornings. No more Nick to call up at work and laugh over a silly thing Cara had done. No more Nick to read to Fred at night.

Stop him, Andie, you can't let him go, stop him stop him stop him . . .

'Don't—' she started to say.

'Can I just ask one thing?' said Nick. 'Can you not invite Jonathan over until we've sorted things out? For Fred's sake.'

'Nick – we're not together any more. It's all over,' she stuttered.

Nick gave her a look.

'Nick – please don't go.' Andie broke; she ran to him and he circled his arms around her and they hugged tightly. 'Please stay,' she whispered, 'please let's talk some more.'

Nick kissed her on the forehead gently. 'I think, like you said, we need a bit of time apart.' And then, as though he was thinking of Jonathan's hands on her, he suddenly pushed her away and picked up his case.

'You're enjoying this, aren't you?' Andie cried. 'Punishing me. You won't stay and talk things over; why won't you?'

Nick shook his head in disbelief. 'Andie, you're the one who asked me to go,' he said, and then walked out.

Andie stood, listening to the sound of the car reversing out of the driveway. And then there was nothing but silence, as if the whole house had tensed in its foundations and drawn in a gasp. And then exhaled slowly, everyday noises rushing back into her consciousness: the clock, the hum of the fridge, the scratch of the dogs' claws in their baskets down the hall. And Fred upstairs, moaning for his dad to read him a bedtime story.

41
Cara

I took a deep breath and reached out to lift the knocker. Then I curled my hand away and let it drop to my side. Then I reached up again . . .

I was standing outside Sean's house, my suitcase by my feet, wondering whether I dare risk being cheeky enough to ask him to let me stay when the last words he'd said to me were the distinctly unpromising: *I want you to leave me alone.*

I could hardly believe how quickly everything had snowballed since I'd made my confession to Andie yesterday.

I'd been stunned as I'd stood in my bedroom and watched Nick leave the house and heave a suitcase into the back of his car. It just didn't make any sense. I'd thought my confession would be a trigger that cleared the air, not a catharsis that led them to divorce. And how could Andie do that when she'd been seeing Jonathan? Couldn't she see how irrational she was being? It looked as if I had mucked up again; mucked up big time.

But though torrents of guilt kept sweeping over me, deep down I still felt a sense of release. Andie would have found out about the kiss sooner or later; it was better to have got it out in the open.

Even so, I woke up the next morning feeling decidedly nervous about facing her. I reached instinctively under my pillow for my Tarot cards; then I realised that I'd thrown them away. I felt so naked and lonely without my magical friends. I looked out of the window, desperately searching for some magpies to give me an indication of how things might go . . . but all I could spot were a few fat pigeons squabbling over a crust of bread.

Okay, I thought, taking a deep breath, *just be brave. Just go down and explain everything again. Keep explaining it to her until she finally understands it really was no more than a kiss.*

As I walked into the kitchen the next morning, I suffered a shock. Andie was humming along to a song on the radio and making a *cooked breakfast*. And as the DJ came nattering on and made a quip, she *laughed*. A miracle at the best of times, but even more strange when your husband has just walked out on you.

Maybe Andie was just glad to be rid of him. Maybe, in fact, she was going to be stronger without Nick. Or maybe she was just covering up?

Fred didn't look quite as happy.

'Morning, Cara,' said Andie brightly. 'D'you want some breakfast?'

'That would be lovely,' I said, my voice catching with nerves.

Andie, being Andie, ended up burning everything. But I ate it all the same. Fred, however, was not impressed.

'I don't want a cooked breakfast, I want cornflakes,' he said in a sulky voice.

'Sure,' said Andie brightly, getting up and fetching a bowl and some milk. I shot Fred a reassuring smile but he merely scowled at me.

She put down his cornflakes but as soon as she had poured the milk, Fred said: 'I don't want cornflakes, I want Coco Pops.'

Andie swallowed. I saw her scratching a rash on her hand that had swelled up over night and I opened my mouth to suggest some ointment, then shut up. It wasn't my place to interfere any more.

'Sure,' she said, 'anything for my darling boy.' She ruffled his hair and he pulled away, looking angry. Andie gave him a look which would normally have quelled him but he merely glared back.

A new bowl, filled with Coco Pops. A fresh spoon.

'I don't like this spoon,' Fred moaned as Andie started to pour the milk. 'It's too spoony.'

'Fred, it's just a spoon.' I heard the ragged edge to her voice and I realised with quiet sympathy that it was all an act, she was only just holding it together.

'I DON'T LIKE THIS SPOON!' he said, and suddenly he knocked the bowl over, sending milk splashing across the table.

We all froze, watching the milk slither and slide over the table edge on to the floor. Fred sat, wide-eyed, waiting to lose a year's pocket money or worse (if anything could be worse). But Andie merely said brightly, 'It's fine. We can skip breakfast. Go and get dressed. I thought we could go to the park today, darling.'

Fred stared at her, bewildered and frightened. I realised that he wanted her to tell him off. He knew that something was wrong and he wanted the boundaries of his world reasserted. Then he turned and fled upstairs, his footsteps galloping up the stairs.

Silence. Andie cleaned up the milk. Her hands were shaking slightly.

'So . . . did everything go okay last night?' I asked delicately.

'Cara, you're going to have to leave.' She got straight to the point. 'It's nothing for you to get upset about, but everything's changing and we need some space and . . . well . . . to be honest, I don't think we're going to have the need or the money for a nanny any more. I also think Fred needs to be with his mother right now.'

'But – but –' Guilt clawed at me and I was close to tears. 'I'm really sorry – all of this is my fault . . . but it really was just a kiss. If you'd listen to me—'

'Don't be silly,' she said briskly. Then she patted my arm. 'Look, I accept it may have been no more than a kiss. But really, Cara, things haven't been going well between me and Nick for a long time and though your "little accident" didn't exactly help things, I don't want you to blame yourself for everything. I'll give you a nice reference. D'you have anywhere to go? Because,' she went on hastily, looking slightly panicked, 'I know your contract says a month's notice, but—'

'Of course,' I said quickly, drying my eyes. 'I'll go at once.'

Though I had no idea where the hell to go.

Upstairs in my room, I packed numbly. I couldn't work out why my suitcase was a lot lighter than when I'd arrived. Then I realised it was because I didn't have any of my magical equipment.

I tiptoed out of the Wilkinses without even saying goodbye. And now I was standing in front of Sean's house.

I took a deep breath and, raising my hand, knocked on the door . . .

42

Andie

Andie blew her nose and picked up the phone, dialling 1471. Still no Nick.

She glared at the phone. She felt infuriated by his silence. *Why* hadn't he rung? What was he *thinking*? Didn't he want to know how Fred was? Didn't he want to collect his stuff?

Or maybe he would only do everything through a solicitor from now on. Maybe she'd just receive an envelope in the post in a few weeks' time asking her to sign in the right places.

Suddenly she felt panicky. She picked up the phone, about to dial Jonathan's number, then put it down. No. She knew she was fragile at the moment, and even though part of her whimpered for Jonathan's warmth and kisses and support, another part of her stayed stern and strong and held her back. The moment she went back to Jonathan she'd set their relationship alight all over again, and she couldn't get involved. Not right now. It wasn't fair on Jonathan, it wasn't fair on Nick, It wasn't fair on Fred.

All the same, she ached for someone to call, for someone to confide in; her feelings were writhing inside her in a hot mass of anxiety. Yes, she had plenty of female friends: Suzanne, Maggie next door, a jumble of mothers. But she didn't *want* to confide in them. She was too ashamed, too proud. She didn't want them to know Nick had gone, to whisper about her behind her back.

Suddenly inspiration grabbed her. She sat down at her bedside table. She drew out a sheet of blue paper and picked up her pen.

It was a technique a friend had given her a while back, when she had been suffering from post-natal depression.

'What you should do,' her friend had said, 'is sit down and write about how you're feeling. Let it all gush out and you'll feel so much better.'

Andie had been cynical at first but to her surprise it had worked. And now she felt she ought to do the same with Nick.

Dear Nick . . . She broke off. Maybe this was silly; maybe she should go downstairs and hug Fred instead. But then she scrawled a few more words down, and a few more followed. And more, and more, and more. Suddenly it all came rushing out in one big flow of ink.

Dear Nick

I'm not sure quite where to begin with this letter, and you'll probably never read it anyway . . .

So I may as well start by plunging in at the deep end. I know you're really shocked about Jonathan. I know you didn't expect me to ever be the disloyal one. But I guess that's my point, Nick. I feel that you took me for granted, that you assumed that whatever happened, I'd just be there for you. But I guess I hadn't been happy for a while when I met Jonathan.

The thing is, I don't think I ever really forgave you for the affair you had all those years ago, and that's

414

what this all comes down to. I know it's my fault because you kept saying 'Let's talk about it' and I kept refusing, sweeping it under the carpet, saying it was fine, let's just forgive and forget it. But I never did forgive or forget. I never trusted you again. I didn't have an affair with Jonathan because I was really tempted, or because I wanted our marriage to end. I think it was just to protect myself. Does that make any sense? I was convinced that, sooner or later, you were going to have another affair. And this was my way of being tough, so that when that moment came, I could think, 'Well, I haven't been loyal either, I've got someone else on the side too.' And so I don't know if you can forgive me for it, because I've never been quite able to forgive you, but I guess if we sat down and talked everything through, we might understand the reasons why.

I'm sorry I kicked you out. I know now that I was completely over-reacting about Cara. I feel awful. Though part of me still feels justified. I mean, it takes two to tango and she should never have been sitting outside with you having an intimate chat. But yes, I know I went over the top. I know it was just a kiss, and I know you were drunk. And I guess you had your reasons . . . didn't you? You haven't been happy lately with work and instead of helping you, I just bullied you, and I'm sorry for that. I realise I haven't exactly been wonderful either.

You know, we used to be so good at communicating. I know that my parents were never happy, but they never expressed it; they just kind of carried on putting up with each other. But I think our generation is different. Nobody wants to put up with anything any more. And I remember early on in our marriage that we agreed that we didn't want to follow in our parents' footsteps, that we would always tell each other every single little thing we were feeling. We'd even write them down, like an agenda, and discuss each point together, and though it seemed comically businesslike, it did work. I don't know how or why we stopped doing that, but I think that's how this all fell apart. I don't know what you're thinking any more – when I found out how much you hated your job, it came as a complete shock to me. And I guess there's a lot of things I've been unhappy about which I haven't told you. I just feel I've never had much of a career, since I had Fred so young, and I guess that's why I turned to teaching. I've never really felt you've taken me seriously. I just wonder if we sat down and I could tell you all these things to your face, and you could tell me everything . . . I wonder if we could repair things.

Because I miss you so much, I can't tell you how much.

D'you know what happened this morning? I was in the bedroom and wondering if I was going to have the guts to call you. I suddenly found myself opening the wardrobe and looking at all your things. Wondering why you hadn't come to collect them.

And then I took out one of your suits and tried it on. It was too big – baggy at the sleeves; the pockets seemed huge. And then I caught a whiff of your scent on the collar and it made me want to cry. A second later, the scent had vanished into thin air. I kept sniffing the jacket, trying to bring it back, but I couldn't. And then I took all your clothes out of the wardrobe and spread them out on the bed and

416

remembered all the different times you'd worn them, all the things we've shared together, and I just thought – this is such a waste. We've been through so much together, why throw it all away now?

The house is so empty without you. It's like walking around a museum, a place that isn't mine any more. I missed you so much this morning when I woke up and the bed was so empty and cold; I missed you cuddling me to warm me up, your toes curling against mine. I missed you at breakfast time; I missed nagging you to eat healthily and telling you to give up smoking. I can't bear to move any of your stuff, the things you forgot to pack. Your toothbrush in the bathroom, your shoes by the stairs, your umbrella lying in the hallway. It's as if you've died and this house is a treasure-trove of your existence. I'm terrified I'm never going to see you again and I can't bear that, I'd rather die than that.

She stopped, the words suddenly drying up. She put down her pen, flexing her cramped fingers. She felt exhausted, but cleansed, as though she had been suffering a nasty illness and the first sensations of good health were tingling around her body. She picked up the letter, reading over it. Halfway through it got too painful and so she left it on the side and got up. She'd had enough therapy for one day.

She remembered Fred and their fight at breakfast with a nasty pang. She thought of his hurt, crumpled face. How could she have been so horrible to him? This was really all her fault – she needed to sit Fred down and talk to him, explain everything, call Nick on his mobile and make the first move herself, no matter how painful it was, and get Fred to talk to him too. She hurried down the stairs. She couldn't hear any noise from the TV and she felt that intuitive motherly leap of panic. *Where is he?* A familiar series of paranoid images cut and pasted from a selection of Hollywood movies flitted across her mind: someone slipping through the back door; Fred being taken away in the back of a car. *Don't be silly*, she told herself. *He's probably just fallen asleep.*

In the living room, the TV was blank, for the video had reeled to an end. And Fred was nowhere to be seen. Andie felt the panic flower.

She hurried into the dining room. No Fred.

'Fred?' she called up the stairs. 'FRED?'

But his room was empty too. His baseball cap was lying on the bed and she picked it up, clutching it tightly.

She tried the other bedrooms and the bathroom. Empty. Hysteria was threatening to suck her in like quicksand but with a huge effort she pulled herself together. *Stay calm, be logical.* Where else? Cara's room! Of course! She hurried up to the attic, crashing open the door. The room had already acquired an emptiness and the feel of Cara – her vivaciousness and *joie de vivre* – had been replaced by a cold feeling of impersonality. Andie ran to the window. From here she could see every inch of the garden and she could see that Fred was nowhere to be found.

43
Cara

I pushed Sean's front door and it swung open. I heard a jazz tune snaking out from the kitchen, a saxophone and a piano circling around each other.

'Sean?' I half tip-toed, half ran down the hallway to the kitchen.

I stopped short.

Sean was wearing a pair of khaki shorts. His skin was brown and smeared and smudged all over with dirt. He was drinking from a bottle of Coke and reading a book entitled: *A Girl's Guide to Modern Witchcraft*. When he saw me, he stopped short and looked decidedly sheepish, as though I'd just caught him reading a porn mag.

'I—' He broke off, seeing the look on my face. 'Cara, are you okay?'

My eyes fell to the kitchen table. There was a stash of books with shiny cellophane-wrapped covers and Richmond library stamps: *Wizarding, Love Spells, A History of the Golden Dawn* . . .

Then, behind me, I heard another knock on the door, and a frantic voice calling, 'Cara? Sean?'

Exchanging bemused glances, we hurried down the hallway.

It was Andie. She looked terrible. She'd been crying and as she pushed a bunch of curls behind her ear, I saw her hands shaking violently.

'Have either of you seen Fred?' she asked.

'No,' said Sean, and I shook my head.

'He's gone missing,' she said. 'He's not in the house and I don't know where he's gone!'

'I'll just take a look in the garden,' said Sean. I waited by the doorstep as he went out to the back, ineffectually calling out Fred's name. I felt awkward just being in Andie's presence. As she jiggled from one foot to the other, I shot her a reassuring smile but she didn't respond.

'Oh God – it's no good,' she muttered, and raced over to the house on the other side of hers, hammering on the knocker. I crossed my arms, a breeze prickling goose-pimples over my arms, as I watched Andie and Maggie exchange staccato conversation. Then Andie came running back.

'Maggie saw Fred wandering down the road a few minutes ago,' she cried.

I felt my heart clench with shock.

'Don't worry, don't worry,' I said. 'We can take Sean's car and drive about looking for him, okay?'

We all hurried to his Beetle, leaving John Coltrane to improvise to an empty kitchen. Andie looked so anxious that I reached over and grabbed her hand. She winced, then pulled it away. I wondered if I was ever going to be forgiven.

We crawled along familiar streets, gazing out of the dirty car windows. Andie wound down her window, poking her head out so that she could crane her neck as far as possible.

420

Sean drove past the high red brick walls enclosing Kew Gardens. Tourists strolled past in sunglasses and flip-flops. Andie let out a cry, spotting a flash of blond hair – but the boy swung around and we saw it wasn't Fred.

I leaned back into the seat and closed my eyes, gently muttering his name. Normally I would have been able to dig into my heart and find an intuition instantly. But my magical skills were rusty; they needed time to be roused again. *Fred, Fred, Fred.* I kept silently dropping his name into the well of darkness. And then it came. A flash of something. Darkness, criss-crossing. A tree; Fred's jumper snagging on it. My heart leaped – when a hand curled around my wrist, squeezing tightly – I let out a cry –

'*Cara!*' Andie screeched. 'Don't fall asleep, we need to look for him!'

A tree . . . could Fred be in Richmond Park? I felt doubt fill me . . . if I was wrong and sent us all on a false trail . . . if only I hadn't let my magic grow weak . . .

In the rearview mirror, I saw Sean watching me with a curious frown. Then he dug out his mobile and tossed it into Andie's lap.

'Shall we call the police?' Andie sobbed.

'No, call Nick,' said Sean tersely. 'He might know where to look.'

Nick? For a moment I thought Andie was going to hit Sean over the head with the mobile. But then she punched in his number, turning away and talking to him in a low voice.

'He's at Peter's house,' she said. 'It just a few roads from here. Turn left at the T-junction.'

Nick was waiting outside in the street. He looked terrible: unshaven, new flecks of grey shining like bright coins in his dark hair, his face pallid with tiredness. As he slid into the car, I smiled at him. He didn't smile back. I guessed that since I'd told Andie we'd shared a kiss, I wasn't exactly his favourite person.

I watched Nick and Andie exchange tense hellos and then look each other up and down, prickling with hurt and love.

'How come he ran away?' Nick asked as Sean drove off again.

'Believe it or not, Fred's not in a very happy mood,' said Andie. 'We were waiting for you to call.'

Silence.

'Well, I was waiting for you to call,' said Nick steadily. 'Let's not forget that you're the one who threw me out.'

Please don't argue, I prayed. To my relief, they fell into another silence, staring out the windows anxiously, searching, searching.

'Oh God, I need a cigarette,' Andie moaned.

'So do I,' Nick groaned.

She dug into her handbag but all she could find was an empty packet of Silk Cut.

'Here.' Sean took a roll-up from behind his ear and passed it to her. Andie and Nick exchanged doubtful glances, then lit up, passing it back and forth like students.

'Don't worry, we're going to find him,' Nick said to Andie.

'How the fuck d'you know?' Andie cried. 'We might never . . .' She trailed off, swallowing, staring out of the window. But then she reached out and grabbed Nick's hand and held it so tightly that her knuckles protruded like sticks of chalk.

I closed my eyes.

Fred . . . Fred . . . Fred.

This time the vision was lucid and powerful. I saw him scrambling through trees, twigs tearing his shins, his

422

jumper snagging on a branch. I saw the ripple of water, the flash of a white wing. And then suddenly the water surged over me, filling my lungs and blocking my throat and shaking its watery noose around me—

I opened my eyes, gasping. As I came to, Andie and Nick's conversation trickled into my consciousness.

'I'm sure he would have gone to a friend's house,' said Nick. 'If he's not next door with Maggie and Emma then he could be with Richard.'

'Or Gavin.'

'No, Richard. He's nearer, we'll try him first.'

'We have to go to the Thames,' I interrupted in a shaky voice. 'I know he'll be there. I took him there all the time to feed the swans, he loved them.'

'I doubt it,' said Andie. 'Fred wouldn't go to the river all by himself.'

'He would,' I insisted. 'We have to hurry, please.'

'I think Cara could be right,' Nick said at last. Andie looked furious that he'd sided with me and dropped his hand abruptly.

I didn't care. We just had to get there before it was too late.

In the woods, I paused for a moment to catch my breath, staring up at the sky through the criss-cross of branches.

'Are you sure this is the right way?' Nick bellowed behind me. He was wheezing now, his lungs raw from too much smoking.

'This is the way I take him to see the swans,' I panted.

We hurried on, down the path, past a bench where an old lady was sitting, crumbling bread for the ducks, Andie stumbling and Nick catching her. *Oh Dionysius,* I kept praying, *please can we get there in time, please can we get there in time . . .*

'Oh.'

We were here. I gazed down at the riverbank, the grass and reeds flattened from all the times Fred and I had sat there, feeding the swans. I swallowed, my head swivelling, searching for footprints, some sign that he had been here . . .

'I'm sorry,' I said. 'I thought—'

'For God's sake, this is a complete waste of time!' Nick snapped.

'No – if we just look a little further—' I protested.

'It is a fucking waste of time,' Nick repeated. 'Jesus, Cara, this is all your fault. D'you know why Fred's run away? Because he's not with his father when he should be. And we know why that is.'

I stepped backwards, feeling his words pour over me like bile.

'Because you had to go and tell Andie some half-baked story about us kissing. Nothing happened that night, you know it didn't, so—'

'Shut up!' Sean yelled. 'Look!' He had found Fred's jumper, snagged to a zig-zag of brambles.

'Oh my God! Fred!' Andie called.

Fred, Fred, Fred, we all called.

Then we heard a voice shout: 'Mummy!'

We hurried through the trees, following the path to another clearing.

It was unbelievable. Fred was sitting by the river. His shoes were by his side and his grey shocks were rolled neatly into them. He was dipping his toes in the water, gently flicking ripples over to a swan.

'Hi Mum!' Fred called. 'And Dad! Hey, Dad, this is my swan.' He shot us all a big smile that stank of guilt.

Andie was too choked up to speak. Then she burst out: 'Don't you ever, *ever* run away like that again.'

Fred's face crumpled into tears. Andie moved towards him but he scrambled to his feet, swerved out of her embrace and ran off, leaves and dirt sticking to his wet feet.

'Oh Jesus,' Nick muttered, following after them.

'Fred, Fred – I didn't mean – come back!' Andie called after him, crying.

Nick nearly caught him but Fred swerved back on to the path. He jumped into the river with an almighty *splash!* He flailed about and then started to sink, fingers clawing the water. Within seconds it had covered him. A trail of green bubbles popped to the surface.

'He can't swim!' Andie cried hysterically.

'Oh God!' Sean started to pull off his trainers but Nick got there first. He yanked off his shoes without bothering to untie the laces and jumped in. He came up, slicking back his hair. He was oblivious to the fact that he had broken the line of cygnets and disturbed the swan. Just as Nick tugged Fred to the surface, the swan retaliated: it stretched out its huge wings in a theatrical display of white fire and then – *wham!* – beat them into the water, sending violent waves crashing over Nick's face. Fred started to cry and Nick clamped a hand over his mouth, shushing him desperately. Nick tried to ease backwards towards the reeds; the swan advanced. I watched them in horror, remembering a newspaper article I'd read describing how the blow from a swan's wing was powerful enough to kill a man.

I pinned my eyes on its black beady ones. I thought of being back in the school, in Andie's classroom – it seemed so long ago, years before any of this had happened – and the way I had calmed the angry cat. I tried to remember how I'd done it . . .

'Do something!' Andie begged Sean.

Sean looked helpless. Then he padded forwards in his yellow socks, crouching down by the reeds.

'Here,' he called gently, 'here, here.' He dipped his fingers in the water; the ripples spread out, the cygnets bobbing on the circles.

No! I thought. I saw the swan's pupils dilate in anger. *Remember,* I told myself desperately, *remember how it's done.*

And then I heard my grandmother's voice, soft and quiet, telling me to let go. I stared at the swan and silently chanted a spell, feeling the soothing caresses whisper from my lips . . .

It was the perfect cover. As Sean sat and cajoled, I let my magic flow, calming the swan, relieving her of her fear and drawing it back into myself. The swan rounded up her cygnets and gently led them back down the river.

Nick pulled Fred out and Andie clasped them both tightly, teeth chattering, wet hands circling each other. Sean and I watched in exhausted relief. Slowly, we made our way back to the car.

On the way back, Nick, Fred and Andie sat in the back. Fred sat on Andie's lap; Nick curled his arm around her, leaning in and gently stroking Fred's head from time to time. Fred started giggling; then Nick laughed and Andie joined in too. I looked over at Sean and smiled; he smiled back, reached over and gently touched my cheek before putting his hand back on the wheel.

We pulled up in Cherry Tree Lane. Nick carried Fred into the house. Andie followed them, then stopped and turned back to give Sean a tight smile.

'Thanks so much for the lift, for everything,' she said. She flicked me a glance. 'By the way, Cara, when you, er, left, you forgot your umbrella and coat – you can just pick them now if you like.'

In the hallway, Andie took Fred's wet clothes off him as quickly as possible. I picked up my coat and umbrella and asked if there was anything I could do to help, but she shook her head coldly. I asked if I could use the bathroom and she gave me a look as if I'd just asked to poke around in her underwear drawer, then nodded and said, 'Okay, but be quick. I want to get Fred into the bath rightaway, don't I, you naughty little boy . . .'

After using the bathroom, I paused in the upstairs hallway. Nick and Andie's bedroom door was slightly ajar and through the slit I saw Nick's dark profile. He was still wearing his damp clothes, shivering violently, a small pool of water darkening the carpet. He seemed deeply engrossed in a letter. I recognised Andie's handwriting. He was reading it very quickly, drinking in the words like wine, his hands shaking. Then I heard him sobbing.

I hurried down the stairs and returned to Sean's house.

I sat in Sean's living room feeling exhausted, listening to his quiet voice on the phone as he called up Maeve; Fred's running away seemed to have scared him, ignited his fatherly instincts.

He came back into the living room a few minutes later.

'Phew, what a night, hey?' he said, slumping down on to the sofa and starting to roll a cigarette.

'Yeah . . .' I trailed off awkwardly. Now that all the drama was over, I sensed we were going to have to have a discussion about witchcraft. After all, I hadn't even officially asked Sean if I could stay over yet, though he seemed fine about me being here. I waited for him to broach the subject, but he picked up the *Radio Times* and started to flick through it.

'Sean!' I burst out, unable to stand this procrastinating, 'look, I'm sorry I lied to you about being a witch. I hope you understand why I did it.'

The hurt flashed in his eyes again. 'Not really,' he said.

'Come on, Sean, I'm only human! What would you have done in my position? Look at me! My dad left me the day I was born, my mother is a witch and completely insane, and my grandmother owns a shop, a family business, where we sell anything from wands to dead animal paws. I mean, it's pretty freaky.'

'Not really,' said Sean, rolling his cigarette.

'*Not really?*'

'Cara, it's nothing. Witchcraft is fashionable. And every family is dysfunctional these days. I'd probably have been more freaked out if you'd told me you had two happy parents with great jobs. Jesus, I got fucking ragged in the playground because my mother was a dinner-lady. Having a witch for a mother is cool by comparison.'

What? His examples were pale pastels of embarrassment compared to the glaring primary colours of my mother.

Then relief trickled through me, cooling the anger. Hang on. Sean had basically said that he didn't think I was a freak. Yes, he was still cross with me but he didn't mind the witchcraft. And that was a start . . .

We both stared at each other with nervous uncertainty. I nearly cursed out loud when we were interrupted by the phone.

'It's your mum,' said Sean.

Instantly, anger flared up inside me. I could just hear her rasping voice crowing that she'd always known my job wouldn't last. Or maybe this was all the result of another one of her curses.

'Tell her I don't want to speak to her,' I said abruptly.

Sean made up a rather lame excuse, then said with a frown, 'She's ill, or something. I think you should talk to her.'

'What?' Suddenly I felt the bottom drop out of my world. 'Ill? What?'

'Cara – I've been calling everywhere, trying to get hold of you!' It wasn't my mother – it was my grandmother – and she was sounding very muddled. She was phoning to tell me that my mother had had a stroke.

44
Cara

On the way to the hospital, Sean and I didn't speak. Every now and again I was aware of him shooting me a nervous glance or gently rubbing his hand on my shoulder. But I couldn't look at him or I'd start crying, and I couldn't cry, I had to be strong for her. Besides, I didn't *deserve* to cry. *I've been so horrible to my mother over the last few months,* I wailed inside. I'd assumed her aches and pains were just theatrics. I felt tears brimming up into my throat, mixing salt with my saliva, but I forced them back down. Why hadn't she *told* me? Or maybe she'd tried to and I'd shut her out. Every time she'd called me at the Wilkinses I'd been in a hurry to get her off the phone. The tears tried another route, spilling up into my eyes, but I blinked them back fiercely. Sean drove past a row of peeling railings. I looked up and saw the hospital.

We spent about twenty minutes scurrying around the long white corridors feeling like Alice In Wonderland. Finally, we located Mum's ward and Dr Nessa O'Neil, a large Irish woman with a cheerful disposition.

'Is she okay?' I cried. I kept thinking of all the things I'd read about strokes: people in comas, people being paralysed down one side of their bodies, losing their memories, not being able to talk.

'She's not too bad,' the doctor said. 'Don't worry, it was just a very mild stroke. She'll be fine in a few days.'

'But I thought a stroke was . . .' I gulped in relief. 'Serious.'

'It is serious,' she said sternly, 'but strokes can come in all shapes and sizes. Sometimes they're devastating, sometimes they can be so slight a person can have a stroke without realising it. Your mother certainly realised hers, but it wasn't severe by any means. You can go in and see her now.'

I crept into the hospital ward. She was lying in bed, looking terribly fragile. I went to her side and took her hand. I didn't know what to say, except a lame, 'Are you okay?'

She nodded and then closed her eyes.

Over the next couple of hours, a steady stream of friends appeared to see my mother. I was touched by how quickly they'd come, how upset they were; though the hospital staff were somewhat bemused by the odd selection of people coming through their swing-doors. First there was Kieran, checking to see Sean was okay too, brandishing a large bunch of purple grapes which he proceeded to gobble up himself; my grandmother, flitting back and forth with tired, frenetic energy; several witches from our local coven and even my mother's old enemy, Morgan Le Fay. They'd all come as soon as they'd heard the news, bypassing the nurses who'd decreed that only blood relatives be allowed in with charms and hypnotism.

As I gazed around at them, I felt pride leap in my chest – *so many people loved my mother* – followed by guilt, and then irritation. My mother, dropping in and out of sleep, occasionally woke up and managed to shoot them all an exhausted smile; she couldn't summon the energy for words. I felt her fingers rub restlessly against mine and I sensed she ached for the peace of sleep.

Someone tapped me on the shoulder. It was Sean, bringing me yet another styrofoam cup of tea. I took it and put it down on the bedside table blankly. I turned to narrow my eyes at the crowd.

'How can she sleep with them all chattering?' I whispered crossly.

'All right.' Sean turned, surprising me with a wonderful display of protective aggression, waving his arms at everyone and calling, 'Mrs Broad is very tired and I think she needs some peace. Why don't you all come back tomorrow?'

Everyone looked rather sheepish and trailed out. I turned to Sean and said in a trembling voice, 'I can't remember it.'

'What? What?' He curled his arm around me.

'There was a spell . . . to help her . . . I threw away my Book of Shadows . . . What if she doesn't make it? It'll be all my fault . . . my magic's all rusty . . .'

'Cara, you don't need to worry,' Sean said gently. 'I just spoke to the nurse and she said your mother's going to be fine. Modern medicine might not be the same as magic but it can do the trick, you know.'

We were interrupted by the door swinging open. Yet another visitor. He was wearing purple robes and had a bunch of flowers that were singing a 'get well soon' song, the stamens curling, petals swirling.

'Rufus!' I noticed Sean do a double-take, realising who he was. 'Thanks for coming,' I continued. 'Mum is stable but I think she needs some rest.' I eyed the flowers pointedly.

'Oh, thank God.' Rufus put the flowers by her bedside,

weaving a fresh charm so that they softly sang a lullaby. In her sleep, my mother smiled. 'Well, I won't stay then,' he added. 'I hope she gets better soon.'

Rufus held out his hand for Sean to shake; Sean responded reluctantly. 'Well done for winning Cara, by the way,' he said in a matey voice that made me wince and yet touched me with his sincerity. 'I could never even get her to go out on a date with me.'

Sean looked rather stunned as Rufus left. Then we gazed each other, forgiveness and understanding flowing.

At dawn, my grandmother returned to the hospital after catching a few hours of sleep. I'd fallen asleep leaning over my mother's bed, my face nestled next to hers, my blonde hair entangled with her grey tresses. Sean was sitting behind me, his head on his chest, snoring loudly. As I woke up, I felt panic scamper around my body. Then relief: *They'd said she was going to be fine.* And then a sledgehammer of tiredness. It burned like sand in my eyes and a lump of exhaustion pulsed behind my forehead.

'Cara, you must go home,' my grandmother insisted. 'Come back later in the afternoon, darling.'

We were about to leave when she suddenly pulled me back for a 'word'. Sean nodded and waited patiently outside.

'Cara, I just wanted to mention,' she said. 'When you came by my shop and you accused your mum of, er . . .'

'Oh yes, that,' I said, wincing painfully at the memory. For one horrible moment I thought she was going to say that all the stress I'd created had caused the stroke.

'She didn't really put any spells on you, you know. With the amount she drinks, she really wouldn't have the skill. All the things that went wrong were your own fault, Cara,' she said.

'But . . . why did she say . . . she told me she had!' I protested, feeling awful.

'I don't know. I think she was just upset that your magical powers had been, er, less than efficient and she didn't want you to feel so terrible, so she went along with you and pretended she was partly to blame.' Seeing my face, my grandmother lightened up. 'Don't look so worried. Now go and get some sleep.'

'But I have to tell her I'm sorry,' I burst out. 'I've been so horrible . . .' I trailed off, seeing that my mother was now deep in sleep. I would have to save my apologies for later.

Sean drove us through the dawn-dappled streets. London was surreally quiet. I watched litter dancing along a pavement and felt numb. As Sean clicked on his indicator to follow the route back to Richmond, I stopped him.

'I want to go to my home,' I said, 'and I want you to come too. Please.'

It felt odd walking down the silent street of terraced houses in Shepherd's Bush, pushing the creaky black gate, going up the grey stone steps and reaching under the flowerpot for the spare key (the pot had been charmed so that if a burglar tried to take the key, it would seize his hand). Inside, everything was a real mess, covered with dust and black cat-hair. The kitchen was full of old boxes and used dishes. I stood up and gazed around at the chaos, swallowing.

'You okay?' said Sean.

'Yes. I'm just tired. I need to sleep.'

'Sure. Well, I guess I'd better get back, but call me as soon as you wake up and—'

'I want you to stay,' I said, tugging his hand. 'I don't want to be alone.'

I went up to my bedroom but, since the lodger had moved on, my old bed was covered with junk. I dragged two sleeping bags and some rather musty blankets down to the living room. I took the sofa while Sean offered to sleep on the floor.

'If I fall asleep, will you put a spell on me so I don't wake up for a hundred years?' Sean teased me. When I didn't laugh, he said quickly, 'Look, what I wanted to say earlier when we were talking about the witch thing was . . . well, I'm okay with you being a witch. I think it's cool. I mean – those talking flowers Rufus brought in! God, I wish I could charm flowers – imagine how much more fun gardening would be!'

I was so tickled that I managed a soft laugh and he grinned back.

'And I could charm my mower to work by itself and sit about sun-bathing while it handled the lawns. Anyway . . .' He smiled, and I smiled back, too tired to summon up any words. 'Goodnight,' he said awkwardly. 'Or rather, good morning.'

But when I pulled up the blankets, I felt hot and itchy and couldn't sleep. I felt as though guilt was devouring me. Look at this place! Look at the mess, the dirt! My mother wasn't coping well at all, even with my grandmother checking up on her. She wasn't eating properly, she wasn't looking after herself; the cigarette packets and bottles on the kitchen table indicated just what kind of 'healthy living' she was managing. And I'd deserted her! Buggered off to the Wilkinses because I was too selfish to acknowledge that she needed help; refused her calls and pushed her away and then unfairly accused her of ruining all my spells when it was just my own ineptitude. And finally the tears that I'd been holding back poured out and I cried quietly, hoping I wouldn't wake Sean.

435

But it was too late. I heard from the rustling of his blankets that I already had. I sniffed, closing my eyes and pretending to be asleep.

I felt the covers lift up, a cool rush of air followed by the comforting warmth of his body. 'I'm just here as a friend,' Sean whispered. I clung to him, crying my heart out, and he held me tightly, hugging away all the shock and pain and sadness. And then, as the rest of London woke up, hooting and commuting, my tears ebbed away and we gradually dropped off to sleep, nose to nose, our breaths mingling softly . . .

45
Cara

Sean woke me with an excited smile on his face.

'Look!' he said, pointing to the window.

I opened my eyes groggily. Since the day after my mother's stroke I'd been staying at Sean's house, and every night found myself sinking into such heavy, deep sleeps – no doubt due to the exhaustion and trauma of the last few days.

I went to the bedroom window and looked out. At first I couldn't work out what Sean was pointing to. Then I saw: Nick's car was in the driveway. He was passing things from his car to Fred, who was carrying them back to the house: a pair of sunglasses, a carrier bag of clothes. And Andie stood in the doorway, smoking and smiling at him nervously. I turned to Sean and grinned. It looked as though Fred's escapade had been a blessing in disguise after all.

My mother was being released from hospital today and Sean was mowing more lawns, so we spent the day apart.

I spent the morning cleaning my mum's house and shopping. I went to the supermarket and came back with four carrier bags full of proper food. I poured all her half-drunk bottles of wine down the sink and tossed her cigarettes into the bin.

I was cleaning out my old room, making up a bed so that I could stay for the night, when I came across a very old tin box that had been shoved down the side of the bed. It had once held sweets and an old-fashioned logo was stamped across the lid. I let out a gasp of nostalgia. This was my first 'magic' box. As I opened it up, the colours of memory came seeping out: the thrill of my first magic box, of putting my first bottle and tiny wand in it. I closed it gently and put it into my bag. Okay, so I'd got rid of all my magic things . . . but I could always start again.

By the time my mother turned up in a taxi with my grandmother, she was in top theatrical form. She got the taxi driver to practically carry her to the front door. I told myself to stop being mean – she *had* been in hospital after all – but when she asked him in for a drink I felt it was really too much.

She seemed touched by the fact that I'd cleared up, but to my shock and dismay she told me that she didn't need me to stay overnight.

'You go back to Sean,' she said, waving her hand airily. 'During my hospital stay I quite got into watching *WestEnders*. I'm going to have a long hot bath and then settle down to watch an episode.'

I mistook her remark for a barb. 'Mum, I'm not going out with Sean,' I protested. 'Look, I know things didn't work out with Rufus but I'm willing to give him another try. I mean, I'm sure I could learn to like him.'

'Cara,' she said, her voice softening. 'I've never heard such nonsense in all my life. You and Rufus are not meant to be. Now go and enjoy yourself with Sean.'

Finally, an hour later, I reluctantly left her behind. As

I was swept up into the thumping flow of commuter traffic, I couldn't help feeling tearful again. I'd hoped that my mother coming home would be the perfect opportunity for us to bond together. But we were just the way we'd always been; awkward, talking at cross-purposes. And I hadn't even said sorry for accusing her of ruining my spells. No wonder she didn't want me to stay.

Back at Sean's, I'd hoped to sink into bed for an early night, but to my surprise Sean suggested we take Fred out to the movies.

'I saw Andie earlier today and she mentioned that she and Nick needed a bit of time to themselves, so I offered. D'you mind?'

So we took Fred off to the cinema. When we got to the Odeon, while Sean and Fred went off to get popcorn, I went to a payphone to call my mother, like an anxious parent fussing over her child. So, as you can imagine, I was taken aback when a male, Irish voice answered the phone.

Oh God, I thought. *This is unbelievable.* Where on earth had she got him from? And what if she'd started drinking again? I pictured her sitting on her sofa, waving a gin and tonic, on the verge of collapse, only this time she might not survive.

'It's Cara,' I said rather hysterically. 'I'm her—'

'Oh Cara!' The voice sounded unnervingly familiar. 'Cara, what can I do for you?'

'Kieran?' I said incredulously. 'What are you doing there?'

I heard my mother in the background and he passed the phone over to her. 'It's all right, darling,' she said, 'Kieran has been looking after me.' She pulled away from the receiver, 'Darling, put those flowers in the nice purple vase under the sink, not the white one.'

439

Darling. She'd called *Kieran* darling. So this was why she'd wanted to get rid of me. I felt ill. Kieran and my mother.

'Mum, if he's harassing you, I can come over and make an excuse,' I said.

'Cara, of course he's not *bothering* me. He's brought a nice bottle of non-alcoholic wine and a video to cheer me up, haven't you, sweetie?'

'Mum, did you see what he did in hospital? He ate all your grapes! Look, maybe I should come over anyway, just to check—'

As the pips sounded, I hastily slotted in another pound.

'Cara,' she said gently, 'I'm fine, really. Stop fussing.'

'Mum, I just wanted to say – I didn't say it earlier – I know you didn't do the spells – I'm sorry.' I blurted it all out in a splurge.

'Cara, it's fine. Really, it's all in the past. Now call me back tomorrow and tell me how it went with Sean.'

The pips went again. So I said goodbye and stood there blankly, receiver still sweaty in my palm, watching Sean help Fred carry a huge tub of popcorn and them flicking a few pieces at each other in a mock fight. Then Sean ruffled Fred's hair affectionately and Fred grinned up at him. It was strange that, after so many shocks, life had slid so rapidly back to normality. I'd been so convinced my mother would be changed by her experience, that she would turn into a celibate teetotal saint. And yet, deep down, part of me was glad she hadn't. She was still the witch I knew and I loved. She was still my mother.

We got seats towards the front of the cinema, munching popcorn and watching the ads.

'Your bloody grandfather is preying on my mother!' I whispered to Sean.

'Oh God! I told him to lay off her . . . Look, if it's any consolation, he's liked her for months,' Sean whispered. 'He spotted her that time she came over to keep an eye on you, and he's been going on about her ever since.'

'She's in a very delicate state. If he hurts her, I shall put a very nasty spell on him,' I sniffed, though I felt a little better. At least Kieran's affections sounded genuine.

I suddenly became aware of Sean staring at me. I turned to look at him. A funny smile was tugging at his lips. On the other side of me, Fred wriggled in delight as the film started.

'What?' I whispered at Sean. Then I shut up. Suddenly the silence throbbed between us. And then he started to kiss me. I struggled in surprise, but he put his arm around me, pressing his fingers against the small of my back and pulling me close. I felt my desire turn into anger. *He's just taking advantage of me,* I thought furiously, pulling away. But when I looked up at him, I saw tenderness in his eyes. He stroked my jaw gently with his finger.

'Oh God, you're so lovely,' he whispered, before leaning in for another kiss. 'I know this isn't the time or the place, but sod it, I've been wanting to do this for ages. I can't hang on any longer.'

'You two!' Fred poked us. 'You're *kissing*!'

We broke apart, biting back sheepish smiles. My head was reeling. I couldn't believe that after all my hoping, all my worrying and wanting, it was finally happening. Sean had made his move. I frowned; I couldn't help wondering if my mother was working her magic again. Then I smiled at Sean and figured that if she was, I definitely owed her one.

The film started. It was lovely being in a cinema with children. The atmosphere felt completely different from the serious silence of watching an adult film; the kids laughed and shrieked and booed and filled the auditorium with an enormous sense of innocent joy. But I couldn't really concentrate on any of it. I kept gazing up at Sean, and then we started kissing and Fred sighed, 'Not again.'

'This is *so* embarrassing,' I whispered.

'So what?' said Sean.

And that was how it was for much of the film. Everything felt blurry, as if the rest of the world was out of focus, unimportant. Just me and Sean, in our little bubble of bliss, finally realising and expressing how much we cared for each other. We couldn't stop kissing. It was magnetic. Every so often we'd break off and have a bit of popcorn and smile at each other and shrink into our seats with embarrassment, but soon we found our lips meeting again, soft and tender. We couldn't stop touching each other. He threaded his fingers into mine. He stroked my arms and my neck. His jeans were rough against my bare legs. He tasted sweet and sour, of salt and popcorn. I wanted to take him home and eat him.

However, after a while Fred started to throw popcorn at us and we worried that we were corrupting him, so we sat back and tried to be good. And so we managed to keep our hands off each other for the rest of the film, though I have to say it was so hard I had to put a binding spell on my fingers.

Sean pulled his car up into his driveway while I dropped Fred off next door. As I took his hand and led him up to the house, I saw Andie and Nick through the curtains, playing chess together.

Andie could hardly believe how excited and happy Fred was.

'Mum,' he cried as she scooped him up into her arms. 'We threw popcorn and Cara and Sean *kissed*!'

442

'Oh, did they now?' Andie said, smiling at me knowingly. I smiled back in relief. I could tell at once that something good had happened between her and Nick, that they'd started communicating and had taken the first steps to repairing their marriage. In the space of a few days, Andie had relaxed: there was a floral softness to her face, a redness in her cheeks, a happy slackness around her mouth.

Just as I turned to go, Andie said, 'By the way, thanks for, you know, helping us to find Fred. I must pay you for looking after him tonight.'

I watched her in amazement as she fumbled in her purse. 'Andie, don't be ridiculous,' I said. 'Really, it's fine. Don't worry about anything. Everything is going to be all right.'

'You know,' she swallowed. 'Maybe in a few weeks, when things have settled down, you could . . . well, we're going to have to get another nanny and Fred does so like you . . .'

'I'll think about it,' I said hurriedly, hiding my stunned shock.

'Great!' she said.

Outside, I paused on my way back to Sean's house. What a night. First Sean finally makes a move on me and now this. Everyone was being so *nice* to me. Everything I wanted was coming true, only it was starting to irritate me because it was all so unexpected. Since when did anything this good ever happen to me? I almost wanted a bird to poo on my head or something, just to make me feel I wasn't in a dream.

Still, I was flattered by Andie asking me back. I wasn't sure how I felt about it, but I tucked it into the back of my mind for later: for now I had to think about Sean.

A few minutes away from him had given a chance for my lust to quell and my reason to come into play. Now doubts were filling my mind. How many times had Sean and I been through this before? Friends and then lovers, lovers and then friends, the seesaw constantly tipping up and down depending on his mood. How did I know he wasn't going to change his mind tomorrow morning? I was tired of having my emotions kicked around all over the place like a football.

But when I got into the kitchen and saw him standing there, eyes shiny with love, I couldn't resist him. Within seconds we were kissing again.

Then Sean broke off. 'This is all very weird, isn't it?' he said, running his fingers through his hair and looking at me from under his lashes.

'But a good weird,' I said.

'A *very* good weird.' Suddenly Sean did a funny little jig around the kitchen, sending me into fits of laughter, which finally ended in him coming and putting his arms around me. His hands roamed through my hair, slid down my back and trailed around the waistband of my skirt. 'Hang on.' He suddenly stepped back, all sparkly-eyed with excitement. He looked like a little boy on Christmas Day. 'Sit down, wait there!' He darted out, stumbling up the stairs three-at-a-time.

I waited, wondering what on earth he was up to. Above, I could hear the sounds of running water and creaking floorboards. Finally, he called down: 'CARA, it's reeeady!'

Upstairs, I found Sean wearing nothing but a towel around his waist. He led me into the bathroom and I gasped with delight. A bath was running, swirling and shimmering with the rainbow ripples of essential oils. The air was steamy with a chaos of scents: lavender, sandalwood and white musk. He had lit about a hundred tiny candles, some new, some melted stumps, and placed

444

them all around the bath so that waves of light and shadow rippled across the walls.

'I saved all the candles from the dinner we never quite had,' Sean said shyly.

'Yes.' I let out an embarrassed, apologetic laugh. Then I blushed as he came up behind me, circled his arms around my waist and whispered in my ear, 'Of course, if we want to get in before the water gets cold, it would help if you took off all your clothes. I can help you out if your buttons get a bit tricky . . .' But as his fingers fumbled with the buttons of my cardigan, I remembered how, when I'd turned into a man, he'd said he *didn't even fancy me*. And I pulled away, turned to face him and crossed my arms.

'I'm not sure if this is a good idea,' I said.

'Oh?'

'The last time we got into the bath . . . when we had those crazy cocktails . . . you didn't want to know me . . .'

'Cara, we were very drunk,' said Sean in surprise. Then he clicked. 'Cara, you're not thinking that I pulled away because I didn't fancy you? God, I was dying to have my wicked way with you. But you don't like drinking much, and you seemed a bit gone, and I thought that if I took advantage of you when you were in such a state, you might wake up and regret it and think I was a total bastard. I couldn't tell if you were all sexy because you really liked me or because I'd got you drunk, and I liked you so much that I felt I wanted to go to bed with you because we both really wanted to, not because we were both wasted.'

'Oh.' I smiled with relief.

'Why, what did you think I was thinking?'

'I thought . . . I just . . .' Suddenly I felt silly and paranoid. 'I thought you thought I was a bit of a dog or something.'

'Cara!' Sean grabbed me in an indignant hug. 'I think you're *gorgeous*.'

'But why did you tell Ralph that I wasn't your type?'

'What? Oh, when we went for drinks . . . Well, I was pissed off. You hadn't turned up to dinner – I realise now with your mother that it was a genuine emergency, but I thought you were making an excuse. I mean, you escaped through the *toilet window*. And when this Ralph guy, who isn't actually your brother—'

'He's a friend,' I said hastily – I had a feeling Sean wasn't quite ready to hear about mystical sex changes yet; that would come later, when he'd got a bit more used to me.

'Look,' he continued, 'I was just trying to pretend I didn't care for you. I think I'd better explain my behaviour . . .'

Yes, I think you better had, Sean, I thought.

'I know I've come across as a bit hot and cold at times, and it's not what you think. I'm not some bastard who's going to use and abuse you. It's just that . . . after Laura . . . I've been so muddled. I got hurt. We've been divorced a while now and I still feel that I'm a failure. When I was a kid, I had all these ideals about a good career and a good marriage and everything – and here I am, mowing lawns, with nothing but a divorce certificate. And then I met you . . . and I worried I was going to blow it again.

'It was when we were in hospital that I changed my mind. I was so scared by what had happened to your mother that it just reminded me how short life really is. I realised that by shying away from any form of relationship, I was going to go through life feeling miserable, and that I was about to throw away something really rather precious.'

I was deeply touched. I knew how hard it was for Sean to make that speech, to open up. And I looked into his eyes and realised for the first time that his actions had

446

been motivated not by cruelty but fear; that in many ways he was even more vulnerable than I was. I smiled, put my arms around him and gently kissed him. 'Okay,' I said, 'let's have a bath.'

We lay there for hours, talking and kissing and gently splashing each other. I nestled into the warm wet cave of his body, my head against his chest, and he circled his arms around me.

'D'you know, Andie offered me my job back!' I said. 'Can you believe it?'

'Really?' Sean was amazed. 'After everything . . . God, it's because they pay you so little,' he said. 'And you're so good.'

'I'm not sure I'm going to take it,' I said. Sensing his worry, I added, 'But if I get another job, I will stay in the area,' and he grinned in relief.

'How d'you feel about them now?' he asked.

I thought for a few moments. 'I think I came to live with the Wilkinses with this naïve ideal that they were going to be a perfect happy family, and I've never had a father so Nick became a substitute. I can't help feeling disillusioned now I've found out they're in such a state. It just makes me think *why?* Why do perfectly good marriages and relationships go so sour and what can I do not to end up like that? Sorry, that sounds a bit heavy, doesn't it?'

'No, not at all,' said Sean. 'After Laura, I've been thinking the same. I think the key is simply good communication. Being honest and saying exactly what you feel. The moment you start withholding things and burying them beneath the surface, it creates a wall between you that gets bigger every day, until one day you realise you can't see over the top . . . I think Nick and Andie have realised this, and they will sort it out

447

eventually—' A sudden bang downstairs made us jump. Sean quickly called down, 'I'm in the bath, okay, Kieran? And I'm going to be here all evening,' he added with a whisper, stroking my tummy and then playfully caressing my breasts. 'Mmm, they're so lovely.'

'No, they're not,' I moaned. 'They're much too small. Another curse from my mother—' I broke off with a cry as Kieran opened the door and walked in. For a moment he gawped at me, then hurriedly picked up a towel. Sean cupped a handful of water and splashed it at him.

'I told you not to come in, you fecking eijit.'

'Well, you didn't say you had a lass with you, did you? If so, I would have brought my camera. Only joking, only joking,' he backtracked, seeing our faces. 'By the way, Cara,' he winked at me before closing the door, 'I think your breasts are wonderful too. Though they're not as nice as your mother's.'

'*Kieran!*' Sean howled. 'Oh God, I'm sorry, Cara. You complain about your mother – just imagine what it's like having to put up with that.'

'Oh, don't worry,' I laughed, twisting my head back for a kiss. 'I think I could learn to live with it . . . but what about me?' I asked, bringing up another question that had been lurking in my mind. 'What about me being a witch, and my family? Can you learn to live with that?'

'Sure,' said Sean. 'Look, I did kind of guess you were . . . D'you remember that night you stayed here? I saw you sitting in your bedroom, utterly engrossed in making this black penis out of a candle. I realised then something was up, but I didn't like to say.'

'Oh God – I was doing a spell on Nick's penis.'

'*What!*'

'Don't worry, it's okay now. I was just a bit pissed off.'

'Remind me *never* to upset you.' Sean paused, worried.

'So what happened to it when you did that spell?'

'What?'

'To Nick?'

I looked deep into his eyes and said sadly, 'It fell off.'

Sean gulped. Then, seeing the look on my face, he smiled in relief, albeit a wobbly smile.

'Sean, it was just a dark moment in my life. I use magic for good things – to help people. I want you to know I'd never ever use magic to hurt you. Anyway, I was kind of planning to give it up . . .'

'Oh, don't give it up!' Sean cried. 'I think if you've been given a gift, you should use it. Come on, show me something. Do some magic. I'm never going to get used to it unless you actually show me, am I?' he asked nervously.

I paused, pondering. I felt nervous too. I had to give him a gentle introduction to my powers; something not too extreme, something to impress but not scare him off. I could lift up a bottle of bubble bath with my eyes and tip its greeny potion into the bath, showering us in bubbles. Or I could put a spell on the taps so that melted chocolate came out of them (yum!). Then I turned and smiled at Sean. I knew what to do. I leaped over and gently kissed him, and as I did so I let all my love flow from my heart in a stream of ambrosial honey, filling his mouth with a delicious taste. His eyes widened in shocked delight; then he smiled and we carried on kissing, a witch and a human, in perfect harmony.

Epilogue
A few months later . . .

I gazed at my reflection in the mirror. I was wearing a dark suit with a cherry-coloured blouse and high heels; I looked smart, professional and, above all, deceptively normal. My hair rather spoilt the effect by straggling around my shoulders.

I clicked my fingers and with a touch of magic it furled into a bun. No, too prissy. I clicked them again and it divided into two plaits. No, too jailbait. I clicked again and tried an elegant chignon. There, that was more like it. As a few strands wisped down, I clicked a last time and sealed them into place.

I went downstairs to the kitchen. I'd only been living in Sean's house a short while but I had already transformed it. For one thing, it was marginally less messy, though I can't say I was any kind of proper girly homemaker; Ikea blinds and tasselled cushions were not my forte. However, I did feel I'd contributed plenty of nice 'touches' to the place.

I boiled some water and opened up a drawer. On one side it was labelled 'Sean', containing all his tea-making equipment: a mega box of tea, some brown sugar and his crusty old turquoise mug. On the 'Cara' side was a box of my favourite bat-wing tea bags, several little droplet bottles to give my tea a different 'mood', and a magical mug that re-filled itself as soon as it was empty. I made two cups of tea, then there was a clatter on the stairs and Sean came tumbling into the kitchen, his face haggard.

'Interview . . . interview . . .'

'Relax, darling. It's only early,' I said. 'We've got several hours to go yet.'

Sean looked relieved. As he woke up properly, he looked me up and down and gave me a teasing wolf-whistle.

'God, there is *no doubt* you're going to get your new job,' he said.

I'd applied for a job with a family three streets away. It was only part-time, of course, so that I could come home in the evenings to my darling, delicious Sean.

'And you'll get yours too,' I said, touching his cheek and passing him a mug of tea to make him feel better. Unfortunately, I gave him the wrong one. He took a gulp, eyes watering, and passed it back. 'I'm sure you could get used to it if you tried,' I chided him, slightly hurt.

'Cara,' said Sean, sliding his hand up and down my back. 'It's a bit . . . um, *leathery*. Besides, I'm a veggie now. Um, sort of. Anyway, are we still on for Candlemas?'

'Sure!'

It was so funny; Sean relished all the magical festivals and now he was the one who ended up dragging *me* along. I couldn't believe how much he enjoyed them; he seemed to find our rituals and robes and potions wonderfully fascinating.

We stood in the kitchen, sipping tea and teasing each other over who was the most nervous. We were both interrupted by the flap of the letterbox. Sean cocked his head at me; I whistled and two letters, a catalogue and a postcard came dancing in. I sent the catalogue scuttling into the bin with a frown, sent the letters into Sean's hand and held out my hand for the postcard. Unfortunately, it was only a little one and couldn't quite jump up high enough – it kept trying and then flapping back on to the floor. I bent down and it jumped up, wriggling a grateful thanks.

'Oh my God, it's from Mum and Kieran!' I cried.

'Oh wow,' said Sean. 'God, these bills are horrible. If we don't get these jobs, Cara, you're going to have to magic up a money-press.' He slurped his tea. 'Read it out then.'

'*Dear Cara,*' I read, '*Kieran and I are having a lovely holiday in Italy. I've never been here before and it's divine! We are even thinking of retiring here together and buying a little farm. We've looked at a few places – I will send you the photos. Kieran has a nice tan and looks terribly dashing. He is happy, though he did get cross with me when I put a spell on the Tower of Pisa. How was I supposed to know it was meant to be crooked? I thought it was going to fall over, I was just trying to help. Anyway, I have been very good and not drunk a drop or smoked for two months, so you can stop fussing about me now. I am starting to think perhaps men are not so bad after all. Lots of love, Mum.*' I shook my head, laughing. 'God, they're such a pair.'

'They probably say the same about us,' Sean grinned. 'Anyway, I must shower.'

I cooked up breakfast, humming along to the merry hiss of the shower. Then I heard the sound of Sean nervously testing out riffs on his new sax. I'd been giving little offers to Dionysius at my altar every day for the last week; though I'd steered clear of doing any real magic, for I knew Sean had to prove himself by himself. Even so, I hoped my prayers had been heard, for I was acutely aware of how fragile his confidence was. It had taken me ages to persuade him to go and perform at the jazz club in Camden and now Sean was going to audition for an agent who had spotted his 'potential'. If he did well, he might end up playing all over the country, releasing a CD and being featured in every car advertisement on TV.

Sean came in, looking smart in beige chinos and a tie and we ate breakfast. Time had rushed by; now it was time to go.

On the doorstep, we exchanged kisses goodbye.

'Good luck,' Sean whispered, stroking my hair back from my face. 'You'll be great. Just try not to turn them into a cat by mistake or something!'

I laughed and then he kissed me deeply.

'Good luck,' I whispered, kissing him back.

As he drove away, I reached out with an invisible hand and tooted his horn. Sean shook his head, laughing; he hated it when I did that.

I strolled down the road, tweaking the clouds to allow some sunshine in. How funny – not so long ago I walked down this road on my way to my interview with the Wilkinses. I'd been so nervous; the 'real' world had seemed a minefield of scary challenges and characters and I'd been convinced I'd never fit into it. Funny how quickly life can change, how we rise and fall through so many snakes and ladders to fulfil our dreams and desires. But we get there in the end . . .

As I passed by the Wilkinses' house, I saw them through the window and gave them a wave. They waved back, grinning.

Though I'd been tempted to go back to them, I felt that now their problems were over they seemed a bit . . . well . . . *boring*. I pulled a piece of paper out of my pocket, checking out my new family: Mr and Mrs Young. Mr Young was unemployed and recovering from a nervous breakdown; Mrs Young was a mega-career woman at a woman's magazine. Two children: Kelly, aged thirteen, who was refusing to speak, and Brian, aged six, who had been expelled from three schools. The last two nannies had left within two weeks due to low pay, a bad atmosphere and kids that were impossible to control. Now that was what I called a *challenge*. As I turned the corner into their road, I heard the Youngs arguing, angry voices spilling on to the street, and I repressed a whoop of anticipatory delight.

I could feel the magic tickling my fingers, just waiting to be unleashed.

This was going to be fun . . .